MAIL

GIRL

A NOVEL

JIM TRAINOR

**UpNorth
Press**

BOOKS BY
Jim Trainor

Grasp: Making Sense of Science and Spirituality (2010)

Waverly's Universe (2012)

The Sand People (2013)

Up North (2014)

The Mountain Goat (2017)

68 (2018)

Mail Girl (2021)

MAIL GIRL

A NOVEL

Mail Girl is a work of fiction.
Characters, places and incidents are the products of the
author's imagination, and any real names or locales
used in the book are used fictitiously.

Mail Girl

For information contact
UpNorth Press
www.JimTrainorAuthor.com

ISBN-13: 978-0-578-83177-0

For MST

Part One

TRAVAIL

I don't want to end up
simply having visited this world.
Mary Oliver

Chapter 1

Shelby

Except for the mailbox at 113, the scene along Drury Lake Road was as it always is. Quiet. Serene. A picture postcard, some have called it. Soaring maples and oaks provide a canopy over the narrow road, almost creating a green tunnel in the summer. The road is two-way, but has no center stripe, and its winding narrowness requires cars to pass with care.

The boat ramp at the west shore of Drury Lake is accessed from this road, and it's one of the few centers of activity on a summer day. Drury Lake is one of fifteen thousand lakes in Wisconsin and is little different from most of the others, but its tranquil shoreline of stately trees and abundance of smallmouth bass bring the fishermen in on the weekends.

The homes along Drury Lake Road are mostly old cottages like 113, their age revealed by weathered sidings and mossy roofs. They were built back in the day by families whose children, now grown, have left for careers in Chicago or the Twin Cities. Although many of the cottages are used only on summer weekends, there is a handful of full-timers, mostly elderly, puttering in their gardens, feeding on memories of water skiing, laughter-filled barbecues by the lake, and children who do not visit anymore.

The mailbox at 113 was no different from the other mailboxes along Drury Lake Road—a standard metal box, like you'd find at Home Depot, mounted on a four-by-four post. But the mail hadn't been collected for days. It was so chock full, the door wouldn't even close completely. It wasn't a big thing, and no one passing by noticed the mailbox at 113—they were focused more on dropping a Rapala lure in front of a hungry bass.

But Shelby noticed. It was her job to notice.

Chapter 2

"I'll have the same thing," Shelby said, adding a nervous laugh, after Tisha had just ordered the fried haddock. Not that Tisha's words were funny, but their waiter, Rick, who looked like he could be a tight end for the Packers, was enough to evoke her nervous laughter. "And another Happy Heron," she added, nodding toward her empty beer glass.

Shelby Sims and Tisha Reynolds were Friday night regulars at The Quartermaster, here for the best fish fry in town, not to mention the good assortment of beers on tap and the woodsy, homey ambiance that always lifted the spirits. They took in the scene from their regular booth, paneled in knotty pine, with red-vinyl-covered seats. No different from any other Friday night, the place was packed and so loud it almost drowned out a Luke Bryan song about being with his girlfriend in the back of a pickup on a starry night.

"So, you got your route tomorrow?" Tisha asked. Tonight she wore that shimmery white blouse that looked like silk, with white buttons up to the neck. With her black hair pulled tight behind her head, she had the elegance of an ambassador's wife in London, not a clerk at a post office in rural Wisconsin, the person you met when you went in to mail a package or purchase stamps. And she didn't look a day over thirty, although she was the same age as Shelby—thirty-seven.

"No," Shelby said. She worked five days a week as a rural carrier—she delivered mail—and sometimes worked on

Saturday. She took a foamy sip of the Happy Heron that Rick had just set in front of her.

"Plans for the weekend?" Tisha sounded concerned. One of the few African Americans in town, she stood out in rural central Wisconsin, where over ninety percent of the population were white—Shelby had seen that fact somewhere—mostly of Polish or German descent, mostly Lutheran or Catholic.

"Not really," Shelby said, looking away to show how uninterested she was in this conversation. "Guess I'll just play it by ear."

"You could come to church with me." Tisha extended this invitation almost every Friday night. She'd come here out of college to take a management position in some business that folded, then stayed because her husband had a good job. When their marriage crumbled, Tisha still didn't leave, because—she told people it was because of her church and her friends, but it was more complicated than that.

Shelby rolled her eyes.

"So, what will you do?"

Give it a rest, Tisha, thought Shelby. "Some gardening maybe—it's supposed to be nice out this weekend. Maybe some reading." She was working her way through Richard Russo's novels.

"You know, you need something more than your children."

Tisha referred to the people along Shelby's mail route as her "children," because she showed so much concern for them. Maybe it was a dig, but Shelby took it as a compliment. She often stopped to visit with someone working in the yard, often carried the mail to the doors of the more elderly residents. For Shelby, this was just caring service, but, of course, it was more. It was also her social life. No one seemed to mind, except Seymour Johns, the postmaster, when she got back late from her routes. There had been more than one reprimand in the past. "I'm doing okay," said Shelby.

"Yeah, I know you're doing okay. After all, you got me." They clinked their glasses together so hard that beer from each glass sloshed onto the table, producing more laughter. It was hard to stay gloomy at The Quartermaster. But Tisha wasn't ready to let it go. "You trained to be a nurse, Shelby. You should probably be doing that, you know."

Tisha should talk. She'd gone from manager to postal worker. "I like what I'm doing," Shelby said.

"I mean all the nurturing you do with your children … yeah, you should be a nurse."

"Maybe we're just meant to be mail girls," Shelby said. She hoisted her beer in a here's-to-you gesture, then added, "We could do worse."

It was still light when Shelby got home at nine. She hurried past the full-length mirror just inside the door, but risked a quick glance. Her glasses reflected back at her, masking her emotive dark eyes, her best feature, she thought. Michael once said they made her look cuddly. She moved on, not wanting to check out her meet-a-cute-guy outfit—the sleek black tights and the tight red tunic. Seeing herself now was the last thing she wanted.

Yeah, she always went out dressed like she was ready to party and start a wild romance. But that never happened. She'd spend the evening talking to Tisha, greeting a few friends— mostly workers she knew from downtown—and getting buzzed on two Happy Herons. Maybe she was going through the motions of trying to meet someone again, but down deep she knew she still wasn't ready.

Tisha seemed to have no problem meeting great guys, and she was always trying to get Shelby to break out of her boring pattern. Problem with Shelby was that her not-ready phase had lasted for three years, ever since she'd started at the post office.

Sometimes she hated that mirror. As she leaned against the kitchen counter, she wondered why. She wasn't bad looking at all. Yeah, her brown shoulder-length hair was too plain. And there was a little more breadth in her butt than she'd prefer, but, hell, last week, someone on her route said she looked like Marissa Tomei.

She poured a glass of water from the leaky tap—probably needed a washer or something. She should call the landlord, but it wasn't that bad yet. She turned to survey the tiny kitchen. Her mom said you can tell a lot about people by looking at their kitchen. Hers wouldn't get high grades. It certainly wasn't a kitchen from the Food Network, but it wasn't a pigsty either. Sure, the cracks in the Formica counter were hard to clean, and there was no dishwasher or disposal. No array of delicate pendant lights illuminated shiny stainless appliances—her appliances were white and old. Her grade for the kitchen? Maybe a C+. Better than average. Slightly.

She wiped a dried coffee ring from the counter, left from her morning cup. Maybe it's not fancy, but it can be clean. She may be helpless in other areas, but she wasn't so helpless she couldn't keep her kitchen—her C+ kitchen—clean. What was really missing from the kitchen were the memorabilia: the family photos, a toddler's artwork tacked to the fridge with magnets—she shook her head, as she headed for the bedroom.

What the kitchen needed could not be found in a remodel. The deeper longings are never satisfied by granite countertops.

A half-hour later, she climbed onto her bed—it was too hot to get under the covers—and opened *Nobody's Fool* on her Kindle.

Chapter 3

I t's almost expected of us to complain about Monday mornings—getting up early, returning to the grind after a carefree and fun weekend, getting the old engine running again.

But Shelby loved Monday mornings. By six, she stood at the kitchen sink, listening to the hissing Keurig spurt out her second cup of French Roast, while munching her steel-cut oats, with craisins and skim milk. She was ready for work in her light-blue letter-carrier shirt, featuring the blue-and-white United States Postal Service eagle-logo patch over her left pocket, and neatly pressed darker-gray slacks. Shelby worked to project a professional image. She was representing the Federal government and took that responsibility seriously.

She was at the post office by seven. Mornings were hectic, and the two hours of sorting and casing the multitude of flats, packages and mail, while chitchatting with her coworkers, were invigorating and mentally exhausting. The Amazon boxes, which had arrived at the post office by 4:30, added greatly to the volume of her deliveries. They now comprised probably two-thirds of all her packages, and she hoped that the increased volume would prompt the post office to acquire a mail truck for her routes, so she could retire her old Buick, which had been experiencing occasional loss of power lately.

But Shelby was a subcontractor, not a regular USPS employee, so she was required to use her own car. Anyway, she got mileage for using her car, and that extra cash helped.

Although Tisha clerked at the desk up front, she was in early, too, to help sort the mail. Rudy and Liz, the other letter carriers, worked across a large worktable from Shelby and Tisha. Rudy was balding, probably fifty, married with a couple of teenaged kids. He was always chatty, but usually wanted to talk politics, which caused Shelby to tune out. He had seniority on Shelby and had a way of letting her know that he carried more authority than she had, like the way he always addressed their boss as Seymour, while everyone else addressed him as Mr. Johns. A great name dropper, Rudy loved to remind everyone about the important people he knew. While sorting mail, he would often say something like, "So, I bumped into the mayor yesterday. Had a great chat." Or, "So, old man Thenis was out yesterday. Asked my opinion about ..." And he would drone on. Thenis owned the local Chevy dealership, and it seemed unlikely he'd be seeking Rudy's opinion about anything.

Liz rarely spoke. She was nearing retirement and added little to the conversations—probably dreaming about a condo in Tampa. But the busy pace of the morning and Tisha's cheerful presence made the environment a happy one. It helped that Seymour Johns, the postmaster and Shelby's boss, wouldn't be in until eight.

Around a quarter to eight, Tisha headed up front to prepare the counter for the opening of the office. A couple of minutes later, Liz headed for the bathroom. As soon as they left, Rudy came around to Shelby's side of the sorting table, carrying an armload of Amazon boxes. As he passed by her, she felt his hip rub hard up across her backside. Before Shelby could react, it was over, and Rudy had moved to the far end of the table.

Maybe Rudy lost his balance—the space between the table and the wall was narrow. But then Shelby saw Rudy's gaping grin, like he knew she really enjoyed it. Shelby couldn't breathe, much less say anything. She wanted to puke. *That scumbag is married, has kids. If his wife knew* …. She tried to speak, but no words came out. Her mouth felt full of cotton. She shook her head and looked down. She should have said something. All this Me-Too talk and here she was, a sniveling coward.

Getting out onto the road helped distract from the ugly encounter with Rudy. She wouldn't have to see him for the rest of the day. She should tell Seymour or, at least, Tisha. Should she confront Rudy, make sure he knows his behavior wouldn't be tolerated? She felt her hands shaking at this prospect. She just wanted to put it out of her mind.

Shelby had two routes today. Each route contained about 150 mailboxes and would take about four hours, depending on how many visits she made along the way. She'd rack up about fifty miles on the Buick.

Other than its recent loss-of-power issues—and those didn't happen often—the Buick was a good vehicle for a mail carrier. With its strobe light fastened to the roof and its US Mail sign attached to the doors with magnets, it looked quite official. And its cushy bench seat was comfortable for a long day behind the wheel. When she'd started her job, she'd had extra gas and brake pedals installed on the passenger side, like a driver's-ed car. That cost fifteen-hundred bucks, for which the post office reimbursed her. Shelby had become proficient at driving the car from the passenger seat, handling the steering wheel with her left hand and leaning out the passenger window to place mail in the boxes.

The first route this morning was the most rural, out west of town. Shelby was never asked which routes she preferred. They were handed to her by Johns when she started.

So, Shelby wound up with the rural route that included Drury Lake Road. It was seen as one of the least desirable, because it was farthest from the post office and the narrow road could be icy in the winter. Liz also had remote routes out among the farms on the far east side of town. But Rudy had the routes that included downtown—where he could run into the mayor and Mr. Thenis—and the one upscale neighborhood where most of those business and political people lived. Once, Shelby had heard Rudy quip in the mail room, with a smug arrogance, "Hell, this is a post office, not the freaking French Foreign Legion. No way in hell I'd be blowing my time on those remote routes."

But Shelby loved the route along the three miles of Drury Lake Road. Sometimes she'd pull into the Drury Lake boat landing, which was usually empty on a weekday morning, and bask briefly in the beauty of the northwoods lake. If it was sunny, she might stretch out for a few minutes on the hood of the Buick, arms spread over her head. Last week she'd seen a bald eagle, soaring slowly over the lake, free and unconcerned.

Even more than her brief respites at the lake, she enjoyed visiting with her "children," as Tisha called them. Along Drury Lake Road, the residents—mostly retired—greatly appreciated seeing her. Shelby suspected her visits might be the only human contact some of these people would have all day. The other night at The Quartermaster, someone said that most people aren't that interesting. BS. Everybody is interesting, if you look closely.

She stopped to visit with Jenny Balcom, planting marigolds by her front porch, and checked in on Darlene Otis, just back in her home from rehab, after her recent hip replacement.

It was nearly eleven when she arrived at 113, Allen Riley's
house. The box was still full. He hadn't picked up his mail
since last Wednesday. Shelby parked the Buick in the narrow
driveway leading back to Mr. Riley's cottage. Most likely, he'd
gone away for a few days and hadn't filed a hold-mail form.
Many people do that. But she decided to check on him
anyway. She was trained to do a welfare check on residents, if
there was any concern about their well-being. This involved
knocking on the door and calling out the person's name. She
wasn't authorized to enter the house.

Shelby knocked several times. "Mr. Riley," she called out.
No answer. She made her way around to the rear of the house,
squeezing through a tight passage between the house and a
head-high wood fence, clambering over vines and knee-high
weeds, watching for poison ivy. She knocked on the back
door. Nothing. She tried to peer into the windows, but
curtains were drawn on all of them.

She turned toward the small backyard. Grass that needed
mowing stretched to a low wooden fence encompassing the
rear of the property. A small tool shed sat in one corner of the
yard. Beyond the fence were thick woods. Shelby walked the
perimeter of the yard and looked into the unlocked tool shed,
which was empty.

Shelby spoke frequently with Mr. Riley. He'd only been in
town a few months and had told her he was renting the home.
Wouldn't he have mentioned leaving town for a few days? She
walked back to the front of the house and over to the
detached garage. Shielding her eyes from the sun, she looked
into the small window in the side door to the garage. A car was
there. Might Mr. Riley have more than one car? Maybe
someone had picked him up.

Shelby collected the mail from the mailbox and left a note to inform Mr. Riley that he could pick it up at the post office. She decided to leave today's mail—some advertising flyers—so tomorrow she could tell if he had picked it up. She paused at the door of her Buick and drummed her fingers on the roof, while she surveyed the quiet neighborhood and wondered what more she could do. Maybe Mr. Riley had fallen inside the house and couldn't call out. Could he have walked to Drury Lake and drowned? Or perhaps he was injured on another property nearby? No. Someone would have spotted him by now.

She got back to the post office at 5:15. It had just closed, and Seymour Johns was the only person left in the building, sitting at his desk with a military straightness. When he saw her, he glanced at his watch and shook his head slowly.

Shelby ignored his displeasure. "Mr. Johns, we've had some mail collecting in one of our boxes for several days. Can we check if there was a mail-hold card turned in, and we somehow missed it?"

Seymour Johns rose from his desk and led the way out into the service area. "113 Drury Lake Road," Shelby said, leaning in to view the stack of yellow mail-hold cards that Seymour was flipping through.

"Nothing here," he said, as he turned toward her. "Anything else, Shelby?"

She should say something about Rudy's bad behavior. She cleared her throat, then hesitated. "Nope. See you in the morning."

Instead of heading back to her car, Shelby crossed the street to the police station. She was glad to see Sergeant Derek Daniels behind the glass window. He'd been dating Tisha for a while, and Shelby knew he'd do his best to help her.

"Afternoon, Shelby," he said. "What brings you in here?" Derek was a rugged, good-looking guy. Tisha had a knack for dating rugged, good-looking guys.

"Derek, I was wondering how a missing person gets investigated." She told him about Mr. Riley's mailbox. "Is there something you can do to check things out?"

Derek stood and came out through a side door, so he could speak to Shelby face to face. "Unfortunately, there's nothing we can do, unless a friend or family member reports him missing. That hasn't happened."

"Yeah, but I'm not sure Mr. Riley has any family or friends around here."

"Shelby, the police can't go barging into someone's home just because he goes away for a few days. He's probably up north, fishing with a friend."

"So, there's nothing you can do?"

"No, and there's nothing we should do at this point, if you're suggesting we go into that house or something like that." Now the cop leaned toward Shelby, his eyebrows raised and his hands on his hips. "And you know, Shelby, you shouldn't go into that house, either. It would be trespassing."

Chapter 4

Shelby's normal upbeat mood was subdued the next morning when she arrived at work, because she'd have to see Rudy. Not that she was afraid of him physically. She'd been a softball jock in high school and could probably duke it out with the flabby-gutted Rudy. It was because of the power he held over her—with his seniority, they both knew he could probably have her fired with just a few words to Mr. Johns. So, she had done nothing yesterday when he had rubbed against her, and that had allowed him to claim some sick kind of superiority over her, which he'd already been claiming anyway.

She was glad to have Tisha and Liz there and worked to have them lead the conversation. "So, Liz," she said, "counting down the clock to retirement?"

"Eight months and 22 days." Then with a laugh, which was rare from Liz, she added, "But who's counting?"

At seven forty-five, Tisha headed up front to get the counter ready. Shelby regretted not having told her about Rudy's misconduct yesterday. She tried to keep Liz engaged in conversation, continued to ask questions about retirement planning. Rudy busied himself in the work, thankfully, and paid little attention to the two of them.

Then Liz announced, "Be right back. Potty break," and disappeared around the corner.

Shelby stiffened, kept looking down at her work, but watched Rudy from the corner of her eye. As soon as Liz was out of sight, Rudy came around the table toward her. Shelby

turned toward him, as she backed away. She finally found
words. "Stay away from me," she stammered.

"Oh, come on, Shelby, you know there's something going
on between us."

Shelby shook her head emphatically, but couldn't speak.
Then Rudy leaned forward and trailed a finger along her
cheek. She continued to back away, glancing around for a way
out, a way to slip away around the work table and out of the
room. But she was now backed into the space between the
wall and a huge filing cabinet. There was no place to go. She
was cornered. Trapped. Her chest exploded with terror, as
Rudy moved in. She shook her head. This can't be happening.
"No. No," she tried to say, but all that came out was a guttural
whimper.

Rudy stepped closer and leaned in, cupped her chin in his
palm, as if preparing for a kiss. It was a big mistake. Shelby
was almost pinned to the wall, but there was enough room to
lean back and plant one leg behind her, like a softball pitcher
ready to uncork a fastball. With blinding speed that the
unprepared Rudy could not anticipate, she swung hard at his
face.

She gasped at the immediate explosion of blood from
Rudy's nose, as he stumbled backward. Both hands went to his
face and his eyes showed shock and panic. "You bitch," he
blurted, "what the—"

"Don't you ever touch me again." Her words came out as
a growl.

Rudy was silent for a moment, then turned and hurried
toward the bathroom. Shelby stood immobilized, then grabbed
an armload of boxes and raced out to the Buick. On her way,

she looked into the lobby—she needed to tell Tisha what just happened—but Tisha was already busy with a line of patrons.

Shelby's right hand throbbed in pain. The rest of her was shaking. She sagged behind the wheel of the Buick and wanted to cry, but the tears wouldn't come. Maybe a part of her felt vindicated about standing up to the disgusting Rudy, but a bigger part quaked in terror. If Rudy complained, she would be fired for sure. With assault on her record … dear God. She gripped the wheel and shook it. "This job," she sobbed out loud, "is the first good thing I've had in so long."

Maybe he would not speak up, maybe he'd be too embarrassed that he'd been taken down by a girl. Maybe his male pride would protect her. Even so, even if Seymour Johns never knew what happened, Rudy would make her life a living hell. He would undermine her and work to get her fired. And Seymour would listen. Dear God, she hadn't been thinking clearly. How could she? If she'd just thought about it for two seconds, she'd have done something else.

Focusing on her routes—on her "children"—helped, and a few miles out, she was already doing better. But today she skipped the rest stop at the Drury Lake boat landing.

The mail at 113 had not been picked up. Shelby strode purposefully to the door and knocked. "Mr. Riley," she called out. No answer.

To the left of the front door, a wood planter that ran the length of one side of the house was filled with purple petunias in full bloom. She recalled Mr. Riley telling her how much he loved his purple petunias, had had them at every house where he'd lived. Mr. Riley had beamed when he talked about his flowers. One day he'd said, as he brushed a finger across a velvety petal, "Petunias require harmony and peace to flourish." Looking at them now calmed her. Shelby found a hose and watered the plants, beginning to wilt in the summer heat.

She rested her hand on the front doorknob, hesitated, then gave it a twist. She jumped back when the handle turned. The house was unlocked.

Shelby did a slow three-sixty on the porch, as she pondered what to do. Derek Daniels' words rang in her ears: "It would be trespassing." She massaged her sore right hand, then pushed the door open and went in.

There was concern about Mr. Riley's welfare, she'd say. Although she was not authorized to enter a resident's home uninvited, she'd heard of letter carriers doing it, when they thought there might be an emergency. Was this an emergency? She could make a plausible claim that it might be, but mainly, she needed to do something bold, something to get the ugly confrontation with Rudy out of her mind.

The musty-smelling living room was a small square, typical of the unimaginative designs of these old cottages. The house was dark, with curtains pulled and the walls covered in dark, fake-wood paneling. The room was sparsely furnished. A sagging sofa and upholstered chair, badly stained and ripped, looked like pieces that folks set out by the curb for some needy person to pick up. She called out his name again. Nothing.

Shelby decided she wouldn't touch anything—fingerprints, you know—just make a quick inspection. She entered the kitchen, stepping cautiously, bracing herself to encounter blood on the floor or a dead body. She chided herself—she'd seen too many British mysteries on PBS.

Beyond the kitchen, a dark hallway led to a bathroom, a utility room, and two small bedrooms. The house was depressingly claustrophobic and made her own house seem palatial in comparison. It was hard to imagine a refined man like Mr. Riley living here permanently.

It didn't take long to check out the bedrooms. One room was empty, the other contained a double bed, a cheap dresser and a small desk. The bed was unmade, but nothing in the room looked unusual. No drawers pulled out with contents strewn across the floor, no broken furniture that would indicate a struggle.

Shelby recalled her conversations with Mr. Riley. Once she'd asked where he had lived before he arrived here. He'd said something evasive, like, "Oh, I've been in a lot of places." On another occasion, she'd asked if he had any family, which produced a shaky laugh and words to the effect that it was a long story. When she asked him why he had moved here, Mr. Riley had said something like it seemed he'd spent his whole life waiting. Shelby wondered now what he had meant by that. Riley looked old enough to be retired, but Shelby had never learned what he did for a living. Despite all their conversations, she now realized that she knew very little about him.

Mr. Riley hadn't received much mail over the past few weeks. She would know—she sorted it every morning. Mostly ads, some utility bills. She couldn't recall him ever receiving a personal letter or a package.

She considered going through the dresser and desk drawers, but this would violate her no-fingerprints caution and definitely be further entry into trespassing territory.

Back outside, Shelby tested the side door of the garage. Locked. But she had fulfilled her duty, verifying that an ill or, God forbid, a dead Mr. Riley was not in the house. She should feel good about her accomplishment. Why didn't she?

Even with Shelby's unscheduled tour around Mr. Riley's house, she was back at the post office before five. Tisha was still at the window and there were no customers. "I need to talk," said Shelby.

"What's up, hon?"

Shelby first told Tisha about her experience at Mr. Riley's house, working her way up to telling her about the run-in with Rudy.

"You actually went in? Did you pick the lock or break a win—"

"It was unlocked."

"Still. You could get into trouble for this, you know."

"I'm more worried about Mr. Riley. Maybe he—"

"Maybe's he's on a trip, visiting family, or in the hospital, or—"

"I called the area hospitals, while I was on the routes. No Riley at any—"

"He could be a million places, Shelby. Let's not jump to—"

"I'm not jumping to—"

"Just don't tell Seymour what you did, okay? You know he'll show you no mercy. He's been in a foul mood all day, anyway."

"Oh? What about?"

"Don't know. He wasn't saying."

"So, there's one more thing." Shelby paused, and she was shaking. Tisha's eyes grew wide, as if bracing for a bomb to detonate. "This morning after you left to open up ..." was how she began. She told Tisha everything, including the rubbing incident from the previous day. Finally, she said, "Tisha, this scares the crap out of me, but, if I know Rudy, his pride will take over. He'll tell everyone he ran into a door, got a bloody nose. But I wanted you to know. Don't find yourself alone with him."

Tisha's mouth had dropped open. "Shelby, I can't believe you didn't tell me this morning. Oh, hell, you need to go tell the boss right now. Don't mention going into that house, but you've got to tell him about Rudy before that jerk invents some lie about you. I wouldn't put it past him."

Shelby groaned. "I don't think he'd—"

"Go, tell him right now, Shelby. You need to protect yourself."

"Okay." Shelby let out a big sigh that said the last thing she wanted was to talk to Seymour about the morning incident.

"I'll be here if you need me," Tisha said, as Shelby headed back toward Seymour's office.

Seymour Johns stood in the doorway to his office. Before Shelby could speak, Seymour said, "Come in, Shelby. We've got to discuss a problem."

Chapter 5

"Close the door," Seymour said. He didn't invite her to sit down. He stood behind his desk, fists clenched at his side. "What in the hell are you doing? Assaulting another employee. What has—"

"I want another female present," said Shelby, with a fake-calm voice. She hoped that Tisha would be called in.

The exasperated Seymour stepped to the door and called down the hall. A few seconds later Liz appeared.

"I would prefer to have Tisha here, if—"

"I've chosen to ask Liz to join us." He nodded to Liz to take a seat, as he returned to behind his desk, where he remained standing.

"Let me tell you what happened, Mr. Johns. You see—"

"What happened is pretty clear, Shelby. One of our employees had to go to the ER with a broken nose. He's pretty shaken up, and—"

"Broken nose?" Shelby interrupted. "Dear God." She looked at Liz, hoping for some help, but Liz stared at the floor. "I'm entitled to tell my side of the story, so I need you to listen." After a moment of silence in the room, she added, "Okay?"

Seymour let out an exasperated breath that suggested he'd just as soon fire Shelby on the spot and get it over with. "Okay," he said.

Shelby leaned a hand against Seymour's desk, suddenly feeling like a grapefruit was rolling around inside her stomach. "It began yesterday when we were doing the morning sort." She told the whole story, and when she had finished, she said,

"So there you have it, Mr. Johns. I was accosted twice by Rudy. I was trapped and afraid. I did what I needed to do to protect myself."

Seymour turned to Liz. "Did you see any of this?"

Liz, who still had her head down, looked up briefly. "No, sir, but apparently it happened when I was out of the room."

"Well, that's a fine situation. Your word against—"

"I thought I'd find you in here," blurted Rudy, as he pushed the door open and stepped into the postmaster's office. "I don't know what kind of lies she's telling you, Seymour, but I don't feel safe with a violent person in the office."

Shelby felt her face flush as she turned toward Rudy, who had a huge bandage over his nose. It seemed larger than it probably needed to be, she thought, and, in spite of the dire situation, she wanted to laugh. "That's ridiculous, Rudy, and you know it. You came on to me, touched me twice without, and I repeat *without*, my permission. If there's anyone who doesn't feel safe in—"

"That's not true! Any of it," Rudy shouted. Now he turned back to Seymour. "Don't you see what she's trying to do? Telling these lies, trying to ruin me. Trying to hurt my family. I've got two kids." Now he touched his nose. "I see only one victim here, Seymour."

Seymour looked down at his desk, then over at Liz, who still stared at the floor. He clearly didn't know what to do. Shelby noticed the plaque on his desk—it had probably been a gag gift—that read, *I'm the boss: I said maybe and that's final.*

Shelby spoke up again. "I repeat, Mr. Johns, I did nothing wrong. Just stood up for—"

"Nothing wrong, my ass. What do you think *this* is?" Rudy touched his nose again. "Physical assault. That's what it is. Oh, and I know why she did it, too. Everybody knows. She's jealous of my seniority, and she'll do anything to take me down."

"That's absolutely not—"

"If it were up to me, she'd be thrown in—"

Tisha burst into the office. "I heard the shouting, and I thought I needed to be here." She gave Shelby a you-go-girl look, as she waved a sheet of paper toward Seymour Johns.

"She doesn't need to be here, Seymour," Rudy protested. "She's Shelby's friend. You know what she'll say."

"Tisha," Seymour said in a fatherly way, "maybe it would be best if you—"

"I'm not going anywhere, Mr. Johns. And I brought Shelby this grievance form—she held it up for everyone to see. She has a right to protect herself."

Rudy shook his head, like he was appalled at the injustice he was enduring. "I'll make this simple, Seymour. I cannot continue to work in such a hostile, dangerous environment. I'm the one who should be filing a grievance. So, it's either her or me."

The self-righteous, lying ass, thought Shelby.

Seymour let out another big sigh, probably stalling for time. Maybe he was praying for an earthquake, which would rescue him from having to make a decision. Finally, he said, "I'll have to get HR guidance from regional before we go much further here. But I think I'm going to have to place you on leave, Shelby, until we can review this."

"No, that's not fair," said Tisha. She took a step toward Seymour, then stepped back.

"I need my job, Mr. Johns," said Shelby, trying to keep her voice from shaking.

"Shelby, if there was inappropriate behavior, and I'm not saying there was, you should have come to me about it. Violence like this"—He nodded toward Rudy's nose—"has no place here."

"Touching me without my consent should have no place here, either. What I did was simply protecting myself, and I do not apologize for it." She was trembling.

Seymour looked left then right, as if help might be arriving from an unexpected source. Then he looked over at Rudy's nose. "I don't really have any choice, Shelby." There was a bit of a whine in his voice, like he was the one everyone should feel sorry for.

Shelby could see how this was going to play out. "Will the leave be paid?" She already suspected what the answer would be.

"That would be like vacation, wouldn't it, Shelby?" Seymour laughed, but no one joined him in the laughter. Then he looked around nervously. "Like I said, this is above my pay grade."

"Look, Mr. Johns, I did nothing wrong, and I need my job."

"I'll say it one more time, Seymour," Rudy bellowed, "it's her or me. And if it's me, you can bet your sweet ass there's going to be a lawsuit." He folded his arms across his chest in confidence.

Seymour looked at Shelby like a doctor coming into the waiting room to break the bad news, but said nothing.

"I've got two weeks' vacation, Mr. Johns. Can I just take that instead of leave?"

Seymour was quiet, chewing his lip, like he didn't know what to say. "Uh …." Seymour looked first at Rudy, who grimaced, then at Liz, who still had her head down, as if seeking their input. "Well, usually, you have to put in a request ahead of time, but I guess I can let you take your vacation days instead. That doesn't mean you're off the hook, Shelby. I've still got to report this to regional."

Shelby didn't wait to hear any more. She nodded to the exasperated Tisha, and together they walked arm in arm out the door. She held her head high, trying to project dignity, hoping her knees were not wobbling visibly. *I'm screwed.*

Chapter 6

Shelby and Tisha headed straight for The Quartermaster. They ordered Happy Herons, then Tisha placed a hand on Shelby's arm. "That really sucked," she said. "That idiot Johns doesn't know what he's doing, and you can be sure that the powers that be at the next level up are going to rip him a new one, when they find out how he handled this. I say get a lawyer who'll make Seymour regret the day he fell for dear old Rudy's lies." She looked out the window, shook her head, then added, "That scumbag, Rudy. I'd like to punch him in the nose myself. And maybe take a swing at Seymour, too, while I'm at it." Her features were pinched, like she might be about to cry.

Shelby wanted to cry, too. "I've really blown it, Tisha. I'm going to lose my job, and maybe arrested. Nobody's gonna believe me over him. Why did I have to hit him?"

"You hit him because you had no choice. You were backed into a corner. You weren't going to talk your way out of what Rudy had in mind. Look, you're going to come out on top of this thing. But, worst case scenario, even if you did lose your job, what you didn't lose was your dignity." Tisha now held Shelby's hand in both of hers and squeezed tightly, then she laid the grievance form on the table between them. "Now, let's fill this damn thing out, and you send it in tonight."

"But I'm just a subcontractor, not a member of a union or—"

"That doesn't matter, Shelby. Just fill it out. You have rights, no matter what your job title is."

When she got home, Shelby paced the floor, too nervous to sit. She had to stop shaking. She pulled out her phone and brought up Emmylou Harris on Spotify, playing it through the Bluetooth speaker atop her fridge. She scrolled through Facebook, paused to read the latest post from Sedona, her cousin out in Loveland, Colorado, who'd just gotten home from Singapore. Now she was off on yet another great adventure, up in the Rockies. She shook her head, fighting back tears.

Shelby lifted a half-full bottle of chardonnay out of the fridge and poured herself a glass. She switched off Spotify—Emmylou was just too depressing for tonight. She headed toward the living room but stopped and gripped the edge of the countertop for support, as an unwanted memory flashed through her head—Michael and her baby. It was a familiar stab, like a knife cutting to her soul. Three years ago, the memories incapacitated her, almost destroyed her. They still returned, always at low times. Now, the memory flashes were brief, though just as painful as ever. She knew they would pass, but that they would return.

Tisha was always telling her that she needed a plan, that she could do more. Should've been a nurse, she liked to say. "I'm okay," Shelby would always reply. What Tisha said was true, of course. But she had no plan. What she had were more longings than any kind of plan.

If she was planning anything, it was probably her next regret.

Now she tossed atop her bed, unable to sleep. She'd struggled to get into *Nobody's Fool*, but her brain was still replaying the events of the day. Things that were said, things she wished she had said. She should have stood her ground better in Seymour's office, not let Rudy run roughshod over her, like it now seemed he had.

God, she shouldn't have hit him. She broke his nose and most likely her own future. She drew her body up into a fetal position, knees under her chin, and sobbed. The tears subsided after a while and were replaced with something else. She rolled onto her back and stared at the ceiling. Undergirding her despair, there was a sense that, for once, she had stood up for herself. Despite Rudy's lies and self-justification, he now knew that there could be consequences for his misconduct. Maybe next time, he'd think twice and keep his dirty hands to himself.

But that didn't help much right now. She got up, paced her house again, once more stared into the refrigerator, like she might discover some magic elixir that would take away all her problems. She turned on the tube and scanned through the channels, then clicked it off. She paced some more. She needed to get her mind off the mess she was in.

She forced her thoughts to Mr. Riley and the peaceful image of him talking about his beautiful purple petunias. Where the hell had Mr. Riley gone? Sure, there were many easy explanations: the fishing trip up north, whatever. None of them seemed quite right to Shelby.

She pulled on blue jeans and a faded T-shirt, then headed out.

On the way to 113 Drury Lake Road, Shelby passed a Kmart, still open. She turned the old Buick into the parking lot, and twenty-minutes later emerged with her new flashlight—a super-bright tactical flashlight, the label had claimed. It sounded like one the British TV detectives would use to explore a deserted warehouse at night. She also purchased a three-pack of latex gloves.

She wasn't sure why she was going back to Mr. Riley's house, but her intuition told her that something was wrong. Weren't the most successful of the British TV cops the ones who trusted their hunches? Plus, what else was she going to do? Writhe in bed, reliving the horror of the morning?

Shelby had never been down Drury Lake Road at night, and she was surprised how completely dark it was. No streetlights, and the few occupied homes that might have lights on were set well back from the street.

She killed the headlights as she approached 113 and gently eased the car door closed as she got out. She adjusted the new flashlight to its narrow-beam setting. A wider beam might be more easily seen by a neighbor. This was unlikely, she knew, because the house to the left of Mr. Riley's house, 111, had been empty all summer. The property to the right, 115, was an undeveloped, wooded lot. There should be no one around to see her, but she would be careful. The last thing she needed now was a police cruiser rolling up, while she was illegally inside the house. Wouldn't Rudy just love that?

At the door, she pulled on her latex gloves. The package said they were for dishwashing, but Shelby would use them for tonight's sleuthing.

The front door pushed open easily, as it had earlier today, and she stepped inside. She scanned the small living room with the flashlight, not flipping any light switches. Unsure what she was looking for, she peered behind the old sofa and the upholstered chair, probed under the cushions. Nothing. She scanned the walls with the flashlight. No pictures that might cover a note or a hidden niche. There was no TV and no bookcases. Mr. Riley seemed like a man who would like to read.

The place felt depressing. Reeked of loneliness. Shelby rubbed her chin with a forefinger as she considered the blank walls. He had said he was waiting. But for what? To die? For someone or some news? Maybe Riley was lonely. She recalled asking him once if he'd been married. In a typical Riley way that didn't directly answer your question, he'd said, "Marriage just wasn't for me." Yet, Riley didn't seem lonely. She closed her eyes and envisioned him caressing the delicate petunia blossoms. There was no anxiety about him—he seemed at peace.

It helped that she'd been in the house earlier, so she knew her way around in the dark. In the kitchen, she opened cabinet doors. Only a few inexpensive dishes. The refrigerator contained little food. Some ground meat from the Piggly Wiggly, several pieces of fruit, a milk container. The milk carton was full. She checked the expiration date—last week. She checked the date on the meat—a week old.

As she turned away from the fridge, she noticed the wall calendar, mounted to the side of the fridge with magnets. One of those big calendars that shows all twelve months. The only entries were for Tuesdays, every week, beginning in February, around the time Mr. Riley moved into the house. The most recent entries were: "gardening-12," "sculpture-12," "history-12," and "Art." The last entry was the day before he'd stopped collecting his mail. Perhaps a relevant clue. Shelby checked her hunch on her phone. She found that the library offered a weekly noontime (hence the "-12") lecture on Tuesdays. The last four topics listed on Mr. Riley's calendar, in fact, corresponded to the lectures at the library on those dates: hydroponic gardening, Wisconsin history during the Civil War, Greco-Roman sculpture, and European watercolor paintings. Not much of a clue at all, but Shelby smiled at the thought of Mr. Riley attending these programs.

The kitchen drawers provided nothing of interest. In fact, it was unusual how little information they did contain. No bills, no phone numbers jotted on a notepad, no business cards. The waste basket under the sink was empty.

On to the tiny bathroom. The cabinet over the vanity contained nothing personal or suspicious. No prescription drugs, no mysterious syringes, not even any interesting OTC meds.

She heard something. She killed the flashlight and pressed herself against the bathroom wall. It was quiet. No sound except for her shallow breathing. There it was again. She took a quiet step toward the front door, in case she needed to make a run for it, then flashed the light into the hallway, where it reflected back from small beady eyes.

A mouse. Just a mouse, but somehow, her reaction to the noise had triggered an adrenalin surge. And a chilling awareness that she was in this old house, alone, at night.

There was nothing of interest in the bedrooms. She went through the pockets of the few clothes in the closets. Nothing. She looked through the nightstand next to the bed—there was no book he'd been reading, no photographs, nothing personal.

She was about to leave the bedroom when she noticed a white cable, plugged in beside the bed. It looked like a charging cable for a mobile phone. She knelt to study it closer. The end of the cable was not the kind of connector that charged a phone. It was for a Kindle—she had one just like it. This would explain the absence of bookcases. If Mr. Riley was the victim of foul play or an accident, would he have taken his Kindle?

Now she stood back by the front door. She'd learned little from her covert adventure. A wave of nausea swept over her, as memory of the incident in Mr. Johns' office replayed itself again. She willed it away and stepped outside and headed for the garage.

Shelby tested the handle on the side door to the garage, as she had earlier—locked. Around the other side of the garage was a small slider window, about five feet above ground level. She wedged her car key into one side of the window frame. It moved, and she was able to slide it open. With a jump, she launched herself up and into the window opening, then pulled herself through, lowering her body carefully into the darkness of the interior.

She panned her flashlight around the garage. A shelf at the front of the garage held a few garden supplies, but the garage was otherwise empty, except for the car, a Jeep Wrangler. It was a narrow one-car garage, typical of these old cottages, with barely enough room to squeeze around the car. She studied the vehicle closely, unsure what she was looking for, checking the wheel wells, where the TV detectives often found hidden packages. At the rear of the car she noticed the license plate—New Mexico. Mr. Riley had never told her where he was from.

She opened the driver's door and flashed her light into the vehicle, breathing a silent prayer: *God, don't let Mr. Riley be in here.* He wasn't. There was nothing in the car. She peeked into the glove box. A manual for the Wrangler. Nothing else. No proof of insurance or registration. That was odd. It was as if the house and vehicle had been sanitized to remove every trace of Mr. Riley's existence.

She started to close the car door, then had one more thought. She leaned down and raised the floor mats. Under the driver's-side mat was a card. She leaned in to look closer. Plastic, laminated. She picked up the card and examined it in the light from her flashlight. Across the top was printed

"Pajarito Ski Area Annual Pass." Below those words, "2016-17." A ski pass from three years ago to a place named Pajarito Mountain.

What she saw next caused her to gasp. She almost dropped the card. It was issued to a Victor A. Marshak. And above the name was a small slightly fuzzy photo of Mr. Marshak, like a driver's license photo. But there was no mistaking what she saw: Victor A. Marshak was Mr. Riley.

Chapter 7

She had just stepped out of the garage door, when she saw a light in the window of the house next door, 111. No one lived in that house. It had been just a flicker, like someone had turned on a flashlight, then quickly turned it off. It couldn't have been a reflection from the road. There was no traffic.

Shelby clicked off her flashlight and pressed herself against the side of the garage, while she tried to decide what to do next. Was someone watching her? Was Mr. Riley, er, Mr. Marshak, hiding in that house? Or was it someone else? Or was her imagination just running wild?

Two minutes later, Shelby stood at the front door of 111. *This is really crazy.* After a deep, mind-clearing breath, she knocked, then called out, "Mr. Riley, are you here?" No point revealing that she knew his real name. "Mr. Riley," she called again. "It's Shelby, the mail girl. Are you okay?"

Nothing.

She went around the side of the house to the window where she'd seen the light. Slipping up quietly, she peeked in one corner of the window. No light from inside. She held up her flashlight and illuminated the interior. The room furnished with a few simple pieces, but showed no evidence of anyone being there recently.

Shelby returned to the Buick, puzzling over the flash of light she'd seen. Maybe some kind of weird floater in her eye, a reflection that scattered off the lenses of her glasses, maybe a lot of things. She dismissed them all. She was certain that she had seen a light in the empty house next to 113.

An hour later, Shelby sat at her dining room table. She'd pushed aside the vase of fresh peonies from her garden to make room for her laptop, and was following the paths that Google led her down.

Typing in the name Victor A. Marshak led to a professor of physics at the University of California, Berkeley, from 1990 to 2012. A short bio stated that he was an expert in quantum entanglement. There was no mention of why he apparently left Berkeley nearly seven years ago. Maybe he retired?

She had to pay three bucks to access an online white-pages from 2010, which showed a Victor A. Marshak with a Berkeley, California, home address. It said he was 54 years old. That would make him 63 today. Too young to have retired from Berkeley in 2012.

A search of obituaries led to an Arthur Marshak, who died in 2002. The notice listed him having a son, Victor. It also listed a daughter, Olivia, Victor's sister, from Golden, Colorado. Was that near Loveland, where Shelby's cousin, Sedona, lived? Shelby had never been to Colorado. Shelby found an Olivia Marshak on Facebook, but there was no personal information available to non-friends.

Shelby learned that Pajarito Mountain Ski Area is in Los Alamos, New Mexico, near the famous science lab. Consistent with the New Mexico license plate she'd seen in the garage. Had Marshak gone to work in Los Alamos from Berkeley?

She brought up the website for the Los Alamos National Laboratory. There was no online employee directory, which did not surprise her—she knew that Los Alamos was where the atomic bomb was developed, figured they worked on top-secret things. She typed Victor A. Marshak into the search bar on the home page, but needed a password to see any results.

Shelby's search could find no other listing for Marshak's name. But she already had plenty.

Next, she looked up quantum entanglement in Wikipedia. It had something to do with quantum physics, about how subatomic particles that had been related to each other in the past, when they were close together—like in the same atom—remain connected with each other forever, even if one particle is moved far away from the other. The article was too complicated for Shelby to follow completely, even though she'd done well in high-school physics. Maybe it simply meant that the things you were born with and the things you have done will always follow you. You can run but you can't hide. She knew that was true. She remembered one of her father's favorite country songs from Merle Haggard, "The Roots of My Raising Run Deep," about a man returning home after being away for many years to discover that the things he had left long ago still affected him deeply.

She leaned her chair back on two legs and hummed the old Haggard tune, while she rubbed her chin between her thumb and forefinger. So, Mr. Riley, who loved the purple petunias in front of his tiny cottage on Drury Lake Road, was really a big-time scientist, who, as best Shelby could tell, had not been heard from for a long time.

Out loud, she said, "Well done, Inspector Sims."

She leaned forward over the table, resting her chin on her palm, as she stared at the screen and pondered the deeper implications of what she'd learned. Maybe Marshak moved from Berkeley to Los Alamos to work on some kind of top-secret stuff, something to do with quantum entanglement or whatever. Maybe he was being chased by the FBI or terrorists or corporate thieves. He had to change his name. Maybe the flash of light she saw in the window next door was .... She slammed the lid of the laptop shut. *For God's sakes, I'm really going off the deep end now. I'm Shelby Sims, not Miss Marple.*

Chapter 8

In the house at 111

He had been watching the house for two days. He'd been through the house, but had found nothing. He was ready to abandon his watch, but then the woman appeared. She'd come twice, gone inside, snooped in the backyard. The first time she wore the uniform of a postal worker. Maybe that was her job, but he couldn't be sure. The second time she'd come, tonight, she'd killed her headlights before entering the driveway—this wasn't a postal inquiry or a social call. Why was she so interested in this place? What was she looking for? More importantly, who was she looking for?

He would have to find out why she was here, what she knew.

Chapter 9

Shelby

Six a.m. on Main Street. The Mug Shot, a coffee shop across the street from the post office and next door to the police station—hence, its name—had just opened. Shelby had already ordered a large extra-bold, when Tisha, wiping sleep from her eyes, slouched into the seat across from her.

"Six freaking a.m., Shelby. This had better be really good," Tisha said.

"I've got a new plan," Shelby said.

"A new plan? It's about time." She ordered a tall latte, then narrowed her eyes toward Shelby. "You sent in the grievance, right? And I hope you're calling some hard-ass lawyer today."

"I mailed the grievance on the way home. But, I'm placing the lawyer thing on hold. I'm heading out this morning."

"What? Heading out where? Hell, I need my coffee."

"Not a hundred percent sure, yet, but maybe Loveland, Colorado, or maybe Golden. Never been to Colorado."

Tisha placed both palms flat on the table and sat up straight. "Are you crazy, Shelby? Don't you think you need to … Colorado?" She shook her head like that might rid her brain of the silly words she'd just heard.

"Just listen. I'll explain. Last night I couldn't sleep, so I went back over to Mr. Riley's house, and—"

"For God's sake, Shelby, you need to get that lawyer, and … you really are channeling your Xena-the-Warrior-Princess, aren't you?" Tisha rolled her eyes like she was in the presence of a lunatic. "Or have you just gone bat-shit crazy?"

Shelby wondered for a moment which description really was her, then manufactured a laugh at Tisha's theatrics. "Just listen. Okay?"

Tisha's latte arrived. "I hope I ordered a triple-shot," she muttered, as she took her first sip. "Seems like I'm gonna need it."

Shelby told the whole story of last night's sleuthing, then said, "So, I've got two weeks of vacation, if you want to call it that. I'm heading out to Colorado. I'll see my cousin Sedona—haven't seen her in years—and I'll see if I can find Mr. Marshak's sister, who I hope will lead me to Mr. Marshak."

"But you're—"

"And I'll get to see the west, which I've always wanted."

"A brilliant plan, Shelby—oh, wait, that isn't a plan, that's just crazy. So, what if you find this Mr. Marshak, and he doesn't want to be found? What if he's some embezzler running from the law?"

"Well, I'll just talk to him about purple petunias and head home." Tisha's eyebrows were raised again. "Look, Tisha, maybe this is crazy, but I need to get out of here. I can't be hanging around, waiting for Mr. Johns to call."

"But, Shelby, don't you—"

"Tisha, I need to clear my head. I need to do something—what else am I going to do?"

Tisha took another sip of her latte, set it down and folded her hands in front of her. "Maybe you're right. But you know I'm going to worry about you, heading off to parts unknown in that old Buick of yours."

"I'll text every day."

"It doesn't matter what I say, does it? Seems like you've got to do this." Tisha reached across the table and squeezed Shelby's hand. "Geez, if I had any vacation, I'd come with you. Wouldn't we cause some trouble?"

"Like a scene from *Bridesmaids*?" Shelby asked, and this got them laughing, which provided needed relief.

"I gotta say," said Tisha, "you do look like a girl headin' out on a road trip." Shelby wore a sky-blue tank top over khaki cargo shorts, perfect, she'd concluded, for a long drive on a summer day. Then Tisha added, "I'm still not sure if you're running after something or just running away."

"What difference does it make?"

"When you're just running away, you have no destination."

Shelby gave a slow nod that said she understood and that she wasn't sure which it was—running after something or running away.

"I'm not sure you're going to find this Mr. Riley, but I hope you meet some good-looking dude who'll sweep you away. When are you leaving?"

"Right now."

"Right now? As in, this very minute?"

"Yep."

"You're messing with me now, aren't you? I seem to recall you taking two hours just to select one outfit for the evening. And you're already packed for two weeks?"

Shelby looked down at her mug, as she recalled Michael once joking, "You should never have so much stuff that you can't pack it all into the back of your car and be gone in twenty minutes."

But then, that's pretty much what he did.

She needed a refill. After she'd raised her cup to the waiter, she said, "Remember, I've got a big old Buick. You can pack a lot of stuff in it. Didn't require much thinking—just pretty much threw all my decent clothes in there." Fueled by a little booze and lots of adrenalin last night, she had, in fact, quickly filled two large duffels—she hadn't used them since her move to town—with most of the summer clothes she had.

"So, this is real. Good God, you really had better text me every day. Shelby, this scares me."

"I know."

There were a few more words, a long hug, then they left, Tisha across the street to begin the morning mail sort—Shelby wondered if Rudy would be in—and Shelby off to Colorado.

In the car, before she pulled out, Shelby reflected on her decision. Yes, she would see Sedona, and she would find Mr. Riley. Or whoever this man is. As far as she could tell, he had no friends. Except maybe her. Maybe the people on her routes really were her children. Maybe Mr. Riley, or Marshak, was in trouble. Had to leave suddenly. Maybe he needed help. Who would help him, if it wasn't her? And—she sagged behind the wheel—who would help her?

As she pulled out onto Main Street, she noticed a man in a parked car—a gray sedan, maybe a Toyota. Was he was watching her? *You paranoid fool. That's something that happens in the British mysteries. Not in a backwater town in central Wisconsin.*

Chapter 10

Andrew

Two days before his fall, Andrew Logan was absorbed in the challenge of starting a campfire. He had set many campfires in his life, but none in the last ten years. Sure, he remembered the principles—make a teepee with the wood, have plenty of kindling underneath—but this apparently wasn't like riding a bicycle; you do lose your ability to do it.

It was the fourth night of his backpacking trip, and every afternoon there had been brief-but-intense thunderstorms, which drenched the landscape and made it impossible to find dry wood. But this afternoon he'd been fortunate to scavenge a few downed branches from under the protective overhang of a large pine, enough for a small fire.

It wasn't that he needed a fire—he had his Jetboil, a miniature propane camp stove, which was fine for cooking meals, and he had the right clothing to keep warm and dry. He wanted a fire. He wanted to gaze into the twisting flames and swirling colors, into the heart of the inferno. He had things to figure out, a future to discern, clarity to grasp. And maybe those could be found while staring into the mystery of a campfire, alone, on a quiet night in the middle of nowhere. Twenty-seven miles from the trailhead, where his old Tundra was parked, he was just now getting in touch with the solitude, getting in touch with himself. It was what Maureen had counseled him to do, and, tonight for the first time, it seemed like she had been right.

The whole purpose of this trip—an open-ended, solitary backpack into the mountains—was to contemplate and pray in the quiet of the wilderness. But so far, his plans had flopped.

He should know something about contemplative prayer—he was a priest, after all—and he did. In his earlier years at St. Timothy's Episcopal Church, he'd taught classes on all kinds of prayer practices during the adult-education hour after the service, but he struggled to make them work for himself.

His church should have been a place for contemplation—an oasis of quiet and peace—but over the past few years it had become the major source of noise in his life. As Andrew leaned over the fledgling fire, blowing and waving a hand to get some air flow, the unwanted image of Buck Martin returned. Buck was the owner of the local Mazda dealership and a member of the vestry, the lay leadership council of St. Timothy's. Andrew was back at the most recent vestry meeting, where Buck was holding court, as usual, about the church budget.

BUCK (making eye contact with all the vestry members): It should be obvious, but we need to run this church like a business. It's no surprise the budget is in the toilet.

ANDREW: The church is not a business, Buck. It's a community built on faith.

BUCK (shaking his head in disappointment): Andrew, we brought you in here to fix this church. Get more families in the pews, especially young ones. Get the budget up, so we don't need to dip into the endowment every year. That hasn't worked out.

Buck never called Andrew, "Father Andrew"—it was always just Andrew. In the Episcopal Church, some parishioners with a more Protestant upbringing called him

Andrew, which was fine with him. Others with a Catholic background called him Father Andrew, which was also fine. But, with Buck it was something else. He never ceded any authority to Andrew, even seemed to resent the authority of a priest. It was unclear whether the other vestry members agreed with Buck's rantings about church operations, but they seldom spoke up, afraid, apparently, to challenge the aggressive Mazda dealer.

Buck was emblematic of a greater problem. Andrew wasn't cutting it anymore—maybe he never had. Maybe it was time to move on—hell, he'd been there eight years. Move to another church? Or maybe to another vocation. Maybe he was washed up.

Andrew shook his head, like he could shake away the image of the judgmental Buck leaning back in his chair with that smug look, his fingers steepled in self-satisfaction. Like he could shake away all the doubts about his ministry that had crept upon him over the past few years, like a stalking predator.

Andrew turned on his knees, away from the struggling fire, not to pray, but to watch a tiny green beetle clambering over a piece of his firewood. "Good evening, Mr. Beetle," he said, "you probably couldn't care less about my whining, could you? I hope you have a good night."

He turned back toward the fire, unlaced the stiff Merrell hiking boots, peeled off thick wool socks, and massaged his feet that were sore after today's long hike. Another recent conversation—with Maureen, the senior warden of St. Tim's—calmed him. Seventy years old, Maureen had been at the church for at least half her life. She'd seen it all, through the good times and the difficult times—in season and out of season, as St. Paul had written. Wise and considerate, Maureen was the only person who knew that Andrew might not be coming back.

MAUREEN: You need to get away, Father, have some time to yourself. Take a few months to figure things out. You're due for a sabbatical, and I'd say you've earned it.

ANDREW: But there's so much work that needs to be done.

MAUREEN: The church will be fine. It's in God's hands, you know.

ANDREW (sputtering): Of course, but ... but ...

MAUREEN (with a twinkle in her eyes): Father, I shouldn't have to remind you that we already have a savior, and it's not you.

A wall of tall trees, now becoming black at nightfall, encircled his campsite. Above them, a few evening stars were already out, and a full moon would be up soon. The green beetle, he noted, had successfully made its way across the piece of pine. He leaned toward the diligent bug. "You see, Mr. Beetle, it's going to be okay, after all." Andrew would have laughed out loud at his friendship with the shiny insect, except he usually wasn't the kind of person who laughs out loud.

With the campfire now burning well, Andrew sliced open a foil packet of freeze-dried beef burgundy and stirred in the boiling water from the pot on the Jetboil. The whishing of the stove and the gurgling of the boiling water joined the only other sounds of the night: an occasional pop from the fire and the faint whisper of the evening breeze in the pines.

He ate his meal in silence.

Pleased with himself for the good supper and the cozy campfire that warmed him, he leaned back and took in the magnificent night sky. The great streak of the Milky Way washed across the darkness above him. Andrew knew that calling it the Milky Way was incorrect—this was just one arm of the Milky Way spiral galaxy, which comprised all the stars he could see on this night. He also knew that all the stars visible to the eye, perhaps ten thousand, were just the tiniest portion of the hundreds of millions of stars in this one galaxy. And he knew that this vast galaxy was just one of billions of other galaxies. He smiled. His physics training was serving some useful purpose.

Andrew studied the pockmarked full moon, now rising above the trees, and pondered what lessons it held for him. That moon had been banged around plenty, pounded by meteors for eons but had not lost its beauty, its ability to whisper soothing encouragement to the romantic heart. Maybe that's who he was—banged up, but still useful.

Andrew had settled into a pattern in just four days. Hiking until mid-afternoon, reading until it grew dark, then quiet time under the night sky. While his planned sessions of contemplation and prayer had not yet been the medicine he'd hoped for, his hiking had. And already the medicine was having effect. The earthy crunching of his lug soles on the rocky trail; the out-of-breath exhilaration as he topped a pass and was treated to a great view; the endless, glorious night sky—these were the holy canticles that had stirred him.

He yawned, as a welcomed sense of peace settled into him. The first time in four days. Campfires will do that. An owl hooted not too far off in the forest.

He had fallen asleep in his down bag, next to the fire, when he bolted awake. A woman was seated on a rock by the fire, her hands extended toward the flames to capture the warmth. Good God, it was Nicole Loverby, the heart throb of most of the boys in high school. Nicole wore shorts and a red sleeveless blouse on this chilly night. He noticed the goose bumps on her smooth arms.

He looked around, as if someone were playing a trick on him. "Nicole?" He'd barely ever spoken to her in school.

She looked down at him. "I had a huge crush on you back then," she said. She had long blond hair, just like he remembered.

What was going on here? Andrew surveyed his surroundings again, expecting to see someone filming this prank or preparing to attack him, then looked back at Nicole. "You did?"

She gave him a smile that to his inexperienced eyes seemed seductive.

He climbed from the sleeping bag and took a step toward her. "I had no idea. Geez, I never even thought of approaching you. You were kind of out of my league."

Nicole arched her delicate eyebrows in a way that said, you've got to be kidding. "I wish you had approached me."

Andrew nodded, his mouth hanging open. "Why are you here?" he finally said. He knew this wasn't real. But Lord, it seemed so real.

"I'm cold."

"Let me get you something." Andrew dug into his pack and pulled out a fuzzy fleece. He started to place it around her shoulders, but stopped and handed it to her. He knelt in the dirt across the fire from her.

"You look the same, Andrew," she said, snuggling into his fleece.

That was ridiculous, of course. He hadn't seen Nicole in over twenty years, since graduation. But oh my, she sure didn't look forty. "And you look, well, great."

"You're out here alone, Andrew." Her large eyes bathed his face. "But you don't have to be alone."

Andrew hadn't kissed a woman in, like forever. He tried to craft a response, but just nodded.

"So I guess I should be going then." She stood, those long cheerleader legs as sexy as ever. She handed the fleece back to him. "Thanks for helping a girl get warm."

Andrew jumped to his feet. "Nicole, you don't have to go."

She turned and walked toward the forest, with Andrew unable to turn his eyes from the sway of her shapely body. He took a few steps toward her, then stopped.

At the edge of the clearing, she turned and gave him a come-to-me invitation with a wiggling index finger. Then she stepped into the darkness of the trees.

Andrew dashed after her, but she was gone. He called her name, but all he heard were the whispers from the pines.

What the hell was going on? A dream? Maybe from the melatonin the doctor had suggested to help him sleep? A loneliness-induced fantasy? Was there something wrong with the beef burgundy? Maybe a reaction to the altitude? There were plenty of explanations. Or was he losing his mind? He'd heard about early-onset Lewy Body dementia. Maybe that was it.

He couldn't accept that somehow this was a real event involving a real person. He turned slowly, scanning the perimeter of his campsite, where the reach of the flickering light from the fire was swallowed by the blackness of the night. He needed to sit.

The reality of his encounter with Nicole now caused him to shake. Whatever this was, it shook him to his core. But he wasn't sure he wanted the memory to end.

Chapter 11

S unrise in the mountains is a sublime matter. Maybe it's something about high altitude air. Maybe the lower atmospheric pressure and the lower oxygen concentration contribute to a giddiness. Maybe it's the absence of pollutants.

Andrew stirred at first light, under the plastic tarp stretched with bungies between two trees, and watched the sunrise from the warmth of his sleeping bag. On a morning such as this, it was hard to feel burdened, difficult not to feel one with the world. It would be easy to shoulder that forty-pound pack with a quick lift, like it was nothing, and envision a vigorous trek today. Objects stand out with a crisp clarity on mornings such as these. Maybe one's life stands out with a crisp clarity, too. It is almost impossible not to be stoked.

Memories of the strange encounter with Nicole had faded in the morning sunshine. Last night, as pleasant as that had been, had spooked him, left him on edge for any sound that might emanate from the forest around him. He'd finally been getting into a contemplative space, when sexy Nicole appeared and destroyed all that.

But this was a new day. Preparing his pack in the morning brought satisfaction. That you can load everything you need for living—shelter, food, clothing, toiletries and even reading materials—into a sack you can carry on your back is a pride-worthy achievement.

Most of Andrew's backpacking equipment was old stuff he hadn't used in years. He'd had to work hard to find it all, buried away at the back of a high shelf in the garage. His old sleeping bag had been musty, but, after airing it out on his back porch for a day, he deemed it usable. The tent was another matter. Apparently, it had been stored wet and was now caked in disgusting back mold. It went straight into the dumpster. He'd considered getting a new one, but couldn't bring himself to shell out two-hundred bucks—that's how he settled on a simple tarp and bungies, which so far had worked fine. He did purchase the new Jetboil, which replaced the old white-gas stove that hadn't been used in a decade and looked unreliable, maybe even unsafe.

Andrew's clothing for the trip had also been a challenge. At church he wore a black clergy shirt—short sleeve in the summer, long sleeve in the winter—with a narrow white tab collar. Black pants. Mostly slacks, but on more casual occasions, black Levi's. Black Rockports. This was his wardrobe, the clothes he wore every day, even on his day off. A parishioner once asked him if he slept in his collar.

It felt strange but liberating to be away from all that. Blue jeans on the cool evenings, hiking shorts during the day. A T-shirt and a new long-sleeve cotton shirt from Cabela's, with an embroidered insignia that said 'Guide Wear,' there no doubt to project the image of a rugged outdoorsman. On this glorious morning, who could argue that he wasn't? He had a fleece—the one he'd offered Nicole—a sweater and a waterproof Gore-Tex parka, which came in handy on the rainy afternoons. These clothes, other than the Guide Wear shirt, had laid around the rectory for years. His only other purchase was a new pair of hiking boots, the waterproof Merrell's, which at ninety bucks was more than he wanted to spend.

As he sipped coffee brewed on the Jetboil, he pondered his day. A topographical map lay spread open on his lap, but it would probably go unused today. He relied instead upon a GPS-based map on his phone—he'd even packed a miniature battery pack that should keep the phone charged for at least another week. Today, he'd log about eight miles, which would take him into the Black Elk Wilderness, a rugged region dominated by massive granite outcroppings and vast forests of pine. The region was heavily travelled by backpackers in the summer, but Andrew had planned a route through one the more remote portions of the wilderness, across a high pass that would lead him to a meadow near a creek, which one online review called stunning.

Now, he pulled out a small journal, where he'd decided to record his observations, fears and hopes, and prayers each day during the trip. He should write something about his encounter with Nicole, but all he could come up with were his reminiscences about dating women over the past ten years. That didn't take long. He laid his pen down, as he recalled a meeting with Fr. Ken, a Capuchin friar, who he visited monthly for spiritual guidance.

ANDREW: I haven't kissed a woman in at least five years. It's not that I didn't want to, don't get me wrong. (Was he blushing?)

FR. KEN: Go on.

ANDREW: Being a single priest is hard. When I—

FR. KEN (laughing): I know about that, Andrew. At least, you Episcopalians are allowed to marry.

ANDREW: When I was newly ordained, I dated some, but it was hard. I never dated anyone from the church—that would be a recipe for disaster. But, even when I dated someone who wasn't from the church, I felt like I was under a microscope. And, as time wore on, my interactions outside the church became fewer and fewer. My only friends, my only contacts, were with people in the church or other clergy. That was a mistake, I knew. So, I haven't kissed a woman in five years at least.

FR. KEN (shaking his head): Great attitude, Andrew. Five years, huh? Sounds like you're going for ten.

He set his journal aside and brought up *The Book of Common Prayer* from the app on his phone—as he'd done each morning on his trip—and found the place where Morning Prayer begins. He had intended to pray the traditional morning liturgy each day of the trip, but this morning was no different than the others. He would barely get past the opening words—"Lord open our lips," with the response, "And our mouths shall proclaim your praise"—when he'd become distracted by a blue jay chortling in the overhead branches of a pine, a chipmunk scurrying across his campsite in search of a meal, the breeze slowly swaying the upper reaches of the forest canopy. He'd initially felt guilty about these distractions—why couldn't he focus on his prayers? But maybe these distractions weren't really distractions at all, but actually evidence of his praise to God. He could present himself to the love of God with his mouth in Morning Prayer, or he could immerse his whole self in that love all around him.

He stuffed the phone into the front pocket of his hiking shorts, where he could easily access the GPS, loaded his pack onto his shoulders and headed out. It was a clear sunny morning, but he kept his Gore-Tex rain parka strapped to the top of his pack, where he could easily get to it. There would be storms later in the day.

Chapter 12

*Hiking on a rough mountain trail takes skill. It requires a
balance of keeping your eyes on the trail versus enjoying the
view. If you don't want to stumble on the uneven rocky surface or trip on a
tree root, you'd better watch where you're placing your feet. It is possible to
have a perfectly safe hike by only watching the trail, but never get to enjoy
the natural beauty around you. It is also possible to spend so much time
watching the distant mountain peaks, the gurgling beauty of a mountain
stream, or keeping an eye out for a buck peeking his head out from behind
a tree that you stumble on a boulder and find yourself flat on your face.
After many years of hiking, I've found this balance.*

Andrew wrote this from the dry sanctuary under his tarp,
beside a quiet meadow that was getting soaked by the
afternoon storm. He chewed the end of his ballpoint pen, then
added, *Too bad that I can't find such balance—caution vs enjoying the
beauty—in the other aspects of my life.*

Damn, he was going down his path of self-pity again. He
finished his journal entry with, *Maybe I should write a book titled
Learning to Whine.*

He set the journal aside and gazed out onto the meadow,
pelted by rain. He picked up Muir. Andrew was a priest—he
should have been reading Thomas Merton or Julian of
Norwich or the Bible, but he needed a break from his normal
habits. He needed a break from theology, biblical commentary,
ethics and morality, and the lives of the saints. Instead, he'd
brought along John Muir's *My First Summer in the Sierra* and
Aldo Leopold's *A Sand County Almanac.*

He underlined a sentence that made him grin. Muir wrote, "Another glorious day, the air as delicious to the lungs as nectar to the tongue." John Muir had travelled solo through the Sierra Nevada Mountains of California—had it been on a glorious day such as Andrew had just experienced, when he wrote these words? He flipped back to an earlier page to another underlined passage, savoring the words again. "Oh, these vast, calm, measureless mountain days ... days in whose light everything seems equally divine, opening a thousand windows to show us God." A great sigh released the tensions he'd been carrying.

He looked out onto the meadow—wild green grasses and June wildflowers popping up everywhere. No other camper in sight. He was alone here. And yet he was not lonely. He couldn't think of any place he'd rather be, and he was certain that Muir would agree. He'd been more lonely in a room full of people. But here, there was a kinship with a great community of living things. Even though he could not see them, he knew that near him now were red-tailed hawks, mule deer, foxes, coyotes, mountain lions, and even green beetles like he'd befriended last night. They were here, like him, sitting out the storm in the forest that surrounded his little meadow.

At the crack of thunder, a tiny lizard scampered from behind the nearest tree and headed for another nearby place of safety. It froze in its tracks when it saw Andrew.

"Hey, Ms. Lizard, don't be afraid," he said.

The lizard remained motionless.

"What can I do for you? What? You want me to sing a song? Sure. What? A Christmas carol? But, it's summer, why would you ... well, okay, if you insist." He cleared his throat before starting.

"We three kings of Orient are

Tried to smoke a rubber cigar.

It was loaded and exploded.

Now, we're—"

The lizard darted away. "Hey, come back, I wasn't finished."

The lizard gave him one more quick look, then disappeared behind a rock. "My, you are one picky lizard," Andrew said. He rolled onto his back and looked up at the plastic tarp, sagging slightly from the pooling rainwater. He smiled at the silly version of "We Three Kings" he'd learned in the schoolyard in fifth grade. Yeah, he could ham it up in front of a lizard, but it was different with people.

He remembered being in a large group in the parish hall last year, while "All You Need Is Love" played on a boom box. Everyone began rocking from side to side and clapping as they sang along. Andrew stood there, frozen like that terrified lizard.

He exhaled a troubled breath, as he wondered why he could preach in front of a congregation, read the last rites amidst a grieving family, and lead the liturgy every Sunday, but struggled to be himself in casual interactions.

The rain let up in late afternoon, but there was no dry wood available for a fire tonight. He ate soup—powder mixed with water and heated on the Jetboil—and crackers, as he watched night fall on the meadow. A few bats circled overhead at dusk, and he heard a pack of coyotes howl somewhere far off.

He had just rinsed his plastic dinner bowl and the soup pan and was putting them away in his pack when he saw her. She sat on a large boulder ten yards away, facing away from him. He stood and cautiously walked toward her. Maybe it was

Nicole again. As he neared her, she turned to face him. Dear God, it was Sharon.

He shuffled from one foot to the other, as she stared up at him. "What are you doing here?" he asked.

"It's been a while, Andrew."

Andrew was silent. Sharon wore Levi's and a dark blue puffy vest over a wool shirt, just like she had when they'd gone backpacking back before grad school, back when they'd first met in sophomore calculus. She looked good. Her brown hair was brushed back, like she was facing into a strong wind. He'd always liked that look. Her large green eyes, which could flash anger, then instantly melt into gentleness, were glued on him.

"Out here alone, huh?" she asked.

"Yeah." Good Lord, he hadn't seen her in years.

"A lonely place."

"I guess."

"I know about lonely."

"You've said that before." He didn't trust himself with her. It would be too easy to get drawn in by that innocent face.

"Still, you don't like to hear that, do you?"

He wasn't going down that path again. "You're looking well, Sharon."

"I take care of myself."

"You always did."

"Somebody had to take care of me."

After more silence, Andrew said, "Look, I know I wasn't a very good husband." She had that loopy smile, like she'd been drinking. He loved that smile.

"No, you weren't. Newsflash, I wasn't so great either."

"How's Sean?" Andrew had not seen his best friend—former best friend—since Sharon left with him.

"He's fine. A very successful physicist."

"I'm not surprised." He worked to keep his voice at a monotone, unconcerned level. Sean and Andrew had been classmates in college and during that one year when Andrew was going for his Ph.D.

"So tell me now, Andrew, after all these years, why did you do it?"

"It" was going to seminary, leaving grad school in physics to pursue becoming a priest. "It's a complicated answer," he said. He'd had this conversation with her too many times.

Sharon winced, as unsatisfied as she had been when he'd first broached the idea to her in their second year of marriage.

But the answer was complicated. Why did he do "it?" Of course, he knew the answer. There had been for him as much clarity in this decision as for anything else in his life. It started when a fellow student invited him to a Canterbury Club meeting at the university. It was an informal evening gathering sponsored by the local Episcopal Church. Andrew had been reluctant to go, then gave in. He'd invited Sharon to go with him, but she said no way. What he discovered at the meeting changed him: students and faculty asking and pondering hard questions about the world, about life, about God's role in all this. Andrew had been intrigued enough that he joined his fellow student at church the following Sunday, although he hadn't been to church in years. Again, he had invited Sharon to go, told her about how meaningful the meeting had been. But Sharon had said something like, "I got burned by church a long time ago, Andrew. There's no way I'll ever darken the doorway of one of those places again."

One time at church and Andrew was hooked. It was like something he'd always longed for had been presented to him. He couldn't articulate what that was, but he found it in the liturgy and the prayers, in the music, in the fellowship, even in the way the sunlight streaked through the stained-glass windows.

At the church, Andrew learned about the priesthood of all believers, that the ministry of every lay person was needed as much as that of an ordained priest. But that wasn't enough for him. He wanted everything he did to be connected with this new-found faith journey. He fought the idea, fought it hard, but ultimately he knew what he had to do: whatever was necessary to become a priest. He had no choice.

He was never successful in explaining his newfound passion to Sharon, but then the most important things in life are often hard to explain. While Andrew struggled with the answers to the questions Sharon asked, she seemed to gradually accept his new calling. Yet, while Andrew was beginning to see the Light, Sharon was beginning to see Sean.

Only a year after that fateful evening with the Canterbury Club, Andrew had become convinced he was called to become an Episcopal priest. It wouldn't be that hard, he had told Sharon—the seminary was just a few miles away from their apartment near the university. He had begun a discernment process with the vicar and other parishioners and had met with the Bishop and the diocesan commission on ministry. Then a year-long field assignment in another church flew by. All these things happened so quickly that their memories were a blur to him now. Perhaps the process had gone too fast. Perhaps the commission on ministry should have told him to slow down, take more time to be certain.

But soon he had dropped out of the Ph.D. physics program and headed to seminary, while Sharon headed to Sean's apartment.

It was almost impossible to focus on learning Greek or anything else at seminary, while he was grieving the loss of Sharon, dealing with anger and guilt at her taking off with Sean, and the sense of rejection from his parents, who sided with Sharon and hounded him to come to his senses about this seminary fiasco and go crawling back to her.

And the seminary was not happy about Andrew's divorce. In their eyes, this wasn't the best way to start a life called to serve God. There were meetings in closed-door offices before disapproving glowers and accusingly raised eyebrows. He remembered this being a time when he sweated a lot.

But he was, in fact, called to serve God's kingdom. At least back then, he profoundly believed that this was so.

Sharon's eyes were locked onto him through this time of silence. They betrayed no emotion. Finally, she said, "Of course, I didn't expect any new insights from you."

Andrew looked down at his feet, as he pondered Sharon's presence. Was he in fact standing on the edge of this beautiful meadow talking to himself? Or, was there something more going on? He looked back up, expecting that she might have vanished, but she still sat there, watching him. "I'm sorry, Sharon," he said. He'd never said this before, but now it felt like the right thing to say. The true thing. "I did what I needed to do then, but maybe I didn't think enough about your needs. I am sorry."

Sharon stood and hugged herself, like she was chilled. "I didn't expect you to say that. But, I'm glad you did. For the record, I'm sorry, too."

Andrew wanted to reach out and touch her, but he didn't. Instead, he watched in silence as she turned and walked off into the forest.

Now he was alone again. Andrew hurried to his pack and pulled out the journal. He wanted to write about the meeting with Sharon. But he didn't. Maybe it was too painful, too disorienting. Instead, he wrote about physics.

Physics. I was pretty good at it. Got good grades in undergrad school. Was good at manipulating equations. I could get the right answer on exams, and the prof would say well done. But I never really understood it at a deeper, intuitive level. Yeah, I didn't understand physics very well, but then I didn't understand a lot of things very well. Like how to relate to other people or how to feel comfortable in my own skin. People have asked me how I could walk away from something based on data, experiments, and reason for something so ancient and unprovable as religion. Good question. Bottom line: faith grounded me, gave me something physics could not, a better sense of where I fit into the universe. Still, I think about physics, visualize those beautiful equations, and wonder how life might have been if I'd stayed on the other path.

He closed the journal and stared off into the darkness. Wasn't he on a vision quest? A vision quest is about vision, and isn't vision about looking forward? That's what Andrew needed, a look forward. But all he was doing was looking back.

Chapter 13

S omehow it got to be morning. He'd had a fitful night, reliving the visit with Sharon. Or was it a visit? Most likely, it was a dream, but, in any case, his encounters with Sharon and Nicole were not the kind of thing he could ever share with another human being. Imagine what Buck Martin would have to say about this. He had read the accounts of near-death experiences, out-of-body experiences and so on. Were any of these things credible? Some scientists, he knew, argued that a certain chemical released at the time of death can produce hallucinations that pass as real experience. Maybe something similar was happening to him.

Focusing on the day's plan helped. Today's hike would take him deeper into the most remote part of the Black Elk Wilderness, up over Marmot Pass, into an area lightly traveled by hikers. He hoped he could again make camp before the afternoon thunderstorm hit, and that required an early start. He'd save his journaling and prayer time until the afternoon. Two energy bars with his coffee served as breakfast. Then he shouldered his pack and headed out.

The trail climbed steeply from his campsite, switchbacking up a high granite cliff that rose above the surrounding forest. He paused at mid-morning along the top of the cliff and took in the view. The craggy summit of Black Elk Peak rose far across a broad canyon. Two turkey vultures soared near him, scouting the terrain below for a snack. Only a few small white clouds on the horizon hinted at rain. Yet,

Andrew knew it wouldn't be long before a thunderstorm would roll through.

He recalled that one of the Church fathers had said that the glory of God was a person fully alive. Working up a sweat in the brilliant sunshine, winding his way up a steep trail through the pines—what a contrast to his usual inactive regimen of slouching over his computer for hours preparing sermons or editing the church newsletter, flattening his butt in a folding metal chair at vestry meetings, not to mention all those second helpings of chicken casserole at the frequent potlucks. Today he was fully alive.

As Andrew hoisted his pack back up onto his shoulders, two hikers emerged from the forest on the trail ahead, the first people he'd seen along this stretch.

"Good morning," came the cheerful greeting from a man, while the pair was still a ways off.

Andrew watched as the man and woman approached him. They were slender and looked fit, each walking with trekking poles. Only the wrinkles on their faces suggested they were older than one might imagine from their fitness.

"Good to see another hiker out here," beamed the man. "I'm Phil, this is Jenny." His face was shaded by a weathered Tilley hat.

"Andrew," he said, nodding to them both. "You come over Marmot Pass?"

"Yep," said the man, "just now. Beautiful up there." He gazed out over the panorama that lay before them. "View's even better than this."

"Just be careful on the trail," added Jenny. "It's washed out in some places." She and Phil both wore khaki hiking pants and faded long-sleeve shirts similar to Andrew's Guide Wear shirt. Clearly, they were veteran hikers—wiry and tanned, unlike Andrew, who was pale and could stand to lose ten pounds.

"Thanks for the heads up. Have a good day." Andrew edged away toward the trail up Marmot Pass. Even though he was a pastor, whose job involved making chitchat with many people, he preferred to be alone.

"How long you out for?" asked Jenny, adjusting a yellow bandana that surrounded her long gray hair.

"No set schedule," said Andrew. "Probably a couple of weeks."

"Nice," said Phil. "Lots to see around here. We're retired—high school teachers for thirty years over in Kalispell—now we get out as much as we can. What do you do?" Phil and Jenny seemed ready to settle in for a good visit.

"I'm a pastor," said Andrew, tugging at the shoulder straps of his pack, indicating he was ready to head out. "Well, better get moving, if I want to be in camp before this storm hits."

Phil gave the sky a wary look. "Don't think you're going to beat it today, I'm afraid. I'd say we've got about an hour. But I see you've got rain gear."

"Looks like you don't have poles, though," said Jenny, raising one of her trekking poles. "These babies really came in handy up on those nasty spots."

"I'll be careful," said Andrew. He nodded and stepped out onto the trail. "You guys have a good day."

From the cliff-top the trail disappeared into dense forest. In the darkness of the canopy, it was still wet from the daily rains, but Andrew's Merrell's were doing a good job, so far, of gripping the muddy trail. His online map indicated there was about three miles in the forest before the trail climbed up to

Marmot Pass. The scenery and the adventure of being in this remote region kept at bay any thoughts of Sharon or Nicole or his mess back at St. Tim's.

An hour later, at a fork in the trail, the rain started, and Andrew slipped into his Gore-Tex rain parka. It gave him satisfaction to see the Gore-Tex label that proclaimed "Guaranteed To Keep You Dry," affirming his confidence that his equipment was impervious to the onslaught of nature, even a torrential cloudburst in the mountains.

Uncertain which branch of the fork to take, he pulled out his phone to check the GPS again. No signal. He didn't remember seeing the fork on the map. He pulled out the paper topo map from a side pocket of his pack, holding it close to keep it from getting soaked. It was difficult to find his exact location on the map because the dense forest prevented him from visually locating landmarks—a peak, a canyon, some distinguishing feature that would help him pinpoint his location—but the map showed no fork, either. He considered his options. He could retrace his steps, but he wasn't out here to backtrack and miss some of the most scenic country in the region. He decided to take the left fork, as it headed uphill, most likely toward Marmot Pass.

He felt a surge of excitement at the prospect of getting lost. He had everything he needed for survival, including a week's worth of food. He was completely self-sufficient. Perhaps getting lost was just what he needed, a chance to truly disconnect from the world.

As the trail climbed the side of a high ridge, the slippery stretches became more frequent. He recalled Jenny's trekking poles, and, yes, he could use them now for balance and stability. Several patches of trail were completely washed away, and Andrew crossed these stretches with great care, often needing to scramble uphill above the trail to traverse around the washout.

After he crossed each difficult spot, he'd turn to admire his accomplishment. It felt good. Out here in the boonies, he could see all his other problems in a different light.

Fr. Ken, his spiritual advisor, had once pointed out that all Andrew's problems were first-world problems. As a priest, he was well aware of the needs in the world around him—even in his parish: people who didn't have enough to eat, people who did not feel safe, people who were discriminated against and marginalized, people dealing with loss. He had none of those problems. A queasiness in his gut marked his shame that he had become so wounded by his stagnation and sense of burning out in his job. Maybe that's why backpacking was so rewarding—it put you back in touch with the more primitive needs: food, shelter, and safety.

Soon the thunderstorm had passed, and the sun peeked through the last straggler clouds and filtered down through the trees. Raindrops continued to drip from the pine needles, and a mist swirled around him.

He stopped to remove his Gore-Tex parka. It was already warming up, and his shorts and Guide Wear shirt, with sleeves rolled up, would be ideal for the rest of his jaunt over the pass. He unshouldered his pack and leaned it against a tree, then removed the parka.

He was leaning forward to attach the parka to the side of his pack when it happened. One heel slipped out from under him on the wet surface, and he went down hard onto his knees. Before he could rise, his momentum had carried him backward toward the edge of the trail. Instinctively, he lunged for his pack, a tree, a rock, anything to hold onto, but his hands came up empty. In an instant, he was over the edge, on his belly, careening feet-first into the dark, forested canyon.

Chapter 14

Shelby

Heading out across the country without a firm destination or perhaps even a legitimate purpose may seem like a great idea to a free-spirited college kid. But for a thirty-seven-year-old woman who'd never been west of the Mississippi, the idea stirred a fair amount of fear this morning. It had seemed like a great idea last night, as she was studying the maps on her computer, with a beer and a glass of chardonnay in her, after a day when she'd been assaulted, humiliated and probably fired.

It was natural for Tisha to worry, Shelby knew, but her objections to her leaving had shaken her resolve. Shelby had stood her ground during their coffee this morning, put up a front of determination and fearlessness, but now, as she considered the concerns of the person she respected most in the world, she wasn't so sure. Maybe she'd make it out to the state line and turn around. She was free to do that, she reasoned, and this freedom helped keep her fears at bay and pressing westward. She certainly was no Xena the Warrior Princess, like Tisha had joked. But dammit, she wasn't crazy, either.

This wasn't really about sleuthing. Not about latex gloves and fingerprints. Not about high-power tactical flashlights probing the darkness of some spooky building. It was about her needing to get away from the gut-wrenching stress of waiting to hear if she'd been fired. And yes, it was also about her "children." Looking out for them. Being a responsible friend. And, okay, it was also a little bit about sleuthing. And maybe also because she was lonely. Were Miss Marple and that woman on *Murder She Wrote*—Shelby couldn't remember her name—ever lonely?

The northern half of Wisconsin in June is a lush green. The scenery is not dramatic—no stunning skylines, no snowcapped peaks or breathtaking canyons—but pleasant, soothing. Shelby used the Google Maps app on her phone to guide her along a network of state highways toward Eau Claire, where she'd head west on I-94. In Minneapolis, she'd either continue west on I-94 into North Dakota, or cut down to I-90, which would take her through South Dakota. She'd never been to either state. She'd make the decision when she got there.

Other than filling the tank of the gas-guzzling Buick, Shelby didn't stop often. Once at a pull-out to take a selfie against the scenic backdrop of the St. Croix River, where she crossed into Minnesota. The other time at a rest stop for a potty break and to send a text to Tisha, with the selfie, saying she was doing great. She also texted her cousin Sedona, letting her know she was coming to Loveland. She didn't say when she'd arrive—she didn't know, and she didn't want to know. She would fight off her tendency to over-organize. She would be a free spirit, like Sedona.

Three hours later, after battling the urban freeway networks in the Twin Cities, it felt good to be back out in the country, in southern Minnesota, where the green woods of Wisconsin had faded into fields of yellows and ambers.

She wished she had an audiobook. The 2002 Le Sabre had no USB or Bluetooth through which she could connect her phone to the speakers, just a CD drive. She leaned across and dug into the glove box—she was good at driving with her left hand—and pulled out a CD, apparently the only one in the car. But it was a good one: Emmylou Harris, *Quarter Moon in a Ten Cent Town,* and soon she was bouncing in her seat and wailing along with Emmylou to "Two More Bottles of Wine." She'd heard the CD a million times, but she played the whole disc twice. Then she scanned through the few radio stations she could pick up out here in the heartland, mostly political talk shows and Christian radio, and clicked the radio off.

She had decided to take the southern route across South Dakota, and by three-thirty she'd made it to a KOA campground outside Sioux Falls. The old Buick had performed mostly without a problem, although there was a moment on the interstate south of Minneapolis, when the car momentarily lost power, similar to what she'd experienced along her mail route. It had lasted only a second or so—enough to alarm her—but hadn't occurred again in the last three hours of today's drive. She probably should have had it checked out before she left.

Any concerns about the car were offset by her accomplishment of finding a good campsite for only thirty bucks. It was close to showers and was nestled safely among big RVs, where families with children tossed Frisbees and charming retired couples in lawn chairs sipped wine. The campsite cost far less than a hotel room and was safer than a roadside rest, where God knows who might pay her a middle-of-the-night visit.

She'd have to sleep in the reclined bench seat, but that would be fine—she was exhausted after four-hundred eighty miles and eight hours of driving.

The new scenery, the challenge of route-finding, the tactical decisions about where to stay, even worrying about the

Buick, had successfully displaced, at least for now, thoughts about Rudy and his big bandage and dirty hands, the prospect of losing her job, Tisha and her doubts about the trip, and even the mystery of Mr. Riley.

Shelby walked with a new confidence along the gravel path to the shower room, nodding at other campers. She was in the freaking middle of nowhere, and she loved it. The shower was great, as were her spirits. She made funny faces in the mirror, while putting on her sleepwear—sweat pants and a drab sweatshirt—and sang another verse of "Two More Bottles of Wine." She was on a road trip.

The walk back from the shower took her past giant RVs the size of Greyhounds, small pop-up trailers, and even a few tents. The atmosphere was friendly, almost celebrational. Everyone here was traveling somewhere; out here on I-90, their destinations were probably far away. What a collection of exciting stories were likely embodied in this small community, thrown together for one night. And she was part of it.

As she made the turn onto the gravel path that led back to the Buick, her phone beeped. Text from Tisha. *Loved the selfie of you against the scenery. Looking forward to a selfie of you against some six-pack scenery wearing tight Levi's.*

Shelby, rocking with laughter, looked up from her phone just as a football sailed past her, barely missing her head. As she turned toward where the ball had come from, a young boy, going full-tilt, collided with her, almost knocking her over. Shelby caught the boy in her arms, and it took a burst of her strength to keep them both from toppling over.

"Are you okay?" she asked the child, as she knelt to look him in the eye.

The boy looked at Shelby with surprise in his face, but said nothing. His dad was by her side quickly. "Are you okay, Chad?"

The boy looked up at his dad and nodded, as Shelby stood. "Gee, I'm so sorry," the man said. "I'd have never thrown that pass if I'd seen you coming around the corner. You all right?"

Shelby's eyes were still on the boy, Chad, this healthy, energetic, good-looking child. She'd held him in her arms. He was probably about five, the age her child would be now. "I'm fine," she said.

The man and his son walked, hand-in-hand, back to their campsite. Shelby stood motionless, watching them, glanced toward the sky, then continued back to the Buick.

Later, at sunset, Shelby sat at the picnic table next to her car, chewing on a Luna Bar and sipping a blue PowerAde Zero—she'd tossed a case of each in the back of the Buick before she left—and studying Google Maps on her phone, when the man approached her.

"Gonna sleep in that thing?" he asked.

She didn't look up. "Yes."

"Good luck with that, young lady," he said. Now she looked up at a graying guy with a paunch and a green John Deere logo cap. He let out a chuckle to convey his amusement with this camping newbie.

"I'll be fine."

"Probably gonna get uncomfortable later on," he said, nodding toward the Buick.

"I'll make do," she said with disinterest.

"You should have a little trailer to pull behind that thing."

Shelby shrugged.

"Where you headed?"

She was certain that the man meant no harm, and her natural response would be to tell him where she was going, be polite, maybe even ask his advice. But not today. It was none of his damn business where she was headed. "Just traveling. My car's fine."

"Well, actually, if I were you, I'd probably get a campervan. Yeah, that'd make the most sense for you. Be happy to fill you in on—"

"Like I said, I'm doing fine. I don't need a—"

"Well, actually, it can be dangerous for a single gal to be—"

"I'm rather busy right now, sir, so if you don't mind." She lowered her gaze again. Tisha called it mansplaining—you don't get to be thirty-seven without having to put up with more of it than you'd like. Shelby smiled, as the man left—she knew that calling him "sir" would take the air out of his swaggering.

Shelby had no trouble falling asleep. She'd even had the foresight to throw her favorite blanket—an old Tartan wool blanket that reminded her of her mother—into the back seat, and it felt good now, wrapped around her. Then the chatter began. At some campsite nearby, a loud, animated conversation had begun, punctuated with raucous laughter, the kind usually produced by lots of alcohol. She tried to ignore it, but soon she heard the strumming of a guitar and voices butchering "Oh, My Darling Clementine." She checked her phone. Ten-fifteen. Didn't the campground quiet hours begin at ten? She pulled the blanket up over her ears and tried to sleep, but the drunken laughter and bad music were too much.

She got up and moved to the picnic table, diving into *Nobody's Fool* on her Kindle. Then, her sleep ruined for a while, she headed out for a stroll around the campground. The noise from the neighboring site had now subsided. Most of the RVs, fifth wheels and trailers were dark, their tall silhouettes like the nighttime skyline of a small city.

Just a few sites down from hers, she saw another car, with no tent or trailer, pulled into one of the sites. Someone else sleeping in their car—she wasn't the only loser in the campground.

It was a gray sedan. The silvery windshield cover prevented her from seeing inside. Was it the car she'd seen as she was pulling out this morning? Those late-model Toyotas, Nissans, and whatevers all looked alike—there was no mistaking an old Buick. She continued on around the campground loop to where she could see the rear of the car. She turned toward a large fifth wheel opposite the car, like she was admiring the big RV, then, as she turned back, quickly snapped a photo of the rear of the car, a Camry with Minnesota tags.

Chapter 15

The start-up roar of a big diesel jolted Shelby upright from a deep sleep. It took her a moment to realize where she was. Sometime in the night she'd switched from lying back in the reclining seat to stretching out across the bench seat. It was still uncomfortable, as there wasn't quite enough room to fully extend her five-eight frame.

She climbed out of the car and stretched, her muscles stiff. The old guy with the John Deere cap had been right about sleeping in the car. Back from the bathroom, she pondered her day. Instead of planning her route last night, she'd spent her time with Google Maps following the extent of I-90 across the country. The interstate runs over 3,000 miles from Seattle to near Logan International in Boston, not to mention the KOA outside Sioux Falls. These folks around her—packing up and starting those big diesels—could be heading anywhere. She stretched again and gave out a long yawn. And here was this girl from Wisconsin, who'd never been anywhere really, out in the midst of all the excitement.

Although she'd studied where I-90 went, she wasn't sure where she was going. She'd be heading west on I-90, then at some point—she hadn't figured out where yet—she'd cut south toward Colorado. She was determined to be spontaneous—Sedona would be impressed. Loveland, Colorado, would be her first major stop-over, but she wanted to take her time getting there, with so many things to see in between—the Badlands, Rapid City, Mt. Rushmore, the Black Hills. Places she'd heard about her whole life.

Her breakfast was an Egg McMuffin and black coffee from the drive-thru at a McDonald's near the interstate. Shelby rarely ate fast food, but this was part of her guilty indulgence, munching on the sandwich, as she merged into the sparse I-90 traffic headed west. She toasted the day with her coffee—that's what she was: headed west.

I-90 is a straight shot across the flat plains of eastern South Dakota. Two hours into the drive, she'd already listened to the Emmylou Harris CD two more times and heard the farm reports from several local AM stations. Now she enjoyed the silence. There wasn't much to see out here: an occasional billboard, a truck passing her—the speed limit out here was eighty, but she kept her old car at seventy.

It was over 300 miles from Sioux Falls to Rapid City, a lot of time to think. A lot of time for reliving memories, for assessing the present, for wondering about the future. This was more than a trip, she thought. Symbolically, it was a statement. She was seizing something new, instead of having to settle for the less exciting path, as she'd always had to do—not having the money to get her nursing degree at UW and settling for an AA in nursing from a community college, then dropping out of that. Losing a fiancé, then a child. Shelby eyed the endless landscape speeding by, like time passing, like her life passing by. She forced herself to focus on the road ahead, a horizon coming toward her fast, bringing with it things that are new. Life must be about more than surviving loss.

A trip west was just what she'd needed, and she hadn't realized it until now. She lowered her window and let the hot, dry South Dakota air blast her face, like a pressure washer ripping away the dirty layers of regret. She was free and wild, like a pioneer woman facing bravely into a new world.

Hell, there was nothing wrong with her that riding off into the sunset on the back of a Harley wouldn't fix. And maybe that was what she was really doing out here. Even if she was taking baby steps. She remembered Tisha's cliché response when she'd anxiously taken her first turn driving her Buick from the passenger side with her left hand. "Gotta walk before you can run," she'd said. Maybe that's what she was doing heading out into the open west, as open as her plans. Maybe this was just the first step on her way to great new discoveries about herself. Or not. Maybe this was just the thrashings of a fool. Gotta walk before you can stumble.

Tisha. Perhaps the most amazing person she'd ever known. Confident and wise. And funny. Those high, regal cheek bones and large dark eyes that could melt you with their warmth or burn you with their intensity. And her spectacular black, almost iridescent, hair. Most recently, Tisha had worn it pulled back into a tall bun behind her head. In the past, she'd worn her hair in a stunning Afro, and, Shelby's favorite, what Tisha called a halo braid.

They'd met at the post office three years ago, when Shelby was hired as a contract employee. Tisha had already been there two years and was a regular USPS employee. They hit it off immediately. Slowly, Shelby had learned about Tisha's unusual background. October 23, 1983. That date stuck in Shelby's mind, because it was so important to Tisha. That's the day a truck bomb exploded in Beirut, Lebanon, killing over 200 Marines. One of them was Tisha's father. She was six months old at the time. She'd been born in a Black neighborhood in Milwaukee, but a couple of years later, her widowed mom married the realtor, a White man, who had sold her house, and they moved to the north shore suburbs, into an almost all-White neighborhood.

So, although Tisha was Black, for as long as she could remember she had lived in White communities. Once, Tisha said to Shelby, "You'd think I'd fit into both worlds, but the sad truth is I don't fit into either. I'm a Black girl who could never be White, yet I don't know how to be Black. I grew up in a White neighborhood, played with White kids, had White dolls, went to a White school, even dated White guys. Didn't matter—I'm not White and I can never be White. Folks always look at me differently. I was called the N-word in grade school by other kids. Sure, I had friends, but others treated me as inferior. I was used to cops stopping me when I was walking in the neighborhood, just blocks from my home, and grilling me about what I was doing in this part of town. Back then I didn't even know that was wrong."

Shelby had asked, "Did you ever go back to your old neighborhood?"

Tisha looked down, shaking her head. "No. My grandparents had a falling-out with my mom when she remarried and moved away. Then when my mom died—I was sixteen—I lost the last connection with my roots."

Shelby shook her head now. So freaking what if I lose my job, she thought. Compared to what Tisha's gone through, that's just crap.

It was only about a month ago when the subject last came up about what it was like being one of the few African Americans in town. It was at one of their Friday nights at the Quartermaster. Tisha usually emphasized living in the present and going for the possibilities of the future—she didn't believe in brooding about the past, but that night she got into it good. Shelby had again asked Tisha why she stayed in their little town, and she wanted to hear more than her usual bullshit answer about staying because of church and friends.

Tisha stared into her beer and was silent for a bit. Then she said, "I'm just a few generations removed from relatives who were slaves, who were treated as property. Relatives who trembled with PTSD and no doubt passed it down the line. This place, this town, isn't my true home, but it's as good as any place I've lived. Frankly, I don't know where else I could go." Then, Tisha had said, "Do you know how many Black people there are in this town?"

"Not very many, but I don't know the number."

"Eleven."

Shelby wasn't surprised the number was so low, but she was surprised that Tisha knew what the number was.

"I regret that I know that number," Tisha said, emphasizing her displeasure with a grimace. "I shouldn't have to."

"I hate that you've been discriminated against."

Shelby remembered that at this point Tisha looked away. Shelby had followed her gaze toward the head of a big eight-pointer, mounted helplessly on the knotty-pine wall behind the bar. The glassy eyes of the poor creature stared back at them.

Tisha shook her head as she looked back at Shelby. "You see, when I get started, I always wind up a mess. Feeling angry. Wounded. Isolated. Not where I want to be."

"I'm sorry Tisha, but I want to know about you."

Tisha let out a huge sigh that was either a surrender or a refueling for the battle, before she continued. "Most of the time it's okay, but then some clerk who doesn't know me will give me the once over when I walk into their store, watching me like they're expecting me to shoplift. Like they're afraid of me. I'm used to having people act awkward around me, like they don't know what to say to someone who's Black, like they don't know I'm just an ordinary person."

"Oh, Tisha." Shelby took one of Tisha's hands and held it in both of hers.

"Oh, it's not everyone, just a few."

"Still, I hate hearing this, Tisha. You're the best person I know."

"The discrimination is real," Tisha said. She sagged like she was exhausted. "But it will be better someday, I pray. Meanwhile, I can't let it defeat me."

"You're always so positive. How do you manage that?"

Tisha let out a troubled laugh. "I've learned how to survive anywhere, but I'm still looking for a place where I can thrive."

"So, why do you stay here?"

"It's the same everywhere," Tisha said, with a hopeless frown that evolved into a smile. "And, anyway, where would I find a friend like you to go drinkin' with on Friday night?"

Shelby took the last sip of the now-cold coffee and watched the flat South Dakota plains fly by. Too bad Tisha didn't have any vacation days. She glanced over at the empty passenger seat and imagined her there. Laughter, singing—the miles would fly by.

Shelby considered turning the car around and heading home. Then she gripped the wheel harder. She could not let her resolve falter now. It helped to review her plans again. Maybe after she saw Sedona and found Mr. Marshak's sister, she'd head on down to Arizona to visit her parents. They'd sent her photos of their little condo in Sun City—they'd only been there a year—and invited her over and over again to come visit.

Maybe that wasn't the best subject to pop into her head. It wasn't that long ago—when they still lived in Oshkosh—that she'd moved back in with mom and dad. It was during that down time. She'd been thirty-two then—good God, behaving like a helpless child. What would she say now? That she'd been sexually harassed and probably fired? She could see them now: her mom, wistful and passive, worrying and emotional; and her dad, strong and opinionated, ready with explanations and judgment. At his worst, belittling. "How could you let that happen to you?"

But, hey, she was heading west. Away from Rudy, the impending loss of her job and perhaps some kind of criminal charge. Maybe she was like a fugitive fleeing the hounds or a desperado on the run from the law. Maybe that should provoke some kind of adventurist adrenalin surge, but right now it just caused her to shake. Her mother's worried face popped into her mind again: "Oh, Shelby, you'll get through this somehow."

Shelby. Strange name, she thought, then laughed, amused by the things that flit through your mind, like a swarm of butterflies, while you're driving across the endless flats of South Dakota. She wasn't sure how she came by her name, but when she was growing up, her father liked to mention that she reminded him of the country singer Shelby Lynne. He loved Shelby Lynne, even though most people had never heard of her. Dad had always been a big country-music aficionado, knew all the singers, even the obscure ones—back before country music was mainstream cool, back before guys in muscle shirts and big cowboy hats that hid their faces could pack stadiums with 20,000 screaming fans. Back when you wouldn't dare admit that you liked country music. Sort of like admitting that you liked the taste of Spam or that your dog slept in the bed with you.

Shelby's dad loved Shelby Lynne's smoky, sultry voice and often claimed that she should have made it big. Shelby Lynne was pretty, and maybe that's why her dad said she reminded him of his daughter. But he also lamented how Shelby Lynne had lots of unrealized potential. He'd shake his head at the injustice of it. Maybe he was shaking his head about his daughter, too. Unrealized potential.

Her phone beeped—another text from Tisha. *So, still shaking a bit. At lunch today, Derek popped the question!*

Shelby pulled into the next roadside rest. **Derek Daniels,** the sergeant at the police department, was certainly a good guy and a hunk. But she wasn't sure how Tisha felt about him. She texted back: *Tisha! I'm shaking too! So exciting. Did you give him an answer?* She ended the text with a heart emoji.

Tisha's response came in moments. *Not yet.*

Then a minute later, Tisha texted again, with no mention of Derek. *It's always easier to advise you what to do.* A smiley-face emoji was inserted here. *Enjoy your drive today—rest up for that candlelight dinner with some buff cowboy. Rudy—sorry to spoil your romantic dinner—called in sick today. Probably building his case as the wounded victim.*

Shelby punched in Tisha's number. It went to voicemail, of course—Tisha was at work. She left a message: "Hey, Tisha, call when you can."

Not yet. That's what Tisha wrote.

They'd already been living together for two years, when Michael said something like, "So, you think we ought to go ahead and tie the knot?" They were out to dinner at Pizza Hut for his birthday.

Shelby had said, "Are you asking me to marry you?"

"So, what would you say if I was?"

She'd waited for something like one freaking second before saying, "I'd say yes."

He'd hoisted his PBR and said, "Well, I guess that settles it."

She should've said, "Not yet."

Yes, she should be back home, hanging out with Tisha, working through important stuff, and here she was wandering aimlessly off into the unknown.

As Shelby pulled back onto the interstate, she lowered the window and let the warm summer air blast her face again. Was it the text from Tisha, or the travails she had left behind, or maybe this wild open country that was causing her emotions to bounce all over the map? After all, it was emotions that had brought her out here, not some careful analysis.

What was it that Tisha asked at the Mug Shot? Was she running after something or just running away? For now, even running away felt like enough. She was trusting her intuition, and it felt good.

What is intuition, anyway? Is there really such a thing as women's intuition? She'd heard that phrase all her life, but right now she suspected it was total bullshit, a sexist label attributed to women that implies they lack the rational deductive skills or education to make decisions that are not based on emotion, hunches or whims.

Was she a feminist? Probably not, she concluded. She'd rarely been one to rock the boat or make a scene. Geez, she was one of those women who ended her statements around men with an apologetic laugh that said you don't have to take me seriously. She wrinkled her nose in disgust.

When she took that swing at Rudy, maybe she was taking a swing at those times in her life when she had acquiesced, caved, didn't speak up. And maybe more was broken by that swing than Rudy's fat nose.

Yes, she believed in intuition. Maybe she had it, maybe not. Women's intuition? That was akin to attributing a sixth sense to your dog.

She had just passed the exit to Murdo, South Dakota—noteworthy, according to the gaudy billboard, for a pioneer auto show that promised fun for the whole family—when she saw the orange sign: *Road Construction 12 Miles Ahead, Expect Delays*. She glanced down at Google Maps, open on her phone on the seat next to her—no surprise: a long stretch of red ahead, with a forty-minute delay. The app also showed an exit, six miles ahead, for a state highway slanting off to the southwest toward Colorado. An easy call.

South Dakota 78 was a two-lane highway with little traffic, winding through the rocky open country south of Badlands National Park. It should bring her out to a connecting highway that would lead her right into the Mt. Rushmore area. Shelby's pulse quickened, as she spotted pronghorn antelope grazing near the roadside and a huge bird, maybe an eagle, perched atop a rancher's fencepost. Mountains on the horizon, backed by a spectacular thunderhead, created an iconic western landscape. She had made the right decision, leaving the big trucks and construction delays of I-90 behind. At the entrance to a dirt road leading off to nowhere, she pulled over and took another selfie, then texted it to both Tisha and Sedona with the message: *Me in God's country. This is so great!*

As she accelerated back onto the highway, she felt the hesitation of the Buick. She had pressed her foot down on the gas pedal, and nothing happened. A shaft of panic jolted her, but then the car's power returned and everything was normal again. Maybe she should return to I-90, she wondered, where there were other motorists to help, in case the car broke down. But that was already a good fifteen miles behind her. What would Sedona do? She would keep going toward that beautiful horizon and have the car looked at the next Buick dealer, although Shelby had no idea where that would be.

The road began to climb gently toward the mountains, with sagebrush giving way to hillsides dotted with pines. There was almost no one living out here. No towns since she'd left the interstate. Shouldn't there be towns along a state highway? An occasional cabin or distant water tank was the only sign of civilization. She checked Google Maps again, but the screen had gone blank, with a little spinning arrow indicating no data. *Damn.* She checked the phone signal: nothing. Shelby tightened her grip on the wheel, remembering how her father always criticized electronic devices like GPS. She could see him now, shaking his head and proclaiming, "What's wrong with a good road atlas?" She didn't have a road atlas.

The thunderheads were getting closer—she expected rain soon.

Wasn't there a sign a couple miles back that said there was a town up ahead—was it called Omega? She couldn't remember how far it was. She would stop there and regroup. Fortunately, the Buick now sounded healthy.

As the highway topped a low pass, the storm hit. Lightning strikes came like a machine gun barrage, illuminating the cloud-darkened landscape like a strobe light. One struck so near that the car shook. A pounding rain, loud and dense—the wipers could not keep up—forced Shelby to the side of the road. She killed the engine and waited.

Within minutes the storm blew over, and shafts of sunshine now streaked through the clouds—someone had called it God light. A magnificent rainbow arched the highway, which Shelby took as a good sign. She snapped several photos that she would text to Tisha later. When she started the car, it emitted a growling sound like a snarling dog. Then in the rearview mirror she saw the plume of white smoke behind her.

She left the engine running, as she walked around the car, looking for a clue to the problem. She popped the hood, but couldn't see anything amiss, cursing herself for not knowing much about engines. She checked her phone again—still no signal. Maybe she should stay here by the road and wait for help. She leaned against the car, fingers pressed against her temples like she had the mother of all migraines. How far was it to Omega? She peered down the road, but could see no sign of civilization. But it couldn't be that far, could it? She'd try to make it. Maybe there'd be a Buick dealer there.

The car sputtered along, shaking, belching white smoke. She kept her speed down, and fortunately, there was almost no traffic—still, she worried about being rear-ended by a Peterbilt going eighty. Then she noticed the temperature gauge. The needle had moved way over into the red.

A billboard advertising the Omega Diner, two miles ahead, buoyed her spirits. Another billboard promoted Omega Garage, specializing in all vehicles. Shelby let out a laugh, wondering if you specialized in all vehicles, how could that be specializing? But mostly, her laugh was of relief. Help was near.

When she arrived in town, her buoyed spirits sank. Omega seemed to be no more than a small cluster of shacks, many apparently abandoned and near collapse. She briefly wondered who delivered the mail out here. There were two businesses. On her left, the Omega Diner was closed and looked like it had been closed for years.

On her right was the Omega Garage. Shelby wanted to cry. The garage was a sagging structure, surrounded by old vehicles, some without wheels, supported on blocks. Apparently, the Omega Garage was part garage and part junkyard.

Shelby pulled the Buick up to an open garage door, stepped out and surveyed her surroundings. Shaking her head, she poked her head in through the open door into a dark interior. Except for the faint sound of Lee Greenwood singing "God Bless the USA" somewhere far off, there was no sign of life. "Anybody here?" she called out.

"We're not open today," came a voice from the back.

Shelby considered leaving, but where would she go? "I need help," she said.

A light came on in the garage area, as a woman, wiping her hands on a towel, stepped toward her. "What kind of help?" she asked.

"I'm having problems with my car. There's white smoke coming out, and it's overheating. And it loses power sometimes."

"I'm afraid the mechanic, my husband, is away visiting his brother out in Boise—won't be back for three days."

"I don't know what to do."

"I'm Brenda," the woman said. She wore a tattered flannel shirt over blue jeans. Her short gray hair hung straight. Her big green eyes were kind.

"Shelby." She looked around the interior. Old engine parts lay everywhere. "I can't wait three days." Of course, she could wait—she had no schedule—but there was no way she was going to wait here.

"Sounds to me like you've got a blown head gasket. And, I hate to say it, maybe some engine damage."

Shelby had heard about blown head gaskets. She didn't know what they were, but she knew this was bad. "What do I do about that?"

"Start it up and let me listen to it."

A few minutes later, back inside, Brenda said, "Yep, I'm pretty sure Flo would say it's at least a blown head gasket."

"Flo?"

"My husband. Oh, he's Florence—everybody calls him Flo. Kind of a boy-named-Sue thing, I guess."

"So what should I do?"

"That's an '02, right?"

"Yes."

Brenda busied herself in a book behind an unpainted plywood counter. "Yep, I figured as much." She gave Shelby a mournful look that said she had some bad news to share. "Problem is, Bluebook here says your old Buick isn't worth much more than two grand."

Shelby didn't like where this was heading.

"And, I can't say for sure—Flo could—but a new head gasket, installed, is gonna cost you about the same."

Shelby rested her hand atop a rollaway tool chest, just in case she was going to faint. She should have had the Buick checked out before she left. Had the head gasket examined. Hell, she should have had *her* head examined. She checked her phone again: No signal. "I don't suppose you have WiFi here?"

"Usually we do, but that storm knocked it out. You can use our phone, if you want."

"That would be very nice." Shelby already had her laminated insurance card out, as Brenda led her back into another room, full of scattered papers, auto parts, and greasy rags.

She was lucky to get through, after being on hold for only ten minutes. "I'm broken down out here in South Dakota, and I want to check if my insurance has towing coverage," she told someone named Toby. She had to hold for another ten minutes before learning that she had no coverage for roadside assistance, which would include towing or a rental car while her vehicle was being repaired.

When she hung up, she turned back toward Brenda, who'd been watching with a concerned motherly look. "So, how much would it cost for you to tow my car to the next town? And just where is the next town? I mean one where I could get my car fixed. Oh, hell, I'm not even sure what I'm asking."

"Oh, Shelby," said Brenda, laying a gentle hand on Shelby's arm. "I'd be happy to tow you, but Flo's got the wrecker. And, since that's our only vehicle, I can't even drive you anywhere. And the next nearest town is Bridger, a real nice place. Twenty-three miles."

Shelby turned and faced the door, hands on her hips.

From behind, Brenda said, "If you like, you could stay here with me until Flo gets back. You'd have to sleep on the couch, but I'd make you real comfortable."

"That's very kind of you, Brenda," she said, turning back toward the woman. "But I'd really like to move on, if I can."

She drummed her chin with her forefinger, like she was drumming up a new idea. "Isn't there some kind of additive or something you can put in the gas tank or whatever to keep my car going for a while?"

Brenda thought this over. "Well, I've seen Flo use some stuff before. He just calls it gunk." She gave out a brief laugh. "And you put it in the radiator, seals up cracks and leaks, I think. At least, it's supposed to. I've never used it myself."

"Have you got some of this gunk?"

"Hmm, let's look. I'm not sure where Flo keeps some of these things," she said, as she began digging through the mess. Shelby joined in, even though she wasn't sure what she was looking for. "Ah ha," Brenda almost screamed, "I think this is it." She held up a can for Shelby to inspect.

They studied the instructions for a long time. "So, it says it's only good for a temporary fix," Brenda said. "You still want to try it? Might get you to Bridger. Or not. I'd worry some—there's nothing but wilderness between here and there."

"Surely, it's not too bad. I'm on State Highway 78, aren't I?"

"'Fraid not. You must have missed that turn about ten miles back—easy to do. Bet it was in the storm. This is just a county farm road—not even sure it has a number any more, everybody just calls it the Omega Road. Not much traffic, as you can see."

Shelby stared out at the empty highway for a moment, then looked back at Brenda. "Sure, I'm ready to risk it," she said, with fake confidence. As the gunk glugged its way into the radiator, Shelby made small talk. "So, how'd this town get its name?"

Brenda was watching the fluid ooze from the can, being careful not to spill any. "The bible. Remember? The alpha and the omega."

Shelby must have given Brenda a puzzled look. "Get it? Alpha means the beginning. Omega ... I mean, just look around."

"But it's your home," Shelby said. "How long have you and Flo been here?"

Brenda scratched her head. "Must be twenty years."

"Before that?"

"Rapid City. Flo worked at the Chevy dealer there. Got a chance to have his own business down here." She waved a hand in a sweeping gesture. "Hasn't always been easy, but like you said, it's home."

The Buick started right up, sputtered a bit, but there was no white smoke. "Brenda, I think you did it. I'm so thankful. What do I owe you?"

"Oh, it's on the house, hon. But, you watch out. That can said "temporary fix," so I say get this buggy checked out when you get to Bridger. Okay? Like I said, you're welcome to stay here. No charge for that, either. I'd cook us up a nice supper."

Shelby stepped in and gave Brenda a hug, then pulled back to see the mistiness in Brenda's eyes. "I won't forget this," she said.

Five minutes later, Omega had already disappeared from her rearview mirror.

Chapter 16

The Buick was running better, but Shelby wasn't. Maybe the gunk had been a miracle drug for her sputtering car, but where was the miracle drug for her sputtering life? The thought of Brenda, lonely, living out here, trying to make the best of it, only brought her down further.

Maybe she wasn't that different from Brenda. Always had to settle for less. Suck up the disappointments. Lower expectations. The big breath she exhaled was like the air gushing from a balloon that had brought joy at the birthday party, but was now expended and forgotten in some corner of the room.

She rolled down her window and screamed into the wilderness, "Why in the name of God am I out here?"

The screaming felt good. She raised the window and focused on the driving. When she got a phone signal back, she'd call Sedona. Lordy, how long had it been since she'd talked to Sedona? The energetic and bubbly Sedona talked a mile a minute and was always full of ideas and new plans. She treated Shelby like a sister, confiding in her about her work and her love life, seeking guidance from her, good grief, as if she were some expert. Sedona would be her miracle drug.

It raised her spirits to review what fragment of a plan she had. So, after seeing Sedona, she'd head south to find Olivia Marshak, even though, now that she was actually not that far from Colorado, this was sounding like a poor idea. What the hell was she going to say to her? And why would Olivia Marshak be inclined to say anything to this nosey stranger inquiring about her brother? Other than she lived in Golden and still went by Marshak, Shelby knew nothing about her or how to locate her. But she'd come this far—she was going to find her. She'd know where her brother is, maybe why he left Wisconsin. If Shelby had a brother, she'd know. Even if this was the most foolish idea she'd ever had, even if she learned Mr. Riley really was on a fishing trip up north, she wasn't going to back down now. She'd done that too many times, but that was in the past.

The road climbed steadily out of Omega, up into dense stands of conifers. She wished she knew more about trees— were these pines? Or spruces? Or maybe cedars? Then she encountered her first switchback, which challenged this flatland girl. Should she brake? Downshift? Slow down? But after several of the switchbacks, she felt like she'd gotten the hang of it, started to realize this was fun. She checked her phone again. She'd love to send Tisha a selfie from up here. But still no signal.

Then she saw it in the rearview mirror. White smoke belching from the rear of the car. She'd been monitoring the temperature gauge ever since Omega, and it had been fine, but now it was creeping up, nearing the dangerous red zone. She checked her odometer—she'd come eleven miles from Omega, almost halfway to Bridger. Too far to walk back if she had to. She should have stayed with Brenda.

She decided to press on, even if this meant destroying the car. Brenda had told her that a new head gasket would cost as much as the car was worth, so what did she have to lose? And what else was she going to do? Park here and find a cozy grizzly bear den to bed down in?

Shelby pushed on for another mile or two, until smoke began pouring out from around the hood. Terror surging through her, she immediately pulled off onto the shoulder. A badly running car was one thing, a car fire was something else entirely.

Shelby jumped from the car, then leapt away. She knew from the TV mysteries that it could blow at any moment. She shook her fist at the sky, then shook her fist at the Buick. One of the great luxuries in life is to have someone to blame it on. She didn't have that luxury.

As smoke continued to spew from the engine compartment, she considered opening the hood to hasten the cooling, but was afraid that she could be blasted by boiling steam. She looked up and down the road. No traffic. She checked her phone again. No signal. She had no plan, could formulate no plan, her mind awash with fear. The only thing that came to her was something that Michael had said in those last days: "Needy is the worst thing a woman can be." She had fought off the tears long enough. She leaned her elbows on the roof of the car, buried her face in her hands and sobbed.

A vehicle was coming. She heard it up the road, but she couldn't see it yet. She wiped the tears from her eyes and quickly grabbed a long-sleeve shirt from the back seat to cover her tank top. This was about the last place she wanted to project a sexy image.

A black pickup appeared from around the switchback and slowed to a stop next to her. A dark-glass window went down, as a man with a bushy beard and a backwards ballcap leaned toward her. "Hey, lady, you having some trouble?"

Shelby crossed her arms over her chest, which seemed to be the area the man was checking out. "I'm okay," she said. Her stomach clenching like a fist, she willed herself to lock into his gaze with a cold steeliness, unafraid.

"Don't look okay to me. Seems like I see some smoke comin' out of your engine. I'd say you need some help."

"I said I'm okay."

"Why don't you hop in, and I'll get into town in no time. Always like to help out a young lady in need."

About the last thing Shelby was going to do was climb up into the cab with this guy. Probably some fiend who'd take her to a filthy cabin and chain her to a bed as a sex slave. "My ride's on the way." She held up her phone, as if she'd just made the call. "Be here any minute. In fact, I thought you were them." She used "them" to add to the intimidation factor, if indeed there was any intimidation factor with this dude.

"Have it your way, bitch." The man rolled up the dark window and sped off. Shelby watched him disappear down the road, praying he wouldn't turn around.

Now it was quiet again. What was going to happen next? The gray sedan from the campground? She felt a chill on her spine.

The sound she heard didn't come from the road at all. She turned toward the dense, opaque woods. There was something in there. She hurried around to the side of the car away from the trees, to have a shield between her and whatever was making that sound. Maybe just a squirrel or raccoon. But this wasn't the pitter-patter of little feet. There were snapping branches and the loud crunching sounds of each footfall. Something was coming her way. It was something large.

Chapter 17

Andrew

Andrew had fallen a long way. He felt no pain yet, but he knew that would come soon. He was injured. Probably seriously, maybe fatally. In these moments before the adrenalin wore off, he could view everything objectively, more as a witness than as a participant. Yet, his churning brain could not assemble the pieces of what had just happened. There were only explosive gushes and brief flashes of memory.

It had happened so fast. He should have been screaming during the fall, but he'd made no sound—there wasn't even time to be afraid. The first part of the fall was on his belly on a slick surface, perhaps muddy or wet rock, which caused his body to accelerate. Then he hit a bump—a rock, a tree root, he couldn't tell—and he was airborne before coming down hard in a tumbling motion, so fast he could not get a perspective between horizontal and vertical, completely out of control. He slammed to a sudden stop, the impact driving shock waves through his body.

He was now wedged helplessly into a wide crack in the side of a granite wall that fell away into the canyon at about a forty-five-degree angle. On his belly, facing into the abyss, he was like a luge racer poised at the top of the course.

Still, he didn't scream, but sucked deep gasps through his mouth. He was still breathing, he realized, and that realization made him almost euphoric—he was alive.

Now the pain was beginning to escalate, like the sound from a train approaching from far away, so faint you can barely make it out, then growing, growing, until it overwhelms everything else, shattering eardrums and rattling your bones.

Was he safe? What held him in place? Maybe only a twig, ready to snap and send him on down the canyon wall in a fatal plunge? These were not rational ponderings, as much as they were his shaken reflexes filtered through the smothering cloak of panic, which now was seizing control of him. Rational, connected thoughts could not get a toehold in his head.

He had to get control over the panic. The only words that came to him was the Jesus Prayer: *Lord Jesus Christ, son of God, have mercy on me, a sinner.* Over and over, he breathed more than said these words. Over and over.

Slowly, the raging out-of-control panic began to subside. He could feel his ability to think return. But he kept saying it, afraid to stop. *Lord Jesus Christ, son of God, have mercy on me, a sinner.*

Only now could he begin to assess his injuries. His whole body pulsed with pain. Wedged into the crevice in the granite, he was nearly immobilized. But, he could shift his body enough to see it. There was blood everywhere.

Chapter 18

A ndrew was held in place in the crack by a narrow lip of granite. The challenge was to get free, without falling again. He pushed himself up with both arms—they were still functioning—to raise his upper body over the granite lip. It was surprisingly easy.

Gravity had almost killed him, but now it helped him. His body slid out of the crevice onto a narrow ledge a couple of feet below. He went down onto his side, recoiling in pain. He did a quick inventory: rough abrasions everywhere, almost all bleeding, but he found no severed artery that was gushing blood. He ran his fingers over his scalp. No bumps or wounds that might indicate brain injury. He was uncertain whether he'd lost consciousness. There were probably broken bones— he couldn't tell. His whole body hurt like hell.

He planted his palms flat on the cool rock, sucking in air in panicked gasps. He had to stay calm, although everything inside him was driving him toward freaking out.

He returned to the Jesus Prayer, trying to stay still, as any motion hurt. Even in crisis, his mind noted how the Jesus Prayer was often used as a centering tool in contemplative prayer, and how this prayer, which had failed him in meditation, was now what enabled him to hang on.

Was the pain subsiding or was he getting used to it? His ability to hold a coherent thought seemed to be returning. He checked his pockets. His phone was still there, intact, functioning, but there was no cell or GPS signal. He tapped in 911—nothing. Patting his pockets, he realized he also had his wallet, safe in the zippered hip pocket of his hiking shorts. Aside from the phone and wallet, he had nothing else. Damn, how easily he could have stuffed a couple of energy bars into his pockets. And, he could sure use that ibuprofen that was tucked away in his pack.

He needed a plan. Otherwise, he was going to die right here, which, with the cool night ahead and his lack of warm clothing, wouldn't be long. He mouthed the Jesus Prayer again as he tried to consider his options. There were only three: stay here, climb back up to the trail, or go on down into the canyon.

The best plan was to climb back up to the trail, where everything he needed for survival lay. He peered up through the trees and rocky outcrops, but couldn't see his pack or any sign of the trail. How far had he fallen? Maybe a hundred feet? It might be impossible to get there, but he would have to try.

The other two options were obviously bad, but he needed to consider them anyway. His ability to reason was no doubt impaired, so he needed to take it slow. Careful and deliberate. He could not afford a mistake.

What if he stayed put? That was the easiest option. But wouldn't he just die here? His only hope would be that someone would come along the trail, see his pack and call out. He had seen Phil and Jenny, after all, so there were people in this wilderness. But he'd seen no one else in two days, and Phil and Jenny had said that they'd seen no one.

He called out, "Help. I need help," and his words reverberated in lonely, eerie echoes off the canyon walls. Then again. Only echoes. What about a signal fire? That was likely impossible with everything around him wet.

Remaining here would just slowly deplete his energy, which was probably already oozing away at a high rate due to

shock and maybe the early stages of hypothermia. Andrew
didn't know much about shock, but he was likely suffering
from it. He did know what hypothermia was. Clad in only
shorts and a shirt, and with the dropping temperatures of the
upcoming night, he would inevitably be swept away into the
dreamless sleep of death.

What about going downhill? He peered down into the
dark forest below, but he couldn't see far. It's a canyon, so it
might terminate at a river, which would lead to lower elevation
and perhaps help. Maybe that would be—no. Most likely, he'd
just be descending into more remote wilderness. Damn, he
could use that topo map, safe and secure in the side pocket of
his pack.

It was settled. His best chance to survive, maybe his only
chance, was to climb back up to where his pack lay.

He bit down hard on his lower lip to fight back tears, as
he reviewed the fall again. What a dumb ass he'd been. He
breathed out a breath that was almost a sob, but then became
the Jesus Prayer again. No use beating himself up. That would
only further deplete his energy, his ability to think straight. If
he couldn't get back up to the trail, he probably wouldn't make
it to morning.

There was no time to waste. He pushed himself up from
where he lay on his side, then immediately screamed, as a jolt
coursed through his body like someone had sledgehammered a
spike into his leg.

His ankle. *No. Please, God, no.* He went back down to a
sitting position and tested the ankle. Another knife-stab of
pain. Is it broken?

If he was going to make it up the side of the canyon wall, he would have to crawl. There were maybe four more hours of daylight. Would that be enough? He needed to start now.

Andrew rolled over onto all fours, keeping his left ankle slightly elevated. It was a ten on the pain scale, but he had to push through that. He set out, mumbling the Jesus Prayer like a mantra.

There was no way he could ascend the steep rock face directly above him. So, he crawled laterally a few yards to the base of a pine, which gave him something to cling to, then pulled himself out onto a gravelly slope, covered with pine needles. Immediately, he began to slide on the wet surface, and panic surged through him again. A desperate lunge enabled him to wrap his arms around a nearby tree trunk. He lay there, immobilized, until his shaking stopped. He tried several other routes, but each was too slick from the afternoon rains. This wasn't going to work.

Knowing he had no time to lose, Andrew found branches under a nearby tree, then spread them out as a mat atop the surface above him. He hoped this might provide enough traction for him to crawl without slipping. But the branches weren't much better than nothing.

An hour after setting out, Andrew was still near the ledge from where he had started, and he'd significantly depleted his energy.

He cried for help again, but all he heard were the lonely echoes. He leaned back against a tree trunk and looked to the sky, which was now a cloudless blue, showing no trace of the recent storm. So, this is where I wound up. Stranded on a mountainside with no way out. Where was this God he had preached about for the past eight years? Andrew had dedicated much of his life to convincing others of God's existence. But is being convinced that God exists enough? Unless that God is actively in the midst of our messiness, slogging with us through the swamps of failure and loss, sitting beside us as we await the results of the MRI, holding onto us on a dangerous mountain side, then who cares?

He had experienced the immanence of God—one of those fancy seminary words for the nearness of God—or at least he had convinced himself that he had. He recalled those times when prayer drew him into God's arms, made him feel loved, safe. That night before his discernment weekend. He was at a rustic retreat center, awaiting his interview the next morning with the Commission on Ministry, which would determine if he would move ahead into the ordination process. Andrew had been filled with so much doubt that night that he planned to inform the committee the next morning that he would withdraw from the process and continue his physics studies. In the middle of the night, in a dream, he heard a voice say, "Get up and read Mark 1:16." Andrew had bolted awake, fearing that some stranger was in the room with him. "Who's there?" Silence. No one there.

He got out of bed, found a bible and looked up Mark 1:16. The verse began a passage telling of Jesus' call to his disciples. They were fishermen—they had another vocation, like him. *And Jesus said to them,* the text said*, "Follow me and I will make you fish for people." And immediately they left their nets and followed him.* Andrew was shaking, as he set the bible aside. The next day, his doubts erased, he entered the process for ordination. He had been so certain. But what about now?

He gazed down into the canyon. That was really his only option, wasn't it? To descend into the darkness, farther away from his warm sleeping bag, his Gore-Tex parka that was guaranteed to keep you dry, the fleece that Nicole had worn, away from his Jetboil, his food and water bottle, his tarp. Those things were now part of his past.

He recalled Jenny's trekking poles. The pine branches. Maybe he could use two of the most sturdy branches to take the weight off his injured ankle and give him stability as he descended. It would be slow and dangerous, but it was his only option now. In the midst of fear and panic, he felt a glimmer of excitement—he had a new plan. A crappy, probably hopeless plan, but it was a plan.

Chapter 19

Flat on his face. Andrew hadn't made it twenty feet down the fall line before he fell. He had planted one of the branches solidly—so he thought—but when he leaned his weight onto it, it skidded across the surface of a wet rock, and down he went. Shaken and concerned that he may have further injured himself, he lay on the damp ground, angry at himself, before struggling to stand. He would fall two more times over the next twenty minutes. After the third fall, lying on his back, he looked back up to where he had begun the descent—he'd come down no more than fifty feet.

But Andrew was a quick learner, and he quickly figured out how to plant a pole and test it before trusting it with his weight. He traversed the slope back and forth, zigzagging slowly down the uneven terrain, like a sailboat tacking into the wind. His hands were already raw from the rough bark of the poles, but this minor pain was the least of his worries.

If this weren't a survival march, Andrew could enjoy the beauty of this place. Lush green pines all around him, sunlight mystically filtered through the canopy, the air thick with a moist pine scent.

One lucky break: puddles of rainwater in the hollows of rocks and logs meant he would not die of thirst. This did not console him much, as there were plenty of other ways he could die here.

The concentration required to safely descend the steep slope had distracted him from worrying about how he was going to survive the approaching night. But now the temperature was already falling, as the sun had dropped behind the ridge above him. It would be dark soon. He had begun to shiver. He knew he was headed for hypothermia and that he would die without an external heat source, because his body's ability to generate heat would soon be shot.

Maybe there. Under that huge pine. Fallen pine needles had piled up, like a snow drift, against the trunk. He eased his injured body down into the pine needles and, to his relief, was able to bury himself, with only his face exposed. The needles seemed to be good heat insulators, and the way they piled gave them a natural loft like his puffy down bag. It wasn't long before the shivering subsided, and for the first time in an hour, he was warm. He would survive the night.

Andrew would have been elated about improvising his accommodations, except he was starving. He had found water and he had found a warm bed. Could he find something to eat? He remembered that TV show. The guy who lived off the land. Bear something. Bear Grylls, that was it—he could have handled this. He found bugs or lizards or berries to eat. Andrew wished he'd actually watched that show now—he'd just paused on it occasionally, while switching between news channels. Maybe he could find a lizard. Ms. Lizard? So, you hated my Christmas carol … now I'm going to eat you. He wasn't yet desperate enough to eat a lizard, even if he could capture one, but if he could make himself smile, maybe this would help stave off his terror.

He'd wanted to be off the beaten track. Tonight he was— in a place where probably no human being had ever been. He listened to the evening sounds: a woodpecker drilling out a meal before dark; small animals he couldn't see, scurrying in the understory, probably ground squirrels or chipmunks. Just before he'd reached his pine-needle abode, he'd seen a solitary mule deer that had locked eyes with him for an instant before bounding away.

He tried to distract himself from thinking about food, but his thoughts went to his injuries, which wasn't much better. He was lying in a relatively level spot with his left ankle elevated, so the pain, which had been a ten, was probably down to a seven. He wondered if he'd be able to sleep. He almost laughed—sleep deprivation was the least of his problems.

As dire as his situation was, Andrew felt like congratulating himself. He had fought off the pain pretty well. He was, after all, a bit of a hypochondriac, which was something recent. There were those three times in the last two years that he'd gone to the ER with chest pains. Each time they said his heart was fine. But he hadn't been convinced, so he'd insisted on tests, and the cardiologist reluctantly gave in. There were echocardiograms, treadmill EKGs, even an angiogram. Everything had checked out. It was only after all those tests that a doctor diagnosed his problems as gastro-intestinal reflux, caused by the mixture of too much stress and too much coffee. He'd tried to do better about his hypochondria, had sworn off looking up every little twinge on WebMD, where flow charts guided you from symptoms to diagnosis and inevitably pointed to cancer or heart disease.

Andrew forced his thoughts to the wilderness around him. What about all those solo trips Muir made into the wilderness? Was he ever injured? Feared he was going to die? He recalled a famous line from Muir that he'd memorized years ago: *Climb the mountains and get their good tidings. Nature's peace will flow into you as sunshine flows into trees. The winds will blow their own freshness into you, and the storms their energy, while cares will drop away from you like the leaves of Autumn.* Sure, you can say those things when you're sitting around the campfire, chewing on something tasty, with your warm sleeping bag nearby. He felt no good tidings from the mountains tonight. The words of Muir no longer comforted him.

Just hours ago, Andrew had celebrated the wilderness as his friend, his gentle, beautiful companion. He'd learned in seminary that the beauty of nature was one way of knowing that God exists. He was fond of Romans 1:20, where Paul says bluntly that anyone looking at the beauty of nature must know that God exists.

So, where was God now? This same natural world now threatened him, like a heartless assassin stalking from the shadows. Perhaps God was laughing at him, enjoying his struggle against death. Maybe God was indifferent, occupied with other, more important things.

Tonight, Andrew had little interest in a distant God, far off, gloating over his accomplishments of creating the fabric of the universe. He needed a rescuer. Somebody who could help. Right now, he needed somebody who gave a shit.

Another line, this one from Aldo Leopold, popped into his head: *I am glad I shall never be young without wild country to be young in. Of what avail are forty freedoms without a blank spot on the map?* He'd loved that line at one time. What a crock it seemed to be now.

What he needed right now was a non-blank place on the map. More than any sublime wilderness panorama, how about a dusty road and a run-down gas station? Hell, he'd be glad to see Buck Martin right now. He'd throw his arms around him in a bear hug. Maybe even buy a Mazda.

Chapter 20

Wː hat jolted Andrew awake in the predawn wasn't a noise—it was the large yellow eyes. It felt like a basketball had inflated inside his chest. A mountain lion stood not ten feet away, watching him. Sizing him up. It was huge, sleek and muscular, with a furry tan coat that looked like rough sandpaper. The big cat didn't roar, no saber-teeth were bared. It was in stealth mode, its fuzzy ears peaked high to catch any minute sound from its prey. The big yellow eyes, almost glowing, were locked on him. Maybe this was another vivid dream, like Nicole and Sharon. But, damn, this looked real. Then the cat took a slow step toward him and crouched, as if it was preparing to attack. Andrew had read that in a mountain lion attack, you should make noise, wave your arms, look large. But he couldn't move. He couldn't breathe. The mountain lion eased forward another step.

Then the lion stood, turned and disappeared into the forest.

Dear God, even the predators felt sorry for him.

Andrew remained motionless, waiting for the big cat's return. After a good half-hour, he stirred and attempted to rise, watching for any motion that might indicate the lion was back. He'd slept with his leg elevated, and now the pain was just a dull throbbing. But when he tried to stand, an arrow of crippling pain pierced through his leg.

The wilderness morning that he had extolled just yesterday wasn't as enchanting without his warm clothes and his Jetboil, although the pangs of hunger had moderated somewhat from last night. Andrew had occasionally fasted as a spiritual discipline, and he knew that the first day of a fast was the worst. Yet, he was weaker today. Just lifting his pine-branch trekking poles from the bed of pine needles was almost more than he could manage. At some point, maybe today, he would collapse and lie there until death mercifully took him.

He listened carefully to the morning silence, hoping to catch the grumble of a truck on a distant highway, a gurgling stream, anything that might give him a clue that he was heading toward something, instead of just deeper into the endless forest.

The day marched on. Like yesterday, he moved slowly, each step downward into the canyon a great effort of planting the tree branches, then leaning his weight on them and hobbling forward a foot or so. The pain of his injuries almost didn't matter anymore.

The afternoon thunderstorm came like clockwork, and he sat it out under a large pine. Before dark, he found another heap of pine needles to bury himself under, with only his nose and eyes exposed. He watched the vast night sky. What does the universe care about one life? Did the stars pause in their motion to take pity on his plight? No. They moved according to the grand design, unaffected by things so trivial as his needs. Relentless, governed by equations not decisions, by physics not feeling, perfect in their unalterable motions, never stopping by the side of the road to give a drink of water to the thirsty. Not caring one way or the other about a soul lost in the mountains. His mind bounced through all these scrambled thoughts. How many others tonight were cold? Hungry? Lost? Not even missed. How was his situation, sadly typical in the world, a big deal? He could cry out to God, "Why me?" and the answer might likely be, "Why not you?"

These mental thrashings took him toward sleep, but he fought it, fearing the mountain lion, which had likely been stalking him all day, might return. A memory of a conversation with Maureen comforted him.

MAUREEN: Look, Father, you're a good priest. I always judge a priest by one thing.

ANDREW: Which is?

MAUREEN: Would I want that priest at my bedside when I'm dying? I don't want a priest who knows all the right words to say. I don't need a priest who can shout down Buck. I want a priest who really believes all this stuff about God. That's why I'd want you, Father.

He looked to the heavens again and began to pray. Maybe he was uncertain about God, but he prayed any way. God was the last thing he had.

He remembered that his phone had a downloaded *Book of Common Prayer*. He pulled it from his pocket, found the app, and turned to the last rites, which the Prayer Book calls Ministration at the Time of Death. As a priest, he was practiced in reading this beautiful rite at the bedside of a dying person. Tonight he would read it for himself.

He read the words aloud, slowly.

At the point in the liturgy where the Lord's Prayer is said, Andrew paused. He'd visited Alzheimer's patients in nursing homes who couldn't speak, could no longer recognize their loved ones, but could whisper the Our Father. "Our Father, who art in heaven, hallowed be thy name …" If he was going to die, he would die with a prayer on his lips.

Sleep was about to overtake him, in spite of the likely nearness of the mountain lion, but he forged ahead to read the concluding prayers of the last rites:

Into your hands, O merciful Savior, we commend your servant Andrew. Acknowledge, we humbly beseech you, a sheep of your own fold, a lamb of your own flock, a sinner of your own redeeming. Receive him into the arms of your mercy, into the blessed rest of everlasting peace, and into the glorious company of the saints in light.

He sagged into the pine needles, nearly spent, as he breathed out the final words: *May his soul and the souls of all the departed, through the mercy of God, rest in peace. Amen.*

Chapter 21

Andrew awoke with a start. There was movement. The mountain lion was back.

He tried to focus his eyes in the dark, but could only make out a shadow. He grasped one of the pine branches, held it like a spear. This is it, he thought. Yes, he was weak, but he would make a last stand—the mountain lion would have to earn its dinner.

But it wasn't the lion. What he saw terrified him even more. It was a man.

As Andrew watched, flames shot up from a fire the man was poking at with a stick.

"Who are you?" Andrew's words came out in gasping bits.

The man said nothing, continuing to focus on the fire.

Andrew sat up, pine needles falling away from his body. "How did you start a fire out here?"

The man continued to poke at the coals. "The fire's almost out," he said, without looking at Andrew. He poked some more. "But not quite."

"Who are you?"

The man's face was dark, with a short beard. His hair was long. He wore jeans, a wool shirt, and scuffed-up hiking boots.

"Who are you?"

"I am …"

Andrew's eyes narrowed as he sat up straighter and leaned forward. "You are who?"

"I am."

It hit Andrew. "How did you start a fire out here? It's so wet."

"I'm pretty good at starting fires almost anywhere."

"Why are you dressed that way?"

"What way?"

"Modern, I guess. Like a hiker."

"I've always liked to hike."

"I mean your clothes. I always pictured Jesus wearing—"

"Why wouldn't I wear these clothes, Andrew?"

Good Lord, he knows my name. "Well … uh …." He remembered the scripture that said that through Him all things came into being. That would apparently include clothing from REI.

Jesus continued to poke the fire, as Andrew went silent, at a loss for words. Finally, Jesus picked up a flute—had that been the stick he was poking the fire with?—and began to play. It was a haunting melody. A familiar melody.

"I didn't know you played a musical instrument."

"I play all the instruments, Andrew."

Andrew couldn't place the familiar tune. Then it came to him. It was the accompaniment for one of the anthems sung in the Good Friday liturgy. He remembered the words: *We adore you, O Christ, and we bless you, because by your holy cross you have redeemed the world.*

"You want me to go back to St. Timothy's, don't you."

"Do you want to go back?"

Andrew didn't answer immediately, but then said, "No … I mean, I don't know," his empty gut churning as he said the words. He added, "But I will, if you want me to."

Jesus was silent.

"They need me. I took a vow at my ordination."

"They'll be fine, Andrew."

"How do you know?" He instantly realized this was a stupid question.

Jesus said nothing.

"Maybe you've given up on me."

"Maybe you've given up on yourself."

"What do you want, Jesus?"

"What do *you* want?"

"Uh, I'm not sure. What should I do, Jesus?"

Jesus grinned. "Get up and read Mark 1:16?"

It was like he'd been kicked in the stomach. "So, that really was you." He looked around sheepishly. "You said to your disciples, follow me." Andrew looked directly at Jesus, hoping he might be impressed that he was quoting Scripture. "I haven't been very good at following you."

"You followed me here."

"What?"

Jesus was silent.

"Jesus, what should I do now?"

"What do you think you should do?"

"Well, right now I'm afraid I might die."

"You will."

"I mean soon, like being attacked by a mountain lion or simply starving to death or hypothermia."

"Do not be afraid, Andrew. Just sit with me and watch and pray."

Words from the Garden of Gethsemane, thought Andrew. Then Jesus poked at the fire again—the flute was again a stick—and watched the flames dance. The golden light flickered on his face and created catchlights in his eyes.

Andrew wanted to ask more. He needed more answers. But maybe just being here at this moment was all the answer he needed.

He began to nod, then his eyes closed and his head drooped. He came awake with a start. He hadn't meant to fall asleep.

Jesus was gone.

It had been the best sleep he'd had in a long time.

Chapter 22

Just below his pine-needle bungalow of last night, the canyon wall he'd been descending for two days—or was it three, or maybe only one?—suddenly bottomed out at a small creek. He had made it to the canyon floor. This would be the place. The words of an old Gospel song soothed him now: *Gonna lay down my burdens, down by the riverside.* He leaned his pine branches, which had by now become his friends, against the trunk of a pine and lowered himself to the edge of the creek. It was peaceful here, the little creek gurgling around boulders on its way down to who knew where. He watched a small twig carried by the current, making its zigzag journey, careening off rocks, and spinning in the whirlpools and eddies.

The terrain of the canyon floor was not as steep as the rugged wall he'd just descended, but it would be more difficult to negotiate, as it was choked with large boulders. With his bad ankle, he'd never make it through the boulder field. The forest was more dense here along the creek, forming a canopy that almost blocked out any sunlight. It was cooler here. In only shirt and shorts, Andrew shivered. There was little he could do to stem the onslaught of hypothermia.

He turned and gazed back up the high canyon wall. Somewhere up there were his pack and all his tools for survival. And yet, here he was, almost dead for sure. But he had made it to the bottom. He nodded with approval of his accomplishment to a squirrel that watched him from a tree trunk.

The swirling of the water was like the swirling in his mind, still reeling from the mysterious encounter last night. He could approach it with the analytical skepticism of a physicist, biased from the get-go because things like this just don't happen, or he could trust his senses, trust his heart. And his heart told him that he'd had an encounter with God. But why had Jesus appeared to him? The words that stuck with him now were, "Do not be afraid."

That gave him comfort. But not enough to displace the gloomy reality that he would die here alone. He couldn't imagine being any weaker. He couldn't imagine going any farther.

He had been with many people at the time of death, so this time held little surprise. He knew that such occasions were often times of grace and prayer and love. Love in the midst of tears.

This would be the day, he was certain. His injuries, the impending hypothermia, and his hunger had taken their toll. Or maybe he hoped it would be the day. Why not die peacefully here? Perhaps he could hold on for another day or two, weakening further each day, but why not lie down here? It would be easy to fall asleep and never awaken. He'd be free from the wrenching hunger in his belly, the throbbing pain in his ankle, the mountain lion, the fear.

But his physical weakness was made worse by something else that haunted him this morning. Brought on by the middle-of-the-night visitor? Or maybe the nearness of death? He was so alone. He hadn't called his parents out in California in months. They would never know what happened to him. How long would it be before they even learn that he was missing? Before anyone knew he was missing or where to look. There was no loved one who'd have to go through the grief cycle over him. Maybe Maureen. He had no real friends, other than the parishioners. They would call it a tragedy, attend the beautiful memorial service, but, while saddened, they'd go on with their lives, relatively unaffected.

The last thing you have to hold onto is something with a heartbeat. Andrew wouldn't have that.

He didn't even have a dog. If he got out of this, somehow, he'd get a dog.

Andrew knew, as a pastor, how important it was to just sit with a person who is dying or grieving. Words are optional. The nearness of a caring being is what's important. There would be no one sitting beside him. No tears. No one holding his hand. No one saying prayers or singing hymns. No one reading to him. No one … no one loving him.

It would not be hard to slip away by this peaceful stream, but the memory of Jesus kept returning. It wasn't so much what he said—he didn't say that much—or how he looked, although there was something about his eyes—maybe it was the fire that gave them a laser intensity. It was that Jesus had showed up at his weakest and most frightened point. God had not forgotten him. Parishioners had told him of loved ones seeing Jesus shortly before they died, and he'd never quite known what to make of that. But he had just experienced it.

What did it mean? Andrew struggled to his feet, leaning against a tree to favor his ankle. He reached for his poles. Well, it meant that he wouldn't sit down here to die. He wasn't supposed to give up. He would go on until he dropped.

He barely moved, as he struggled across the boulder field in the canyon bottom. The afternoon storm came again, but today he plodded on through it. He got soaked and that would hasten the hypothermia, he knew. "I have fought the good fight. I have finished the race," he said out loud, quoting St. Paul.

He fell again. Had he blacked out? As he looked up through the dark canopy of trees, he saw it. There was light up ahead. A surge of excitement flooded his body. He knew what it was. He'd studied near-death experiences, even known several people who'd shared theirs with him. There was always light. This was it.

Oh, God, it's so beautiful. It's what he had hoped for.

As he emerged into the light, almost blinded, he saw an angel, standing behind an altar, its long hair streaked in sunlight, welcoming him home.

Then, all was black.

Chapter 23

Shelby

When a series of unfortunate events has you on the ropes, you can either panic or push the panic away with a pleasant thought. Shelby tried to savor a memory—was that just two days ago?—of hoisting a Happy Heron with Tisha. God, she'd love to be laughing right now with her, joking about hot guys and tapping her toe to Kenny Chesney. Not stranded in the freaking middle of nowhere, with a busted car and something big lumbering toward her from the dense forest beside the road.

She braced her hands against the roof of the Buick, pulled off on the gravelly shoulder of the mountain road, and squinted through her wire-frames at the woods, where whatever it was was getting closer.

She swallowed something that felt like a baseball when it emerged from the trees—a brown furry creature, up on its hind legs, its front legs raised like a grizzly moving in for the kill. It was large, but … it wasn't a grizzly, it was … what? She pressed her glasses more firmly onto her nose and leaned in to see better, as her hand moved to the car-door handle, ready to dive into the safety of the Buick.

But then the creature fell, not twenty yards away. It hit hard, falling face first into a small creek that poured out of the trees.

Dear God, it was a man. He lay still. Shelby's fear shifted instantly to compassion. She moved around the Buick in a flash, bounded down the rocky shoulder of the road and knelt in the water, where the man lay, face down.

It wasn't fur. It was mud and pine needles caked all over the poor man. She placed a tentative hand on his back. "Are you okay?" Hell, it was obvious he wasn't okay. She raised the man's head to make sure he wouldn't drown in the shallow water. She knew the risks of moving an injured person, but rolled him onto his side, in case he had aspirated water.

He was a mess. The caked mud and pine needles masked abrasions that had bled significantly. He wore a tattered long-sleeve shirt and shorts, woefully inadequate for a cool afternoon. Two fingers against his muddy neck confirmed a pulse. Shelby cradled his head and laid her ear close to his mouth—he was breathing. She poured a cupped-hand of water over his face, wiping away the mud. What the hell had happened to him? "Sir, I need you to wake up."

Who was this guy? Maybe an escaped convict, running from the hounds? No, the shirt and shorts and hiking boots told her it was something else. Still, this wasn't an ordinary guy you just encountered in the deli section at the Piggly Wiggly. Frankly, a grizzly might have been less scary. She had to be careful. Shelby checked her path back to the Buick to make sure she had a good escape route, in case he lunged at her.

The man stirred. Despite his terrible state, he gazed up at Shelby with a peaceful expression. Even through the pine needles and mud, his face glowed.

"You are so beautiful," he said.

Chapter 24

Shelby scanned his body for injuries. Dried blood caked his shirt, but she couldn't find any active bleeding. His injuries appeared to be at least a day old. His skin felt cool. Hypothermia. "Sir, can you tell me what happened?"

The man looked disoriented. "Is this ... heaven?"

Shelby ignored his loony question. "Sir, I'd like to move you to my car, but you need to tell me if you are injured."

He took some time to process the question. "My ankle. Broken."

Shelby ran her fingers over both of his ankles. "I don't think you have a broken ankle. Probably just a bad sprain."

"I don't?" The man looked even more confused. "Who are you? Are you real?" He was shivering.

"I'm Shelby Sims, and I'm very real. Do you think you can stand up? You can lean on me, while I get you to my car. We've got to get you warm. I'm worried you may be in the early stages of hypothermia."

"I'll try," he said.

Shelby got one of the man's arms over her shoulder, as she wrapped her arm around his waist, getting mud and pine needles all over her shirt. "Okay," she said, "we've got to climb up this little embankment. Think you can do that?"

The man nodded. Shelby, the former softball pitcher, was strong, but this wasn't going to be easy. He was a big man, probably six-two. Somehow, she got him to the car, got the door open while holding him upright. She paused for a moment, thinking she should spread something on the seat—

this guy was going to make a mess. She scanned the interior of the car, then, seeing nothing she could use, settled him into the seat. She hurried around to the driver's side, opened the door, then stopped. Was it safe to be in a tight space with this filthy stranger? She shook her head—she might regret this—then climbed in. She made sure the door didn't latch when she pulled it closed, in case she had to make a run for it, and positioned herself at the edge of the bench seat farthest away from the man.

"Just lie back and relax. You're going to be okay." Even though the outside temperature was dropping in the late afternoon, the Buick still sat in direct sunlight, and it was warm inside. She dug out the Tartan wool blanket from the back seat and spread it over him. "Have you had anything to eat or drink?" she asked.

"Hungry," the man said in a whisper. His head rested against the window, his eyes closed.

"Maybe you should have something to drink first." She held out a bottle of PowerAde Zero. "Don't drink too fast; it'll make you sick."

Then Shelby leaned into the back seat again. "I'm afraid all I've got to eat are these Luna Bars." She peeled the foil wrap off one of the energy bars and handed it to the man, then peeled open several others. "Sorry I can't offer you a cheeseburger."

The man nodded gratefully, as he crammed the first bar into his mouth. "Try not to eat too fast," she said. But within seconds he'd scarfed down two more.

The man then downed the rest of the bottle of PowerAde without taking a breath. He lowered the bottle and looked at her. "Where are we?" he asked.

Shelby let out a nervous laugh, as she shrugged. "Good question. We're on the Omega Road, headed to Bridger, somewhere in South Dakota."

The man's uncertain eyes said he didn't know where that was. "I'm Andrew Logan," he said. "Are you a doctor?"

"I've studied nursing."

"I thought I was dead." Andrew offered a thin smile. "I thought you were an angel."

She chose to ignore the comment. "Is your ankle still hurting?"

"Just a throb now, but it's been pretty bad."

Shelby uncapped a container of Tylenol. "Take these— should help." She handed him two of the capsules with a second PowerAde. "Can you tell me what happened?"

Andrew looked toward the forest, as he gulped down the pills and half of the second bottle of PowerAde. He shook his head slowly, but didn't answer.

"Were you in an accident?" Andrew now turned toward Shelby. His dark brown hair was matted onto his head. With the mud and pine needles and abrasions masking his face, it was hard to tell, but Shelby guessed he was about forty. "Are you going to tell me what happened?"

"Yes," said Andrew, nodding, like he was working up to speaking. "I was backpacking." He shot a glance toward the forest. "Up there somewhere. I fell." Then he turned toward her. Again he said, "I thought I had died. I thought you were an angel."

Shelby shrugged and looked away briefly. "Well, I'm no angel, but I guess it's a good thing I was here. I don't think you would have lasted the night."

"You're sure you're real?" When Shelby didn't answer, he added, "What are you doing here?"

"I'm headed out to Colorado, and my car broke down here. Head gasket, I think."

Andrew stared at her, but said nothing. Then he looked down at his body. "I'm really a mess, aren't I?" He wiped some of the mud and pine needles from his arm.

Shelby gathered up three empty PowerAde bottles scattered around the interior of the car. "I'm gonna run down to the creek and get some water for you to wash with. I've got a towel in the back seat." Andrew nodded, as Shelby jumped out and headed for the creek.

When she returned, Andrew had opened the passenger door and turned his body so that his legs hung outside. Thoughtful move, she thought, given his state, not to get water all over the interior. Andrew removed most of the muck with the water and towel. Then Shelby pulled a plastic container from the backseat and handed it to him. "Here are some baby wipes," she said. "You can use them to finish your clean-up." She stayed outside on the driver's side of the car to allow Andrew to bathe in privacy.

She leaned her back against the car and stared down the road. It was deathly quiet. Wait 'til Tisha hears about this. *So I met a guy. He's gross and smelly and he looks like Bigfoot.*

She almost laughed out loud, considering the text she might send. *But he thinks I'm an angel and I'm beautiful.*

Chapter 25

"I think the Tylenols are starting to kick in," Andrew said, when Shelby climbed back into the front seat. "I'm feeling a little better."

"You're starting to look presentable, too," she said, laughing, "more like a human and less like the swamp thing."

Andrew didn't share in the laughter. "I still feel pretty gross."

Shelby rummaged around in one of her duffels, then handed Andrew a deodorant stick. "I have an extra one of these," she said.

Andrew flashed her an embarrassed look. "Thanks," he said.

"And here." She handed him a tube of toothpaste. "You'll have to use your finger," she laughed again, "I'm not sharing my toothbrush." Andrew's brown hair was fairly long, but matted down, and he had a few days growth of stubble that toughened his fair complexion. His blue eyes looked inquisitive, with a trace of sadness, but maybe that was because he'd just come through a life-threatening ordeal.

Andrew nodded, then looked down at his feet. "What's this?" He gestured toward the extra gas and brake pedals on the passenger side.

"I use this car for mail delivery."

"Oh. I thought maybe I was still delusional. You work for the post office? I thought you were a nurse."

"Studied nursing," Shelby said, not interested in pursuing this topic. "I'm a mail carrier now."

He nodded like he understood, although he probably didn't. "So, is someone coming to fix the car?"

"Afraid not. No cell signal."

Andrew pulled his cell from his pocket, then shook his head. "Mine's dead."

"There was smoke coming out from under the hood. I was afraid to drive it any farther."

"Good Lord. How far to get help?"

"I just came from a little town about twelve miles back, and there's another town, Bridger, about twelve miles ahead. As far as I know, there's nothing in between."

"So, we wait for someone to come along."

"Unless you're up for a twelve-mile walk." She laughed again, but stopped because Andrew hadn't yet even smiled. "You know anything about cars?"

His grimace said he didn't. Then he said, "Couldn't hurt to take a look under the hood, though. No smoke now."

Two minutes later, after Andrew had gamely hobbled to the front of the vehicle, they stood peering into the engine compartment, neither of them speaking. Andrew gave a perfunctory poke at a couple of wires, maybe because a guy is supposed to know what to do under the hood of a car. He nodded, like his brain was churning with analysis.

"Like I said, I think it's a blown head gasket," Shelby said.

"Hmm. I don't even know what that is. Sorry." He gave her a helpless look. "Have you tried starting it again?"

Back in the car, Shelby cranked the engine, but now the Buick wouldn't even start. She mumbled a few obscenities, then tried again. Nothing. She pulled the key out of the ignition. "Just great." She threw the keys onto the dash. "Well, this sucks."

"I wish I knew how to help." Andrew craned his neck to look back through the rear window, as if a car might be coming. "So, I guess we just wait, huh?" He slouched back into the seat, like he was settling in. Within moments, he was asleep.

Shelby studied Andrew's face, as he lay back in the seat, his head turned toward her. His mouth was opened slightly, as he breathed softly in deep sleep. He must be exhausted, she thought, trying to wrap her mind around the ordeal he must have endured. A few pine needles still clung to his cheeks. She was tempted to brush them away, but didn't.

Shelby settled back into the seat, too, with a big sigh of defeat. All her plans, her silly, poorly conceived plans—her trip to Loveland to see Sedona, tracking down Olivia Marshak, her hunt for Mr. Riley, all her sleuthing fantasies—crushed by a dead car. She pushed away the path down which these black thoughts were leading her, and in moments she was also asleep.

She awoke when she heard him stir. How long they'd been napping she wasn't sure. He was looking more alert, which she took as a sign that the threat of hypothermia had passed.

"Sorry I drifted away on you," he said, sounding apologetic.

"No problem. I hope you're feeling better." When he nodded, she added, "So, tell me about yourself, Andrew. What were you doing out here?"

He shook his head slowly, then looked toward the dense forest, from which he had emerged just a short time ago. "I was up there. Up in the Black Elk Wilderness, had a long trip planned. Needed quiet to do some discerning about my life.

I'd been out almost a week, when I slipped on the muddy trail and went over the edge. Fell a long way." He was more chatty now, which was a good sign, too.

"And you couldn't get back up?"

"It was too steep and slippery, and I was injured. Thought my ankle was broken."

"How's it feeling now?" Shelby leaned forward to take a look. The swelling was noticeable. "Damn, I should have wrapped that thing right away. Wish I had an Ace bandage." Looking around for something she could use, she pulled a long purple scarf from one of her duffels. She remembered buying it to wear over her black cardigan for some romantic dinner that never happened. "Put your leg over here, we'll get you taken care of. Not as good as a compression bandage, but it ought to help with the swelling."

While Shelby wrapped Andrew's ankle with the scarf, snug but not too tight, he said, "You're good at this, you know. Why didn't you go into nursing?"

"It's a long story. Does that wrap help your ankle feel better?"

"Yes, it does. Thanks."

"So, are you from around here?"

"About three hundred miles south," he said.

"In Colorado?"

"Afraid not. High Plains. In Nebraska."

"Never heard of it."

"Not many people have. It's out in the plains, a long way from anything else."

"Why do you live out there?"

"That's where my job is."

"Which is …"

"I'm a priest."

Shelby hoped her immediate wince hadn't been visible. "I see." She cleared her throat, as she tried to imagine this stubble-faced guy with pine needles still sticking to him wearing a clergy collar. "You mean, like in the Catholic Church?"

"I'm an Episcopal priest. Rector of St. Timothy's in High Plains."

Shelby had had a few friends over the years who went to Episcopal churches. "They're the ones who can get married, right?"

Andrew nodded yes.

"So, are you married?"

He shook his head like he was about to share a disappointment. "No."

Shelby fidgeted in her seat. "A priest, huh? So, maybe I should make a confession?" she giggled, certain she was making an ass out of herself.

Andrew let out a little grunt, and stared out the windshield. "Maybe you should—I don't know. Maybe I'm the one who needs to make a confession."

"Do priests make confessions?"

Andrew flashed her a raised-eyebrow look that said, *You've got to be kidding.* "Of course they do." Then he looked straight ahead again.

They sat in silence, watching the late-afternoon sunlight silhouetting the tall pines off to the left and casting golden streaks across the road.

Finally, Andrew turned toward her. "So, where are you from?"

Shelby was about to answer when they both heard it. The distant growl of an engine. A vehicle was coming. They spun toward the sound behind them. A car.

Shelby jumped from the Buick and waved both arms toward the car, still a ways down the road. Although it was now near dusk, the car's headlights were not yet on. The car slowed as it approached.

A jolt shot through her, as the car pulled to a stop alongside the Buick. A gray Camry. Shelby backed against the Buick, her breath heavy as she waited for what would happen next. The dark-tinted windows prevented her from seeing inside. Then the car sped off. Shelby couldn't make out the license in the poor light, but she was pretty certain it was a Minnesota plate—maybe the same as the car from the KOA last night.

Chapter 26

"Why didn't they stop?" Andrew asked, after Shelby was back in the car. He apparently saw she was troubled. "Are you okay?"

Shelby turned toward Andrew and told him the whole story, beginning with her unauthorized visits to Mr. Riley's house back in Wisconsin; her finding out that Mr. Riley was actually a Mr. Marshak, who was an expert in quantum entanglement. She paused at that point. Maybe Marshak was some fancy scientist, she thought, but what she remembered now was the love he showed for his purple petunias. Then she continued with the account of her sexual harassment and probable termination at the post office; her decision to go to Loveland to see her cousin Sedona, then find Mr. Riley's sister; and her sightings of the mysterious gray car. He sat in rapt attention, as she told the story, even during the few silent interludes when she had to pause for an emotional break. She concluded with, "Maybe I'm just being paranoid, and maybe it's just a coincidence, but you've got to admit, seeing this same car again is a little creepy."

Andrew still had the Tartan wool blanket around him. He pulled it closer, as it was beginning to cool down in the car. Shelby had slipped into a fleece and a pair of Levi's over her cargo shorts. "I don't think you're being paranoid," he said. "It's strange that the car stopped, then sped off. You mentioned that this man—Marshak?—worked in quantum entanglement?"

"You know something about that?"

"A little. I took a quantum physics course once."

"It's about how particles that once were close together retain their memory of each other, even if they're moved far apart. Right?"

Andrew's mouth fell open a bit. "That's a pretty good definition. Did you study—"

Shelby put her hands up like stop signs. "Oh, no. I skimmed a Wikipedia article." She gave out an apologetic laugh, then stopped, realizing she had nothing to apologize for. "So, tell me more about quantum entanglement."

Andrew rubbed his chin with a forefinger. "Well, it's a complicated topic. And it's more than just some intellectual curiosity. It's the basis of a new way to send ultra-secure encrypted messages, called quantum communications."

Shelby nodded attentively, as she tried to follow Andrew's description.

"I've heard it could have great national security implications. Imagine battlefield communications that cannot be intercepted and decoded. Something many countries are probably working hard to develop. Or maybe steal. Do you think that might have something to do with that mysterious car? Something to do with this Marshak?"

"Maybe. I thought about that." She hugged herself, suddenly feeling colder. "Or maybe it's some stalker spotting a woman travelling alone."

"Yeah, that's a scary thought," he said, nodding his head with concern.

She pulled the keys off the dash and tried to start the car again. It groaned as the battery cranked, but still wouldn't start. "I wonder if the heater will work without the engine running." She switched the heat on, but only cold air came out. "Damn

… oops, sorry, Father … do people call you Father? Anyway, I think we're gonna get cold tonight."

Andrew cracked a smile, his first. He must be feeling better. "Yeah, some people in my church call me father, but you can call me Andrew."

"Does anyone ever call you Andy?"

Andrew winced. "No. Andy sounds too much like Andy Griffith or Andy Rooney, good ol' boys who'll slap you on the back. I'm hardly a slap-you-on-the-back type."

Shelby had already figured that out. "You said you had some discernment to do up in the mountains. What was that about?"

Andrew trailed a finger across the green and red squares on the Tartan blanket. "This is a beautiful blanket."

It was wool, in a plaid pattern like a Scottish kilt. Dad had given it to Mom a long time ago, before Shelby was born. It had warmed Shelby not only with the tightly woven wool, but also memories. They had gone to Scotland—Dad wanted to visit the Scotch whisky distilleries, Mom just wanted to gaze out onto the sea. Her mother said the blanket was from the Outer Hebrides—she would say this like they were holy words, like that place was the most magical in the world. After Shelby was born, they never traveled overseas again, or much of anywhere else. "My mom and dad got it in Scotland, a long time ago. They gave it to me when I graduated from high school. It's pretty special."

Andrew nodded his appreciation. "So, yeah, I was doing some discernment. I'm trying to figure out my future in the church."

"What have you figured out?"

"It's still a work in progress, I guess."

Shelby was silent, waiting for Andrew to say more.

He turned his head forward to gaze out through the windshield. "I've been at the church for eight years. When I started out, I was a greenhorn, naïve and energetic and full of ideas and high hopes. I had plans to fire up the congregation, bring new people into the church, really make a difference in people's lives. I thought my preaching and teaching would be enough to turn the church around." He shook his head, like he was trying to shake away an unpleasant memory, then turned to look at Shelby. "Hey, you don't want to hear this crap."

Shelby was surprised a priest said *crap*. "Yeah, I do want to hear. Anyway, you got a better idea of what to do? We could play gin rummy, but we don't have a deck of cards." She gave him a smile meant to be encouraging.

"I never liked cards anyway," he said, managing a weak laugh. "Look, I normally don't talk about these things with people. I have a spiritual advisor, Father Ken, who I—"

"A spiritual advisor?"

"That's a person you talk to about your life. They listen and help you understand your life from a standpoint of God and faith."

"I could use one of those. Anyway, keep talking."

Andrew gave her a penetrating look, like he was trying to figure out who she really was. "So, like I said, I've been at the church for eight years. Came in with a head of steam, convinced folks would be pouring in to have their lives changed. But that didn't happen. We've got fewer members now than when I started."

Among the things that Shelby least understood was church. She'd gone to a Lutheran church a few times back in high school, but all she could remember about it was checking out the place for cute boys. And Tisha was always inviting her to go to church, but she avoided those invitations. It wasn't that she hated church—she just had no interest in it. Her parents had never gone to church, had never mentioned anything about faith or God. Maybe she didn't know about church, but she knew some things about life, about disappointment, about failure. "So, you must be pretty discouraged."

"In some ways, yes. In other ways, my ministry has been very rewarding. Like, when I get to say prayers at the bedside of a dying person, or baptize a baby, or dig into the Scriptures to prepare a sermon. I love those things—they are what I'm convinced I was called to do."

Andrew looked bothered, and Shelby wanted to lay a hand on his arm, but she didn't. "Those sound like important things," she said in a whisper.

"They are. But there's more to being a priest than that. There's administration, budgets, settling disputes, promoting the church—I haven't been very good at ... hell, I guess I've been terrible at those things. People are saying—"

She cut in: "How do you know you've been terrible?"

"Oh, it's easy to see."

"What are you going to do?"

"That's what I was trying to figure out up in the mountains."

"Sorry your trip got interrupted. Maybe you—"

"I saw Jesus up there." His eyes were locked on her, then he looked away.

Shelby edged back toward the car door. "What?"

"I shouldn't have told you that. You'll think I'm crazy." Andrew let out a self- deprecating laugh. "The last thing you need is to be stuck out in the boonies with a lunatic."

"What do you mean you saw Jesus?"

"I know this sounds crazy—maybe I was delusional, maybe it was just a dream. It was after my fall. I was cold and hurt and scared. I awoke in the middle of the night and there he was."

Shelby wasn't sure what to say. Maybe Andrew, in fact, was a lunatic. "What did he do?"

"He sat by a fire and talked to me."

"He talked to you?"

Andrew nodded.

"What did he say?"

"He said to not be afraid. Oh, Lord, I wish I hadn't told you this. You don't believe me. You probably think I'm insane, but—"

"Yeah, maybe I don't believe you, but I also don't disbelieve you. Does that make sense?"

"It's just that it sticks with me. I decided I wouldn't ever tell anyone, but then I told you." He shot her a sheepish look. "I'm sorry, I won't mention it—"

"I'm glad you told me. Maybe you were delusional, but I gotta say, 'don't be afraid' sounds like pretty good advice."

Andrew rubbed the stubble on his chin with two forefingers. "Yeah, but I haven't been very good at following it."

Shelby looked down. "Me, neither," she said, almost in a whisper.

The temperature was now starting to drop in the early evening. Shelby turned toward the rear and dug through her duffels, emptying almost everything out onto the back seat. Tank tops, blouses, shorts, skirts, sandals—everything she needed for going out for margaritas in Loveland. She was wearing her warmest garment, a polyester fleece. "Geez, I feel so stupid. Here I am, a Wisconsin girl, and I brought no warm clothes." Images of her dad and Michael, slowly shaking their heads in disapproval, flashed through her mind.

Andrew still had the Tartan wool blanket wrapped around him, and Shelby was doing okay in her Levi's and the fleece, but she knew this wasn't going to be sufficient to get them through the night.

Andrew watched Shelby, as she rummaged through her bags. "Why don't you take the blanket? It's really quite warm."

"Thanks. I'm okay for now. I wish I had some warm clothes to offer you." She gave out a childlike giggle, which drew a smile out of Andrew. "I don't think you'd be able to squeeze into one of my tank tops."

Andrew studied the floor of the Buick. "No floor mats?"

Shelby shook her head slowly. "Yeah, we could use them for warmth. But this old clunker hasn't had floor mats for years."

Her glasses were already fogging up. She pulled the wire-frames off and wiped them on the front of her fleece.

"Are you near-sighted?" Andrew asked.

Shelby shifted in the seat and brushed a wisp of hair from her face, aware that Andrew was examining her. "Yes," she said. "Worn glasses since the eighth grade." She could remember when she first showed up at school with her new glasses. She had dreaded that day, certain the other kids would ridicule her, call her "Four Eyes" or some other humiliating name. But to her relief they'd paid little attention to her glasses. Truth was, they hadn't paid much attention to her on any other day, either.

She pulled the glasses back on, pushing them up on her nose and pressing the bridge into her forehead, which she often did when she was nervous or uncertain. "They came in handy when I played softball, though." She told Andrew how, as a softball pitcher in high school, she had a blazing fastball. She would intimidate the opposing hitters by leaning in and squinting, like she couldn't see the plate. Like she'd soon be sending a heater wild, on a collision course with the batter's head—although she never did that. "It's hard to hit a line drive," she laughed, "when your knees are wobbling."

Andrew seemed fascinated. "Sounds like you were a terror." After a pause, he said, "I never played sports in high school. Guess I was too much of a nerd."

"So, you never had eyesight problems?"

"Guess I'm lucky. They say when you hit forty, though, which I did two months ago, your eyesight goes to pot. So, I guess I should be preparing, huh?"

"Oh, great, you're telling me that when I hit the big four-oh, my eyesight's going to get even worse. Thanks a lot."

They sat in silence for a while, then Andrew said, "What did you mean, me neither?"

"Huh?"

"When I said I hadn't been very good at not being afraid, you said me neither."

"I don't really want to talk about me, if that's okay."

"No problem."

There was more silence, as they watched night fall around them. Shelby hugged herself for warmth, as she stared out through the driver's side window, which was already fogging up from their breath. She rubbed some condensation away with the sleeve of her fleece.

At least I didn't see Jesus, she thought, and almost laughed. Problem was, she needed to see someone. Someone telling her to not be afraid.

"Here," Andrew said.

She turned to see he had raised the edge of the blanket to share with her.

"Scoot over a bit," he said.

She didn't refuse.

Chapter 27

"All we need is a drive-in movie," said Andrew, as they huddled together on the bench seat, under the blanket, facing the fogged-up windshield. Snuggled would be too strong a word, as Shelby was careful not to touch Andrew, and he was also respecting her boundaries.

Shelby let out a nervous laugh at Andrew's attempt at humor. "I'd say we've got time for a double feature."

"So, I could run over to the concession stand and pick up some popcorn. You want butter, Ms. Sims?"

Shelby liked being called Ms. Sims. "We don't want to be spoiling our appetites, you know. We're going to that fancy restaurant after the movie."

"Ah, yes, you are correct. I wonder what will be on the menu tonight."

She held her chin between her thumb and forefinger, like she was in deep deliberation. "So, I understand the chef has some special menu items for tonight. We will start with a nice tossed Luna Bar salad, with your choice of dressings. Then he's serving up a succulent filet of Luna Bar, cooked medium rare. He'll be pairing that with their fine Chateau du PowerAde."

"And for dessert?" Andrew asked with a straight face.

"Ah, the best is saved for last. I understand they're serving an award-winning Luna Bar cobbler."

"Sounds delicious. Will we need reservations?"

"You're in luck. I called ahead." Shelby couldn't remember the last time she'd been to a nice restaurant. Back before her breakup, before her pregnancy.

They feasted on Luna Bars and PowerAde. Afterward, Andrew said, with a silly grin, "Well, Ms. Sims, that was the best date I've been on in a long time."

Shelby felt her cheeks warm, as she looked at him with raised eyebrows. It was now completely dark, and he wasn't much more than a dark shadow next to her.

"To tell you the truth, I haven't been on a date in years," he said.

She could tell him that she hadn't, either, but she didn't. "And the movies weren't bad," is what she said.

Now they were quiet. Shelby shifted uncomfortably, while Andrew cleared his throat, as if he were awkwardly struggling to find words. Finally, he said, "You never said if you were married."

Hell, she was out here travelling alone across the country—shouldn't that be obvious? "Nope."

Andrew manufactured a fake laugh. "Nope, you're not married, or nope, you agree that you never said if you were married?"

"Nope, I'm not married." After a pause, she added, "I almost was once, but …." She trailed off.

"But, what? Hey, forget I said that—that's none of my business."

Shelby stayed silent.

"I was married once."

Shelby turned toward his dark silhouette. "You were?"

"Sharon. We were married for two years. It was a mess. I just—good grief, I'm really spilling my guts, aren't I?"

"You're doing fine," Shelby said. She laid a hand on his arm, then pulled it away quickly.

"I guess after telling you I saw Jesus, any topic ought to be fair game, right?" He manufactured another shallow laugh.

"So, what happened to Sharon?"

Andrew's heavy sigh said his answer was a complicated one. "It was after I decided to leave grad school in physics and go to seminary. She left me."

"Oh, my, I'm sorry. She didn't want you to go to seminary?"

"She hated the idea."

"But you went anyway?"

"I had to do it, I thought I was called by God, I mean I *was* called. I thought she'd come around to the idea … but she didn't. She left me for my best friend."

"Ooh. That hurts."

"Yeah, it did. The other night, up in the mountains, I saw her. She … nothing."

"What?"

"Nothing, it was just a dream."

"So, you're not going to talk about it?"

"Not right now, if you don't mind."

"That's fine." He'd already told her plenty about his life. Shelby gripped the edge of the blanket tight, like she was hanging on for dear life. She needed to do this. Tell it all. Things she hadn't even told Tisha. She would tell this man, this dark shadow next to her, who she didn't know. On this dark night, far from anywhere, she would say the words out loud, hoping they would soar off into the night, carrying her burdens with them. This would be her confession. "So, yeah, I was engaged once. Hell—oops, shouldn't say that in front of a—"

"It's okay."

She gave out a shaky laugh. "I thought it was the real thing."

"I'm sorry it didn't work out. What happened?"

This was a bad idea. "I really can't talk about it."

"I understand. Forgive me for probing into your—"

"I wanted to be a nurse. That was my dream, my passion." She knew this wasn't directly answering his question, but this was where she needed to begin. "My parents were poor. Dad was a pulp-mill worker, and he was unemployed for four years after the mill closed. Lord, I remember how he came home emotionally drained during those years, after his various part-time jobs, like yard maintenance. Mom bagged groceries at Safeway. Neither of them had gone to college." Good grief, she was babbling. "TMI, right?"

"No, not at all. I want to hear all of this." Even in the darkness, she could feel his eyes locked on her, like her story was the only thing that was important.

"I wanted to go to college. I studied the admissions requirements for UW Oshkosh, and I could get in, and it was close to home, so I wouldn't need to pay for room and board. And it has a good nursing department, but the tuition was over six thousand a year—no way could I afford that. So, I went to work, instead, to earn money. Worked as a janitor in a doctor's office, gave half my income to my parents, who were barely afloat. I worked for years. Sure you want to hear the rest of this sob story?"

"Yes."

"Then I met Michael." Shelby exhaled a deep, cathartic sigh. "He was working on his BA at Oshkosh. I moved in with him. I continued to work and helped him with his tuition."

"So you worked to help take care of your parents and then your boyfriend. Geez, who was taking care of you?"

Shelby shrugged. "I'm not complaining. I was doing okay." Sharing this story now, it was clear that she hadn't been doing okay. "Anyway, I finally got the bucks together to start the nursing program at Fox Valley Tech. That's a community college that I could afford. I think I was maybe thirty."

"So, I take it you didn't finish?"

"I got pregnant." She was quiet for a moment to center herself. "When I told Michael, he freaked out, accused me of tricking him. He left. He just up and left." She was aware that her voice had become shaky.

"That's terrible. But you have a child. That must be—"

"I went into a tailspin. Oh damn, it wasn't a tailspin, it was a real crash. I had a miscarriage." Shelby felt the tears welling up. She squeezed the edge of the blanket tighter—she was not going to cry. "I've messed everything up."

"How can you say that?"

"I really wanted my baby, but I was so bummed out over Michael, I didn't stay emotionally healthy. My diet fell apart. I drank."

"You were dealing with a lot."

"I was pregnant, then I wasn't … started bleeding …got to the hospital …they did a D&C …when I woke up, I wasn't pregnant." Her words came out rapid fire, like she was spitting them out.

"What happened then?" His voice was calm and steady.

She was going to get through this. She needed to get through it, even as more images of those dark times—images she had worked hard to dispel—threatened to again overwhelm her. She closed her eyes. "After I lost the baby, I sank into a real depression. Dropped out of nursing school.

Moved back in with my parents. Didn't work for a long time."
That chapter of her life still shamed her. Strong Wisconsin
girls don't get depressed. They gird their loins, put their
shoulder to the wheel, and keep on truckin' or some such
crap—that's what some people told her.

"Did you get some help?"

"My parents got me to a shrink. Went the full-blown
Prozac route. I don't know where they got the bucks to pay
for it—I wasn't asking very many questions back then."

"So, the therapy helped."

"Eventually I became functional again, got weaned off the
Prozac. Started to work, helping my dad, who, by now, had
started his own yard maintenance business and was doing
pretty well. Last year, in fact, they were able to sell the business
and get a small place in Arizona—I'm happy for them.
Anyway, my dad hired me to help him—planting lawns,
pruning trees, weeding, that kind of stuff. I did that for a
while, then I applied for the post office job. That was three
years ago." She fumbled around in the darkness. "Damn,
there's got to be some Kleenex lying around here somewhere."
She finally came up with the box and blew her nose. "I can't
believe I'm telling you all this." She let out a little giggle. "A
complete stranger."

"Hey, we're not strangers. We've already been on a date."
He was trying to add a little levity into the conversation. It
helped.

Chapter 28

How much later it was, she wasn't sure. She certainly had been asleep. Startled by the sound of his breathing next to her, Shelby bolted upright in the pitch black. It took her a while to realize where she was and who this stranger next to her was. It was colder now. Instinctively she had snuggled closer to the man, closer to his warmth. He stirred and shifted toward her. Then his steady breathing continued.

The middle of the night is a terrible time to evaluate your life. Shelby peered into the blackness around her—it was like a void sucking away the light in her life. She could see her past now, which she'd shared much of with Andrew tonight, with crystal clarity for what it was: a sequence of bad choices driven by fear and foolishness. She knew down deep that this crystal clarity was a middle-of-the-night crystal clarity, which could not be trusted. Yet, it held her prisoner for now.

She shook her head and blew out a breath of disgust for allowing herself to once again fall prey to these midnight times of dread that she knew would recede in the morning light. She reached into the back seat and found her Kindle. Although she had read several of Richard Russo's novels, she wasn't very far into *Nobody's Fool.* Yet, she had already connected with Sully, who leads a dreary life in a dreary town in upstate New York. But Russo's humor lifted Shelby's spirits about her own dreary life. She could laugh about Sully's predicaments, even though she cried about her own predicaments, and this helped her to see, or maybe hope, that she would be able to laugh about her own.

A few pages of Russo were enough—it was a gentle hand taking hers and leading her away from despair. She pulled her corner of the Tartan blanket tighter around her and wondered if her parents ever slept beneath it, huddled together on a cold night. This pleasant thought took her back into sleep.

Sometime later, she awoke again. It was even colder, and the blanket and the nearness of Andrew weren't enough to stave off her chill. Andrew seemed to stir next to her. "Are you all right?" she asked.

"I'm okay," he said in a groggy whisper.

She moved closer to his warm body. This would be so easy. The natural thing to do. Just relax and let it happen. This was in fact the right thing to do.

No words were said, although the intensity and desperation in their breathing said plenty. His face was beside hers, like a couple dancing close, his stubble against her cheek. A quick fumbling with clothing. Fingers tugging buttons and zippers. His hands that had been at his sides were now sliding up under the fleece, caressing her back, pulling her to him.

It didn't last long. It had been born out of sleep and the need for warmth, slowly, in semi-consciousness. Neither would remember who started it, but neither of them fought it off.

Maybe it was her response given to all those who said, "No, you can't"—her clenched fist raised against the cold, against blown head gaskets, gray sedans, the Rudys and the Michaels of the world, against settling for less. Maybe it was her choice of pleasure, even temporary, over suffering. Maybe it was her choice of heart over mind. It was *her* choice.

Or did she just need this, and all other rationalizations and explanations be damned?

In any case, she was now warm for the first time in hours, and a return to sleep came easy.

Something awakened her from deep sleep. It was now light, although she could not see outside—the windows were iced over with their frozen breath. She sat up and ran the back of her hand across her neck, covered with the damned pine needles, and groaned. She looked around to find something to scrape the windows with, but could find nothing. She tried a fingernail, but it was not sufficient to carve through the ice.

Andrew was now awake, too. *Thump!* It was outside on the glass. *Thump!* Someone or something was pounding on her window.

Chapter 29

Andrew

He'd be home in five hours. The route south, mostly down US 385 and 24, was deserted, with long, open stretches. Plenty of time to think. And he had lots to think about.

Some things he didn't want to think about. Like those harrowing three days, injured and without food, on the mountainside, the thoughts of which still made him shake. Like, he groaned, returning to St. Tim's—he'd only been gone a week, but somehow his church and the people there seemed far in the past. It would be good to see Maureen, even though his senior warden would be giving him a chewing out for returning so soon. She could always be counted on to provide a good dose of straight talk.

Of course, there were some recent experiences he would not share even with Maureen. Like the encounter with Jesus. He knew that people in the Bible, like Paul and Peter, experienced visions and dreams that were authentic communications from God. Yet, anyone hearing this story would brand him, with some justification, as a certifiable nut-case.

But, he had told Shelby. Shelby. He could never mention her, either. Interesting, he thought, how the things he couldn't talk about were, in fact, the most important things.

He'd been with Shelby less than twenty-four hours, but— it was too difficult to think about that now. He turned his attention to the sea of rolling grasslands. This is where the high Rockies spilled out onto the Great Plains, the endless prairie. Out here, only a few gentle hills give any hint of the tall mountains two hundred miles to the west. The late afternoon sun cast long golden streaks across this endless grassland, as beautiful and moving as any resounding hymn from a choir.

He arched his back, which was sore from the hard seat of the old Tundra and the bangs and bruises from his fall, and stretched out his left leg as far as his six-two frame would allow. The first aid he'd received in Bridger and the supply of ibuprofen they'd sent him away with had him feeling almost back to normal. He even had a new set of crutches from the Urgent Care, leaned up against the passenger seat, which he was told to hobble around on for the next few days.

This land had once been alien to him. After all, he was a West Coast boy, raised in the Bay Area. Went to college there, right through seminary. He had known the sea breezes off the Pacific, the electric ethnic diversity of San Francisco, and the weekend backpacking trips to the High Sierra that were less than a day's drive from his home. But out of seminary, he'd struggled to find a position. He took a part-time position as a curate in northern California for a year, before the offer from St. Tim's came along. It was the only offer he received. He never understood why he had such a difficult time landing a priestly position. Maybe it was the divorce mess that had colored his early days in seminary. Maybe it was his lackluster performance in the few interviews he had—his inability to cut loose and be the dynamic, outgoing leader that search committees wanted. When the St. Tim's offer came along, they'd been searching for over a year, and the church and he were relieved to connect. It had seemed like a match made in heaven.

But had it been? He pondered that question. Out here along these endless stretches of straight highway, it seemed like he had two options for the future. One was to get back to work and buckle down. Deal head-on with difficult church leaders like Buck Martin. Maybe take courses to learn some fresh ways of church leadership. In other words, do the job he was called to do and stop whining.

The other option was to leave. Either start looking at other clergy openings around the country—he had been at St. Tim's for eight years, after all, and no one would say it was too soon to consider something new. Or, look for something entirely different. But what that would be, he had no idea.

This wasn't the first time he'd pondered this question, of course, and it seemed like today he was no farther along the path toward a decision.

Is my life a test, he mused? Or just a random wandering through the chaos of life? If it is a test, then is it a True-False test? He knew some people who saw it this way. For them, there were right answers and wrong answers, nothing in between. Andrew saw, for better or worse, all the in-betweens—for him, life certainly wasn't a True-False test. Or maybe, life is a multiple-choice test? He knew others who saw it this way. Maybe there is more than one correct answer. The pluralistic approach. Or maybe his understanding of life, of himself, of God was an essay test. Yep, that was him—writing and writing, moving forward, then back, circling around, wondering at the end of all his ponderous prose: what was the question?

Andrew couldn't get very far with these mental churnings, because Shelby kept elbowing her way back into his mind. Lord, had that been just last night?

It had all happened so fast. He'd thought she was an angel, and maybe she was. There was no doubt that she had saved his life. How had it happened that her car would be right there, as if waiting for him, when he stumbled out of the forest? He shook his head, admonishing himself for his tendency to see everything as providence.

Last night was a fog to him now. Andrew had joked with Shelby about being on a date, but in truth it had been his closest thing to a date in a long time. And what about the middle of the night? He exhaled a huge breath, which was the best he could do to articulate his response to that. A wild cocktail of warmth and comfort, out-of-control yielding from a guy unaccustomed to out-of-control anything, guilt, and, yes—he could not deny this—absolute delight.

Then this morning, before they'd even had a chance to speak to each other, there came the thumping on the window—the deputy from the county sheriff's office, making his morning run down the Omega Road.

Things moved quickly after that. The deputy loaded them both into his warm cruiser, piled Shelby's duffels in the back, and whisked them into town. At the station, over bad coffee in Styrofoam cups and a sack of Egg McMuffins, they filled in another deputy, Rhonda, who leaned forward on her elbows over an old metal desk, seeming to hang on every word. It was decided that a wrecker would be dispatched to haul Shelby's old Buick to a local garage, while she sorted out her insurance situation. When Rhonda asked Shelby what her plans were, she had said, with no emotion or any sideways glance at Andrew, "I'll be heading home to Wisconsin."

Those were the last words he heard from Shelby. A young intern named Doug came in to take Andrew to the Urgent Care and then—it was amazing the office would allow this—

drive him up to the trailhead to get the Tundra. Apparently, poor Doug didn't have much else to do. Andrew left with Doug, but at the door turned toward Shelby, who was busy talking with Rhonda. He should have said something.

Maybe she didn't want to talk about it. Maybe she was ashamed or embarrassed—he had no idea. He pounded his fist against the dashboard of the Tundra.

It had been a ninety-minute drive up to the trailhead, where Doug dropped off Andrew next to the Tundra. Fortunately, the key he had stashed in the rear wheel well was still there. After thanking Doug, Andrew had stopped at the visitor center to report his missing pack. A young ranger, who looked like she'd just graduated from college, told him that no missing pack had been reported, but that was not surprising, given how lightly used the trails were in the backcountry. She took down Andrew's contact information, then reassured him that wilderness hikers were honest folks and that his pack would be returned. Andrew had nodded, but was glad that his wallet and phone had not been in the pack. Then he began the long drive home.

Sure, his time with Shelby had been brief, and he barely knew her, but, hell, he should have at least said goodbye. Not to mention talk about what happened last night, the thought of which stirred him, even now, with a guilty glow.

He tried to picture her. Tall and athletic—Lord, she had almost carried him up from the creek bed to the old Buick. He could still remember that much from those delusional first moments after meeting her. Her soft complexion—it was almost impossible not to reach out and touch her. Her wire-frame glasses only accentuated those large gentle, inquiring eyes, like a frame around the Mona Lisa. Was she beautiful?

Not by Hollywood-starlet criteria, but, yes, her look of vulnerability and gentleness, that humor ready to pop you—seriously, filet of Luna Bar. Her brown hair was shoulder-length, natural, just like who she seemed to be—no, wait. She was more than natural. Transparent, that's what she was, transparent and honest. Beautiful? Lord, yes, she was beautiful.

He felt like he was short-changing Shelby with this superficial assessment—all that was missing was some disgusting 1-to-10 score. She was more than that. What he remembered most right now was her warm breath against his cheek, and her soft body pressed against him.

Andrew had done premarital counseling with many couples in his time at St. Tim's. These sessions covered all the issues of marriage—communications, finances, and family planning. There was always a discussion about sex, usually done awkwardly, but respectful of the couple's privacy. He stressed the importance of sex and the sanctity of marriage: how sex was for couples within marriage, for the purpose of children and intimacy and mutual pleasure. If any of those couples knew about his tumble in the front seat of an old Buick, which had nothing to do with children or intimacy or maybe even pleasure, just raw need—he shook his head in amazement.

He turned on the radio, but only one far-away station with a lot of static came in—some country guy, backed by a steel guitar, twanging away. He clicked it off, preferring to drive in silence. The peaceful flute music that Jesus had played came back to him now, and he hummed that haunting melody from the Good Friday liturgy.

Soon, Andrew was singing other songs he knew, and settled on ones he used to play on his guitar. He had played guitar since high school, but never was that great. But, once, at a youth lock-in at St. Tim's, he'd played and sung "Welcome to My World," "You've Got a Friend," and "Bridge Over Troubled Water," songs he'd played many times at home, but never before others. They were songs about human relationships, but the words worked just as well for describing a relationship with God. It had taken a real effort on his part—he could speak before a group, if he had notes, but singing just exposed him too much. But the kids loved it, and Gretchen, the volunteer youth leader, had suggested Andrew play guitar and sing in church. Buoyed by their enthusiasm, Andrew floated the idea to the vestry of working such songs into his sermons.

That had been a big mistake. He recalled the unpleasant exchange:

BUCK (shaking his head slowly, even before Andrew had finished describing what Gretchen had suggested): "I don't know, Andrew. We hired you to be a priest. That means preaching, administering over the plant and budget, fund raising, and visiting sick parishioners. It doesn't mean channeling your inner John Denver."

ANDREW (open mouthed, said nothing).

BUCK (looking around the table at the other vestry members with an authoritarian glower): "Of course, I could be wrong."

Buck never thought he was wrong. The other vestry members were quiet.

ANDREW (after a time of uncomfortable silence): Okay, let's move on. Next agenda item is ....

Andrew never played his guitar in church.

It had not been easy at St. Tim's. From Andrew's perspective, shaped by the lonely stretches of these highways, he saw little new life in a parish community that seemed to want to do things the way they always had, even if those ways had been unsuccessful. He sensed down deep that the problem was not the people or the institution, it was him—his passivity, his lack of the right skills to make things happen, his lack of a burning fire that had been there when he'd begun but was now a dim coal. He recalled what Jesus said, as he tended the fire on the mountainside: "It's almost out, but not quite." Had Jesus been talking about him?

He found little joy in the endless haggling with parish leaders over the color of the new paint for the parish hall or whether to serve ham or bacon at the Shrove Tuesday pancake supper. It seemed to him that he'd seldom been successful in steering their focus away from such things and toward the majesty of God, even though he had worked hard to create new programs, improve his preaching and teach about the necessity for outreach into the community.

What had initially attracted him to church, then to seminary, was the Christian message of hope, joy, love and new life. He still believed that message, but he had worked so hard for what sometimes felt like little or no impact, and he had to spend too much time on tasks that challenged him—administration, conflict resolution, and so on—that the essentials of the Christian message now seemed far away.

Maybe it was his preaching. He had once viewed his sermons as heady and thoughtful. And more than one parishioner had said his sermons were thoughtful. Maybe that was a compliment, meaning his sermons weren't vacuous. But thoughtful could also mean his preaching was restrained, not passionate. Maybe thoughtful meant his sermons gently tweaked the mind, rather than stirring the soul. Rarely had he heard from parishioners after church: "That sermon changed my life, Father," or, "Your sermon really got me thinking," or, "Can I come and talk with you more about God?" No, his sermons were merely thoughtful.

He worked hard on his sermons. He studied the scriptures, read commentaries about them, checked the meanings of key words in the original Greek or Hebrew, carefully chose each word that he would read from his typed manuscript. But, that's all his sermons were, apparently: thoughtful.

Andrew admired preachers who could fire up the crowd, bring tears, mobilize for action, maybe even evoke an Amen. But that's not who he was. He just wasn't able to let it all hang out, to pour his heart out in front of others.

There was much more in his heart. Fire. Passion. Longings. Fear. Love. He tried to share these things, but it was hard. It all stayed in his heart, never to be shared in a raised, shaking voice that could be on the brink of rage or tears. What came out was what was printed on the three pages of 14-point Times Roman, double-spaced text of his manuscript.

He looked down at his hands, gripping the wheel, and they were trembling. He purged his thoughts about preaching with a fantasy of playing his guitar. Playing "Welcome to My World," "You've Got a Friend," and "Bridge Over Troubled Water." In the front seat of the old Buick, next to Shelby.

Chapter 30

It was after dark when Andrew pulled into the driveway of his home, three blocks off the main drag of High Plains. The rectory was a large brick house, built a hundred years ago, with four bedrooms for a priest with a large family. It was separated from the church building only by a small parking lot.

Shelby said she'd never heard of High Plains, Nebraska. Most people haven't, because High Plains is not on the well-travelled I-80 corridor that passes through better-known small cities like North Platte, Kearney and Grand Island. Yet, High Plains had long been a significant city in the western part of the state. At least, that's what the Chamber of Commerce brochures claimed. It was only a little smaller than North Platte, thirty miles to the south. Like North Platte, High Plains grew as a railroad and cattle town, with a little agriculture. Settled in the mid-1800s, only a few of the original downtown buildings still stood, most of them having burned in the disastrous fire of 1908.

The church, like the town, had been founded in the mid-1800s. The current church building was constructed in 1910, after the original building had burned in the town fire. St. Tim's was a pretty good example of Gothic Revival architecture, designed to give those wild-west cowboys as good a taste of merry old England as a limited budget and the limited imagination of western-Nebraska architects could produce. It was hardly Westminster Abbey, but it was, nonetheless, an impressive gray-stone building, with a tall, square bell tower. It always reminded Andrew of a village parish church in England.

The sanctuary had high cathedral-like ceilings, supported by huge oak beams. This dark solemn space could evoke silence, prayer and maybe tears. The altar was carved from limestone quarried from up north. A beautiful oak rood screen, with a tall crucifix, guarded the entrance to the altar area, and a huge stained-glass window depicting the Resurrection, with a majestic risen Christ towering above grieving disciples and sleeping soldiers, filled the rear wall behind the altar. Legend was that the glass came from Italy. In one corner stood the high pulpit, with an elaborately carved frontal depicting the Nativity. The ornate lectern, across from the pulpit, was in the form of a brass eagle, patterned after Reformation churches in England—a place where the Word would be read and hopefully take flight on eagles' wings into all the world.

It was an inspiring place. When Andrew had first interviewed at St. Tim's, someone told him that the steps below the altar were soaked in prayer. Many times, Andrew had knelt on those steps, often alone at night, to pray, and it was easy to feel the presence of those who had knelt here for over a hundred years—in joy, in grief, in reverence.

The rows of hard pews could accommodate over 200 worshipers. In the early days, Andrew had been told, the church was full on Sundays. But it felt somewhat empty on a typical Sunday nowadays, when the congregation of about forty was gathered.

The rectory had been a fancy home when it was constructed, but over the years it had been maintained only by volunteers from the parish, and it showed. The whole house always had a musty smell, which Andrew had been unsuccessful at fully eradicating.

Summers were hot and steamy in High Plains, yet there was no air conditioning in the rectory. Maureen had campaigned every year for a new central-air unit, but it always got cut out of the budget, when the usual annual need for financial belt-tightening arose. There was a window unit, which Andrew had purchased, in the master bedroom upstairs. His study downstairs had only a fan, and those great streams of sweat he generated, while working on summer nights, were not necessarily from the fire of the Holy Spirit.

Despite the updating that had been neglected for decades, the rectory still exuded a stately, though faded, charm. High ceilings, arched doorways, built-in cabinets in the dining room, beautiful-though-creaky hardwood floors, and a massive stone fireplace topped by a beautiful maple mantle made the home a perfect place for the monthly teas of the women's guild, weekly bible studies, and hosting the occasional dinner for the Bishop.

Andrew hobbled into the house on his crutches. He had no luggage. Everything he'd taken on the trip was probably still alongside that wilderness trail. He dropped into a straight-back steel-and-vinyl chair at an old Formica dining-room table, a funky retro piece that people paid big bucks for these days. This table was simply the same table that had been in this room since the fifties. He leaned back on two legs and studied the sparse interior. He'd lived here for eight years, yet had very few wall hangings. A few dark landscape paintings, left by a former priest, were the only art on the walls.

He considered calling Maureen, but it was too late. She always turned in at eight, after watching Anderson Cooper 360.

In bed, unable to sleep, he scanned the nearby bookshelf for something to read. With no sermon to prepare, his usual studying wasn't needed, and his copies of *My First Summer in the Sierra* and *A Sand County Almanac* were along the trail to Marmot Pass. He surveyed the rows of books, all religious titles, by many great authors, across a spectrum of theological viewpoints. Henri Nouwen, Richard Rohr, John Stott, Marcus Borg. None of them made him want to pull a book off the shelf and flip open a page.

He turned his body toward the tall window, where the soft glow of the downtown lights streamed through white-lace curtains, and fell asleep to the drone of the window air conditioner.

Chapter 31

It was three blocks to Henry's, over on Comstock Street, an easy walk, even on crutches. The sign above the entrance of the vintage brick building said, "Henry's, Friends and Food." Andrew claimed his usual spot, in a small booth by a window looking out on the boulevard.

This is where he often worked on his sermons. But, today, he'd left his laptop at the rectory, since he had no sermon to prepare. Fr. Morrison, a retired priest from down in North Platte, was scheduled to fill in for the next eight weeks.

Henry's bustled with activity, as usual, producing a lively din of conversation, clinking coffee cups and shuffling newspapers. Dean Martin crooned "That's Amore" in the background. It was this bustle that Andrew loved and found conducive to writing his sermons.

Paige, the waitress, who also attended St. Tim's, was beside his table immediately, carrying a pot of coffee. She brought no menu or notepad, as Andrew probably knew the menu better than Paige. A few specials were posted on a large chalkboard on one of the paneled walls.

Paige, whose gray hair was bound neatly in a bun, peered at Andrew through pink-rimmed cat-eye glasses, straight out of the seventies. "Father," she said, "did you hurt yourself?"

Andrew glanced at his crutches. "Just a minor slip and sprained ankle. Should be good as new in a few days."

"Well, you gave me a scare. And I didn't expect to see you back so soon. We thought you'd be gone for a couple of months."

"Oh, I'm back a little early. How have you been, Paige?"

"Same ol', same ol,' Father. Kids are bringing the grand-kiddos over from Lincoln this weekend. Can't wait to see those little angels."

"Well, I hope you have a great time with them."

"So, does this mean you'll be back at church on Sunday?"

"Not yet. Fr. Morrison is scheduled to fill in."

"Oh, we'll miss you, that's for sure, Father. So, you gonna have your regular?"

"You know, Paige, I think I'm going to try one of the specials today." He studied the chalkboard. "Maybe that quiche."

After Paige left, Andrew watched the flow of life on Comstock Street. A guy in overhauls was unloading boxes from an Econoline in front of Sam's True Value. An old man on a walker, wearing a sweater even in the summer, was moving slow, maybe headed to the senior center down the block. Other than that, the street was quiet. It was still before nine, before most of the shops opened. But the sad truth was, most of the shoppers were probably gathered at Walmart, on the edge of town.

He pulled out his phone, took a deep breath, and punched in Maureen's number, knowing he would get an earful for coming back so soon.

"Maureen, it's Andrew. Thought I'd let you know I was back in town."

"You're back already? Good grief, Father, it's only been a week. You really are more boring than I thought."

"It's not that I couldn't stay away. I got injured, and—"

"Are you okay?"

There was no use worrying his senior warden with the story of being lost for three days and almost dying, or the crutches he was stumbling around on. "Yeah, I'm fine, just a little banged up from a fall on the trail. Lost my gear, though, in the fall, and that ended the trip. So, what's new around the parish?"

Maureen was taking a little too long to reply. Finally, she said, "I'm glad you're okay, but there is one thing, and it's good you called. I've tried to reach you the last couple of days, but there was no answer."

"Yeah, I was out of range, and then my phone died. What's up, Maureen?"

"Maybe it's best we meet. Have you got time for that, Father?"

"Of course, Maureen. I'm just having breakfast at Henry's. Want to meet in, say, forty-five minutes over at the church?"

"I'll be there, Father. Now, you go and enjoy your breakfast and don't worry about a thing."

His quiche arrived, along with a coffee refill. So, I won't worry about a thing, he thought. But what is that thing I'm not supposed to worry about?

Andrew was at the church in a half-hour and decided to wait for Maureen in the parish hall. They could have met in his office, just off the parish hall, but that space was dark and claustrophobic. Plus, his desk, which he'd left in a mess, held too many reminders of unfinished tasks. None of them was a huge project—he'd taken care of those before he left on his sabbatical—but he knew that once he got back in his office, he'd be sucked into a whirlpool of responsibility. He wanted to avoid that whirlpool for as long as he could.

The parish hall was, in some ways, the most inviting space in the church. The sanctuary, of course, was more ornate and had a special sacred ambiance, but it was dimly lit and formal.

The parish hall, which everyone just called "the hall," was where the social life of the parish took place. The ceilings, over ten feet high, were covered in an antique hammered metal. Tall windows along one wall brought in lots of light. The hardwood floors creaked from the millions of footsteps that had traversed them: the joyous wedding reception attendees almost dancing, the grieving family members moving slowly after a loved-one's funeral, kids bounding in from Sunday School, and the happy shuffling of parishioners gathering for coffee every week after church.

Across the three walls that didn't have windows, there were felt banners from various festivals and celebrations of years gone by, artwork and poems by children, and announcements about church and community activities. Sadly, there were a lot fewer of those kids bounding in than there were just a few years ago, and most of the announcements were about concerts and lectures elsewhere in the community.

The hall made you feel good. Sagging old couches, castoffs from parishioners, were mismatched in color but were comfortable and well-used. The attached kitchen was part of this gathering place, and often the aroma of fresh-brewed coffee filled the air.

Andrew took a seat in a folding metal chair, at one of the dozen round tables in the room. Soon, Maureen came in, walking fast like she always did, and took a chair across from him. She brought out a small stack of papers and centered them in front of her. Maureen Edelman was a life-long Episcopalian. Her husband died long before Andrew showed up at St. Tim's. She was a small, white-haired woman, who some might initially dismiss as another little old lady that a Boy Scout should help across the street. But that would be a serious error in judgment. Maureen was a ball of fire, tempered with intelligence and wisdom. There was no living soul— including his spiritual advisor, Fr. Ken—whose insights Andrew trusted more.

"Father, you have crutches." Maureen's eyes displayed worry.

"Oh, I just sprained my ankle. Nothing really. I'll be off these things in a few days. So, what's up, Maureen?"

"Like I said, I tried to contact you, even though the last thing I wanted was to interrupt your time away. But anyway, here's the situation. Almost immediately after you left, Buck Martin sent an email to the vestry, proposing that the budget be modified to shift outreach funding toward paying off the mortgage on the church building."

Andrew came up out of his chair. "He what?"

"Just let me finish, Father." Maureen spoke with a calm voice, but, of course, Maureen, who never lost control, could probably describe an H-bomb detonation in a calm voice. "So, Buck put in some weasel rationale in his email for not contacting you about this. Some nonsense about how you were away on your well-earned sabbatical, and we didn't want to disturb you with budget details. Since you wouldn't be back for two months, the church needed to act now and not wait for your return. That's what he said." Maureen pushed a copy of the email across the table to Andrew, then continued.

"Buck made some grandiose claim about how the vestry is the business body of the church and had the responsibility to take on this budget challenge without delay." She shook her head in disapproval. "That email sounds good, until you think about it for two seconds. I called it out, just yesterday, for what it was: an end-run around the rector. I said I wouldn't stand for it, but I haven't heard back from Buck or any of the other vestry members yet."

Andrew felt his face redden. "I can't allow this to happen, of course. Those outreach funds help support the food kitchen, the shelter and all kinds of charities around the region. To get rid of the outreach fund is just saying you value financial security over living out the life of a Christian. It's saying you don't want the church to be what the church is supposed to be."

Maureen produced a warm smile, as she leaned back and crossed her arms over the floral pattern of her knit blouse. "That's what I knew you'd say, Father. That's what I hoped you'd say. That's what the vestry needs to hear."

Andrew couldn't sit any longer. He stood, but immediately needed one of his crutches to lean on. "I'm glad I came back, Maureen. This has to be dealt with." He would have to deal with it. He had the authority. He was the one grounded in what a Christian church should be about. This would be a teaching moment for the vestry. Even as these thoughts mobilized him, the image of Buck, the human steam roller, flooded his mind.

"So, what do you want to do, Father?"

"Well, let's see, maybe we should call a special vestry meeting to—"

"Father, don't you think a special meeting gives too much credence to this out-of-line email?"

"Hmm. You're probably right. Maybe we should—"

"Father, I'm concerned about your sabbatical. Yes, this is a problem, but we've had lots of problems before, and we've always come through it. I claim that's one of the proofs that God exists. There's us, so often making bad decisions and screwing things up, but then there's this church that's survived for two thousand years, in spite of us. I say that's pretty good evidence for divine protection, don't you think?"

"Yes, of course, but here's what—"

"The most important thing for you to be doing is what you've been doing. Trying to understand the path forward."

"But, what about—"

"You don't need me to tell you what to do. You're the priest. You're the one who's taken those seminary courses."

Andrew slumped over the crutch. "I'm not so sure that I don't need your advice."

Maureen raised an eyebrow. "How old are you, Father?"

"You know how old I am. Forty."

"Forty. You should get back out there, Father. Have an adventure."

"But, I—"

"Trust me to handle this situation, Father. But, more importantly, trust God."

Chapter 32

On a corner, one block off the main street of Bridger, South Dakota, an old building with peeling paint housed the Greyhound Bus station. Inside, behind a window, an attentive clerk was going through a stack of papers. A board above the window announced arrival and departure times in bright-red-LED letters. The eastbound buses—to Sioux Falls, connecting to points beyond—departed at 8:00 a.m. and 2:30 p.m.

It was 2:45.

The waiting room was a cold-feeling place, with harsh fluorescent lights and a dull concrete floor. A few travelers occupied the two rows of molded-plastic chairs that filled the space. They were the ones who wouldn't be leaving town in their Escalade or flying out on some charter flight to the Twin Cities: an old man slumped in his chair, staring straight ahead, holding a plastic supermarket bag of his belongings on his lap; a teenager sprawled across two seats, chewing gum and looking at her phone; a husband and wife snapping at each other, as they tried to corral two energetic rug rats running up and back between the rows of chairs.

Double glass doors led out back. Outside, there was a roofed-over drive-through bay, where the buses pulled in. It was empty and quiet. Another row of empty plastic chairs was positioned along one end of the boarding area. At the other end was a concrete bench. There was only one person there, a woman with two large duffel bags. Apparently, the 2:30 bus was late.

Andrew saw her notice him, then quickly turn her head away, as if she were pretending to not see him. Maybe he should leave. Give her the space she may want. She probably thinks, here comes the self-righteous priest who has regained his piety and wants to convert this sinful heathen. Now, she had pulled out her Kindle and was giving it her full attention.

"Shelby."

She looked up, feigning surprise. "Oh, it's you. What are you doing here?"

"Where you headed?"

She shot him a none-of-your-freaking-business look, then pushed her frameless glasses up on her nose with an index finger. "Home." She looked back down at her Kindle.

"I was wondering …"

"What?"

"Do you still want to go to Loveland?"

Part Two

REFUGE

Every breath's a gift,
the first one to the last.
Luke Bryan

Chapter 33

Shelby

Shelby had gotten to the boarding area of the Greyhound station an hour before Andrew arrived. She'd purchased her ticket—to Twin Cities, connecting to an Indian Trails bus home—then hauled her duffels outside to a bench near the edge of the boarding platform, the most isolated place she could find.

Yesterday had been a long day. After their rescue by the sheriff's department, and after Andrew had departed, she'd spent much of the day negotiating with the local garage and her insurance company. She still wasn't sure what was going to happen with the Buick. She'd finally left the car at the garage, after forking out $150 for the towing, and after a long conversation with the insurance company, who again verified that she had no roadside-assistance coverage. It was uncertain whether the car could be repaired, or if it could be sold or salvaged as scrap metal. Shelby finally prevailed on the garage owner to hold the car in a lot out back until she figured out what to do with it.

She'd spent the night at a Super-8, two blocks from the garage, but caught a bit of luck, when Rhonda, the deputy who had interviewed them, called in the evening to see how she was doing. "Thought maybe you might need a lift to the bus station," Rhonda said. "Did you say you were going tomorrow?"

"Yes. That would be great. Thanks."

"I gotta say, I admire somebody who heads out across the country like you."

Shelby could picture Rhonda's big, dark curious eyes. "I'd never really been much of anywhere before," she said.

"Takes some guts, though, what you did. Gives me something to think about."

"You lived in Bridger long, Rhonda?"

"All my life." Rhonda followed her words with a self-deprecating chuckle that Shelby recognized.

"And how old are you, if you don't mind me asking?"

"Twenty-six."

"Oh, you're still just a kid. Are you married?"

"Was for a while. Now it's just me and my little girl."

"I bet she's beautiful."

"Yeah, she's my treasure." There was some silence before Rhonda added, "But I get lonely."

Must be lonely now, thought Shelby, if she's calling a stranger at the Super-8. This would be a good time for some sisterly advice, something schmaltzy about not letting go of your dreams. But Shelby couldn't talk about letting go of dreams, because that's what she had done so many times. And that's what she'd be doing again tomorrow, when she climbed onto that bus.

After Rhonda's call, Shelby sat on the bed and stared at the wall.

So much for your sleuthing work, Inspector Sims. Those British detectives on PBS, Detective Chief Inspectors Vera and Barnaby, would not be thwarted by even the most sinister villain—you were done in by a blown head gasket. A few days of excitement, which had not only quickened her pulse, but had diverted her thoughts away from Rudy's groping hands and the imminent loss of her job—all that was over. The image of her vivacious cousin, Sedona, who she would not get to see, now flashed in her mind: the carefree, always successful Sedona versus the klutzy, fumbling reality of herself. The bouncy Sedona, who, like a cat, always landed on her feet, unlike her, who always seemed to land on her ass.

She flipped on the tube, but a few seconds of Big Walt shouting to the viewers to come on down and get the best deal for their old car was enough. She flicked the set off, even as she wondered how much Big Walt would pay for her old jalopy that needed two grand worth of repair.

In the silence, the thought of heading home tomorrow produced alternating waves of dread, resignation, and humiliation. She recalled someone once saying to her during that low time, "Well, at least you don't have cancer, it could be worse." *What an asshole.* At least a cancer patient can have some dignity, can be applauded for her courage. And then she heard Michael's voice again saying to her something like, "You know, there's a billion people in China who don't give a shit about your problems." She remembered thinking at that time, as she watched his smirking face, *A billion and one.*

She wasn't ready to call Tisha. Instead, she tried to amuse herself composing the text she could write: *You said I was crazy, and I guess you were right. So, I was out only one night before my car blew up. Then I had unprotected sex with a dirty stranger I found in the woods. Now I'm coming home on a Greyhound.* The dark humor failed to produce a smile.

God, she wished Tisha was here.

She tapped Tisha's number into her phone.

"Shelby," Tisha beamed, "I was getting worried about you. No calls or texts since yesterday morning. What's going on, girl?"

Shelby hadn't thought through how she was going to explain things. She stammered, "Oh, Tisha, everything's a mess."

There was urgency in Tisha's voice now. "Are you safe? Do I need to call somebody to—"

"No, I'm safe. I'm at a motel in South Dakota."

"Oh?"

"And, I'm coming home tomorrow. On the bus. Don't know yet when I'll get in."

"Coming home? Oh, hell. Okay, I'm sitting down and I have a glass of wine, so let me have it."

Shelby gave out a short laugh. "Wish you could pour me a glass, too." Then she fumbled through a summary of her car troubles, breaking down in the middle of nowhere, Andrew showing up, and their spending the night, almost freezing their butts off, before the cops finally came by. "So, the car's dead, and the repairs will cost more than it's worth. That's why I'm coming home on a Greyhound. My great adventure is over after only two days. God, Tisha, I'm such a loser." She could feel the flood of tears building up.

"Okay, Shelby, let's get a grip. First, you need to know this: you're about the coolest, best person I know. So, wrap your brain around that for a minute. Second, this is just a little setback. You'll get home, you'll get squeezed half-silly in a big hug, then we'll get you remobilized—is that even a word?—and you'll still have time for a new adventure. Hell, having my tail planted on a Greyhound sounds pretty good compared to going in to see your friend Rudy tomorrow."

This got Shelby laughing.

"So, what about that guy you found by the road? Andrew? What happened to him?"

"He headed home this morning. One more thing ... we had sex last night."

"Okay, so there was one good thing that happened on this trip." Then she added, "I'm assuming it was a good thing?"

Shelby waited a second. "Yes. He was a nice guy. Only problem was, I had no protection—so, yet another rookie move by this thirty-seven-year-old teenager."

"Well, we don't have to cross that bridge today, do we? You just get your sweet fanny home. Don't go causing any trouble on that bus. Then we'll figure shit out when you get here. Unless you need me to come over there and get you—you need me to do that?"

"That's nice, Tisha, but I think I can handle the bus trip without screwing that up, too." She was glad she'd called Tisha. She was already feeling better. "You always know how to get me laughing." She was about to hang up when she realized she'd been so wrapped up in herself, she hadn't even asked about Derek's proposal. What a crappy friend she was. "So, dare I ask about Derek's big question?"

There was quiet on the other end. Then Tisha said, "Let's talk about that when you get back."

When Shelby was off the phone, she paced the floor again, peeked out through curtains so dirty she didn't want to touch them, then returned to the bed, where she tapped in a request to Google: *Chance of getting pregnant by having sex one time.* Hell, she had studied nursing. She should know these things.

She knew, of course, that the probability depended upon on the time relative to the woman's menstrual cycle. The probability varies, according to the expert that Google led her to, from near zero on certain days to a peak of 9% during the month.

These pretty-low odds should have comforted her. Even on her most-likely-to-get-knocked-up days, it was less than one in ten that she'd get pregnant. Yeah, she should feel reassured. But she didn't. The only way for her to cope would be to not think about it. That's what she would do—not think about it. Other people could do that, why couldn't she?

Now, Shelby shifted on the hard concrete bench in the boarding area and checked her phone again. Two-thirty had come and gone. The freaking bus was late. Of course.

From out of her periphery she saw him, a man on crutches. Good grief, it was Andrew. *What is he doing here?* Maybe he's taking the bus, too. But didn't he say he had a car somewhere? She hadn't spoken with him before he left the sheriff's office yesterday. She should have, but what would she have said? *Nice knowing you, have a happy life?*

She'd just as soon not see him now. She didn't want to see anyone now. Except maybe the driver of the Greyhound, opening up the cargo door and loading her duffels. She pulled up her Kindle and turned away from the double doors through which Andrew had just come. Maybe he wouldn't see her.

"Shelby."

Oh, damn.

Chapter 34

S helby was flustered when Andrew dropped his bomb, "Do you still want to go to Loveland?" It was the last thing she expected him to say, and she forced herself to be silent until she could get a grasp of what this question entailed. Of course, she still wanted to go to Loveland. But that really wasn't the question, was it? The real question was, "Do you want to go to Loveland with me?"

She shuffled on the bench, without speaking. Andrew looked a lot different now. No mud and pine needles. He wore black Levi's and a pale-blue short-sleeve shirt. As best as she could tell, those were the same hiking boots he'd had on when she found him. His face was fair but sunburned, no doubt from his days in the mountains, and his features were sharply chiseled. His eyes held the same sad look she'd noticed when they'd first met. He leaned forward on his crutches, which she guessed the sheriff's department had help him get. Her eyes met his. "No, I've decided not to go."

Andrew's mouth fell open, like that was the last thing he thought she'd say. *Good. Give him a little jolt, like he gave me.*

Then he nodded, like he understood. "Okay," he said, then paused. "I just thought I'd ask … uh … well, goodbye. I wish you the best." He turned and headed back toward the double doors.

"Wait," she called out when he was about halfway to the doors. He turned and stood there, leaning on his crutches and looking uncertain. "Why did you ask me that question? I mean, why would you want to go to Loveland?"

"May I sit down?" He nodded toward her bench.

"Okay," she said tentatively. Shelby shifted toward the far end of the bench, and Andrew sat at the other end. Her eyes were locked on him, waiting for his answer.

"Well, I drove home to High Plains. I was supposed to be gone two months or so, but I'd only been gone a week. It became clear … actually, Maureen … that's the senior warden … she's the lay leader of the church … anyway … she helped me see that I needed to continue my sabbatical." He rubbed his chin between a thumb and his fingers. "No way I could continue my backpacking trip. So … what was I going to do?" He shrugged his shoulders. "I just figured maybe it would be fun to go to …" He licked his lips, as if they had gone dry. "I guess maybe that was a stupid idea, huh?"

Shelby started to speak, just as the bus pulled in, large and loud, filling the area with the faint odor of diesel fuel.

As the doors whished open, Andrew stood, awkward on his crutches. "So, I guess here's your bus."

Shelby also stood and leaned to grab the two duffels, one in each hand. Then she looked up at him, with a smile. "So, where's your vehicle parked?"

Chapter 35

"You brought a guitar?" Shelby asked, as she piled her duffels into the rear of Andrew's truck, the bed covered by a fiberglass camper shell.

"Yeah, I play sometimes."

"Cool. You had the truck long?" It looked old, with rusted out bottom panels on the doors and a lot of dings. The red paint was faded from too many days in the sun.

"Just a few years. I think it's an '05. Odometer's broken, but it's got a lot of miles. A parishioner gave it to me. Probably figured it was better as a tax write-off. But it runs well." He smiled, like he was preparing a zinger. "Head gasket's okay, I think."

Shelby ignored the good-natured dig. "So, how did you know I was at the bus station?"

"Easy, actually. I called the sheriff's station, and Rhonda told me. I was worried I might miss you, though."

Google Maps said it was a five-hour drive from Bridger, South Dakota, to Loveland, Colorado. Leaving at three—they wasted no time departing the depressing bus station—they would arrive in Loveland by eight.

Andrew's truck made her old Buick feel like a limo. A crack that ran the full width of the windshield made you wonder if you touched it, maybe the whole thing would collapse. The panel above the dash was faded and warped from too much sun. The floor mats were worn through like the soles of old shoes. The bench seat was hard and utilitarian—any late-night shenanigans would be difficult here. Good Lord, why did she think of that? But the truck sat up high, providing a good view of the road.

They'd just made it to the edge of town, which didn't take long. "So, tell me again," Andrew asked, "it's your cousin who lives in Loveland?"

"Sedona. I haven't seen her in, like forever. We stay connected on Facebook." With that, Shelby pulled out her phone and gave out a laugh, a happy laugh, she noted, the first one in a couple of days. "I guess I'd better let her know we're on our way." She keyed in her text: *Headed your way! Should be there by eight! Can't wait to see you. Bringing*—she shot Andrew an appraising glance—*my friend, Andrew. Let you know when we're a half-hour out.* She turned back toward Andrew. "Hope she's home. I haven't been able to connect with her since I started the trip." Yeah, Sedona is spontaneous, Shelby thought, won't mind if we drop in on short notice—unlike me, who is already worrying that she might not be home.

"I think I drove past Loveland once," Andrew said. "Didn't get off the interstate, though."

His comment gave Shelby a chance to give him a long appraising look. He'd said he never played sports in high school. But, hell, he looked pretty fit. Backpacking through the wilderness for days wasn't for wimps, she thought. The stubble had been shaved from his face, and the sunburn was already fading. His face and arms still showed the abrasions from his fall, but they were healing quickly, which Shelby knew indicated a person in good health. His hair, dark brown, was longer than she would expect for a priest. Not wild or shaggy, it was straight and combed back, but long enough that she could visualize it stirring in a breeze or her mussing it up with her hands—*Geez, Shelby.* In addition to the sadness in his eyes, he had a look of … what? Was it fear or longing? Or something deeper? Like beneath the surface there were layers of mystery and secrets. Of course, she understood, their romp in the front seat of the Buick may be coloring her assessment. She grabbed the armrest with her right hand and squeezed it hard. "I've never even been to Colorado," she said. "Can we hear some music?" she asked, reaching toward the radio.

"Of course."

Shelby found only one AM station, coming in with lots of static from Cheyenne. George Strait was singing "Amarillo by Morning." Shelby cranked up the volume. "Oh, I love this oldie. How 'bout you?"

"Guess country isn't my thing," he said, in a restrained way that implied he really hated it.

"Why?"

Andrew squirmed. "I don't know. Maybe it's just too sentimental for my tastes."

Shelby turned the volume down. "You don't know what you're missing. Don't tell me you're one of those Bach sonata types."

This brought a smile from Andrew. He seemed to ponder her comment. "Hmm. I like lots of different kinds of music … just not country, I guess."

It was a brilliant, sunshine-filled afternoon, as they followed South Dakota 89 south through rolling ranch country toward Wyoming. Green, pine-clad hills backed large fields, where horses grazed. Yellow wildflowers dotted the fields, and rustic split-rail fences demarked the property lines. Shelby half expected to see the Marlboro man ride by.

She sent a text to Tisha. *So, the adventure continues. Andrew, the guy from the woods, showed up at the bus station. We're headed to Colorado.*

Within a minute, Shelby had a response. *That's more like it!*

After a while, as gawking at the landscape had replaced their conversation, Andrew cleared his throat and said, "Look, I'm awkward talking about these things, but—"

"Then, let's not." Shelby knew where this was going. This was not the time to talk about the sex. What in hell was there to say about it, anyway? Maybe some BS like, *Gee, it was wonderful* or, even worse, *Was it good for you?* No, thanks. *Oh, I feel so guilty.* No, thanks. *You know, I usually don't*—No, thanks.

"But I need to—"

"No, you don't need to."

"But I never asked if you had protection." His face was full of concern.

Shelby swallowed what felt like a lump in her throat and turned to look out her window. This was not a subject she was interested in exploring, while driving down the highway on a sunny June day. "No, you didn't," she said.

He seemed upset. "I was sleepy, I just didn't—"

She turned her face back toward him. "Don't worry about it." She had decided not to worry about it, and she didn't need to listen to him worrying about it.

Andrew gave her a sad nod, then turned his attention back to the road.

"There is one thing to say," she said.

He looked at her.

"What happened. That was a one-time deal, okay?" It was important to manage expectations. Wasn't it? She added, "Unusual circumstances, right?"

"Okay … I mean, yes, of course. Look, I'd never—"

"Just focus on the driving, okay?"

Chapter 36

The five-hour drive gave Shelby time to formulate a plan. She ... er, they ... would spend a couple days with Sedona, plenty of time for her high-energy cousin to show them around, probably some of the places that Shelby had just explored with TripAdvisor and Wikipedia. The nightlife scene in Loveland apparently was limited—Sedona would know—but nearby Fort Collins, with its big university, would have plenty of fun places. Shelby could drift into a pity party over how little of the university party scene she had experienced, but she wasn't going to let that derail her now.

The really big draw of Loveland—this had Shelby both pumped and intimidated—was the nearby Rocky Mountain National Park. She read to Andrew some of the highlights of the park, as they approached Cheyenne, Wyoming. High peaks over 14,000 feet in elevation—Shelby couldn't imagine that. The highest paved road in the nation, well above timberline, where there were ten-foot-high snow banks, even into summer. And amazing wildlife like elk and moose. Lord, what if she got to see a moose?

A more compelling subject than unprotected sex.

Shelby looked out her window to the west, where a high mountain range was beginning to appear on the horizon—the freaking Rocky Mountains. Tisha had been right. It was just a little bump in the road that had set her back, but she was headed west once more. Her plans, just packaged a little differently from what she had anticipated—she shot a quick glance over at Andrew, focused on driving into the intense afternoon sun—were back on track.

They would party with Sedona, then go find Olivia Marshak. Let the sleuthing commence. Inspector Sims was back. DCIs Vera and Barnaby, watch out.

Chapter 37

"Are you sure this is the right address?" Andrew stood with hands on hips, staring up and down the block, as if on the verge of some profound discovery. They were at the entrance to one of the units of Silver Streak, an upscale condo complex in downtown Loveland.

"Of course, I'm sure." Shelby was checking her phone again. "Okay, so the address I have is from awhile back, but I never heard that she'd moved." Silver Streak, with lots of glass and stainless and tasteful brick accents, was just a block off 4th Street, apparently one of the few happening areas in town. It was easy to envision Sedona, all slinky in some cool outfit and surrounded by hip, laughing friends, making the rounds of the trendy bars there, knocking back exotic cocktails Shelby had never heard of.

They had rung the doorbell, knocked multiple times, then peeked in the windows. The problem wasn't that Sedona wasn't home, it was that the place didn't looked lived in. Advertising blurbs were piled by the door and several leaflets were tucked into the door handle. Shelby scanned through recent Facebook posts from Sedona. She posted often, but there was no indication that she had moved. She found one photo, from a year ago, that showed Sedona with several friends—she seemed to have a ton of friends—clowning it up in front of her home. "Here, look at this," she said to Andrew. "Same place, don't you think?"

Andrew looked back and forth between the photo and the condo. "Yep, this is it. Look at that chipped brick by the front door," he said, using two fingers to expand the photo. Then he reached down and touched the actual chipped brick.

Shelby reviewed all her contact information for Sedona. She had a phone number, which she called and texted again with no response, and the address. It hadn't seemed troublesome at the time, but Sedona had not responded to any of Shelby's recent calls or texts.

A man in running clothes carried bags of groceries toward the entrance of the condo unit next door. Shelby took a step toward him. "Hey, I'm looking for Sedona Jones, who lives here. She's my cousin. Have you seen her?"

The guy set down his armload of bags and looked at both Shelby and Andrew, obviously checking them out. Apparently satisfied they weren't stalkers or repo agents, he said, "Yeah, I remember her. She hosted a block party once. Sedona, yeah that's her. Like the town in Arizona. Now that you ask, I haven't seen her for a while. Maybe she moved out?" He shrugged, picked up his groceries and went inside.

Shelby pushed her phone back into the pocket of her khaki cargo pants, then did a slow three-sixty, shaking her head, like a girl who'd run out of options. She turned toward Andrew. "So, I didn't expect this," she said. "Now what? You hungry?"

"Starving. Let's grab something, and then we can refine our strategy."

Shelby nodded—she was already refining her strategy. Like, now that staying at Sedona's place was out of the picture, where were they going to sleep tonight?

TripAdvisor led them to a restaurant that wouldn't cost big bucks: Door 222, walking distance from Sedona's condo, even with Andrew hobbling on his crutches. They chose the outside seating with cozy tables-for-two right on busy 4th Street. It looked perfect. A waiter brought them water and menus and commented what a beautiful evening it was, but that it was going to get cold again tonight. Shelby already knew what that was like.

They pored over their menus, then sat in awkward silence until the waiter returned. Andrew was probably already refining his strategy, too. This was crazy, she thought. She'd told this man her most intimate secrets the night before last, and now she couldn't think of anything to say.

From the vast menu, they selected several small-plate dishes—tapas—which would hold the cost down. It sounded elegant: smoked salmon, fried avocado, spinach-stuffed mushrooms, and something with an unpronounceable name.

They shared inane chit-chat until the food came. As Shelby started to dig in, Andrew said, "Do you mind if we say grace?"

Shelby already had a mouthful of fried avocado. She quickly put her fork down, thought for a second about spitting the food out onto her napkin, but that would be visibly gross. She swallowed it, trying to be discreet, then dabbed her mouth with her napkin. "Oh, of course. I'm sorry." She brought her hands up into a praying position and bowed her head. She couldn't remember ever saying grace before.

Andrew said a brief prayer that sounded like something he'd memorized. After the amen, Shelby said, "Thank you," trying to sound reverent. She was thinking about how crude she must have appeared with her mouth stuffed with food and whether there was fried avocado streaked down the front of her shirt.

"Hope that was okay with you. Just a tradition for me."

"No problem." She dabbed her mouth again, then spread the napkin over her lap.

The tapas were amazing. Each dish had its own unique sauce, and they both oohed and aahed, a convenient substitute for meaningful conversation.

"Gotta say," Andrew finally said, after they'd had several bites, "I think this beats even the legendary filet of Luna Bar."

Shelby took a sip of her Loveland Aleworks seasonal draft, which the waiter had recommended, then rubbed her chin with her index finger, pretending to be in deliberation. "I don't know. Frankly, I'd say it's close." She didn't want the conversation to be steered toward their time in the Buick.

"So, I guess tomorrow you want to go find that sister of Marshak's ... Olivia?" Andrew asked. With a raised eyebrow, he added, "Hopefully, Olivia's at the address you have."

Shelby gave out a not-really-amused grunt. "Actually, I only know she lives in Golden, Colorado. I checked the map—it's about an hour from here. But ... okay, truth time— I have no address for Olivia Marshak. We're going to have to do some sleuthing."

Andrew fiddled with his knife and fork. Then he smiled. "Good—I guess this really is an adventure, huh?"

They split the bill.

It was now dark. Time to deal with the sleeping issue. After Shelby's earlier slamming the door on talking about their night in the Buick, Andrew obviously wasn't going to be the first to bring the subject up. As they walked back to the Tundra, Shelby stopped and faced him. "I guess we've gotta figure out where we're going to stay."

Andrew's mouth fell open, like he didn't know what to say. Finally, he said, "So, what are your thoughts?"

"Well, I guess we don't have a lot of options. FYI, I'm not staying in the back of that pickup, even if you did have sleeping bags."

"Which I don't, unfortunately… uh, I mean unfortunately because it would save us some money."

"It's okay," she smiled. Shelby was doing the math, and she didn't like what she was coming up with. In the past two days, she'd already shelled out $150 for the towing, $90 for the Super-8 last night, and $110 for the bus ticket. The bus ticket really ticked her off. She had tried to get a refund, but the damned ticket was nonrefundable. Her outlay was pushing $400 in a little over a day, not counting food—cash that a mail girl doesn't easily come by. "It looks like we've got to find a motel. I'm thinking, though, that tomorrow, we might want to get a couple of cheap sleeping bags somewhere and find a campground. I stayed in a nice one a couple of nights ago, only thirty bucks. I can't afford motel rooms every night." She was also pondering whether they would get two rooms or one, but said nothing yet.

"Tell you what," he said, "I'll spring for a room, I mean, rooms, tonight. Why don't you get that trip app out again and let's find something that won't break the bank?"

At the front desk of the A-1 Suites, a budget place on busy Eisenhower Boulevard, the clerk, a young woman, who might have been a student up at Fort Collins, said, "One bed or two?"

Andrew shot Shelby a quick glance. "Actually, we need two separate—"

Shelby cut in. "Two beds." She returned Andrew's surprised look. "Hey, we've gotta save some money. And, besides, we're adults, who ought to be able to behave themselves."

In the small bathroom, she put on the sweat pants and drab sweatshirt that she'd worn at the KOA. It was about as sexless as you could get, she concluded, appraising herself in the mirror. She brushed her teeth, arranged her toiletry bag on the corner of the sink to leave him some room, then re-entered the bedroom, feeling about as exposed as if she were wearing a flimsy negligee. Andrew politely didn't gawk.

"Your turn," she said in a casual, breezy way, trying to deny, even to herself, that she was in a sleazy motel room with this guy. It didn't matter what had happened in the front seat of the Buick, the room was still so charged that she wasn't sure she could walk to her bed without tripping over her own feet. "I left room on the sink for your stuff," she said, all business.

Andrew emerged shortly, wearing a blue-and-gold Steph Curry T-shirt over what looked like pajama bottoms. Shelby had spread her Tartan blanket over her bed to give it a personal feel, and Andrew glanced down at it, as he passed her. Maybe bringing out the Tartan blanket wasn't such a brilliant idea.

She had pulled out her Kindle and was trying to get into *Nobody's Fool*, a title she now noted did not describe her. Andrew had no book. He lay on his back, hands clasped behind his head, which highlighted the bulge of his biceps. After a while, he asked, as he leaned toward the lamp on the nightstand between their beds, "You ready to turn off the light?"

Even with the curtains pulled, there were streaks of light knifing into the darkened room from the street outside and scattering off the cheap popcorn ceiling. He was still lying on his back, apparently with his eyes closed. Was he asleep already? She tried to keep her eyes fixed on the Kindle.

Lord, how was she supposed to go to sleep with this guy in the next bed over? "I guess I never said thank you for coming back to the bus station," she said.

"Thank you for inviting me along on your adventure." He didn't sound like he was falling asleep.

"I'm worried about Sedona." A safe topic.

"Is there a way to contact her parents? Your aunt and uncle, right?"

"I don't have any contact numbers for them."

"Maybe your parents have them?"

"Yeah, but I don't want to …" She didn't want to talk about her parents.

"Don't want to what?"

"Call them now." She exhaled a big breath that fluttered her lips audibly. "They still think of me as some broken down charity case, who can't take care of herself. And telling them I got sexually harassed and maybe fired … well, I don't want to have to listen to them feeling bad for me. Does that make sense?"

"They probably would be easier to talk to than you might think. But, hey, I'm a pastor. I'm supposed to say things like that. Truth is, I guess you'll know when to talk to them."

"And what about *your* parents?"

There was silence. "Yeah, I need to call them. It's been pretty hard between us the last few years. Polite phone conversations every few months. I haven't been a very good son."

"Say more." It was good to have the focus off of her.

"They pushed me away after my divorce. Blamed me for the whole thing. Which maybe they should have. I—"

"No way they should push you away. You're their son. You'll always be their son. They love you."

"You're sounding like the counselor now." She heard a soft chuckle from him.

"Ha, I'm no counselor, for sure, but I do know something about love." Maybe she shouldn't have said that.

"Maybe you're right. When I was out there in the mountains, thinking I was going to die, one of the things that troubled me the most was dying without anyone knowing or caring. I thought a lot about my parents."

Shelby said nothing.

"I haven't talked to them very much. They've got their own lives out in the Bay Area. Seem pretty independent. Not sure my calls make much of a difference."

"That's bullshit and you know it. Come on, Andrew, don't give me—"

"I shouldn't have mentioned them."

"Not mentioning them would be an even bigger mistake. Maybe, you need to go see them. Have a heart-to-heart talk. You're the pastor, you know how to do that."

She heard him shuffle in the bed, probably turning to face her, but she avoided looking at him. "I haven't always been good at heart-to-heart talks, especially when it's with someone I care about," he said.

Shelby sat upright and turned toward him. "Seriously, Andrew. You are an intelligent man. If you don't get over yourself, you're going to go to your grave carrying all that crap." She was getting a little heated, yes, but she needed to say something.

He was quiet for a moment. Then he said, slowly and softly, "You are a wise person, Ms. Sims."

The "Ms. Sims" did it. Shelby pushed away the Tartan blanket and swung her feet to the floor. He still lay on his side, facing her, his head propped up over his elbow. They were silent for a while, then Shelby moved over to his bed, as Andrew pulled back his blanket. She was in his arms. He kissed her gently and tentatively. The next kiss was deep and long.

Then Shelby pulled away, breathing hard, and sat up on the edge of the bed. "This can't happen."

Andrew was quick to respond. "I understand, Shelby. I didn't mean to—"

"Oh, shut up, Andrew. Of course, you meant to, and so did I."

"Well, I …" That's all he said.

"Look, I don't have any protection, okay? Do you? Didn't think so. And, this is a bad idea, anyway, don't you think? We still barely know each other."

"Would you like me to leave?"

She let out a little laugh. "I didn't say that." She returned to her bed and sat again on the edge, facing him. "I said something about us acting like adults. Guess we weren't ready for that, huh?" She laughed again.

"I'll try to do better," he said.

"I know you will." She laid a hand on his arm. "Just don't go calling me Ms. Sims right at bedtime." She gave his arm a gentle squeeze. "Let's go to sleep." *If that's possible.*

Chapter 38

Andrew

It was his second consecutive Sunday away from St. Tim's. The first one had been up in the Black Elk wilderness, which felt disconnected from time. But here, in the small room off the lobby of the A-1 Suites, where the free buffet breakfast was served, he was very aware that it was Sunday. He'd missed very few Sundays in his eight years at St. Tim's. That day was always special for him, so special that the other days of his week were usually seen in the context of the upcoming Sunday. Sunday was the day that his sermon, which he had worked on diligently for maybe fifteen hours, would be delivered. And, although this was a sacred duty, there was always anxiety associated with giving the sermon. But there were other Sunday-related responsibilities, too. Putting together the service was a great project: selecting and organizing the details of the liturgy, music, and prayers; preparing the service bulletin; verifying that the altar guild, the communion-chalice bearers, acolytes and lay readers were scheduled and ready—all these things had to come together by Sunday morning.

But Sunday wasn't just a time when his week's preparation culminated. Most importantly, Sunday was a holy time for which he had been centering himself all week—controversies about roof repairs, floundering pledge income, and the latest email from Buck melted away. This was a time that would be offered to God.

So, he was off-balance and somewhat disoriented on this Sunday morning. Maybe what really had his head spinning were those kisses last night. He looked across the room, where Shelby was pouring batter into a do-it-yourself waffle maker. She wore a V-necked T-shirt, in a pale aqua, over tight Levi's with a sequined design on the hip pockets. White tennies.

She returned to the table with her coffee, while she waited for the waffle. "This place doesn't seem so bad," she said. They had hesitated at the entrance of the breakfast buffet area to check out the cleanliness of the room, given that the motel was hardly the Ritz Carlton.

"So, where are we headed today?" he asked. So far, there had been no mention of the kisses, but he was certain that she, like him, had not forgotten about them.

"I sure wanted to go to Rocky Mountain National Park. But I guess with Sedona not here, we should press on to find Olivia Marshak. And get those sleeping bags. What do you think?"

"Well, my ankle is feeling so much stronger. I think I'm ready to test it on a hike soon, at least a short one. But, I'm up for whatever you want to do." He had ditched his crutches today and was walking, still a bit unsteady but feeling much better. It had been five days since the ankle was sprained and he was pleased how quickly it had healed.

"Why don't we go find Mr. Riley's sister, then we can head up to the park later?" Shelby seemed to be bouncing with energy this morning. A "ding" indicated that her waffle was ready. As she hurried back to the waffle maker, Andrew forced his eyes away from the sequined patterns on her hip pockets and turned his attention to his phone.

He considered sending a quick email to Maureen to see how things were going, but held back. It was the Sabbath. Then he noticed a new email from her in his inbox. It was a short message: *Well done, Father. The note you sent to the vestry before you left was just right. Will let you know when I hear something. I hope you are finding your adventure.*

Shelby returned with her waffle, carrying it before her like she'd found a treasure. "Finding some interesting stuff on your phone?"

He put his phone away, as he exhaled a frustrated breath. "Just checking my email. Had a problem back at the church."

Shelby peeled open a plastic syrup container and poured it over her waffle. "May I ask what kind of problem?"

"Don't want to bore you with church details. But, yeah … we have this guy, Buck, always pushing for the church to be more business-like and less a community of faith."

"Yeah, I know about having to work with people you'd rather not be around. So, what's dear old Buck been up to?"

The coffee was terrible, but Andrew swigged down the rest of his cup anyway. He would likely need to pop a Pepcid later. "As soon as I left, he sent an email to the other church leaders—didn't copy me. Wants to take all the money we've dedicated to helping the needy and use it to pay off our mortgage."

"Sounds like a big-hearted guy." She shook her head in disapproval. "What did you do?"

"I was going to stay and work this out, but Maureen convinced me to continue my time away. So, I wrote an email to the vestry before I headed out, told them that our duty as Christians was to help those in need, and that priority was higher than paying off a mortgage."

"What did they say?"

"Haven't heard back yet. Maureen said she'd handle it. That I needed to trust her and God. That I needed to continue my adventure."

"And so, here you are."

"Yep, here I am."

"Hope you find that adventure."

Her big eyes were full of compassion. It was nurturing just looking into them. "I'm working on it," he said.

Shelby took the wheel for the drive down to Golden. The route took them through sprawling suburbs and small cities, but what made the journey special was the Front Range of the Rockies, the highest peaks still snow-capped in June, towering off to the west. Andrew had spent time in the Sierra Nevada range of California, so he had experienced high mountains. But Shelby was beside herself. "On my," she breathed in a near-reverent whisper, like she had just entered a cathedral, "I've never seen anything so beautiful."

They exchanged oohs and ahhs about the mountain panorama for a while, then Andrew said, "So, you haven't said much about your job with the post office."

"Yeah, it's been good." She manufactured a laugh. "Up until a few days ago, that is. Anyway, I have—maybe I should say *had*—two rural routes, so I get to deliver mail to about three-hundred homes. I get to be outdoors, get to see a lot of pretty country, and best of all, I get to see a lot of nice people."

"You seem really outgoing. You like people."

Shelby seemed to ponder this for a while. "Yeah, I do."

"Do you know what your Myers-Briggs type is?"

She shot him a skeptical glance, with a raised eyebrow, but said nothing.

"Myers-Briggs. It's a personality survey that tells you what—"

"I know what it is. But, no, I've never done it."

"I've taken it several times. And I use it for premarital counseling." Good grief, he was sounding like a pompous ass.

"Good for you."

He deserved her snide remark, and maybe he should just shut up, but he plowed on. "I'm an NF. That stands for Intuitive and Feeling." He wanted to tell her that the NF type was uncommon among the general population, but that many clergy were NF types. Maybe he wouldn't say that now.

"Intuitive and feeling, huh?" She seemed to be thinking that over.

"I'm guessing you're an SJ."

"SJ? That stands for Sexy and Judicious?"

"No, that's not it. SJ stands for …" He stopped, realizing that she was toying with him. Then he said, "SJ types are dependable, altruistic and honest."

She glared at him. "So, you're saying you can summarize who I am with only two letters? Isn't that a little—"

"Oh no," he stammered. "Myers-Briggs is just a—"

"Well, that's better than one letter." She shot him a smile that looked devilish. "Although, if it was only one letter, I guess I'd prefer the S."

"You are quite the joker, aren't you?"

"Joker? Maybe SJ means Sexy Joker?"

He had no words, just an open-mouthed grin. A self-liberating grin. He wasn't sure about the joker part yet, but— he risked a quick glance that swept down her body. *Yes. Lord, yes.*

Chapter 39

Howdy folks! Welcome to Golden. Where the West Lives. Those are the words of greeting on the big sign arching over Washington Avenue, the main street of Golden, Colorado. The quaint-yet-bustling city, sitting in a narrow basin surrounded by foothills that slope up toward the high country, has a wild-west vibe, with many charming old buildings. Yet, there are Starbucks, hip outdoor restaurants, and upscale clothing stores that mark the town as a tourist destination.

They'd made one stop along the way, at a Dick's Sporting Goods, outside of Boulder, where they picked up two sleeping bags and two cheap foam pads, splitting the bill. They found bags rated down to twenty degrees, warm enough to get them through nights like the one outside Bridger. The bags were in the closeout section, marked down from sixty bucks to forty, presumably because they were a distasteful mustard-yellow color. "You sure we should get something so ugly?" Andrew asked.

"Well, we're only gonna use them in the dark, so I don't see what difference the color makes," she said. This got Andrew laughing, and it felt good.

They also looked at tents, but Shelby shook her head at the price tags. She didn't say, but apparently she'd made peace with the idea of sleeping in the back of the Tundra.

Across the parking lot from Dick's was a Rite Aid. There would be birth control there, he thought. He glanced at Shelby, who had also been staring at the Rite Aid. Then she shot him a look with raised eyebrows. "I know what you're thinking, mister. We don't need to go there. We're going to be adults and behave ourselves. Right?" She poked his arm with her elbow.

"Right," he said, with a fake surprised look.

Fifteen thousand people live in Golden. Finding Olivia Marshak would be the classic needle-in-a-haystack problem. Maybe like Sedona, she didn't live here anymore. These were reservations that Andrew kept to himself, while he and Shelby wandered up Washington Avenue, crowded with Sunday visitors, probably from nearby Denver. Families slurped snow cones and munched on burritos, couples sipped microbrews at outside tables fronting chic bars, and shoppers packed the many small stores. Shelby had not taken in much of the lively scene—she was checking Facebook and Google White Pages again, calling directory assistance, even poring over a local phone book she found in a rare phone booth. She'd come up with nothing.

After an hour of this fruitless thrashing, they sagged into chairs at the Starbucks with a couple of black coffees. "Now what do we do?" he asked. "Maybe Olivia Marshak doesn't exist."

"I'm sure she exists." Shelby scratched her chin, like she was trying to dig up an idea. "I wonder what one of the British detectives would do." She followed that comment with a little laugh.

"Huh?" Andrew had no idea what she was talking about.

"I heard you mention Olivia Marshak. Do you know her?" Their barista now stood next to them. Andrew and Shelby exchanged open-mouthed looks.

"Well, sort of," Shelby said. "I'm a friend of her brother, and we thought we'd stop by and say hello on our way through. But I've misplaced her contact info." All this was technically true, if misleading—her best effort to assure the barista that they didn't have malicious intent. It was probably what one of the British detectives would say.

"Everybody around here knows Olivia." The barista didn't say why.

Although Golden is a small city, it is a complex one. Side streets in downtown are lined with modest houses built back in the fifties and earlier, apparently before Golden was discovered. Yet, the downtown area also features fancy condos that made Sedona's condo look plain, and the steep hillsides are dotted with sprawling upscale homes. Narrow roads wind up into these hills. A couple of miles up one of those winding roads, and following the directions the barista had given them, they pulled up in front of a dirt drive that led back into a grove of Cottonwoods. An old house was barely visible through the trees.

"Well, here goes, huh?" Shelby was wide-eyed. "Let's go talk to Olivia."

As they pushed open a wooden gate at the bottom of the drive, they were met by two large, barking dogs. But the barks from the two big Labs were more of a greeting than a warning. A hundred yards up the dirt driveway, they came to a low, rambling home, nothing fancy, fronted by a long porch with two old rocking chairs.

Shelby knocked. They stood for a while before Shelby knocked again. There was no doorbell. Finally, the door opened a few inches. A woman, probably in her sixties, faced them. Her face bore the grooves of time, like an eroded hillside. Gray hair hung down onto her shoulders. She squinted at them with suspicious gray eyes, but said nothing.

Shelby shot Andrew a quick glance before speaking. "I'm looking for Olivia Marshak."

"Why?"

"I'm trying to find her brother. Victor Marshak."

"Why?"

"Uh … I knew him back in Wisconsin, and I—"

"Why should I believe what you tell me?"

Andrew tried to see beyond the woman into the darkened house. He thought he saw movement behind her. The woman pushed the door to narrow the opening.

"Well, I—"

"I don't know why you think I might know this man. Why don't you just go away?" Then she closed the door.

Shelby turned toward Andrew. "What the hell was that about?" she asked, shaking her head.

As they stepped off the porch to leave, Shelby stopped to admire the flower garden. Row upon row of purple petunias.

Chapter 40

They sat in the Tundra, pondering what to do next. Shelby leaned forward over the steering wheel, her fingers steepled, as if in prayer, trying to figure things out. "Why would she be unwilling to speak to us?" she asked.

Andrew had no idea. "It was almost like she expected you to come, almost like she was afraid."

"Yeah, I think she was more afraid than just hostile. I mean, how can we be a threat to her?"

"Or maybe," Andrew ventured, "she really doesn't know Victor Marshak and she wanted to get rid of you."

"Oh, she knew him. I'm sure of that much."

"How can you be certain?"

"The purple petunias. He loves purple petunias."

Andrew recalled Shelby telling him about them in the Buick. "But, still, that could be a coincidence."

Shelby started the Tundra and pulled forward about a hundred yards, then, under the cover of a huge cottonwood, killed the engine. They were in front of a large fenced vacant lot, adjacent to Olivia Marshak's property.

"Now what?" he asked.

She turned to him. "Time for some sleuthing." Whatever she had in mind, it didn't sound like a good idea. As she climbed out of the cab, she asked, "You comin' with me?"

Andrew exhaled a sigh of surrender. Shelby headed toward a wire fence, then climbed over it. Fortunately, it wasn't barbed wire. "Good grief, Shelby, what are you doing?"

"I didn't come this far to give up. And anyway, I'm not harming anyone. Just come on. I want to see that house a little better."

"Why? What do you expect to find?"

"I don't know, but nothing seems to add up. We need more data. Come on."

Andrew climbed over the fence. "Shelby, this is trespassing. We could be asking for trouble." He tried to marshal his best authoritative Father Logan voice, but it came out sounding more like a whine.

"I didn't see any *Keep Out* or *No Trespassing* signs, did you?"

Andrew looked around, like he expected a police car to be pulling up, then nodded in disbelief that he was actually doing this. "Okay, but let's make it fast."

They walked up a gentle hillside toward the rear of the property, keeping large trees between them and the Marshak house. In Andrew's opinion, they were still too exposed. The Marshak woman was probably watching them right now. She seemed like the kind of person who had an arsenal of assault rifles.

They paused about halfway to the fence that marked the rear of the property. Shelby whispered to Andrew, "What do you think is going on down there?"

At the side of the house, a man in a white undershirt, with a red bandana around his head, was loading bags into the rear of a large van. "I say, let's get out of here."

"Not yet. I need to see more." Shelby was already making her way farther toward the rear of the lot. She stopped behind the trunk of a large tree, from where they could look down into the undeveloped wooded land behind the house. Not much to see, except for a car, pulled up into some heavy vegetation. "Let's get closer."

Andrew whispered with urgency, "This is dangerous, Shelby. We'll set off the dogs."

"I don't see them outside."

Andrew shook his head in amazement, and, he had to admit, excitement. He followed her toward the fence line between the two properties. If anyone came out back, they'd see them for sure.

Shelby stopped suddenly, looking back and forth between Marshak's yard and a photo on her phone. She lurched back, like she'd almost stepped on a snake. She turned to Andrew. What he saw in her face was unambiguous. It was terror. "Oh, Lord," she gasped, "it's the gray car."

Chapter 41

They drove without a destination, with too many unanswered questions sloshing around in their brains. Andrew was at the wheel now, giving Shelby needed time to process the recent events. Finally, he pulled off to the side of the highway that connects Golden to Boulder. He turned to her. "So, what are we going to do?"

Her eyes were burning with a mixture of confusion, fear, and disappointment. "I don't know. I don't know what to make of today."

"Here's what I think. When I've got too much stuff churning inside, I think the best thing to do is to do nothing. Take a break and let all the stuff in your head settle down. Then the answer will come." He gave her a solemn look, then cracked a smile. "Actually, that's what Fr. Ken, my spiritual advisor, suggested. I've always been lousy at waiting for clarity."

Shelby reached out and gently touched his face, letting one finger trail down his cheek.

"Now, there you've gone and done it," he said. "I've totally forgotten what we were talking about."

Shelby leaned over and gave him a soft kiss on the mouth. Her lips were moist, and the clean scent of her almost made him faint. She pulled away and said, "Let's go to Rocky Mountain National Park. Let's let those big mountains refresh us."

She sounded like she'd been reading Muir. "Ms. Sims, I think that's a brilliant idea."

Then she was in his arms, and only after many kisses did they pull apart, breathless.

"How am I supposed to drive after that?" he asked.

It was the middle of the afternoon when they arrived in the small town of Lyons, where they turned onto the road leading up over the mountains into Estes Park and then to the entrance of the national park. But a half-hour beyond Lyons, yellow barricades blocked the road. A tired-looking cop came up to their window. "Sorry folks, but the highway's closed ahead."

"There's no way we can get through to the park?"

"'Fraid not. Road's washed out up ahead. Runoff from snowmelt in the high country. And I understand the other highways are closed, too. Probably be a few days, at the least, before we get 'er open again."

Andrew gave Shelby a frustrated frown that said, "What next?" then turned the Tundra around.

Back in Lyons, they found a city park and sat together on a picnic bench. Tears formed in Shelby's eyes, then she shook her head, like she was trying to shake loose a burden. "I hate to cry," she said. "But, everything I try fails. This whole trip has been a joke. My car breaks down, Sedona's not there. Olivia Marshak won't talk to us and apparently she's been following me. And, just to top it off, we can't even go to the damn park. You must think I'm such a fool." Then she was crying.

Andrew let her cry. He was enough of a pastor to know that tears often need to be released, that they can be better than any soap for washing away sorrow. Then he laid a hand gently on her arm. "So, I've got two things to say. First, I for one am pretty glad your car broke down."

This caused her to look up and offer a giggle through her tears.

"And the second thing I need to say is … what would the British detectives do?"

Shelby sniffled a bit, wiped her glasses on her T-shirt and shook back her hair from her face. Then she turned to Andrew. "I'm not yet sure what the British detectives would do, but I know what I want to do. We passed a brewpub a few minutes ago. I say, let's go get a beer."

Lyons is a tiny town on a wild river that pours out of the Rockies. That beautiful river, Shelby had read to him from her phone, brings occasional destruction, the worst in memory being the flood of 2013, when much of the town was inundated and cut off from the rest of the state.

In the late afternoon, they sat with their drafts at Oskar Blues, a microbrewery, which was obviously a local hot spot. The informal, artsy, neo-hippy vibe created the perfect ambiance for planning your future.

They drank their pints in silence, then Shelby set her glass down, folded her hands in front of her, and looked Andrew in the eye. "So, decision time. What are your thoughts?"

Andrew took another sip. "Well, I'm along on your adventure, so you need to call the shots, but, frankly, I'd like to see you shy away from real danger, like going back to where that gray car is parked."

Shelby nodded, like she was giving his concerns serious consideration, then said, "I see three options." After Andrew gave her a go-on nod, she said, "One, we can just go home. But I can't really do that. I've come this far, and … anyway, option two is go back and confront Olivia Marshak, but what would that gain us, and like you said, it could be dangerous. I agree. So, here's a third option. We go on down to Los Alamos. That's where the big science lab is, and it's where Victor Marshak used to work or may still work. I checked my phone—it's down in New Mexico, about a seven-hour drive from here." She folded her arms across her chest and leaned back, awaiting the response from Andrew. "And, your words last night got me thinking—maybe, we could go see my parents afterwards."

"Sounds like you'd—" He was interrupted by his phone's ringtone. "I'm not going to get that," he said, but then took a peek at the phone. Shaking his head, he said, "It's Maureen. I need to take this."

"Hello, Maureen."

"Father, I'm sorry if I'm interrupting your sabbatical time, but I thought I needed to call you." She told him that she had called each vestry member to see how they reacted to Buck's email and Andrew's subsequent email. A majority supported Andrew's position, but the others weren't sure. Meanwhile, Buck had called Maureen and yelled at her, furious about Andrew's email.

"Maybe I need to come back."

"Honestly, Father, I'm not sure. I'll leave that up to you." She sounded worried.

"Let me get back to you in a bit, Maureen. I certainly appreciate you keeping me informed about this."

"You look worried," Shelby said, when Andrew was off the phone. She laid her hand atop his in reassurance.

"Yes, that situation over the church budget is getting messier."

"Do you need to go back?"

Andrew didn't answer. His mind was awash with ways to respond to the situation. He tapped in Buck Martin's number on his phone.

"Andrew, it's good to hear from you," Buck said, in a pleasant Mazda-salesman voice.

Andrew stood and began to pace the area near their table. "Buck, we need to talk about your budget proposal."

"Of course, Andrew. Sorry if that bothered you while you're away on your much-deserved sabbatical. The rest of us are doing our best to hold things together in your absence."

What a crock. "Look Buck, I've got several things to say to you. The first is, I am very displeased by your proposal, done behind my back, to destroy our outreach funds. I'm not—"

Buck cut in. The volume of his voice had ratcheted up a notch. "I'm sorry you're displeased, Andrew, but the truth is—and we'd better face it, and soon—our church is sinking fast because of administrative neglect. Helping others is fine, but throwing our money away on Pollyanna causes, while our big mortgage sits there, is just piss-poor leadership, if you ask me."

Andrew looked down at Shelby. Her eyes felt like a laser beaming power into him. She gave him a slow, confident nod that said she believed in him.

"Buck, that's not the truth at all. The truth is, our mission is to—"

Buck cut in again. He was shouting. "Bull shit. You've got your head in the clouds, and—"

"Shut up for a minute, Buck, and you listen to me. There are—"

"You of all people don't tell me to shut up. Now, you—"

"I just did tell you to shut up. Think you can do that?"

Buck was silent, while Andrew waited a second, calming himself, before continuing. "Here's how it is, Buck. You are entitled to your opinions, and your opinions are valued, but— and get this through your head—you are to never, I said never, try to end-run me again on a financial matter like this. You got that, Buck?"

"Or you'll what?"

He looked at Shelby's face again. "Or I'll invite you to find another church." Andrew wasn't certain he would actually do this, but it just came out.

"I'm going to call the Bishop. He needs to know about the leadership vacuum at St. Timothy's." Buck said this matter-of-factly, like he knew it would intimidate Andrew.

"I hope you do, Buck. Here's his number." Andrew read Buck a phone number.

"You don't think I'll do it, do you?"

Of course Andrew thought he might call the Bishop, but Andrew knew how the Bishop, a Godly and savvy leader, would respond. He wasn't worried. "Sure, I think you will. And I just want to welcome you to do it."

"Well, I …" Buck was stammering now.

"And one more thing, Buck. I don't want you to ever raise your voice at Maureen again. She can take care of herself, sure, but I'm telling you that you are never to yell at her again. Got it?"

There was silence on the other end for a moment. Finally, Buck said, "This isn't over, Andrew." Then he hung up.

Andrew shot off a quick text to update Maureen on the situation, then sat back down. Shelby reached over and took his hand. "That sounded painful. I'm so sorry."

"Well, it was, but I said some things I've needed to say for a long time." He was aware that he was still shaking.

"Do you need to go back?"

Of course, he needed to go back. Andrew took a sip of beer and leaned back, rocking on two legs of his chair like a cowboy who'd just filled an inside straight. "Maybe I do need to go back," he said. As he felt a smile forming on his lips, he added, "But what I'm *going* to do is go with you to Los Alamos, or wherever you want to go."

Chapter 42

Andrew rarely had more than one beer, so another round to wash down a couple of happy-hour appetizers had him buzzed. It was dark when they exited Oskar Blues, and already the Rocky Mountain evening chill was in the air. Shelby snuggled up against him, and his arm came around her, as they walked slowly back to the Tundra. He tilted his head toward her and felt her soft hair against his cheek.

She stopped suddenly. "Do you hear that?"

"What?"

"Music, silly. Let's go check it out."

A half-block down from Oskar Blues, loud guitar music poured from a rustic building that looked like a run-down miner's cabin. A dim neon sign over the door read, "The Rawhide Club."

"Let's go in," beamed Shelby, pulling him toward the door, not waiting for him to respond.

They stood just inside the door to let their eyes adjust to the low light. Round tables-for-two—most of them were occupied—ringed a large dance floor. Against the wall was a small stage, illuminated by multi-colored spots. The stage was empty, except for a keyboard and the mic stands and tall black speakers of a sound system—the recorded guitars they'd heard came from the speakers.

Shelby leaned toward a woman just coming from the restroom, "Excuse me, will there be live music tonight?"

The woman, middle-aged and dragging on a cigarette, wore a colorful sequined shirt and a cowboy hat. "You're in luck, hon, the band starts at eight, should be just a few minutes."

Shelby seemed excited, but Andrew was uncomfortable. Places like this made him squirm. It was too loud, too uninhibited, too ... too happy. Country music, good Lord. He knew Shelby liked this music, so he would do his best to go along with it. He'd rather be with her back in the Tundra, looking for a campsite.

Shelby pulled him toward a table. "This one okay?" she asked. Even in the dim light he could sense her joy. Another beer, listen to a couple songs, then leave—he could get through this.

After the waitress took their beer order, Shelby slid her chair up close to his. She leaned toward him and rested her hand on his. "I just love this. I hope the band is good."

Soon, a woman and two men were up on stage. One man took a seat at the keyboard, the woman and the other man had guitars. After some tuning, the woman stepped to the microphone. She had blond hair piled high, Levi's tucked into pink cowboy boots, and a pink sequined shirt matching the boots. "Good evening, cowboys and cowgirls. Is everybody having fun tonight at the Rawhide?"

A chorus of cheers filled the room. Andrew squirmed.

"I'm Katie, and we're Highcountry, and we're gonna get y'all high on some good music. Hope y'all will get out here on the dance floor with that special one and let the romance begin." She looked back at the other two and nodded, then they launched into a loud, fast-paced country song.

"That's a Miranda Lambert song," Shelby shouted at Andrew, as she bounced on her chair. Shouting was now required to be heard above the music. Andrew nodded, although he had never heard of Miranda Lambert. Several couples made their way out onto the dance floor. He could feel Shelby's body against his side, moving with the music. Andrew didn't belong here. That painful memory from the parish hall back at St. Tim's, with the congregation swaying and singing along to the Beatles' "All You Need Is Love," and him stiff and awkward, resurfaced. He took a swig of beer.

The next song came on. "Oh, I love this one," Shelby roared. She was already singing along with the band. "Let's dance."

Panic surged through Andrew. "Oh, no," he said, shaking his head, "this really isn't my thing." But Shelby was already out of her seat and pulling him toward the dance floor. He followed her—what else was he going to do?

"I really can't dance," he said, once they got to the center of the floor. Maybe he should use his gimpy ankle, which was now feeling okay, as an excuse.

Katie was singing some song about believing most people are good.

"Don't worry, Andrew, I'll show you. This is a two-step. It goes like this. Just follow me."

To Andrew's relief, no one else on the dance floor seemed to care if he was awkward. Shelby patiently demonstrated the two-step, and it wasn't long before Andrew could get around without stumbling or crushing Shelby's white tennies.

When the song ended, everyone applauded, and there was a lot of laughter. Shelby leaned in. "That's a Luke Bryan song, "I Believe Most People Are Good.""

Andrew had never danced the two-step before, in fact he'd hardly danced at all. Certainly never in a country bar with a beautiful girl. "I believe most people are good?" he asked.

He looked around at the smiling faces. Yeah, that may be true, he thought.

"Wanna stay out here for the next one?" Shelby asked, leaning close to Andrew.

"Yes," he said. "Yes, I believe I do."

Katie said, "And now for an oldie, a Buck Owens classic, "Together Again.""

"Oh my," said Shelby, moving in close to Andrew. "I love this song." Shelby seemed to know all the songs, loved all the songs.

They moved slow, Shelby pressed to him. The song talked about tears that had stopped falling, about lonely nights that were now at an end. He had been so critical of country lyrics, told Shelby they were too sentimental. What he realized now was that his objection had never been that the lyrics were too sentimental. What really convicted him now, the very reason he had pushed them away for so much of his life: they were too honest.

Shelby looked up at him as they moved slowly. The room lights sparkled in her brown eyes, taking his breath away. He tried to understand what he saw in those eyes. Not finding an easy answer, he stopped in the middle of the floor, cradled her face in his hands and kissed her.

When she pulled away, smiling, she said, "So, you're starting to like this, huh?"

He didn't know whether she was talking about the music or her. But his answer was the same for both. "Yes," he said, "I'm starting to like it very much."

Chapter 43

Shelby

While Andrew drove, Shelby stretched back in the seat, feet up on the dash, trying to rub the headache out of her temples.

She was still humming the songs from last night. Lord, it must have been midnight when they got back to the truck. She had taken his hands and done a quick two-step move by the door of the truck, while singing some Faith Hill song about suddenly melting into you. She remembered the fire in Andrew's eyes. Who needed Tim McGraw?

She shot Andrew an appraising look, as he focused on negotiating the morning commute traffic in Denver. A couple days without shaving and he was getting that stubble back. The memory of it rubbing her cheek in the Buick caused her to catch her breath. Andrew wore a long-sleeved shirt, sleeves rolled up to just below the elbows, over faded jeans. He was a mysterious guy, for sure. In some ways he was so uptight, but, by the end of the evening last night, she couldn't get him off the dance floor.

Heck, she wasn't that great a dancer herself, hadn't been dancing in years. Michael hated dancing, said it was just making an ass out of yourself in public. And, of course, in those years after Michael, she'd hardly gone out at all. She smiled, remembering Andrew unlocking the door of the truck, then twirling her, and her spinning right into his arms. "Hey, cowboy," she had laughed, "what are we going to do now?"

Finding a campsite had been an adventure. By now she had accepted that they would stretch out their new mustard-yellow sleeping bags in the rear of the truck, even though she had protested the idea just ... was that yesterday or the day before? This was no different than two beds in a motel room, she rationalized.

They stopped back at the city park in Lyons, where they'd earlier seen campsites, but they were all occupied. A check of Google Maps revealed the bad news that the only other nearby campgrounds were up in the mountains, beyond where the road was washed out. It was too late in the evening for much creativity, so they'd pulled off the road into the trees, just inside the national forest boundary.

Before they'd even climbed out of the truck, Shelby had asked, "Do you think it's safe to stay out here?"

"I don't know. Probably pretty safe."

"Pretty safe?"

"Safe as sleeping beside the road up in South Dakota."

"Fair enough," she said.

"And ..."

"And what?"

"You said you wanted a campsite that only cost thirty bucks. This one costs zero."

"But the thirty-dollar one had a shower."

"Maybe it'll rain."

This got them both laughing.

"So, I guess you've slept in the back of this truck a lot, huh?"

"Well, actually, this is my first time."

They had spread out their bags in silence, Andrew, no doubt like her, anticipating what the night held in store. You wouldn't think the dark interior under a camper shell would be that romantic, but she couldn't imagine more electricity if they'd been in an oceanfront suite in Maui. As much as she was drawn to this new cowboy, she couldn't allow the romance to get out of hand tonight. She grimaced, as a memory about the 9% flashed through her head. In their sleeping bags, zipped up, she turned toward Andrew, already facing her. "You recall we decided that we would be adults and behave ourselves?"

"Yeah, afraid I do remember that," he said in a sad voice.

She rolled against him and planted a kiss on his face, missing his lips in the pitch dark. "Let's try to get some sleep, okay? We've got a long drive tomorrow." She was only half-committed to her own firm talk, but she was coming to know that Andrew would honor her words. She'd fallen asleep, as Faith Hill continued to serenade her.

Now she watched the glare of the morning sun reflecting harshly off the tall glass-and-steel skyscrapers of downtown Denver, making her head throb even more. She hadn't had that much to drink last night—what was it, three beers? Yeah, she loved grabbing a couple beers with Tisha down at The Quartermaster, but ultimately she was a lightweight in the drinking department.

She keyed in a text to Tisha. *Crazy trip. So far, my quest has been a flop, but Andrew and I danced 'til midnight last night, so there's that! Update on Derek?* Tisha had just started her day at the post office, so Shelby wouldn't get a response until her break.

South of Denver, Interstate 25 parallels the Front Range, affording grand views of snow-capped peaks. In spite of the views, it's a long stretch of freeway driving, and they had many miles to go. She turned to Google to learn more about Los Alamos. "So, Los Alamos is where the atomic bomb was developed," she said, "but I already knew that much. Guessing you did, too."

"Yeah. I had a professor who worked there. He was always talking about it. Said it was the biggest employer of physicists in the country. I'm looking forward to seeing it."

She turned toward him, studying him. "Here's what I can't figure out about you."

"Uh oh," he said, shooting an apprehensive smile in her direction.

"What I can't figure out is how you would go from physics, that's based on facts and experiments and so on, to something like religion."

"Well, I've asked myself the same question a few times." He let out a quick laugh, then turned serious. "But here's what it boils down to for me. They both seek truth. They just go about it in different ways. Physics relies on the scientific method. Are you famil—"

"I know what the scientific method is," she said, with a bit of an edge.

"And faith relies on several things. The bible. Sacraments. The generations of believers sharing their faith. And the Holy Spirit. For me, it was all those things—and I came to religion as a real novice. Those things gave me the overwhelming sense that God is real. I mean, I still struggle with doubts and there are a lot of things I don't understand or have answers for. But I am certain about God."

"So, your faith doesn't replace your understanding of science?"

"Oh, no. I still love physics, and I miss it sometimes. But I don't believe either of them replaces the other. Faith by itself cannot design a computer chip any more than physics by itself can tell me how to treat my neighbor."

Shelby nodded her interest. He was on a roll, and she loved it.

Andrew pursed his lips, like he was in deep thought. "One famous physicist says, it's all about the particles, and that's all there is. The particles determine everything, he says."

"Like the protons and electrons?"

"Exactly. But, I sense that there is more to it than that."

"Like maybe you're trying to understand not just the particles, but what poetry inspired the particles."

Andrew shot her a surprised glance, his mouth open. "That's one of the best ways of putting it I've ever heard."

"Oh, I'm just a—" She caught herself starting to apologize. She looked down and rubbed her fingers over the worn vinyl of the seat. "Thank you," she said.

Andrew flashed her another smile. "Maybe those particles listen to country music."

Shelby sat up straight, like she was ready to deliver her address at the symposium. In a fake professorial voice, with her nose tipped upward, she said, "But surely you know that country music is just vibrations in the air."

When their laughter had subsided, Andrew said, "You sure you're not an angel?"

It was good to see him laugh. With a raised eyebrow and a wicked smile, she said, "You should know by now that I'm not." Then she laid a hand on his arm. "You've had an interesting life."

He gave her a look that was hard to read. "It's been a lot more interesting lately," he said.

She wanted to snuggle closer to him, but her seatbelt prevented her.

She must have dozed off. She came awake with a start, as Andrew was slowing down. "What's up?" she asked, removing her wireframes and rubbing sleepy eyes.

"Not sure. Everything's stopped up ahead." They came to a dead stop behind a long line of vehicles. "Dear God, I hope it's not an accident. Lord," he prayed out loud, "please be with any people up ahead who may have been hurt."

Shelby turned toward him as he prayed. "That was very thoughtful," she said, when he had finished.

Their progress was slow. Shelby reached over to turn on the radio, then hesitated, giving him an apprehensive look. "Is this okay?"

Andrew smiled. He seemed to have been smiling a lot more the past two days. "Are you asking if it's okay to listen to country?" He raised his eyebrows. When she nodded yes, he said, "Of course. Warning, though, I might have to pull off on the shoulder and twirl you around a time or two."

"I can think of worse things." She flicked on the radio and found a distant station playing an Alan Jackson love song.

As they inched forward, a large portable highway sign with flashing bright-orange letters came into view. *Road Closed Ahead. Detour Exit Now.* "You've got to be kidding me," Andrew said, shaking his head.

Shelby pulled up Google Maps. "Yep, traffic's getting off here. They're rerouting us off to the east." Then she found the Colorado 511 site, which listed road closures. "Well, damn, we've seen this movie before. A bridge is out, due to flooding." It seemed crazy. They were in arid, high desert country, about forty miles north of the New Mexico border on a dry, sunny day. She cast a gaze up toward the high wall of mountains in the western distance, to another world, where snowmelt was gushing into the creeks.

They finally made it to the exit. At the off-ramp, an orange DETOUR sign directed them to the east, away from the mountains. All vehicles were taking this route. A narrower road ran west from the off-ramp, toward the mountains. A battered sign, peppered with rusted-out bullet holes, read *Refugio, 9 miles.* "Hold up a minute, Andrew." Andrew pulled onto the shoulder, as Shelby was scrolling through her phone again. "Here's the website for the *Pueblo Chieftain.* Listen to this. *Floods have washed away much of the small southern Colorado town of Refugio. State emergency services have been deployed to the area. The extent of damage and injuries is currently unknown. This is a breaking story.*"

They exchanged long glances. "Andrew," she said, "it's only nine miles away. There are people hurting up there. Don't you think we should at least go see if we can help?"

Andrew looked out on the line of cars heading toward the detour route to the east and was quiet for a time. Then he turned to Shelby, with a look of tenderness that turned into a grin. "One thing I gotta say. Life around you is certainly not dull." He rolled down his window and extended an arm to alert drivers to his U-turn.

All the other vehicles were following the suggested detour. Shelby and Andrew were heading in the opposite direction, up a narrow road that led toward the high mountains and Refugio and whatever despair was waiting for them there.

Chapter 44

The road to Refugio was paved for the first few miles, then turned into rough wash-board. Andrew shifted into four-wheel drive, gripped the wheel harder, and Shelby hung on tight to the grab bar above the passenger window, as the truck rattled over the uneven surface. The afternoon sun scattered off the cracks in the windshield, making it hard to see the road.

They climbed a narrow ridge, a hundred feet above the river, hidden by stands of trees along its banks. "I can't believe anyone lives back in here," Shelby said.

"Doesn't *refugio* mean *refuge?* This place certainly is hidden away enough to be a refuge."

Around one turn Shelby saw a coyote scamper along the side of the road. She'd never seen a coyote before. She began to point it out to Andrew, but it had already vanished into the scrub brush.

"Wish this odometer worked," Andrew said. "It would be nice to know how far we've gone. Longest nine miles I've driven in a while."

They topped another hill, and there before them was a small valley, through which the river coursed. A few-dozen small homes sat on both sides of the river, connected by a bridge. On the near side, in a square amidst the homes, stood a tall church. From their vantage point, still a half-mile away, everything looked peaceful and normal.

They pulled into a muddy open space at the edge of the village, where vehicles were parked in a haphazard fashion.

Two State of Colorado emergency trucks, a county utility van, several RVs, and perhaps a dozen private vehicles. Two food trucks were open at one edge of the parking area. On the other side of the parking lot was a row of porta-potties.

It wasn't clear where to go. Andrew and Shelby made their way to the opening of a tent, where a young man met them. "Good afternoon, folks. If you're just visiting, I need you to know that this is an active rescue area. What can I do for you?"

"We came to help." They said this almost in unison, then turned to each other with warm, surprised looks.

"Thank you, and thank God," the man said. "We are shorthanded, and we will put you to work. Come with me. The coordinator will have work for you." He took them back through a narrow passageway between two small adobe homes. They came to a group, huddled at a folding table, around a person with a clipboard, apparently going over a checklist of tasks.

"God has sent us more help," he announced.

The coordinator stood and turned to face them with a smile. The smile quickly dissolved, as they stood face to face with Olivia Marshak.

Chapter 45

"Why have you followed me here?" Olivia Marshak, with hands on her hips, leaned toward them, like she was ready for a fight.

Shelby took a step toward Olivia. "I haven't been following you." Olivia Marshak was a formidable presence, but Shelby, the five-eight softball jock, was no slouch herself in the formidable-presence department. She'd had enough of Marshak's crap. "We came here when we heard about the flood. We wanted to help. But I need to ask you the same question, why were you following *me*?"

Olivia backed up a step, raised her head like she was above it all, then looked around at her colleagues, who were staring open-mouthed at the two of them. "Let's find someplace to talk." She turned and headed toward another narrow passageway between two houses. Shelby and Andrew followed. Then she turned toward them. "We have to stay outside, if we don't have masks. Mold." She rested a muddy work boot atop a wooden barrel and glared at Shelby. "Okay," she said. "Talk."

Shelby looked down at her white tennies and realized they weren't going to cut it for the kind of work they might be doing. With arms crossed to project a confident look, she told Olivia Marshak the whole story. Then she took a deep breath and pondered how she wanted to say the next words. "Now I have some questions of you. For one, that gray car in your back yard followed me halfway across the country. FYI, I don't appreciate that, Ms. Marshak. What the hell was that about? I'm ready for some straight answers." She looked at Andrew and was buoyed by his affirming smile.

Olivia Marshak straightened. She wore a stained flannel shirt over ragged jeans. Nonetheless, there was a look of elegance about her. Her chiseled face held eyes that were penetrating. It was hard to look into them very long without turning away. "So, you were my brother's friend?"

"Yes. Like I said, I was worried about him."

"So am I," Olivia said, as she exhaled a huge sigh. Shelby waited while Olivia was silent. "Yes, we followed you. Actually, not me, but Azcue. You'll meet him. He was helping me find Victor. He came down into Wisconsin from Minnesota, where he works sometimes, when we got some information about where Victor might be staying. He found the house you described, but Victor wasn't there. So, he waited. Found a vacant house next door—sure, it wasn't his house, but Azcue has a way of making himself welcome wherever he is." She cracked her first smile. "Anyway, he was waiting there when you showed up. You went into the house twice, he told me. Like you knew your way around. He figured he needed to find out more about you. Then you left town early the next morning."

"So, that was him in the house next door and outside the coffee shop back home?"

"Yes. We had no other leads about Victor's whereabouts. And the FBI hadn't been much help."

"FBI?" Shelby shot a shaky glance toward Andrew and felt her tummy turn over like something was rolling around down there.

"When a scientist working on things with national security implications goes missing, the FBI gets involved. They said he hadn't showed up for work. After they checked his home, they contacted me. Me? I just want to find my brother."

"And so this Azcue followed me all across the country?"

"He lost you in South Dakota. Was really upset about that. So he just came on back to my house." Shelby figured she had shaken the gray car when the Buick was towed to the garage in Bridger. "So you can imagine my shock when you show up at my door. For all I knew, you were some assassin after Victor."

"I'm just a mail girl," Shelby said softly.

Olivia laughed. "I'd say, if you're just a mail girl, then you're one hell of a mail girl."

"What do you think happened to him?" Shelby asked.

"If I knew that, I wouldn't have been trying to find him." Olivia scratched her chin with an index finger. "So, how did you know to come find me?"

"I found your name in an old obituary for your father."

"Clever."

"And I knew his real name—he was going by the name of Allen Riley—because I found a ski pass from Los Alamos." She pulled the ski pass from her wallet and showed it to Olivia.

Olivia Marshak took the card and examined it closely, her brow furrowing as she did. "So, my brother does like to ski, and this is his name on the pass, but there's one problem." She shot a questioning look at Shelby.

"What?"

Olivia handed the card back to Shelby. "This picture. It's not my brother."

Chapter 46

Shelby looked at Andrew—they were both drop-jawed—then looked around like she suddenly didn't know where she was. *What the hell?* As she began to speak, a large man appeared next to Olivia. "Livie," he said to her, "the muckers down at the Herrera house need some guidance."

"I'll get right over there." She turned back to Shelby and Andrew. "So, this is the Azcue I was talking about." Azcue was the same guy they'd seen loading the van outside Marshak's house in Golden. He was a big man, as tall as Andrew, with bulging muscles on ample display in apparently the same sleeveless white undershirt he'd had on in Golden, although it now bore a lot of mud stains. He had an olive face with black hair that poured down to his shoulders from under a red bandana. "I have to go now," Olivia continued. "We've only been here a day or so, and we're still getting set up. If you still want to stay and work, Azcue will give you an overview and get you settled in. There's plenty that needs to be done." Then she turned and left.

After they introduced themselves, Azcue said, "Come." He led them up another narrow passageway. It felt odd: here they were in the middle of nowhere, behind the man who'd been following them in the gray car. Azcue led them into a small plaza and up to the front of a large adobe church, the one they'd seen from the road above town. "This is Iglesia del Refugio," he said. "One of the oldest churches in Colorado. Built back in the 1800s. We can't go in without protection. The health department said it's unsafe because of mold. The river water was three feet up the walls in the church, just a couple days ago. There will be a lot of work to do inside."

The plaza was empty, except for two children, kicking a ball.

Azcue led them past a small house next to the church. "That house was spared by the waters. Father Ruiz, the priest, lives here. You will meet him later."

Then he led them down another passageway to a clearing by the river. Azcue pointed toward the bridge linking the two sides of the village. "The bridge was under water until two days ago. Unsafe to use now, even though the water level has gone down. Crews from the state got the people who live on that side"—he made a sweeping gesture toward the dozen or so houses across the river—"over to here. Everything's unsafe over there." The river was muddy and slow moving, only about forty feet wide. It was hard to imagine how it had been wild and dangerous enough to do so much damage. Debris from several homes that had apparently been swept away by the flood lined the river bank. Parts of walls, wooden timbers, appliances, and personal possessions were strewn like the result of the reckless tantrum of some angry god. Near them, a refrigerator lay on its side, its white metal finish coated in mud, its door ripped open. At Shelby's feet, a child's rag doll lay in the mud, looking up at them with button eyes. She felt tears building up, but fought them back.

"Six people were injured—State and County got them all to the hospital. No deaths, thank God. Pets were lost, though. And some livestock." He said these words without emotion, but his dark eyes projected sadness.

Azcue turned and faced the dozen or so houses on their side of the river. "Over here, everyone is doubled and tripled up in the houses without mold. The other houses were damaged by the water. Even after the water went down, moisture remained, and there is, or soon will be, black mold everywhere. It germinates in twenty-four to forty-eight hours after the water recedes. Fortunately, most walls are adobe, so they just need cleaning with bleach. Adobe's not like drywall that rots and has to be torn out. But the wood beams require scraping to get the layer of wet wood removed."

Azcue spoke with the authority of one who was familiar with this kind of work. "We need help cleaning walls, moving out damaged possessions, distributing food and water and supplies. The people who live here, they can do this work themselves, and they are working hard, but there's simply too much. They need help. That's why we are here." He was silent for a moment, as he looked hard first at Shelby, then Andrew. "You think you can help with that?"

Andrew and Shelby exchanged glances. Andrew said, "We can help."

"Good," Azcue said. He had made no mention of the fact that he had been following them for a thousand miles. "One more thing. Maybe the most important thing. If you're part of Olivia's crew, you must do your work with respect for these people, and do it with patience, love and prayer. We are not their rescuers, we are their neighbors." He looked from face to face, waiting for their acknowledgement.

"Yes, we understand," said Shelby.

Azcue looked down at their feet. "Andrew, your boots are probably okay. Shelby, you'll need something better. You got any boots with you?"

"Afraid not." She shuffled a bit, aware how frivolous her white tennies appeared.

"We've got some extra work boots in the van. What size do you wear?"

"Women's ten."

"Got it. Any questions?"

Andrew spoke up. "Where will we stay?"

Azcue said, "It's assumed everyone brought their own housing. There's no place here for lodging. Will that be a problem?"

Andrew looked at Shelby, who was thinking how comfortable her mustard-yellow sleeping bag was in the back of the truck. She gave him a romantic smile. "No problem," said Andrew. "We'll sleep in our truck."

"So, take a little time to get yourself ready, then why don't you show up at that house over there in about an hour?" He nodded toward a small adobe building. "And we'll get you working." Then Azcue left.

Andrew turned to Shelby. "So, I hope we know what we're getting ourselves into."

"I'm pretty sure I don't know, but I'm excited. I hope we can help."

"This isn't going to Los Alamos, you know."

"I know," Shelby said. "And what Olivia Marshak said about being worried about her brother, and the photo on the ski pass not being him, and the FBI, good grief."

"Do you think she's telling the truth?"

"I don't know. If she is, then Victor Marshak and Allen Riley are two different people."

"And they both are missing," said Andrew. "Maybe Riley was posing as Marshak."

"Maybe, but Mr. Riley just didn't seem like the kind of man who would do that." She shook her head as she looked about in wonder at the small, damaged village around them. "Anyway, maybe helping these people is more important than finding Mr. Riley. Maybe I'm supposed to be here."

"Have you ever done anything like this before?" he asked.

"Nope. I guess, though, that a priest like you must have helped out with disaster responses before."

Andrew licked his lips and looked at his feet. "Truth is, I haven't done anything like this before, either. Probably should have. Maybe this is where I need to be, too."

Chapter 47

As they headed back to the pickup to change into their best version of work clothes, Tisha's text came in. *Cool about the dancing—I smell romance. Strange around here today. Rudy didn't come in. Suspect that ass is playing damaged in prep for a lawsuit. Two new temps here from Green Bay to fill in for you and Rudy. Good ol' Seymour has gone silent. Where are you now?*

No mention of Derek. The post office seemed a million miles away. The rigid Seymour Johns, Liz and her focus on retirement, and that groping jerk, Rudy—they seemed like people she'd known long ago, in some other life. But Tisha—Lordy, she missed Tisha and would love nothing more than to have her here, have her meet Andrew, have her see this new world she had just entered. She typed her response. *We just arrived at Refugio, Colorado, a small village nearly destroyed by floods. Helping with clean-up work. Scared and excited. Missing you.*

They sat on the tailgate of the pickup, pulling on warm socks. At least Shelby had some warm socks. None of the clothes she brought were for the kind of work that likely awaited them—dirty, sweaty, and rough. She dug through her duffels, through long skirts for nights on the town with Sedona, sleeveless blouses ideal for gazing at Mt. Rushmore from the paved path and browsing the gift shop, tight jeans like the ones she had on, sexy but impractical. Nothing was appropriate for shoveling mud. She settled on the most expendable and rugged pieces from her wardrobe, items that would undoubtedly have to be tossed after the work was done. She had not had a shower today, and the prospects for a shower were likely zero while they were here. Not how she wanted to appear before Andrew, but, he was going through the same challenges.

On the way back to the house Azcue had assigned them to, they stopped at one of the two food trucks. Several other people were in line for food. When they got to the window, a cheerful middle-aged woman, her white hair bound by a hair net, greeted them. "Welcome, you two. I'm Cindy. You're new here, aren't you?"

"Just arrived," Shelby said. "So, what's on the menu?"

"Well, it's kind of limited. Sorry. Burgers, cold sandwiches, hot dogs and tacos. No chef's salads, I'm afraid." Cindy laughed. "We're hardly professionals here."

They ordered burgers. "How much?" Andrew asked, reaching for his billfold.

"Oh, no charge."

"Really? How can you do that?"

"This is our ministry. We're from First Baptist in Pueblo. It's our way of helping."

"That's really kind," Shelby said.

"We're all doing our part to pitch in. As soon as Olivia called us, we were right on it. See those solar showers over there?" She pointed across the parking area toward three wooden barricades with water tanks and solar panels above them. That got Shelby's attention. "The Lutherans in Trinidad set those up. Where are you from?"

"We're just travelling and heard about the flood and wanted to help."

Cindy pushed two burgers through the window toward them. "I'm glad you showed up. This is just so sad."

The stroll to the house where they'd be working took them past other small adobe homes, shaded by tall cottonwoods and surrounded by gardens that were now mud slicks. They passed La Tienda, a small general store with a gas pump out front, that looked like it sold almost everything. The store was closed. Muddy stripes about two feet up the walls of the building marked where the flood waters had reached.

The house that Azcue had sent them to was a small adobe building. A mound of items, probably the possessions that had been removed, sat in front of the house, covered by a blue tarp. Even though it was nearly dark inside, with only a few shafts of sunlight coming in through two narrow windows, Shelby could count six people at work scraping exposed wood beams and scrubbing the adobe surfaces. There was a strong bleach odor. A woman wearing safety glasses, a respirator mask and a long white plastic apron turned to greet them. "Oh, you must be Shelby and Andrew," she said. "We're glad you're here. Shelby, Azcue left some boots over there for you, and you'll both need to grab the fashion essentials." Next to Shelby's new work boots—they looked like men's boots and they were well used, she noted—were respirator masks, rubber gloves, safety glasses and plastic aprons. "You'll need to get dolled up, before you can work."

After Shelby and Andrew were fitted in their new work gear, the woman said, "So, here's what we're up to. Azcue or Olivia probably already filled you in. We've already shoveled out about six inches of mud, so you missed the fun part. But don't worry, we've got more houses that still have mud. Right now, we're dealing with black mold. Got to get rid of all of it before anyone can occupy this house. Water got up to about two feet in here several days ago, left everything soaked. Take a look at the exposed wood. Fortunately, it's hardwood, so it's wet only to about a quarter inch deep. We've got to scrape all the wet wood surfaces down to dry wood. Not rocket science. Any questions?" When Shelby and Andrew were silent, she said, "Okay, grab a scraper and dig in." The woman never introduced herself, nor did she introduce any of the others working there. In fact, they were all working so intently, none of them had looked up when Shelby and Andrew entered.

The scraping was hard work. Shelby used a sharp flat-bladed tool to gouge down into the wet wood as far as she could push, then scrape. Wet wood that was removed fell onto newspaper on the floor, and when a significant pile of wet scrapings had accumulated, she would carry the pile outside to where the scrapings were dumped.

After an hour of this work, her shoulder was starting to ache. She found it was easier to scrape by switching hands periodically. In spite of the hard work, she was pumped. She and Andrew glanced at each other every few minutes, toasting each other with their scrapers. The masks ensured that conversation and smiles were out of the question.

The woman came up to her, lowered her mask to speak, and said, "Okay, time to switch with a bleacher. That scraping will wipe you out. We don't need more people in the hospital." So, for the next hour, they applied bleach to all the surfaces—scraped-wood and adobe—using a large brush, laden with bleach from five-gallon drums.

After another hour, the woman stepped to the doorway, removed her mask and said, "Okay, boys and girls, that'll do it for today. Thank you all very much. You are an amazing crew. We've still got a little more to do on this house, so let's meet back here at seven tomorrow. Hope you all come to the service tonight. Get some rest."

Everyone shed their protective gear, leaving it by the door, and stepped outside. Even though no one had spoken during the afternoon of work, there was now animated chatter. The woman in charge stepped up to Shelby and Andrew. "So, now I can greet you. I'm Sarah from Denver, part of Olivia's bunch." Apparently, Olivia knew a lot of people. No wonder the barista at the Starbucks in Golden said that everyone knew Olivia Marshak. "Thank you for helping," she said.

"We are blessed to be here," Andrew said.

"You're right about that. These people need our help, yes. But the truth is, they are giving me far more than I am giving them. Their faith, their love, their joy in the midst of loss—I need what they have."

Sarah introduced them to the other five workers—three volunteers and the couple who lived in the house. Shelby went up to the couple, while Andrew stood behind her. "I'm glad to meet you," she said, extending a hand.

The woman, young and pretty, beamed. "I'm Lupe and this is Tomas." She brushed back long black hair from her face. "This has been so hard. So sad. Everything we own is over there." She pointed to the blue tarp. Shelby noted that there wasn't very much under it. "We don't need to lose our home right now. I'm pregnant. My baby will come in two months. But we are so glad you are here. You are my angels." Then she gave a Shelby a hug. Shelby looked away as her eyes misted up.

When they separated, Tomas spoke up. "We had some sheep and two horses, and we grow our own food. Now all that is gone. We don't know what we are going to do."

Shelby didn't know what to say to people who had lost so much. She laid a hand on each of their arms. "I am so sorry."

"But we still have the most important things," Lupe smiled. "We have each other, and we have the love of our Lord. We will be okay. We are very happy."

Shelby looked at their gentle faces, but could find no additional words. Compared to Lupe and Tomas, she had so much. Yet, could she honestly say, like Lupe, "I am very happy"?

Chapter 48

Andrew

They sat on the tailgate of the Tundra, after changing into clean clothes. By the time they'd gotten their showers, the sun was already setting, and they were told the water-storage tanks were running low. That meant the water was lukewarm and came out more as a drizzle than a stream. Nonetheless, they agreed that they were the best showers they'd ever had.

Their muddy work clothes lay on the ground beside the truck for use tomorrow. In the twilight, the big peaks off to the west had become dark silhouettes. The village was nearly dark, too. Only a few flickering lights came from the homes.

"I never expected I'd be doing *that* today," Andrew said, turning toward Shelby. They had been so busy, they'd had almost no chance to discuss the day's experiences.

Shelby gave out a muffled giggle. "We only worked a few hours, and I've gotta say, that was the hardest I've worked in a long time. My shoulders are killing me. How about you?" She'd changed back into the white blouse over the sexy Levi's she'd had on earlier. Her hair was wet from the shower and hung in strings around her face.

"Yeah, mine are sore, too. And tomorrow we have a full day. Clearly, this isn't work for the faint of heart."

"And yet," Shelby said, "this really touched me in some way I'll be processing for a while. I mean, all that scraping and scrubbing was so mindless and mundane, but it was so important. And meeting Lupe. I really like her." Her brown eyes poured out emotion that made Andrew's knees feel like jelly. He gave a nod that said that he was blown away, too.

"Good evening, folks." A short man in a black cassock stood before them. As they turned their attention toward him, the man continued. "You must be Shelby and Andrew. Olivia mentioned we had some new crew members today. Glad you're here. I'm Father Ruiz." His shaggy white hair hung haphazardly around a deeply wrinkled face.

"We're glad to be here," said Shelby.

"You're the priest at the church," said Andrew.

"That's right. Been here over forty years. I'm eighty-three now. This place is my home. But it's been sad to see this disaster. Never happened before in anyone's memory."

Fr. Ruiz turned and looked out onto the now-dark village. "These people are so brave," he said. "So many have lost all their possessions. Livestock and pets and all kinds of personal belongings. Lost. We've had no electricity for four days—the County guys have been here working on it, but it may be a few more days."

"How are you holding up, Father?" asked Shelby.

"I'm doing fine. Wish I could go into the church. But we can pray anywhere. My loss is small compared to others."

"Where is everyone sleeping?" she asked.

"They're all crowded into the homes that were spared. Fortunately, many extra beds have already been delivered, thanks to the ministerial alliance down in Trinidad. People have been so good."

Andrew pondered the outreach he had witnessed today. The food trucks from the Baptists, the solar showers from the Lutherans, the beds from the ministerial alliance. He wished Buck Martin could see this, as he schemed how to reallocate the outreach funds at St. Tim's. "How does all this stuff get coordinated?"

"Easy, really." Fr. Ruiz let out a laugh of pure joy. "When the water began to rise, and it came so suddenly, we called 911. Then my next call was to Olivia."

"And she organized all this?"

"Pretty much. I knew she could be counted on to pull together help, with compassion. Sensitive and sensible, that's what she is. You won't get her to talk about it—she's too modest—but she's been doing this kind of work since ... hmm, I think back before Katrina. Olivia's the one who knows how to get it done, take care of those things that the government agencies can't do." Then he laughed again, a laugh that conveyed reassurance and peace. "So, what do you folks do, when you're not up to your knees in mud?"

Shelby looked at Andrew. "I work for the post office back in Wisconsin."

"Long way from home," Fr. Ruiz said. "And what about you, son?"

"I'm an Episcopal priest up in Nebraska."

"Hmm, that's interesting. We're having a service in a little while around the bonfire. Usually only do it on Sundays in the church, but since the flood we've been celebrating almost every night. We're all working hard during the day."

"We'll be there," said Andrew, looking over to Shelby for affirmation. She stroked his arm.

"Good. So, Father Andrew, why don't you celebrate with me tonight?"

Andrew shifted uncomfortably on the tailgate. He wanted to refuse, but how could he? "Wouldn't that be a little irregular for an Episcopal priest to assist at a Catholic service?"

"Of course it's irregular." Fr. Ruiz waved an arm to encompass all that was around him. "But then everything here is irregular. The only thing that is not irregular is God's love."

"I would be honored," said Andrew. "I don't have any vestments, though."

"Neither do I," Fr. Ruiz laughed. "The flood took them all. But I do have a couple of stoles. We'll use those. Eight o'clock then? At the plaza."

At eight, Andrew stood with Fr. Ruiz behind a rough-hewn wooden table in the midst of the plaza. Behind them the dark high mountains were like sentinels, guarding the valley. A cool breeze off those peaks was welcome after the warm day. A hundred folding chairs surrounded them—had Olivia brought those in, too? They were all filled. Light from a large bonfire beyond the edge of the seating area flickered on the faces of the people. Andrew noted that he was standing in the middle of a tiny, damaged village in the middle of nowhere, and there were more congregants than St. Tim's had on most Sundays.

While Fr. Ruiz and Andrew waited in silence, Azcue played at a portable keyboard. Did that come out of Olivia's van, too? The songs he played were simple, familiar, beautiful. "Fairest Lord Jesus," "What a Friend We Have in Jesus," "Blessed Assurance."

Then all was quiet. Fr. Ruiz waited for a full minute, allowing everyone to center themselves in the silence. Then he stepped forward to the makeshift altar and spoke, without notes, Andrew observed. "Dear brothers and sisters, it is so good to see you all tonight. It's been another long day of hard work, sweat, and tears. It's been another long day of us all being immersed in this new reality of loss, destruction and uncertainty. It has been another long day, yes, but it has been another day of hope. I look around our beautiful village—our village *is* beautiful, and no amount of mud, black mold and loss can change that. I look around this village and what do I see? The mud, the damage—sure, I see that—but what I see foremost is faith, hope and love—the three greatest gifts that come from our Lord. Those gifts are here in abundance, and you have seen them, too. They are here in the courage of you, the families for whom this is home, working hard, praying hard, loving hard. They are here in the volunteers who are here working beside you. So, tonight, we gather, all of us exhausted, all of us looking at another long day tomorrow. Tonight we gather, confident that God holds us—beaten, muddied and injured, but undefeated—in the palm of his hand, and that nothing, absolutely nothing, even death itself, can ever separate us from the love of God in Christ Jesus our Lord." Fr. Ruiz bowed his head, then raised his arms high and proclaimed, "The Lord be with you!"

Andrew had started the service with shaking knees, but the words of Fr. Ruiz were so calming. He remembered being on that mountainside with Jesus, how Jesus told him to not be afraid. That comforted him now, emboldened him. And he sensed that Jesus was saying those same words to all those gathered here tonight.

A woman from the village came forward to read lessons, then Andrew read the Gospel. It was a familiar passage from Matthew, in which Jesus tells the people, *Come to me all you who labor and are carrying heavy burdens, and I will give you rest.*

Then it was time for the homily. Andrew waited to see what Fr. Ruiz had to say about this moving Gospel. But Fr. Ruiz whispered to Andrew, "I should have asked you earlier, but why don't you say a few words to the people? It is not often that we have a guest preacher."

Andrew felt the same sudden surge of panic that he had experienced when Shelby dragged him out onto the dance floor at the Rawhide Club. He had not studied the Scriptures all week, had no manuscript typed in Times Roman, 14-point, double-spaced. He looked into the face of Fr. Ruiz, prepared to say no. But then he saw the welcoming, affirming eyes of the old man, and he said, "Yes."

Andrew stepped forward, placed his sweaty palms flat on the altar and said a silent prayer, the Jesus prayer that he had said on the mountainside: "Jesus, son of God, have mercy on me, a sinner." He looked up, saw Shelby, her face beaming, seated next to Lupe and Tomas. He was ready to speak, although, so uncharacteristic of Andrew, he had no idea what he was going to say.

Chapter 49

Andrew and Shelby sat in the darkness, leaned up against opposite sides of the fiberglass walls inside the Tundra's camper shell, buried up to their waists in their mustard-yellow sleeping bags. They had walked in silence back from the service, holding hands.

"The service tonight was very nice. It was cool to see you be a priest."

"That service meant a lot." Andrew took a deep breath, like he was preparing to share something big. "There was a time in my life when I was watching the horizon, following the lead of the Holy Spirit, unafraid to launch out into the unknown. Like when I left my physics studies to go to seminary. But then, somewhere along the way, maybe at St. Timothy's, I began to keep my head down ..." He shook his head, as if suddenly saddened by a memory. "Like I was looking for a set of grooves in the path that I could set my wheels into. Tonight helped me to look toward the horizon again."

"Your sermon was very moving, but you're pretty funny, you know."

"How so?"

"That night in the Buick, you said you'd never tell anyone about your seeing Jesus." She reached over and ran her fingers along his neck, making Andrew have to catch his breath. "And then tonight, you told a hundred people you don't know."

Andrew let out a shallow laugh. "Yeah, that kind of surprised me, too. But as I heard those words of the Gospel, about us carrying heavy burdens and how Jesus offers us rest, that night in the mountains just jumped back out at me." He gave her a penetrating look, and even in the darkness he felt her eyes meet his and not let go. "I was carrying heavy burdens, for sure. I'd just read the last rites for myself, and I was preparing to die, soon and alone. And, then, there was Jesus, telling me to not be afraid. I had to share that." He was silent, then added, "Do you think it was okay?"

"You're asking if it was okay?" Now she gripped both of his hands in hers, holding them tight. Then she leaned forward, kissed him softly and said, "It was a lot more than okay. I was sitting next to Lupe and Tomas. When you finished speaking, they were both crying." She pulled back, and even though it was dark, he could see the fire in her eyes. "And so was I."

Andrew remained silent. He'd done enough talking this evening. What he didn't tell the congregation was how he had been rescued by a woman, who he'd initially thought was an angel, who seemed to be placed there to help him. How she led him to a place that was called a refuge.

"You have deep faith in God," she said.

"I have struggled at times with my faith."

"Yes, but your faith has affected your whole life."

He pondered this for a moment. "It has."

"You probably want me to believe what you believe."

"I don't want to push my faith on you. Faith doesn't come from me twisting your arm. I don't want anything to come between us."

"I don't either." She slouched a little deeper into her sleeping bag. "But that you believe something so strongly naturally has an effect on me."

"Say more."

She sat silent for a while before speaking. "I never have thought much about God. It's not like I'm an atheist or anything. My parents never went to church, never talked about God. I did go to church a couple of times, back when I was in high school. Guess you could say God was just never on my screen." She shrugged, then licked her lips. "But now I see you, and it makes me wonder … wonder if I've been missing something. It's just …" She didn't finish the sentence.

It was deathly quiet. Although there were other RVs and campers parked nearby, probably everyone had turned in early after a long day of hard work. "It's just what?"

Shelby pursed her lips, like she was thinking it over. "Like I said, when I look at you I wonder if I've missed something, but then—how do I say this?—I'm all messed up inside, because maybe I'm unworthy of God."

Now she was quiet. After a bit, Andrew said, "Why would you say that?"

Shelby snuggled deeper into her bag. "Hope these things are going to be warm enough tonight." She let out a nervous giggle, then a deep breath. "I don't know. It's just that there have been some hard times in my life, and it never felt like there was someone there for me, certainly not like some real God—like you talked to out in the mountains—looking down on me."

"Have you ever prayed?"

Shelby shook her head. "I don't know how to pray. I'm not a very holy person."

"You just talk to God in your heart. Use your own words. Be honest."

She nodded like she was considering this.

"And as far as being holy … someone once said the glory of God is a person fully alive. I've never known anyone so full of life as you," he said.

She gave out a nervous laugh. "You need to get out more." Andrew joined the laughter. "But that's a nice thing to say."

"Here's what I see," he said. "I see someone so full of life, and I know God is there."

She apparently chose to ignore this comment. "You have faith because you're a better person than me."

"Funny you would say that," he said. "Because I think you're a better person than me."

"Oh, great," she laughed, "two people with low self-esteem."

"Maybe," he said. "Or maybe just two people who really like each other."

She was silent, and he sensed she was considering those words. "I don't know much about faith."

"I suspect you do. You are the one who brought us here. I wouldn't have done that on my own."

"But you have all that seminary education." After another moment, she added, "Tell me about God."

Andrew was quiet, thinking through what to say, realizing how important her request was. He opened his guitar case, which was stowed near their feet, and pulled out his guitar. He strummed it a few times and tuned it. He usually used a small electronic device to tune his guitar, but now, in the darkness, he tuned it by ear. He'd never trusted himself to be able to do that before. "Ever listen to Sam Cooke back in the day?"

"I really don't know where you're going with this. But, yes, of course, I love Sam Cooke. Darling, you send me."

"Why, thank you."

"I mean, I loved that *song*." She gave his arm a little punch.

"I know. I loved that song, too." Truth was, though, *darling you send me* pretty much described how he was coming to feel about Shelby. "But, here's another one of his songs, with me taking liberties with the words." Andrew softly strummed a few chords, then sang:

"Don't know much church history,

Don't know much theology,

Don't know much about the holy book,

Don't know much about the Greek I took,

But I do know that God loves you,

And I know that if you love him too,

What a wonderful world it would be."

When he finished, he was silent, awaiting Shelby's response.

She was quiet, too, then said, "You wrote that?"

"Well, a little bit of me and a lot of Sam Cooke. But, it pretty much tells the truth about God, I think. Yes, I had a fancy education, but at the bottom of it all is knowing that God loves you." Maybe he hadn't really known that until that night on the mountainside.

"I loved it," she breathed.

"So, that song was about God. Here's another one that could be about God, but also about you and me." He was taking a risk here, no doubt, but he was learning more about risk-taking in the past few days than he'd ever learned before. He strummed a few chords, then began singing, "When you're down and troubled ..."

When he finished "You've Got a Friend," he could hear her soft sobs.

Then she moved into his arms.

Chapter 50

Shelby

She lay in the darkness, listening to Andrew's soft snoring next to her on the bed of the pickup. She had told him that she felt unworthy of being loved by God. Maybe she shouldn't have said it. Tisha would chew her out right now. "You're the best thing there is," she'd say. Of course, she'd say that.

But then, Andrew had gone in a direction she had not expected. She had braced herself for a sermon. But when he sang "You've Got a Friend," she simply melted.

They had both fought it off. Andrew had protested, "We have no protection," and she had said something brilliant like, "I don't care," as she unzipped his sleeping bag. And Andrew didn't push her away. Two times 9% is 18%. *Is that how it works?* Oh hell, she didn't want to think about that now. She drifted into sleep, with his words ... "Winter, Spring, Summer or Fall" ... dancing through her head.

Refugio is a forgotten place, only a hundred people, far from the highway. Truly, as its name says, it is a refuge. A last, undiscovered place. But after only a day here, Shelby was already starting to feel like Refugio was the center of the universe.

After breakfast at the food truck, they'd gotten to work at seven. They would finish their work in Tomas and Lupe's house today, then, apparently—they'd been given no instructions yet—they'd move to another house and begin again.

As she began her morning's assignment of more scraping, Shelby recalled how awkward they had been after their night in the Buick. It was different now. Maybe being in a place like the battered Refugio, where pretense and shyness and bullshit have no place, erases things like awkwardness. She looked over at Andrew now, donned in his white plastic apron, respirator mask and safety goggles. Maybe it was Refugio, but maybe it was last night in the back of the pickup, the most romantic night she'd ever experienced.

They worked in silence, the only sounds the scraping of wet wood, the endless scraping, and the sloshing of bleach. The bleach odor was bad, even through the respirator mask. But the mask, she knew, wasn't only for protection against bleach, it was protection against the black mold, which could cause respiratory illness, and, in some cases, even death. As she scraped, she was motivated by thoughts of Lupe's baby living in this house, a place that would be—if she had anything to say about it—a safe and healthy home.

At noon, Sarah, the supervisor, stepped to the doorway and called out, "Okay, folks, lunch break. Rations are on your left, outside. We'll take a half-hour."

The lunches were military rations. Each plastic-wrapped container was labeled MRE. Reading the finer print, she learned that meant *Meal, Ready-to-Eat*. Far cry from the tapas at Door 222 in Loveland. She picked up a bag and found a place to sit on a low adobe wall. She searched for Andrew, but he was busy talking with Sarah.

Lupe came and sat beside her. Inside the bag was an array of items: a plastic container of cheese ravioli, another container labeled simply *Side Dish*, another labeled *Dessert*, a beverage mixing bag, some crackers, a plastic spoon, towelette and other items. An amazing feast in a small bag. She'd never eaten the military rations that troops eat—it was exciting. Where the hell had Olivia gotten this stuff? She smiled, imagining Olivia twisting the arm of some flustered Army lieutenant.

For a few minutes, Lupe and Shelby busied themselves unwrapping the various portions. Then Lupe bowed her head for a silent prayer. Shelby paused, then bowed her head, also.

After the prayers, Shelby asked, "So, have you always lived here, Lupe?"

"Pretty much."

"Where did you go to school?"

"The church school until I was in eighth grade. Went to high school down in Trinidad. A bus took us, about an hour each way. Then I went to the community college, Trinidad State. Got my certificate as a dental assistant. Lived in Trinidad for a while, but then I came home. I want to live here forever. Most beautiful place I can imagine."

Shelby gazed out at the small cluster of adobe homes around her, and, beyond, the high Rockies, still snowcapped. Another world from anything she'd ever known. She turned back to Lupe. "Have you known Tomas for a long time?"

"Since we were kids. My family has always been here. My mother and father still live here. They make beautiful rugs to sell at art fairs in Walsenburg and Trinidad. Learned from our ancestors down in New Mexico."

Shelby wondered what her own parents were doing. Maybe she should see them. Maybe they are lonely.

Lupe continued with her story. "We work hard, but it is so peaceful. Quiet, surrounded by people you love. I help with

the dental care in the village. Dr. Barria—he's the dentist—
comes down from Pueblo once a month, but I can take care of
most of the routine things." Now she laughed. "We're not
really so backward. We have electricity and telephone, and
there's a WiFi hotspot at La Tienda."

"This sounds like a great life, Lupe." She meant it.

Lupe continued. "I know this life is not for everyone, and
I know there are many people who hardly know we exist. And
I know our way of life may not be able to go on forever. But
this is everything I want. Like I said, my faith and my family
are the center of my life. And helping others. It's all I want."

"That's a beautiful story, Lupe. You are quite inspiring."

Lupe took a bite of one of her raviolis, then asked, "So,
why did you come here, Shelby?"

Shelby blurted out an answer. "I didn't know until we saw
the sign and I read about the flood. Honestly, we didn't know
what was here." She knew that this wasn't the real answer, the
deeper answer. Why did you come here? This was an
important question, but she struggled to find words. "Actually,
I guess I was drawn here," she added.

"Why would that be?"

Shelby shook her head slowly in a concession that she
didn't know.

Lupe watched Shelby with interest.

Shelby looked out at the mountains again, as if an answer
might be found there. "Maybe I was looking for something."

Lupe took another bite of a ravioli and nodded, but said
nothing.

Shelby gave out a nervous laugh. "Maybe I've just been
going day to day in my life, trying to get by." Now she looked
at Lupe, whose intense brown eyes were locked on her.

"Maybe I've always settled for less, and I was trying to find more."

Shelby wasn't sure where she was going with this. She stabbed another ravioli with her fork, lifted it to her mouth, then said, "Like ..." She felt her mouth go dry. "Like with my father and Michael. I was engaged to Michael." She set her fork down and stared out toward the mountains again. "I think I was trying to be this happy, cheerful person, which I often am, but not always. I think ... I think I tried too hard to please them." Still looking out to the mountains, she added, "Maybe I need to find out who I can be. Does that make sense?" She picked up her fork again, chewed on the ravioli, waiting for Lupe's response.

"So what you're looking for is your true self." Now Lupe set her MRE aside and said, "Do you love God, Shelby?" She said it as a simple question, like asking if she loved Italian food.

Shelby almost choked on the ravioli. Following her talk along similar lines with Andrew last night, and after years of not thinking at all about such topics, Lupe's question seemed odd. Maybe being in a place of hardship and deprivation naturally brings out thoughts about the bigger things.

Lupe looked hard at Shelby, waiting for her answer.

Shelby cleared her throat, stalling for time. "Well, I'm not sure I love God, because, well, I guess I never really even thought about it." She remembered Andrew's rendition of the Sam Cooke song. She looked down. "Maybe I could love God, go to church and all that stuff, if I ever get my act together."

Lupe took Shelby by the shoulders with both hands, like she might be about to shake some sense into her, but held her gently. "My dear sweet Shelby," she said, "we're all broken in some way. You don't run to God after you get your act together. No. You run to God *in order* to get your act together."

The afternoon shift began, and she had barely spoken to Andrew. As she passed him on the way back into the house, he purposely bumped his hip against hers, and this said as much as any words. She set herself to more scraping, singing "You've Got a Friend," but the conversation with Lupe wouldn't let her go.

They'd been at it a half-hour or so, when a scream caused everyone to turn. A man on the other side of the room had fallen. He was face down, but then he rolled over, the sharp scraping tool protruding from his thigh. Then he reflexively pulled the tool from his leg. The plastic apron had shifted to the side, and a fountain of blood gushed from the slice the tool had made, at least a foot into the air. He lay on the floor, eyes wide, mouth open in a silent scream. For a second, everyone just watched, completely stunned.

Shelby dropped her scraping tool and was instantly at the man's side. "Get some scissors, cloth, tape, first aid kit," she barked. A major artery had been severed. Femoral artery, she suspected. She knew he would bleed out in less than five minutes.

"Help me get his pants down," she yelled. Andrew was by her side to help.

"Where is the nurse?" somebody screamed.

"I'll go find him," someone said and darted out.

"Call 911," somebody else shouted.

"Got it," came from another voice. "But, it'll take an hour before anyone comes."

The man's face had become pale, the pallor of death.

Shelby recalled what she had learned in nursing school. Apply pressure to the artery, stopping the bleeding by pushing it against bone. Immediately, she pressed down firmly on the artery, making sure to keep her fingers between the bleeding site and the heart.

She was covered with blood, which had spurted all over her, even onto her face, but held the pressure. Where the hell was that nurse?

"Help me elevate his leg," she yelled. She needed to get the wound above his heart. Andrew helped her raise the man's leg.

"You'll be okay, sir. I am with you. I'm a nurse," she lied. Her voice was steady, reassuring. "I know what to do. Just lie back. I need you to stay calm. Stay with me." She barked, "Somebody get down here and hold his hand." Lupe was immediately beside him and took his hand. "Sing a song. We need him to be calm." She knew that raised blood pressure would empty him out even faster. Lupe sang a soft baby's lullaby, probably one she'd been practicing, up close to the man's ear.

After what seemed like an eternity, Shelby continued to hold the pressure against the artery, even though her arm was falling asleep with numbness. She stayed beside the man, as Lupe continued to sing and Andrew was saying prayers.

A young man burst into the house, closely followed by Olivia and Azcue. "Here's the nurse," somebody said. A young man knelt down by Shelby. "Fill me in," he said. Shelby told the man what she had done.

"Bleeding seems to have stopped," the nurse said. "Why don't you let me hold the pressure for a while, until the medics get here?" As they switched places, the nurse looked around at the people, who still looked stunned and panicked. "She did exactly the right thing. She saved this man's life."

"See, you're gonna be okay," Shelby said to the man, in as upbeat a voice as she could muster. "We've got the pros here now, and they'll take good care of you. You'll be good as new."

The man reached up and touched Shelby's arm. Color was starting to come back to his face. "Thank you. I'll never forget this," he said.

Minutes later, two EMTs with lots of gear stormed in and knelt beside the man. Shelby stood, as the stretcher was brought in and the man was strapped into place. After the man was carried out, Sarah said, "I think we need a break. God, thank you for Shelby."

Olivia came up to Shelby, with piercing eyes surveying her. "It seems you were amazing. He is very lucky we had a nurse right here."

"Oh, I'm not really a nurse. I only studied for—"

"So, I guess we did the right thing in not checking your diploma before we let you help, huh?" There was now a sly twinkle in her eye. "Shelby, I'd say you are a hero." Azcue stood next to Olivia, his arm around her shoulder.

"Thank you."

"Oh, and one more thing. I don't want to hear any more of that *I'm not a nurse* crap. Now, you need to get cleaned up. You look like hell." She gave Shelby's arm a squeeze. "And did I mention that I am very glad you are here?"

Andrew was next to Shelby now. And Lupe came up and gave her a long hug, in spite of the blood all over her, and they cried together.

Chapter 51

W hen a major adrenalin surge has passed through you, you may be left an exhausted, shaking mess. That pretty much described Shelby, after she had her shower and changed. When she emerged from the solar shower in her clean duds, Andrew was waiting. "Feeling better?"

Shelby couldn't talk about it now. "Yeah, I'm okay. Let's get back to work."

At the house, Sarah met them at the door. "Maybe you two have had enough scraping for one day. You've just climbed Mt. Everest. You need to chill a bit. Why don't you head over to the store? They need some extra help over there."

The store was an emergency distribution center, set up on the edge of the plaza. Food items, cleaning supplies, paper towels and toilet paper were spread out on make-shift tables, sheets of plywood atop saw horses. Their job was to greet residents and make sure they got what they needed, restock the tables from stacks of boxes where extra supplies were stored, and discourage hoarding. There was no charge for any of the supplies. Again, Olivia had somehow pulled strings to make this possible.

This was a different kind of work for Shelby. Meeting people from the village, helping them find what they needed. Laughing with them. It was surprising how much laughter there was. She recalled Lupe's words from yesterday about being so happy, even as so many of their material possessions had been lost.

During a quiet period, Andrew had gotten his guitar from the truck and played softly in the background. Then children began to gather, and Andrew began to sing to them. Songs he made up, about green beetles and lizards and all kinds of crazy fun things that had the kids dancing in hysterics. Shelby mostly stayed busy helping residents, but once she stopped to hear him sing a song to the melody of "Twinkle, Twinkle Little Star:"

> "All the kids were in the square
> Playing with a grizzly bear,
> And a mountain lion, too,
> Sang as she came walking through.
> Then an eagle dipped real low
> Big white tail was quite a show.
> They all danced and sang a song
> 'Bout this world where we belong."

The kids howled with joy and made him sing it again three times.

When he put his guitar away, the children gathered close, tugging at his shirt and pleading for more. "We could sing all day, my friends," he said to them, "but I've got to go to work now. Maybe we can sing some more songs tomorrow."

When he turned to Shelby, he said, "Sorry for not carrying my weight with the store. It just seemed those kids needed some music."

She rested a hand on his arm to acknowledge the importance of the work he'd just done. "That was wonderful, Andrew. Did you make up all those songs?"

"Yeah, just make 'em up while I'm singing."

"You keep surprising me."

"Not as much as you keep surprising me." They would have kissed, but an elderly couple was approaching the tables.

It was getting late, and the supplies were running low. Azcue had stopped by earlier and said another truck load would be arriving tomorrow. The man, bent and old and probably ninety, looked through the items. He placed a hand on the last roll of paper towels. He gave Shelby a mournful look. "We sure could use these towels to wipe up mud in our house," he said.

"Please, go ahead and take them," Shelby said.

"But they're the last ones."

"That's okay. You need them."

The old man withdrew his hand from the towels. "Yes, but someone may come along who needs them more."

As the man and his wife left, with no supplies, Shelby turned to Andrew. "I have seen some beautiful things since I've been here, but that just about topped them all." She looked up toward the high mountains, backlit by the afternoon sun. It felt like something was about to explode inside her. Something long awaited. Something very good.

That evening, they gathered again for worship in the plaza. Fr. Ruiz approached them. "Father Andrew," he called out, waving.

As they stopped to greet him, he said, "I just wanted to say again how wonderful your homily was last night. It touched many people. I've been hearing from them all day. That is what we all need right now—words of hope, not just religious prattle, but authentic from-the-heart words of hope. That's what you gave them."

It was clear Andrew was pleased, but that he didn't know what to say. "Well, I ..." he began, then bit his lip and said, "Thank you."

"I'd love to have you up front with me again tonight, Father, and the people would love it, too. But, maybe you'd like to sit with your wife tonight?"

Shelby looked up at Andrew to see how he would handle the *your wife* comment. But Andrew simply said, "Thank you," then looked into Shelby's eyes.

They found seats near the front, next to Lupe and Tomas. Lupe leaned over and gave Shelby's arm a squeeze.

Like last night, Azcue began with music on the keyboard, several soft melodies that felt comforting. Then Fr. Ruiz began the service. The stunning dark silhouette of the Rockies behind him was as beautiful as Shelby could imagine any church setting being.

Before Fr. Ruiz read the Gospel, he came out in front of the makeshift altar, carrying the red Gospel book in his arms, and said, "We have a special treat tonight for our Gospel hymn." Then he nodded in Shelby's direction, which made her pulse jump. She breathed relief when Lupe stood and went forward. Azcue brought a music stand out and placed it in front of the altar, then began a soft lead-in on the keyboard.

Lupe took her place behind the music stand and looked around at the gathering, with a smile, before beginning the gentle melody, "I want Jesus to walk with me …"

There was no accompaniment—Azcue had stopped playing and sat at the keyboard watching Lupe. Her voice was low, but loud enough that everyone could hear. She sang the words slowly, and there was little doubt that she believed them. After she completed the first verse, she looked directly at Shelby and said, "Would my sister, Shelby, come up and sing the second verse with me?"

Shelby stiffened and suddenly couldn't breathe. Andrew leaned over and whispered, "You don't have to do this, if you don't want."

In an instant that seemed to last an eternity, she closed her eyes and saw the man bleeding to death face-down on the floor. It was that moment when he rolled over and the blood spurted high in a fatal gush. But it was her own face she saw, her desperate face that needed someone to stop the bleeding. She opened her eyes and gave Andrew a nod of acknowledgement, then stood and walked toward Lupe.

Shelby took her place next to Lupe, who put an arm around her. With her other hand, Lupe pointed to the place on the sheet music in front of them. She leaned toward Shelby and whispered, "Pay attention to the words, Shelby. This is just you and me talking to Jesus." Then Lupe began. Shelby joined in, her voice shaky and probably almost inaudible.

The verse began with, "In my trials, Lord, walk with me …" Lupe had said to pay attention to the words, but as she began, Shelby was more focused on just surviving, getting through this ordeal, with a hundred pairs of eyes on her. She leaned a sweaty hand against the edge of the altar, in case she might be about to faint.

She got through the verse okay, without making a fool of herself. She had never considered herself much of a singer, even though her father had said she reminded him of the country singer, Shelby Lynne, for whom Shelby may have been named. By the last line, her volume had increased, probably matching Lupe's.

Then Lupe turned to her. "Why don't you sing the third verse, Shelby? And, remember pay attention to the words— read them, but hear them, too." Before Shelby could protest, Lupe stepped aside and left her standing alone. Shelby scanned the lyrics of the third verse before she began. Then she looked up and sang,

> "When I'm in trouble, Lord, walk with me;
> when I'm in trouble, Lord, walk with me;
> when my head is bowed in sorrow,
> Lord, I want Jesus to walk with me."

When she finished, she returned to her seat, keeping her head down, the line, *when my head is bowed in sorrow, Lord, I want Jesus to walk with me*, continuing to ring in her ears.

She turned to Andrew, surprised to see the tears streaming down his face. "Shelby," he stammered, "that was so beautiful."

She leaned her head on his shoulder. "Last night, you said I should talk to God about my life."

She felt him tremble next to her, but he said nothing.

"That's what I just did," she said.

Chapter 52

Shelby was asleep almost before she had the zipper of her bag pulled up. She had much to talk to Andrew about, and she longed to roll over into his arms. But the overwhelming emotional and physical load of the day was too much. Her exhaustion drove her into a deep, dreamless sleep, and she didn't awaken until Andrew gently nudged her in the morning. "It's six thirty. If we want to partake of a gourmet breakfast over at the roach coach, we'd better get a move on."

Shelby was still trying to pull herself together at the food truck, blowing over the surface of her too-hot coffee, when Olivia came up to her. Olivia looked alert and ready for a busy day. It's hard to call anyone who's wearing grubby work clothes, refined. But Olivia came close to fitting that description. Her gray hair that had hung on her shoulders in Golden was tied back in a pony tail. It gave her a youthful look, but it was her wrinkled face and searching gray eyes that commanded your attention, made you realize that this was a person you needed to listen to.

Olivia greeted Shelby with a warm smile, which took her aback. "You had an amazing day, yesterday," she said. "Topped off by that song last night. You continue to surprise me."

"You're pretty surprising yourself, Olivia. May I ask how you got involved in this work?"

Olivia laughed. Another first? "That was a long time ago. Maybe twenty years. I worked in public relations and advertising. Some snooty firm in Chicago. I hated it, but I was good at organizing and persuading people. Then I went on a mission trip to help build a house for a poor family in Mexico, back in early 2000, I think. I realized that's what I wanted to do with my life. Help others. Use my ability to organize and persuade to get things done. Not to get people to buy some product."

"This is such hard work. You must get tired."

"I do get tired. But I never get tired of helping someone."

"So, you followed your dream."

"Shouldn't everyone?"

Shelby winced and ventured a first sip of her coffee, burning her tongue. "May I ask you another question about your brother?"

When Olivia nodded, Shelby said, "You said Azcue went down to Wisconsin to that house because of some information he received. What information?"

"After the FBI paid me a visit, I checked around in the guest room in my house, where Victor stayed. I found a yellow sticky note with the address of that house on it. Maybe he'd left it there. I debated telling the FBI about it, but decided to ask Azcue, who was coming this way from Minnesota, if he'd look into it. If my brother was in trouble with the FBI, and that address was important, I wanted to know as much as possible about it before telling them. I still haven't told the FBI. Do you think I should?"

Shelby's first thought was about her two illegal entries into the house and that she was glad she had worn the latex gloves. She took another sip of coffee. "I don't know."

Olivia said, "What do you think has happened to my brother?"

Shelby's raised eyebrows said she didn't know. Shelby was still trying to reconcile the photo on the ski pass. "So, you never saw that man on the ski pass before?"

"I don't think so. Why would the pass have my brother's name on it? Could this be some kind of identity theft?"

"I don't know. Have you ever heard of a man named Allen Riley?" Shelby watched Olivia thinking this over.

"No. I don't know anyone by that name."

"Maybe he worked at the Lab? Someone Victor knew?"

"Maybe. Victor never mentioned anyone by that name. I would remember that."

"I came here thinking that the man I knew as Allen Riley was really Victor Marshak, and you could tell me where he is. Now I learn that they are two different people: your brother and the man who claimed to be your brother. And both of them are missing. Do you have a picture of Victor?" It couldn't hurt to verify that Marshak wasn't the guy in the ski pass photo.

"Sure, back at the house, but not with me. He's a big guy, two-fifty, always had a bushy beard, almost bald. There'd be no mistaking him with the man on that ski pass, if that's what you're getting at."

Shelby sipped some more coffee. "Just trying to be certain."

"I'm scared, Shelby. Victor is such a gentle soul. Do you think this Riley might have kidnapped my brother?"

"I'm pretty certain he didn't. Mr. Riley seemed like a peaceful man." The image of him caressing the petal of one of his petunias came into her mind. "With the FBI looking for Victor, might this have something to do with quantum entanglement?"

Olivia's eyes narrowed. "You know about quantum entanglement?"

"Just enough to know it's important." She gave out a self-deprecating laugh. "Read about it in Wikipedia."

"Yes, Victor was always saying how important it is. Said it had military applications, but that he couldn't tell me more."

"When did you see last Victor?"

"Couple months ago."

"Did he seem okay then?"

"I don't know. He hasn't seemed happy for a while."

"Do you have any idea why?"

"I think he was tired of physics. Or maybe all the national security aspects. At one time, it was all he could talk about. The last few times I saw him, he just seemed … tired. Or, maybe distracted is a better word."

"Does Victor have a family? I mean, other than you?"

"No. Victor never married. I think he was married to his work. Physics was his lover."

"I noticed purple petunias planted in front of your house."

Olivia gave her a curious look. "What does that have to do with anything?"

"Did your brother bring you those?"

"Yes, he did. Why do you ask?"

Shelby decided to steal a technique from the British detectives by not answering that question. "So, your brother loved purple petunias?"

"I wouldn't say loved, I don't know. Said he got them from some nursery. He's always bringing me things. He has a big heart. What difference does that make?"

Again, Shelby didn't answer. She took consolation that Detective Chief Inspectors Vera and Barnaby and the other British detectives were often confused, too, had to deal with pieces that didn't fit together. But, eventually, of course, they always solved the mystery. That's what happens on TV. This was real life. Hell, even the FBI had drawn a blank.

There were more questions she wanted to ask the only person she would likely find who actually knew Victor Marshak, but Olivia had already been pulled away by Azcue, who needed to discuss the plans for the day.

Andrew came up to her. "Ready to hit it?"

They weren't sure what Sarah had planned for them today, so they headed to Tomas and Lupe's home, but the crew had already moved onto another house, and Lupe and Tomas were moving their possessions back inside. "Oh, Lupe, you're moving back in. That's so great."

"It's so nice inside now. Maybe you can come over for a visit sometime, maybe tonight?"

Shelby looked at Andrew, who nodded. "We'd love that. Maybe after church?"

Lupe looked like she was ready to dance. "I can't wait."

They made their way back over to the store, where two other volunteers were already working. They were about to move on to find Sarah or Azcue, when several children ran up to Andrew. "Music. Music. Music," they cried in unison, tugging on Andrew's shirt.

"I have to go to work," Andrew said. He glanced over at Shelby with a help-me-with-this look.

"I think you could play them one song before we start work," she said.

Andrew ran back to the truck, and within a minute was back with his guitar. He looked around at the kids. "Any requests? I only have time for one song."

"One that you made up," they cried, almost in unison.

Andrew knelt down near a little girl, probably ten. "What is your name?"

"Rosa," the girl said.

"Okay, then, this song's for Rosa." He stood and strummed a few times, his mind obviously crafting a new song. He looked down at Rosa, then launched into a melody that Shelby didn't know.

> "Out in the mountains there was a kid.
> It was amazing all the things she did.
> Swam the river and climbed the trees,
> Flew a kite in the morning breeze,
> Kissed her dog and picked his fleas.
> Went to the stars and walked on the moon,
> And she did it all while singing a tune.
> Outran coyotes, outflew the birds,
> Sang all the songs she'd ever heard.
> Floated over town like a big balloon,
> And was back for lunch before it was noon."

When he finished, the kids cried, "More. More. More."

Andrew laughed, "I'll do some more later, but now I've got to go to work." He shot Shelby a quick glance. "I'll be right back."

As Shelby watched Andrew lope back to the truck with his guitar case, she pondered how someone who seemed to struggle with spontaneity could, on a moment's notice, rip off a song like the one he'd just sung. Few people could do that.

When Andrew returned, he was talking on his phone, with a worried look. All he was saying was a string of "Uh huhs," interspersed with long periods of listening.

"You say they couldn't medevac him out?"

Oh, Lord. This was serious.

"Uh huh," he said again.

"I will," he said, finally. "Yes, I'll keep you posted." When he put the phone down, he said nothing for a moment, just gave Shelby a sad look.

"That sounded serious," she said.

"Yes. Buck Martin—you remember me talking about him?"

"Oh, yes."

Andrew shook his head, as if trying to come to terms with a truth he'd rather deny. "His son's been in an automobile accident. Hurt real bad. May not make it. He's in the ICU now in High Plains."

"And Buck called you?"

"No. That was Maureen. She suggested that Buck call me, but apparently he was certain I'd blow him off."

"Off course, you wouldn't."

"No."

"And you need to go back. You should go, Andrew. Probably right now."

"I know." His face had reddened and his eyes were getting misty. "I hate to leave here."

"You are needed here, but you are needed there more."

"What will you do?"

She, of course, didn't know. "I could stay here. But I'd have no way to get home." She looked down at her feet, hands on hips, mulling it over.

"I'm sure Azcue could drive you up to the airport, when the work is done here."

Shelby looked around at the little village, which had become like home in just a couple of days. She stepped away from Andrew and paced around the small plaza. Yes, maybe she could stay here. Maybe Lupe would give her a place to sleep, but their place is so tiny, and they're just now moving back in. Azcue had said everybody else was double and triple-bunked. Maybe someone with an RV would have an extra bunk. She looked back at Andrew, whose eyes were locked onto her. She imagined watching his pickup head off down the dusty road, without her. Maybe she should be a stronger, more altruistic person, but she could not bear the thought of continuing here without him. It was over. "I'll just go home, too. I should be back there anyway. You can drop me at a Greyhound station."

"Come with me."

"To your town? High Plains?"

"Yes."

She walked around in a little circle. "And just how would that work?" The reality of their lives was just now awakening her from the dream world they'd been in the past few days.

Andrew licked his lips, as if saying he had no idea. "You just come and ... uh ..."

"And stay at your house? Your house that is right next to the church? This girl you met at the side of the road? This girl you've been shacking up with? How do you think Buck and all his friends at the church are gonna take to that? Think about it, Andrew. You know that's a nonstarter." This had been a romantic whirlwind, but real life can only be ignored for so long. Suddenly she could see with a clarity all that had eluded her these past few days.

"But I don't want to lose you."

"I don't want to lose you either, but let's get real. We've known each other what? A week? And I'm gonna move into your church house? I don't think so. Your church is important. You left physics to serve the church. You endured a divorce to serve the church. I say, let's cut our losses before this thing has gone too far."

"Maybe it's already gone too far."

Shelby agreed, but couldn't say it. She just stood there, staring at him.

"I'll quit. I was thinking about it anyway."

"Don't give me that crap. You can't quit."

"What will you do?"

"Don't worry about me. I can take care of myself. Just take me to the bus station or the airport, whatever. You wanted an adventure. We had an adventure. There'll be good memories." She couldn't look him in the eye as she said these words.

"But we can reconnect after this emergency back in High Plains is over."

Shelby was no fool. She had been at one time. But not now. "Sure. Sure we can. Now let's go tell Olivia and then hit the road."

Chapter 53

Andrew

Andrew strode through the automatic double-doors at High Plains Mercy Hospital, a place he knew well. He'd first swung by the rectory and hurriedly put on a clergy shirt and collar—Buck and Ginger, his wife, would appreciate that—and picked up his usual kit for hospital visits: a communion set, oil stock, small stole, a bible and Prayer Book.

He didn't stop at the reception desk—he had been to the ICU many times over the past eight years. He stepped out of the elevator on the second floor, turned left and headed to the locked door at the end of the hall. He hit the button on the intercom, told the nurse who he was, and was buzzed in.

He found Buck and Ginger in the small waiting room near the entrance. They stood immediately, when they saw him. Buck stepped toward him and offered his hand. "I'm surprised to see you, Andrew." They looked exhausted, with shadows under their eyes. It was obvious that Ginger had been crying. She dabbed her eyes with a tissue.

Andrew shook Buck's hand. "Maureen called me. How is Blake?"

Buck looked at Ginger. "Doctor was here about an hour ago. She said it's still too early to tell. It's—"

Ginger jumped in. "She said we need to be prepared for …" A burst of sobs followed, and Buck put his arm around her.

Buck looked back to Andrew. "Did Maureen tell you what happened?"

Buck was big hulk of a guy. As tall as Andrew, but probably weighing over 300 pounds. Thinning brown hair, peppered with gray. Puffy cheeks. His eyes were slits that were hard to read. He looked like a guy who was used to being in charge, and usually he was. "No," Andrew said.

Buck drew a deep breath to fortify his speech. "Early this morning. Out on Highway 18. Some guy ran a stop sign. T-boned Blake, who didn't have a chance. The guy walked away, of course." He shook his angry face, which had reddened.

Ginger rested a hand on Buck's arm, then said, "He's got lots of broken bones, but mainly his lungs got injured. They called it a pneumo—" She looked at Buck for help.

"Pneumothorax, I think. His left lung was punctured."

Ginger continued. "They did X-rays and a CT scan, then they cut in between his ribs and inserted a tube into his chest." She stopped for a couple of more sobs. Buck had his arm around her now. She continued. "They had it in there for several hours. Now, we're just waiting."

"Can I see him?"

"He's back in Room 4," said Ginger. "They only allow us in for a few minutes at a time. Should we come with you?"

"Yes."

Outside Room 4, Andrew paused, like he always did before entering a hospital room where someone was seriously ill. It was a requirement for him. He was aware of the immensity of the situation, that just on the other side of the door, someone was in distress, maybe fighting for life. On the other side might be a grieving family desperately seeking hope. He could not provide what was needed out of his own power. This was about God, and Andrew took it seriously. Silently he prayed, "God, please send your Holy Spirit to guide my words

and actions, that I might be a blessing to Blake and his family."
Then he entered.

Blake lay in the center of the small dimly illuminated
room. Andrew hadn't seen Blake in over a year, not since he
graduated from high school, but he remembered him as an
active, upbeat kid from Sunday School and then the small St.
Tim's youth group. But here he was now, dangerously injured.
Andrew had visited many people in critical condition, but he
was never prepared for facing a seriously injured young
person. Blake's face was bandaged, his left leg was elevated.
Numerous tubes and wires ran from his body to racks of
flashing and beeping electronic devices around the bed.
Andrew whispered to the family, "Has he been conscious?"

"No," Ginger said. "He's been like this the whole time.
Oh, God, I just want to tell him how much I love him."

"Why don't you do that now?" Andrew moved aside to
make more room for Ginger. "I've learned that the sense of
hearing is often still functioning, even when a person is
unconscious. I suspect he may be able to hear you."

Ginger leaned in close to her son. "Oh, Blake, my darling
boy, I love you so. Please get better. Your dad and I are right
here. And we're cheering for you. Please know that …" She
seemed to run out of words and gave Andrew a helpless look.
Tonight, Ginger wore a sweatshirt over jeans. Her tinted-red
hair had not been tended to recently. Andrew had never seen
her when she wasn't in her Sunday finest.

"Did you want to say something, Buck?" Andrew asked.

Buck looked choked up. He shook his head no.

Andrew placed his stole around his neck. It was blue, the
color that represents healing. He brought out his oil stock, a
small brass container that contained oil for anointing the sick.

He held up the stock for Buck and Ginger to see. "I would like to anoint Blake for healing. Is that alright with you?"

Buck and Ginger nodded yes.

Andrew wanted them to understand what was about to happen. "This oil is not some magic potion, some mumbo jumbo thing we do out of our hopelessness. No, this oil represents our faith, and it has always been accepted as such by the church." He looked from face to face to see if they were following. "This oil is simply olive oil seasoned with some aromatic spices. It is prepared once a year, during Holy Week, at a ritual where the bishop and all the clergy pray that this oil will be a sign of our faith in God's healing power."

"I didn't know that," Buck said meekly.

Andrew went on. "In the bible, James asks, *Are any of you sick? Send for the elders of the church and have them pray over them and anoint them with oil.* And then a few verses down, the Scripture reminds us that *the prayers of the righteous are powerful and effective.*"

He leaned in close to Blake. In a soft voice, he said, "Blake, it's Father Andrew. I'm here to pray with you. And I'm going to put a little oil on your forehead—you may feel a slight touch. And then we'll say some prayers." He waited a moment, then dipped a thumb into the oil, which now filled the small room with its sweet scent. Then he found an unbandaged space on Blake's forehead and, careful not to press hard on the body of an injured person, gently made the sign of the cross. "I anoint you, Blake Martin, in the name of the Father and the Son and the Holy Spirit."

Andrew could have read a prayer for healing from the Prayer Book, and he would later, but now he bowed his head and said, "Gracious and loving God, your beautiful child, Blake, created in your own image, lies here seriously hurt. We pray that as I have anointed him with this holy oil, you are anointing him with your Holy Spirit, which is a spirit of power and love and healing. Heal him, Lord. Please heal him. Guide the hands of the doctors and the staff here at Mercy, give them wisdom to provide the help that Blake needs. And bless his parents, Lord. Give them peace and a solid knowledge of your presence and that you hold Blake and them in the palm of your hand. Thank you, Lord, for your love. Amen."

Then he turned to face Buck and Ginger, as they wiped tears from their eyes. Buck looked defeated.

They returned to the small waiting room in silence. Andrew said, "Is there anything else I can do for you right now?"

Ginger stepped toward Andrew. "You've done a lot. Thank you so much for coming." Buck nodded, but averted his eyes from Andrew's.

"You've no doubt been waiting here a long time. Why don't you go down to the cafeteria and get some dinner? At least, stretch your legs a little. If they have the lasagna, it's pretty good."

Buck and Ginger exchanged glances, then Buck said, "Sure you don't mind waiting?"

"I'm not going anywhere."

After they left, Andrew sagged into the leatherette sofa. He'd just barely gotten back from being on the road for over seven hours today, plus the stopover at Denver International. Shelby had found a cheap Southwest flight online for less than a Greyhound ticket. It would take her to Milwaukee, where her friend Tisha would pick her up.

Leaving Refugio had been quick. They had told Olivia, who understood. She gave them each her phone number and email, then turned and headed off to the day's tasks. They had found Lupe and Tomas and Fr. Ruiz and said quick goodbyes. It was important to connect Shelby with transportation that could hopefully get her home today.

The rough nine-mile drive out to the interstate seemed to go much faster than the drive in. There was little conversation. In fact, their conversation all the way back to the airport was awkward. Competing needs were doing battle in Andrew's mind as he drove. Going back to High Plains was the last thing he wanted to be doing. He fought off the image from last night of Shelby singing alone at the evening church. The words to the song were moving, but he had not been able to take his eyes off her. This tall, beautiful woman, singing from her heart. Strong, that's what she was. And, earlier in Tomas and Lupe's house, how Shelby had taken charge, made things happen, stood toe to toe with death and would not yield. Maybe she was an angel. God, the last thing he wanted to do was say goodbye.

Shelby sat next to him in the Tundra, but she seemed far away. She seemed to have withdrawn into herself. He had glanced over at her frequently, but she was turned toward the window. He wished she would look at him, would lean down toward the radio and tune into one of those romantic country songs.

He couldn't take this silence any longer. "It's not my fault. You act like I have a choice in this."

She looked at him briefly. "You don't have a choice. I understand. It's what needs to be done."

"Why are you acting this way?"

She turned her head toward the window again. "I need to protect myself," she said.

He recalled the dreams in the mountains of Nicole, who'd been the object of his lust, and Sharon, for whom he had thought he still harbored feelings. But their memories had been obliterated by Shelby. He stifled back a sob. Yes, she was in the truck with him, but she was already gone. Maybe she wasn't an angel. But, dear God, she was his angel.

Andrew rose from the waiting-room sofa and walked out into the central area of the ICU. He recognized one of the nurses sitting behind a computer monitor. "Grace," he said, "how are you?"

Grace Mendez was thirty-something and all business. He'd worked with her many times here in the ICU. "Oh, Father, it's good to see you. You're here for Blake Martin, I suppose."

"Yes, just said some prayers for him. Got his parents to go get something to eat."

"Oh, good. They've been here all day. They're a wreck. This has got to be hard on them. That beautiful boy."

He nodded to Grace, as he wondered what Shelby was doing. She should have made it to Milwaukee by now. He pulled out his phone—he had her email and phone number. He could call her right now. But what would he say? What would she say? Would she even answer? Like she said, she was cutting her losses. He pushed his phone back down into his pocket.

He ambled back to the waiting room, just as Buck and Ginger were returning. "No word on Blake," he said. "How was the dinner?"

"Well, it was hospital food," offered Buck, "but we both got the lasagna, and it wasn't too bad."

Andrew manufactured a weak laugh. "Not too bad is quite the commendation for a hospital cafeteria."

They took their seats in the small room. Immediately, Ginger said, "You don't have to stay around."

"I'm happy to stay, if you think that is of some help. Please use me in any way I can serve. I can go find information for you, I can run to the candy machine or get coffee, and, of course, I will say some prayers."

"Thank you again for those prayers," Ginger said.

Buck let out a lasagna burp, and Ginger gave him a chastising look. That seemed to be Buck's comment on the situation.

As they were taking their seats, the doctor came into the room, with nurse Mendez. Andrew and the Martins immediately stood again.

"That's okay. Please sit," said the doctor.

"Doctor, how is he?" gushed Ginger.

Andrew had met Dr. Elaine Roth several times at the hospital. She wore a blue gown and surgical cap, apparently ready to get to work. She had a gentle smile, even in the most serious situations. Her rosy cheeks and large blue eyes made her look like she should be working in an Irish pub. But she had a reputation as perhaps the best surgeon at Mercy. Many times, Andrew had heard it said that High Plains was lucky to have her.

"I'm afraid we need to begin another surgery."

Ginger gasped.

Dr. Roth continued. "His blood pressure has been slowly dropping all afternoon. We fear there is internal bleeding around his heart. We'll be doing a procedure called a thoracotomy. That means we'll be going into his chest cavity to find where the bleeding is coming from and to fix it. If needed, we are ready to do a blood transfusion."

Buck said, "Don't we have some say about this surgery?"

Dr. Roth nodded, like she'd heard this question many times. "Mr. Martin, this is an emergency. We need to start soon."

Buck looked down at his feet. Ginger, said, "We'll trust your judgment, doctor."

Dr. Roth nodded and asked, "Do you have any other questions?"

"What are his chances?" Buck asked. His voice was shaking.

"We don't know yet. Depends on what we find in there. But, Mr. Martin, I'm always optimistic. The surgery will take a couple of hours, and I'll come out as soon as I can and let you know."

"What can we do?" Ginger asked, between sobs.

"You've got Father Andrew here. You're very fortunate. Please pray for Blake and also for our staff and me." The doctor looked from face to face, her blue eyes searching. Then she nodded and left.

Nurse Mendez stepped up. "There are a few minutes before he goes in, if you'd like to see him briefly."

Buck and Ginger stood, terror all over their faces, as Grace Mendez, added, "Father Andrew will take good care of you."

Chapter 54

Shelby

Shelby got home before dark. She dragged her duffels in and dropped them by the sofa. She'd deal with them tomorrow. Then she opened several windows to cool the place off.

Tisha had wanted to go straight to The Quartermaster when they got home, but Shelby needed to crash. On the drive home, she'd given Tisha only a barebones summary of what had happened—she'd spent half the drive from the airport napping from exhaustion that was more emotional than physical.

She paced the small house, not really looking at anything, just moving. Finally, she plopped into a chair and opened the Kindle. She still hadn't made much progress in *Nobody's Fool*. She only got through one page before she laid the Kindle aside and wondered how Andrew was doing at the hospital.

She'd been too mean. But she couldn't get hurt again. She was too vulnerable now. Lost her job. And would she ever be able to find another job with physical assault on her record? Money would soon be gone. She'd have to leave this house, with no place to go. She'd read about people who, overnight, had gone from a good career to living in their car. That could be her. If she had a car. Didn't even have a car—hell, it was still sitting at that garage out in Bridger. On top of all that, maybe she was pregnant. Wouldn't that be the icing on the cake? Maybe she'd have to go live with her parents again. *Dear God.*

But the main thing was Andrew. He had touched those areas, those sensitive areas of her heart that she had worked so hard to heal. Were they healed? She'd told him they should cut their losses. Maybe that was wise, but what a crock it felt like right now. He was headed to be with an injured boy in the hospital. Was that young man going to die? How was Andrew holding up? And with that bully Buck to deal with. She could call him right now, but he was busy with that boy and his family. He didn't need an interruption from her now, and what would she say anyway? Hearing his voice would probably just add to the pain.

She stood and paced some more, then leaned against a wall and hammered it softly with a fist. Yes, she'd only known Andrew for a week. She shouldn't be feeling this way. She was a grown woman, for God's sakes. She should have relationships, like other people do, enjoy herself, then move on. Maybe that was her problem. She couldn't move on.

She closed her eyes. What were those words? *...when my head is bowed in sorrow, Lord, I want Jesus to walk with me*. She shook her head in disbelief—she'd sung those words in front of a hundred people. Even in her despair she had to smile. With her eyes still closed, she sang the words again. Then she spoke them aloud, "When my head is bowed in sorrow, Lord, I want Jesus to walk with me." She was quiet a moment, then added, "Amen."

Her phone rang, causing her to jump.

"Shelby," her cousin Sedona squealed.

"Sedona," Shelby bellowed, pulling herself together and faking an upbeat voice.

Sedona was talking a mile a minute. "Oh, hell, I can't believe I missed you. All my fault ... haven't been checking my media for a while … I'm so sorry … Are you still in the area? Can we get together?"

"It's okay. I'm back home now. Yeah, sorry we didn't connect." Shelby was glad to hear from Sedona, but she certainly wasn't ready for a big conversation right now. "Where are you?"

"I've moved. Well, sorta moved. I'm with Bryce in Aspen. He's got the coolest place."

"Aspen? Like in the famous ski resort?"

"Yeah. Best place there is. We're having a blast."

"What about your job?"

"I can work from home now."

"And Bryce?"

"Yeah, he's a coworker. We hooked up one night after work, and we're still together. Day to day. Live in the moment and all that BS. We'll see where it goes."

Shelby didn't need the image of Sedona and Bryce padding around their condo in their plushy bathrobes, after sex and the hot tub, sipping brandies, as they checked out the high mountains from a floor-to-ceiling window. She had to laugh. Truth was, all that fancy crap held little appeal right now. She'd rather be in the back of Andrew's pickup, on the edge of the muddy parking area at Refugio. "That's great, Sedona."

"But, hey, enough about me. What about you?"

"Oh, I'm doing … actually, I'm doing shitty." It felt good to confess this out loud. "I've lost my job. My car's broken down a thousand miles from here. And I just lost a guy I think I was … falling in love with." *Oh, crap, did I just say that?*

Sedona was silent for a moment. "Wow," she said softly. Then she was quiet for another beat. "You were falling in love? Really?"

"'Fraid so."

Shelby heard a great sigh, then silence from the other end. Then Sedona said, "Just between us girls, I don't really believe in love anymore."

"Oh?"

"Love makes you do things that can wreck everything else."

"Maybe so." It sure was feeling like things were wrecked. She looked up at the low ceiling and shook her head—there was a crack with water seepage that she hadn't noticed before. Maybe things were wrecked. But maybe *she* wasn't wrecked. Maybe what she had experienced wasn't wrecking anything that didn't need wrecking. Images danced through her mind. Lupe, who'd lost everything, saying how happy she was, then asking Shelby if she loved God. A volunteer, giving of his time to help others, bleeding out on a muddy floor. An 83-year-old priest still having the faith to help his people have hope. And Andrew struggling for meaning, fighting his way, injured, down a mountainside. She couldn't picture Andrew in a plushy robe with a brandy snifter. "But maybe the things that get wrecked sometimes needed wrecking."

"Huh?"

"I'm sorry, Sedona, I don't mean to disagree. What you're doing is great. It's just—"

"It's all bullshit."

Shelby stiffened. Was Sedona talking about *her*? She cleared her throat to prepare for what she might say next, but Sedona continued.

"My life. It's all bullshit. Truth is, Bryce is my boss and his wandering eye is legendary. I'm walking on freaking eggshells around here, sucking my belly in, worrying about my breath—I'm barely holding it together. God, Shelby, you've always been my confessor. The one who keeps me honest. The one who sets me straight."

"I'm not so sure, Sedona. I'm barely keeping myself straight."

"What should I do, Shelby?"

"The way you just told me all those things, Sedona—I'd say you know what to do."

"Lord, I wish we had gotten together."

"Me, too. Maybe it's easier to go straight when you're holding hands."

Chapter 55

At noon, The Quartermaster was bustling. After a solitary morning of putzing in the garden and finally making a dent in *Nobody's Fool*, it felt good to settle in at their usual booth. Tisha got there a few minutes later, straight from work. She wore her blue-gray post office blouse over black pants.

"You look tired, Tisha."

"Thanks, Shelby. You could've said, you look gorgeous, Tisha, but, no, you had to say, you look tired."

"I really didn't mean—"

"Oh, shut up, girl, I'm playing with you. Fact is, I *am* tired. Didn't sleep well, but at least I've got the afternoon off."

"Why couldn't you sleep? Because of **Derek**?"

Tisha rolled her eyes.

"What are you gonna do about that proposal?"

"I'm going to say no. Enough said, okay?"

"You're going to say no? Okay, when you're ready to talk …"

Tisha laid a hand on Shelby's. "Don't mean to be grumpy. Just trying to sort things out."

Shelby laid another hand atop Tisha's. "It's okay. I know about trying to sort things out."

Their iced teas arrived. Shelby took a sip and said, "I look at your uni, and it feels weird to be here and not working at the post office."

"Well, it's also kind of weird *working at* the post office right now."

"Rudy still out?"

"Yeah. Like I said, the asshole's undoubtedly working up a big lawsuit. I'm now thinking he won't bother you—you don't have any money. He'll go after the government for not providing a safe workplace."

Shelby shook her head. "Lord, I wish I hadn't hit him."

"Of course you should have hit that jerk. Anyway, like I said, Seymour's acting strange, too. I say, enjoy your time off. Something good may still come out of this." She raised her iced tea, as if toasting the idea that the future may not be so gloomy after all.

They didn't order their usual lunch salads and got the Whaler Burgers instead. When you're dealing with a load of stuff, you need more than a salad. At least, they didn't get fries. As she handed her menu back to the waitress, Shelby wondered how things were going at the food truck today. Were Lupe and Fr. Ruiz missing them?

Tisha leaned forward. "So, you were pretty quiet in the car last night."

Shelby took a sip of tea, set the glass down, folded her hands in front of her, then began to tell Tisha everything. It was a long story that didn't reach a stopping point until they'd polished off the Whaler Burgers. Shelby wrinkled her mouth in displeasure when the story was finished. Good God, it was tinged with so much self-pity.

"Okay, I'm gonna get all learned on you here," Tisha said with a soft laugh. "Remember Macbeth? I think I read it in high school. Hell, I can't remember anything about high school, but I do remember this. Macbeth saying that life is like a tale told by an idiot, full of sound and fury, signifying nothing."

"I remember that. Thanks a lot, Tisha, that's really uplifting for me right now."

"No, seriously. It's about how life should be more than just surviving. I mean, what gives life meaning? Acquiring material goods? A nice house? Money? Vacations?"

Shelby rubbed a rivulet of condensation from her cold iced-tea glass, remembering her conversation with Sedona last night. "Sure. Easy to say."

"Here's what I want, Shelby. I want more than good times, a cool car, and all that. I want to see the warmth in the eyes of someone whose life has been made better because of knowing me. I want to see tears turned into laughter. I want to see hatred turned into forgiveness. I want to see peace in someone's heart, because I want to see peace in my own heart. I need to give love, because I need to be loved."

"Did you hear that in church? Sounds like a sermon."

"A pretty good sermon, though, you've got to admit."

"I admit."

"Yeah, I did hear some of that in church. But I remember it because it's true."

"Is that why you're saying no?"

Tisha gave out a sigh that said she'd rather not talk about it, but she would. "Yeah, maybe. Look, Derek's a great guy. You know that. And I'm tempted to say yes, but ..." She stopped.

"He sounds wonderful," Shelby said.

"He is. I know that in my head."

"So, what's holding you back?"

"Just this much." Tisha touched fingers to her forehead, then her chest.

"Huh?"

"The distance between your head and your heart."

Shelby took another sip of tea, as she considered this. "Yeah, but maybe my problem with Andrew is that it's all in my heart."

"I tell you, Shelby, that is rare. People say don't trust your heart. Usually your parents. I say the head can conjure up all kinds of crazy justifications. But the heart doesn't lie."

All Shelby could do was nod slowly, as she pondered Tisha's words.

"And, all those things I told you that I want. Well, they have everything to do with you, too."

"It just seems like I always screw up."

"Hmm, let's analyze that." Tisha rested her chin on her palm like she was in deep thought. "So, you lost your job because you had the courage to stand up to a predator. You broke down out in the middle of nowhere, because you had charged off trying to help someone you hardly knew. You picked up this Andrew dude because he was hurt, and the Shelby I know can't pass by anyone who is hurting. So, maybe you want to call those things screw ups."

"Okay, Tisha, I hear you. You're always too generous with me. Still, look where I've wound up. I don't know what to do next."

Cocking her ear toward the country music playing in the background, Tisha said, "Well, maybe we should start by just sitting back and listening to Chris Stapleton sing us a love song. Then, after that, I've got an even better idea."

An hour later, they were at Target in Green Bay, wandering through the aisles, checking out clothes and talking about life.

Tisha already had several items in the cart, but Shelby had selected nothing. Finally, Shelby held up a blouse. "What do you think about this one?"

"Ooh, I like it. The cool babe at the beachfront cafe." Tisha tugged at the blouse a bit, checking the fit. "Yeah. I say get it."

Shelby grimaced when she saw the price tag. "Ouch. Thirty-eight bucks. Like I'm almost broke. Better wait until this one goes on sale." She returned the blouse to the rack.

"Oh, come on, Shelby, don't wait for the sale. It may be gone by then. If you want it, I say, pounce on it now."

Shelby left with nothing. In the parking lot, she stopped and turned toward Tisha. With her hands on her hips, she asked, "So, how do you know if it's lust or if it's desperation or if it's love?"

Tisha shrugged her shoulders. "You think I'm some freakin' guru? That's the question for the ages, doncha think? What is your heart telling you?"

Shelby didn't have words. The best she could do was give Tisha a helpless look.

Tisha gave her shoulder a gentle punch. "It's like I said about that blouse you missed out on."

"Huh?"

"If you want it, you'd better pounce on it now."

Chapter 56

Hanging out with Tisha always made Shelby feel better. The one thing she hadn't talked to Tisha about was the God thing. Tisha was such a devout Christian, she would have enthusiastically been all over that. At some point, maybe even soon, she would tell Tisha about her conversation in the truck with Andrew, about Lupe's question about loving God, and singing that song of faith in front of so many people. But she needed more time to ponder these things.

Tisha dropped her at home around seven—they were both really tired. As she entered her house, she tossed her wallet on the dining room table, and the ski pass from Pajarito Mountain slid out across the table. Shelby picked it up and looked at the photo closely. Why would Allen Riley have purposely used Victor Marshak's name? Olivia had wondered if Allen Riley might have tried to steal her brother's identity. This didn't feel right to Shelby. As she studied the photo again, she noted that this man, Allen Riley or whoever that was in the photo, looked happy.

She remembered another detail. At the house, she had found a Kindle charging cord next to Riley's bed. The Kindle was missing. It's unlikely you'd take your Kindle with you, if you've been the victim of foul play or if you were hastily fleeing a terrorist or the cops.

Wheels turned in Shelby's mind. Those detective chief inspectors in the British TV mysteries always had a moment when the light came on. That moment when some seemingly inconsequential event or fact suddenly made everything click, and the genius of DCI Vera or Barnaby came to the surface. They would stare off into space, as the new insight that would solve the case sank in. Those around them didn't understand what was happening, but the viewers knew—this was the moment the detective had figured it out. For Inspector Sims, this was that moment.

She pulled out her phone and scanned through the online Yellow Pages for nurseries in Los Alamos, New Mexico. There was one. She dialed the number. It was six p.m. in New Mexico. Maybe it was still open. *Yes.* A voice answered the phone. "Sorry, we've just closed. We'll be open tomor—"

"Please wait. I'm trying to find one of your employees, who helped me awhile back. Allen Riley. I hoped you could have him contact me."

"Sorry miss, no one with that name has ever worked here. I've been here ten years. I'd know."

Shelby used Google to search for other garden centers in the region. She found one, Morninglight Gardens, in Santa Fe, about forty miles from Los Alamos. She dialed the number, hoping someone would pick up. "Morninglight," a woman said. *Yes.*

She used the same spiel. "I'm trying to find an employee at your nursery, who helped me awhile back. Name is Allen Riley. I hoped you could have him contact me."

"Sorry, my dear," the woman said. She'd struck out again. Then the woman added, "Allen hasn't worked here for months. In fact, I don't even know how to reach him."

Shelby paced in tight circles in her dining room, the adrenalin pumping. *So, in fact, there is a Victor Marshak and there is an Allen Riley, both from New Mexico.*

There was still more work to do. She hit the number for Tisha.

"Shelby, I thought we agreed we were calling it a night."

"How soon can you get over here, Tisha?"

"What? I'm in my jammies."

"Well, get your clothes back on. We've got to go back to Drury Lake Road."

"I should have my head examined for this," protested Tisha, as they headed toward Drury Lake Road. "I thought you had given up on this quest. No, wait a minute, it's not a quest, it's sheer lunacy. If you weren't my best friend, no way would I be out here tonight."

"I'll explain it all later." Shelby checked the pocket of her light jacket and slid her fingers around the tactical flashlight.

Tisha killed the lights, as Shelby directed, a quarter mile from 113. They slid quietly into the driveway.

"Close your door softly," said Shelby, as they got out.

"You're creeping me out," whispered Tisha.

"We'll go inside first."

"I sure hope we get separate cells. I don't want to spend the rest of my life in the same cell with a maniac."

"Shh. Just keep quiet."

Shelby knocked on the door. No answer. The door was still unlocked. Before she pushed it open, she looked around her. Quiet and dark. She studied the window over at 111, where she'd seen the light last time. Of course, that had been Azcue. But she was going to be careful.

Shelby switched on the flashlight, pulled on a pair of latex gloves and handed Tisha a pair, as they entered. "You really went in here, Shelby? This place makes my skin crawl."

Shelby didn't answer. She probed the interior with her flashlight. Everything looked the same as before. She looked again in all the drawers and cabinets. Nothing new.

"What the hell are we looking for, Shelby?"

Shelby had stopped to examine the wall calendar mounted to the side of the fridge. She again studied the latest weekly Tuesday entries for the library lectures: gardening-12, sculpture-12, history-12, Art. She stepped back, rubbed her neck with an index finger, thinking it through. Was it significant that "Art" was the only entry capitalized? And had no "-12," indicating the time of the event, like the other entries? Also, "Art" was the final entry, the day before Mr. Riley stopped picking up his mail. Wouldn't he have listed the future library lectures on the calendar, too, unless he knew he wasn't going to be around? "Shine this on the calendar," she said, handing the flashlight to Tisha. She pulled out her phone and took a photo of the entries.

As Tisha handed the flashlight back to Shelby, she said, "I suppose you checked the trash bins."

"Yes. Nothing there."

"Well, except for this, which was in the trash can under the sink." She held up a slip of paper, apparently a sales receipt. "Maybe nothing, huh?"

Shelby and Tisha studied the receipt closely, then Shelby laid a hand on Tisha's shoulder. "You are freaking amazing."

It was all beginning to fit together now. The receipt that Tisha had found cinched her conclusion. It was from Scheels, which Shelby knew was a high-end sporting goods store about an hour away in Appleton, and it was for an Arc'teryx jacket, which cost a bundle, $600.

"Damn," said Tisha, "six-hundred bucks for a jacket. Guessing you won't find that at Target. Dude's got some elite tastes."

The coat was purchased three days before Mr. Riley disappeared. The most interesting detail listed on the receipt was that the size of the jacket was XXL. Mr. Riley was a small man, no more than five-eight. Olivia had told Shelby that her brother was a big guy. Two hundred and fifty pounds, she'd said. There was no doubt: the jacket was a gift for Victor Marshak.

Back outside, they moved to the side window of the garage. Shelby asked, "Can I use your car key for a moment?"

"Huh?"

Shelby jiggled her hand, wiggling her fingers, as if saying I need it now. "We've got one more thing to check out."

Tisha handed her the key, as she shook her head.

Shelby jimmied the window slider with the key, slid the window open, then jumped and pulled herself up into the window opening, as Tisha groaned.

"Just when I think I've seen it all from you, you have to go and pull something like this. You've got lots of skills, Shelby, but I didn't know one of them was cat burglar."

"Just stay there and I'll open the door for you," Shelby said from the darkness inside the garage.

The Wrangler was still there. Shelby didn't need to look inside. She moved to the rear of the vehicle. "I should have checked this before. It was so obvious."

"What?"

"This." Shelby shined the light on the rear license plate.

"Ooh, that's odd," said Tisha. "From New Mexico."

"I already knew about the New Mexico plate, but that's not the most interesting thing." While Shelby had waited for

Tisha to pick her up earlier, she'd done a quick Google search about New Mexico license plates. "Here's the most interesting thing," she said. She illuminated the sticker at the bottom of the plate, which, she had learned, displayed the county in which the vehicle was registered. It read *Los Alamos*.

"I don't see what the big deal is," breathed Tisha. She was getting impatient.

"The big deal is that Allen Riley lived in Santa Fe County and Marshak lived forty miles away in Los Alamos County. This car belongs to Victor Marshak." Her first smile in twenty-four hours formed on her face. A perfect place to hide a car you never wanted found. No one, not even the FBI, would think to look in a garage at 113 Drury Lake Road. No one. Except a nosey mail girl.

"We've learned a lot here tonight, Tisha."

"We have?"

Shelby looked at Tisha and pronounced, "The mystery of Mr. Riley has been solved."

Chapter 57

Andrew

Andrew stood with Buck and Ginger, watching in silence as two orderlies pushed Blake's bed down the hallway toward the OR. They walked slowly back to the waiting room, an air of fear heavy upon the Martins. Andrew stayed nearby them in silence.

After they were seated, Ginger was the first to speak up. "God, I'm so scared."

Buck shook his head slowly. "We already went through a surgery today, and now this. Internal bleeding, for God's sake." He shot Andrew a sad look.

Andrew had to work to keep his voice steady and reassuring. Blake going in for another surgery was shaking him, too. But he wasn't here for himself—he was here for this family. "Dr. Roth is the best there is. I've been around this hospital a long time, and I assure you that she is outstanding." Then he leaned forward. "I remember a couple years ago when Blake was in youth group." Buck and Ginger turned their attention to Andrew, no doubt grateful for any diversion from the panic that threatened to overwhelm them. "We were talking about courage. The question came up about what would be the scariest thing you could imagine. One kid said the scariest thing for him would be to be chased by a wild animal. Another said the scariest thing for her would be a tsunami. Another said the scariest thing would be to sing in front of school without clothes." This got Buck and Ginger to crack smiles in the midst of their fear. "Then it came time for Blake to share." Andrew sat back quiet for a moment to let the dramatic tension build. "Blake said the scariest thing for him would be to see his mom or dad die."

Ginger let out an audible sob. Buck choked back tears. Then Andrew continued. "Blake's the only kid who said that. But what he said next was the most amazing. He said that his parents had always brought him to church and that he had learned that even if they died, God would be with them."

Buck's mouth fell open, but he didn't speak. Ginger's chest heaved with another sob, but she was able to get out the words, "Blake said that?"

"Yes."

"That is so beautiful," she said.

"He was trusting you to God." He had their full attention now. "And I'm sure that Blake would want you to trust him to God, too."

Buck and Ginger nodded slowly, but didn't speak.

"Might I read a prayer from our Prayer Book?"

"Oh, yes," said Ginger.

He opened *The Book of Common Prayer* and read: "O God, the strength of the weak and the comfort of sufferers: Mercifully accept our prayers, and grant to your servant Blake the help of your power, that his sickness may be turned into health, and our sorrow into joy; through Jesus Christ our Lord. Amen."

Buck cleared his throat, apparently fighting off a sob, and said, "I don't understand why God would take our son."

"There are a lot of things I don't understand, Buck. But I do know this. God loves Blake. And God loves you. Right now, I believe that God is in that operating room, standing side by side with the doctor and the nurses. And God is watching, guiding, inspiring. This I know."

"What can we do?" asked Ginger.

"We can trust that God is holding Blake right now. And we pray." Then he added, "And you are doing that very well, I might add. Blake is very blessed, and he would be very proud of you both."

Now they sat in silence. Nurse Grace Mendez came in with a coffee pot and a stack of Styrofoam cups. "Haven't heard anything yet," she said. "Thought you all might want some java. It's hot. That's about all I can say about it." She set the cups and coffee pot on a small table beside the sofa.

Buck poured himself a cup. Ginger said to Andrew, "I'm glad you're here."

They were silent now, as they settled into a period of waiting. Every fifteen minutes or so, Andrew would open either the Prayer Book or the bible and read a short passage, loud enough that Buck and Ginger could hear it, but not so loud as to be intrusive. His purpose was to provide a peaceful and prayerful but not invasive presence to remind them that God had not abandoned them. Yet, he kept an eye on Buck and Ginger, as they coped with this time. Nervously turning pages in worn magazines. Absent-mindedly staring at the small TV mounted in the corner, as the overnight news host on CNN talked about oil prices. Drinking too much of that wretched coffee. Frequently checking their watches to see how much time had elapsed since Blake went in. Pacing. Trying unsuccessfully to nap.

Just a few nights ago, when Andrew was facing death himself on that terrifying mountainside, Jesus had said to him, *Do not be afraid.* How could he help these people to not be afraid? He didn't have words to teach them. But he could pray. And he could sit with them as they struggled with their fear.

Andrew had seen Buck Martin full of swagger, seeming to enjoy the sound of his own voice, as he lectured the other vestry members on applying a business model to the church. Andrew had so often been the object of Buck's scorn. So often treated as if he didn't grasp the real world.

But this was the real world, where we are ultimately helpless without God. Where we are on an unwavering trajectory toward death from the moment we are born. These are not realities to lament. They are realities that should sober us to realize that the truly important things are not financial bottom lines, or exercising power or getting your way. The important things are having a son who is not going to die prematurely. The important things are all about love.

Andrew continued to pray silently for Blake. He also prayed for Ginger, that she would be comforted. And he prayed for Buck. That this time, as frightening and desperate as it was, would be a time when this hard in-your-face reality would guide Buck to see what is true and pure and sacred in this fragile life. An image swept through his mind: Shelby, kneeled over the injured man in Tomas and Lupe's house, doing the gritty work of saving a life, her hand pressed down upon his hemorrhaging leg, blood splattered on her face. That was reality. That was love.

A line from Scripture came to him, where St. Paul says, *It is no longer I who live but Christ who lives within me.* The old self emptied out—dead. That old self of fear, pride and self-centeredness replaced with the life essence of forgiveness, gentleness and love. That's what he hoped for Buck. What he hoped for himself. What he hoped for everyone.

At midnight, Dr. Roth came into the waiting room and sat down. Everyone leaned forward anxiously to hear her report. "First, Blake's doing okay," she said, "but he's not out of the woods. We have completed the thoracotomy, and it went very well. We found the bleeding—we had pretty good idea of where to look, given the direction of the traumatic impact to his body—and we patched things back together. The bleeding is now under control."

Everyone let out a cathartic sigh.

Dr. Roth continued. "He'll be back in ICU soon, but I'd rather he didn't have any visitors quite yet. Grace will come and let you know when you can see him. We've got to wait and watch for a while. Any questions?"

Buck and Ginger exchanged looks, then shook their heads.

Dr. Roth stood, rested a hand on Andrew's shoulder and said, "Keep those prayers coming, Father. We need them."

They waited another two hours before they were able to see Blake. Dr. Roth was waiting for them in the room. "Come say hello to your son. I think he's going to be okay. But we need to keep the visit brief."

Blake was now conscious. He blinked his eyes in recognition, and a smile formed on his face. Andrew stood at the rear of the small room, while Blake was greeted by his mom and dad.

Minutes later, outside Blake's room, the atmosphere was euphoric, even though it was two in the morning. Ginger almost squealed, "Our boy is going to live. Oh, God, thank you."

Andrew stood silent, letting them enjoy this time of celebration. Then Buck turned to him. "You really helped us get through this. I need to say thank you … Father Andrew."

Chapter 58

Shelby

Shelby stood on the small back porch of her home, tapping Olivia Marshak's number into her phone. It was six a.m. in Refugio, before the day's work began, so maybe Olivia would pick up. She'd be busy this morning, but she would want to hear what Shelby had to say. Olivia would not want any delay in learning about what happened to her brother.

"Hello?" Olivia answered with apprehension.

"Olivia, it's Shelby."

"Oh, good. You made it home okay, I trust. And that young man in the hospital. Is he going to be alright?"

Shelby shuffled her feet. "I haven't heard yet," she said. "But I'm calling about Victor."

"Wait a bit. I'm in a group. Let me get someplace where we can talk." A moment later, she said, "What about Victor?"

"I think I know what happened to him." She sensed Olivia stiffening. "I'm convinced he's okay."

"Tell me everything, Shelby."

"Just a couple of questions first. Do you remember what kind of car Victor drove?"

"Uh … he's had various cars over the years. I think his last one was some kind of SUV."

"Was it black?"

"Yes, it was black."

"It was a Jeep Wrangler. And it's in the garage at that house in Wisconsin. I guess Azcue didn't notice the car when he was there?"

"He said the garage was locked, and he couldn't get it open without damaging the lock."

"I went in through the window."

Shelby could hear Olivia's nervous chuckle. "Azcue is a gifted man, but he may not be the best detective in the world."

"Another question, Olivia, if you don't mind. What was Victor's middle name?"

"What's that got to do with—it's Arthur, after our father."

"Did anyone ever call him by that name?"

"I only called him Victor, but I think some of his friends called him Art. Shelby, this isn't making any sense to me."

"It will when I'm finished. You said Victor was never married. That physics was his lover. Do you know if he was gay?"

Olivia was silent for a moment. "I honestly don't know. Perhaps. He never had a girlfriend, at least not in recent years. What are you getting at, Shelby?"

"Here's what I am convinced happened, Olivia."

Shelby could hear Olivia's anxious breathing.

"There never was any national security crisis that Victor got caught up in, no terrorist or enemy agents tracking him. No wonder the FBI had no leads. Victor left Los Alamos on his own, driving east in that Jeep Wrangler to meet up with Allen Riley in Wisconsin. Maybe he was tired and needed a break from the intensity of working on sensitive national security issues. Maybe his love had turned to purple petunias and the man who grew them. Maybe he was weary of quantum entanglement and longed for some human entanglement."

"So, you think Victor went east to meet a lover?"

"Yes. Either they are lovers or very close friends. In any case, your brother had met Allen Riley in Santa Fe, where Mr. Riley worked at a plant nursery. That's where he got the petunias. Allen Riley left Santa Fe several months ago, and moved into a cottage in rural Wisconsin. That's where I met him. And you need to know that Mr. Riley is very nice man."

"Oh, my Lord, so they rendezvoused at that cottage?"

"I'm convinced of that. I suspect they planned it all out. Allen Riley would leave town a few months before, leaving no discernible trail, so his and Victor's disappearances would not seem connected. I don't know why he picked rural Wisconsin—maybe Mr. Riley had a relative up here or maybe this place was just a good off-the-grid location."

"And Victor told no one?"

"I suspect he told no one because he was involved in the national security work. He may have feared that they would not allow him to leave easily. Anyway, Victor came east to meet Allen Riley. Victor's Wrangler is now parked in Allen Riley's garage here in Wisconsin. Mr. Riley even had the arrival of Victor, who he called Art, on his calendar, so he'd been looking forward to seeing him. And he'd purchased an expensive gift for Victor three days before."

"What about that strange ski pass?"

"That and the purple petunias were what helped me figure out what happened. It's not about identity theft at all. I believe that Victor and Allen went together to get their photos taken for their ski passes. This wasn't some official government ID like a driver's license, so when Victor's name was called for the photo, Allen stepped in. When Allen's name was called, Victor stepped in. They were like silly school kids, probably laughing as they did this. I noticed last night how happy Allen looked in that ski-pass photo. The photo-switch allowed them to have a photo of each other that they could carry with them. A little like high-school sweethearts exchanging class rings to wear around their necks. Maybe we never get too old to be romantic high school kids."

"That sounds believable, Shelby. I just wish he would call me."

"I suspect he will, Olivia."

"Are they there now in Wisconsin at this house?"

"No. They've left in Allen Riley's car. It made sense to leave Victor's car there, where no one would find it. I don't know where they went. Maybe they're up north fishing, or maybe they've gone to Europe."

"What should we do now?"

"It's up to you, Olivia. He's your brother. I've told you everything I know. You could inform the FBI. Or have the VIN on the Wrangler checked to prove that it belongs to Victor, but that would involve the authorities. Or, you could just let them go. Let them be free. I'm guessing they are okay and just don't want to be found. Not yet."

There was silence on the other end. "I think you are right. Maybe he needed a fresh start. I understand that. I believe in fresh starts."

Of course, you do, Olivia, Shelby thought. *That's why you've dedicated your life to giving people fresh starts.*

"Thank you, Shelby. I'm not sure I've ever met a person like you."

Shelby began to offer some apologetic just-a-mail-girl crap, then caught herself. "Thank you," she said.

Olivia was silent for a moment, then said, "I hope I get to see you and Andrew again."

"So do I." *So do I.*

After the call, Shelby stayed on her back porch. So, what difference did solving the case of the missing Mr. Riley make? No foul play was involved. No nefarious schemes were uncovered. No criminals were brought to justice. But it mattered to a sister who was worried sick about her brother. It mattered a lot. Shelby gazed out at her small garden. Maybe she would plant some purple petunias.

Then her phone rang. She checked the screen, and her knees went weak. Seymour Johns.

Chapter 59

Andrew

Andrew sat at his usual table at Henry's. Paige had just delivered his Eggs Benedict. He'd decided to treat himself to a big breakfast, after that long night at the hospital. But now that it arrived, he realized he wasn't that hungry. He'd gotten, what? Five hours of sleep? Now, he would set about his sermon preparation for Sunday. Maybe this wasn't a good idea, but what else was he going to do? He'd already checked in with Fr. Morrison, the fill-in priest from North Platte. Turned out that Fr. Morrison had had an awful week, laid up with the flu, and was relieved to hear that Andrew was back in town.

"I was planning to come," said Fr. Morrison. "Been sicker than a dog, though, and, truth to tell, I hadn't really started on the sermon yet."

Andrew had told him not to worry. Stay home and rest. The last thing anybody at St. Tim's needed, anyway, was an infectious priest celebrating the Eucharist.

The Eggs Benedict shared the table with his laptop and three thick bible commentaries. Yes, it was already Friday and he was tired. He usually began his sermon prep on Monday, but he still had a couple of days. If he worked hard, he could generate his usual three-page manuscript, to be preached Sunday morning. Sure, he had experienced a great deal these past two weeks, and he should tap into all those things for his sermon—surviving a near-death fall, talking to Jesus, working in a flooded village. These were all life-changing experiences.

Then, of course, there was Shelby. What was he supposed to do with that? To tap into any of these resources right now when he was so raw just wasn't possible. He had to stay strong, and that meant emotionally sealing off those radical, overwhelming intrusions into his normal, predictable life. No, he would try his best to keep it all at arm's length, at least for this sermon. The people at St. Tim's were accustomed to his prepared remarks—thoughtful, if unexciting. This is what he knew how to do. Take the safe route. He took one bite of the eggs, then set his fork down. He couldn't do this.

A new plan was needed. The Sunday lessons in the Episcopal Church are taken from the Revised Common Lectionary, used by many denominations, which appoints specific Scripture readings for each Sunday. It runs on a three-year cycle, so the same readings recur every three years. Andrew had prepared sermons on the texts for this Sunday three years ago and six years ago. He opened a folder on his computer desktop labeled "Old Sermons." He never recycled his sermons—that is, reuse an old sermon; that is frowned upon by serious preachers. Preaching should be fresh, relate to the current life of the parish. But his brain was anything but fresh, and it was already Friday. He scrolled through the sermon files in the folder until he found the sermon he'd preached six years ago—the one from three years ago could possibly be remembered by someone. He scanned the three-page document. He would update it a bit, maybe add a new illustration, but, basically, this would be good enough.

He closed his laptop, pushed the stack of commentaries to the far edge of the table and tried to enjoy the Eggs Benedict. But then he pushed his plate away, also, and looked out the window to watch the slow flow of life on the main street of High Plains.

What was it she had said? He could remember her exact words, like they were engraved on his tombstone. "Let's cut our losses before this thing has gone too far."

This thing had already gone too far for him. Maybe he should contact her. He could do it right now. But what would he say? Maybe under the guise of just letting her know how Blake Martin was doing? That would be pretty transparent. What new plan did he have to offer her? Cut our losses. His losses weren't the only thing that felt cut.

Chapter 60

Shelby

It felt weird walking into the post office on Friday afternoon, not wearing her official USPS attire. She waved at Tisha, busy at the front counter. She'd called Tisha this morning about the meeting Seymour Johns had asked her to attend. Fortunately, she picked up, even though she was working at the front counter.

"Shelby, what is it?" she had said in an urgent whisper. "You know I'm working and not supposed to be on the phone."

"I just got a call from Mr. Johns."

"Oh, crap. What did he say?"

"He wants to meet with me at two today. In his office."

"Excuse me, sir, I'll be right with you," she said in her normal business voice, then returned to the whisper. "Did he say what for?"

"He didn't say."

"Damn. Do you need me in there with you?"

"No, I just wanted you to know."

"Lord, Shelby, I wish you'd gotten a lawyer. So, don't say anything, okay? Don't admit anything. He'll probably have some legal wingnut in there with him, might be taping the whole thing. Okay?" She raised the level of her voice: "Yes, sir, I know. It's an emergency. I'll be right with you." The whisper returned. "I've got to go, Shelby. I'll be praying."

"Me, too," she said to herself.

Seymour Johns' office was down the hall, and this meant she might run into other employees. She didn't want to see

Liz, and she was uncertain what she would do if Rudy appeared. She kept her head down and walked fast. Johns' door was closed. She checked her watch, two p.m. exactly. Shelby breathed a silent prayer and knocked.

"Come in."

Shelby pushed the door open and stepped in. Johns was seated behind his desk, looking down at some papers. No one else was there—no lawyers, no Rudy, no policeman to arrest her. She exhaled a shaky breath.

"Sit down, Shelby," he said without looking up.

Shelby had never met with Mr. Johns when she wasn't wearing her official postal-service uniform. Today, she'd worked to find something that was tasteful, conservative, and very gender neutral. She took the chair on the opposite side of the desk from Johns, kept her legs uncrossed, and folded her hands in her lap like a dutiful student.

Johns continued to pore over his paperwork for a minute or so. Tisha had said Seymour was acting strange lately. What in hell was she about to encounter?

"So, Shelby," he finally said, as he looked up, avoiding eye contact. "Your vacation is about to end."

"A few more days, Mr. Johns."

"So, here's the situation. What you did in hitting another employee was completely out of line."

She wasn't going to agree with this statement. She stayed silent, kept her eyes on him, tried her best to look unflappable.

"A lot has gone on since you left," he said, blowing out a big breath with these words.

For God's sake, Mr. Johns, just say what you need to say.

"And, so as a result, I'm prepared to hire you back as a regular USPS employee, full time with benefits."

"What?" Shelby almost fell off her chair.

"And since Rudy will be taking a new position, I'd like you to take the more senior position he previously had at the post office."

A new position? Her stomach churned at the thought of that asshole getting promoted. All she said was, "I see."

"And of course, in accord with Federal wage guidelines, you will be in line for a pay increase."

This was sounding better. She was still shaking, and she was aware of sweat on her forehead and dampness under her arms. "When will this start, Mr. Johns?"

"Monday. We can talk more about your new compensation details then and about your additional responsibilities." Johns stood, signifying the meeting was over.

Shelby stood, too. She could have said "Thank You" or "See you Monday" or even "Have a Nice Weekend," but instead she just nodded and left.

Oh, my God, I have my job back! Even better, a new job with benefits. She leaned against the wall outside Johns' office and let this sink in. He hadn't said anything about Rudy's charges of physical assault or her grievance, and she hadn't been able to ask. She thought about going back in and turned toward his door, then decided to let it go.

Shelby turned toward the front entrance of the post office and almost knocked Liz over. "Oh, excuse me, Liz. It's good to see you," she lied.

She started to step around Liz, but Liz said, "Can we talk?"

"Uh, sure." What she didn't need was an update on Liz's retirement plans in Florida.

Liz led the way into an unoccupied work room, then closed the door. "I'm so glad to see you, Shelby."

"I'm glad to see you, too." Hadn't she already said this?

"What you did has had a big impact on me." Liz looked hard into Shelby's eyes.

"Oh?"

"When you hit Rudy, it shocked me at first, but then it woke me up."

"What do you mean?"

"Three years ago, just before you came, Rudy assaulted me."

"Oh, my Lord, Liz. I'm so sorry."

"I never spoke up. He told me that no one would believe me over him. And I suppose he was right. So, I never said anything."

Shelby's mouth had dropped open, but no words came out.

"I had been so scared of him. The only way I could survive was to think about retirement, about being somewhere far away from here. But then I saw your courage, and it inspired me. Even at this late date, I had to say something. I'm so sorry I didn't speak up that day when you were placed on leave, Shelby, but I just couldn't yet. It took time, but I got my courage up."

"What happened?"

"I got a lawyer, and she and I went in to see Mr. Johns."

"Good for you, Liz."

"We told him what had happened, that Rudy was a predator who had now assaulted two female employees. And that it would no longer be tolerated."

"Oh, my gosh."

"As you know, Mr. Johns is hardly a decision maker, so he squirmed, said he didn't know what to do."

"Isn't that just like him?"

"Then my lawyer reminded him that any charges against Rudy would likely include him, for shielding a known predator—with two witnesses ready to testify."

"I wish I could have seen that."

Liz produced one of her rare smiles. "Yeah, it was pretty great."

"So, what happened to Rudy?"

"The lawyer really scared Mr. Johns into doing the right thing. He called me in last Monday and told me that Rudy had been terminated."

So, Rudy's new position that Mr. Johns mentioned would be in the unemployment line.

Shelby enveloped Liz in a hug and felt her weeping against her shoulder.

Chapter 61

Andrew

Andrew followed the same schedule every Sunday morning, and today was no different. He rose at six—he had set an alarm the night before, but awoke as always before the alarm sounded. He always skipped breakfast, but carried his first cup of strong French Roast into his study, where he'd go over his sermon. Usually, he'd make last-minute changes to the manuscript, but today he didn't have the initiative to mess with the recycled sermon from six years ago. Reading it over this morning left him uninspired. If he was uninspired, how was the congregation going to react to it? He leaned back in his office chair and yawned. He remembered an old joke he'd heard in seminary: the first rule of preaching is to never yawn during your own sermon. This provided him with a much-needed chuckle.

He walked across the small parking lot to the church an hour before the service was scheduled to begin. This was a time when he could be there by himself. He walked around the sanctuary, then sat in an empty pew for a while, gazing up at the stained glass and praying. He rarely got to sit in the pews. Then he made sure doors were unlocked and that windows were opened. The church had no air conditioning, and now, in mid-June, it would be uncomfortably warm inside by the time the service was over.

He placed the typed sermon manuscript on the pulpit and arranged it in his customary way, so he could read it while maintaining at least some eye contact with the people. He went through the sermon one more time. He was now feeling qualms about using an old sermon. What if someone remembered it?

By now, the altar guild members were beginning to show up. They had a lot of work to do. Check the altar linens. Check the levels in the liquid-wax candles on the altar. Prepare the Eucharistic vessels. Assure that appropriate quantities of wine and bread were readied. Lay out the priest's vestments. Mark the various books from which the liturgy and the lessons would be read. Andrew had great respect for this team of people, mostly women, who worked so hard behind the scenes, rarely receiving or expecting much acknowledgement for their important work.

A bit later, the organist arrived, and Andrew went over the music with him. He was 87 years old and predated Andrew at St. Tim's by many years. He was hardly the world's greatest musician—though word was that he had been quite a notable musician in his youth—but he was loved by everyone, and that's what mattered most. St. Tim's had no choir. There had been an excellent choir—Andrew had been told—back in the seventies, when the church was bustling, but now, with only forty or so in the pews on Sunday, the idea of a choir only came up as a wistful comment on rare occasions.

Then Andrew verified that the bulletins were in place at the two entrances to the sanctuary. He checked the bulletin to see who would be serving as acolytes, chalice bearers, lay readers, ushers.

Twenty minutes before the service began, Andrew put on his vestments, starting with a white cassock alb, fastened by a rope cincture around his waist. Over that was a priest's stole— he would wear his green stole today, for the Season after Pentecost. Then he pulled the chasuble, the vestment symbolic of the Holy Eucharist, over his head and let it drop down over his shoulders. A Sunday did not pass, when this act did not remind him of his ordination, when the chasuble is first placed on the new priest.

Fifteen minutes before the service began, Andrew gathered the altar party—the acolytes and chalice bearer—with him in the sacristy for a prayer. He always used the same prayer he'd memorized from the Prayer Book. As he recited the prayer today, an image of Shelby fluttered through his mind, and he was tempted to forgo the rote prayer in favor of something spontaneous. But he didn't.

Ten minutes before the service began, Andrew stood beside the massive entrance doors at the rear of the church to greet parishioners as they arrived.

Precisely at ten, an acolyte pulled on the heavy rope connected to the bell up in the bell tower. It rang three times, once for each member of the Holy Trinity. Then the organist began the opening hymn, and the procession—an acolyte carrying a tall cross, followed by the chalice bearer, then Andrew—made its way toward the front, as the congregation sang.

He stood on the steps of the altar and began the liturgy. Some priests, he knew, began the service with an informal greeting, "Good morning, hope you're all doing well. It's wonderful to worship together on such a beautiful day" and so on. Such an opening appealed to Andrew, but at one time such superfluous chit-chat, as he had considered it, seemed too casual for something as solemn as celebrating the Holy Eucharist. He no longer felt that way—and longed, in fact, to be more relaxed and spontaneous—but he continued, nonetheless, to follow the routine he had followed for eight years. "Blessed be God, Father, Son, and Holy Spirit," he read from the Prayer Book. After more prayers and the singing of the Gloria, Andrew took a seat for the lessons to be read.

After the lessons, the organ began the intro for the Gospel hymn. Today it was "I Want to Walk as a Child of the Light." Andrew read a passage from the Gospel of Luke, and it was time for the sermon.

Andrew took his place at the pulpit, said a brief rote prayer, then began to read his sermon, based on a verse from the Old Testament lesson, from the Book of Isaiah. *Fear not, for I have redeemed you, I have called you by name.* He began his sermon with a little background on Isaiah the prophet, about the time in which he lived, and the cultural world of Israel in those days. Then he began to take apart the verse and proceeded to explain what the Hebrew word for fear meant in context of the world at that time. All these observations came from the biblical commentaries he'd studied during the week, in this case, of course, six years ago. He only occasionally glanced up.

He was beginning to assess what the political leaders of the day thought about Isaiah, when he risked one of his glances at the congregation. His heart almost stopped. There, in the back row, sat two women. One was tall, with black hair piled high. The other woman was—oh, dear God—Shelby.

He was unable to continue. He looked to his left, then his right, then looked down. Then he looked back at his manuscript. The 14-point Times Roman double-spaced text seemed blurry, unreadable. His mouth had gone dry. He reached for the glass of water he always kept next to the pulpit and nearly emptied it. He held onto the sides of the pulpit with both hands, afraid he might be about to faint.

He looked to the back of the church again. Maybe this was a vision, like Nicole and Sharon popping up unexpectedly. But no—the two of them were still there.

Suddenly, he knew what he had to do. He stepped to the center of the altar steps and said to the organist, "Would you play that Gospel hymn once more?" Then he said to the congregation, "I'll be right back."

Andrew walked slowly, with as much poise as he could muster, to the door leading into the sacristy, amidst confused looks and a few audible gasps from the congregation. Then he bolted through the exit door at the far end of the sacristy and, hitching up the hem of his cassock alb so he wouldn't trip, sprinted across the parking lot to the rectory.

In less than two minutes, an out-of-breath Andrew returned to the altar area, and stood quietly as the organist completed the last verse of the Gospel hymn.

He walked slowly to the center of the steps, bowed his head for a moment, then spoke. "That lesson today, *Fear not for I have redeemed you, I have called you by name*, talks about fear, and God saying that we need not be afraid because he is faithfully looking out for us. I have been afraid too many times in my life. I can't begin to tell you how many times. So many times that it seems like my whole life has been dominated by fear. Fear of failure. Fear of being exposed as unqualified. Fear of letting you down. Fear of what may happen next. Fear of many things. And I suspect, and in fact I know, you have lived with fear also."

Andrew kept his eyes away from the back row, but looked down instead to the front row, where Buck and Ginger sat, having taken an hour away from their vigil at the hospital. Their eyes were locked on him.

"Let me tell you," he continued, "about a recent experience." He told them, in the same way he had told Shelby and the congregation at Refugio, about his travail on the mountainside, how he thought he was about to die from cold or hunger or an attack from a mountain lion, how he had read the last rites to himself. Then he told them about meeting Jesus in the middle of the night. "I swore I'd never tell anyone about this. Everyone would think I was crazy. But then I told one person." He risked a glance to the back pew. Shelby was still there. "Jesus and I talked for a while, then he said, 'Andrew, do not be afraid.' And the next day, I stumbled out of that dark, terrifying forest into the sunlight and was rescued. I said I would never tell anyone, because of my fear of being laughed at. I am now convinced that Jesus wanted me to tell everyone. That is his message, through me, to you. Do not be afraid. He has redeemed you. He has called you by name. In other words, you need not be afraid, because this Jesus, the almighty loving God, is your friend. And this redeemer and sustainer loves you more than you can imagine."

Then Andrew pulled a chair to the center of the altar steps, sat and picked up the guitar he'd just fetched from the rectory. He strummed a few chords, then began to sing, "When you're down and troubled …"

When he finished "You've Got a Friend," he should have been shaking. What he had just done was so out-of-the-box, had once been scoffed at by Buck Martin and the vestry. He had never played before the congregation. Andrew had not asked the vestry for permission to play today. But he knew now that he had never needed such permission in the first place. Yes, he should have been shaking, but he was not. He looked over at Buck, who was smiling, while wiping away tears with the back of his hand. Ginger had her arm around him.

Andrew should have been shaking, but he was not. Why would he? He had long known it in his head, but today he knew it in his heart. He wasn't shaking because he was clinging to his friend, who took all his fear away.

Chapter 62

Shelby

The four of them sat at a round oak table at Henry's. Andrew was across from Shelby, with Tisha and Maureen on either side of them. It looked like any after-church lunch gathering, but all of them knew this was much more than that.

Shelby still hadn't had a chance to touch him or speak to him privately. When Tisha had gone up to the altar rail for communion, Shelby stayed back. She wasn't certain she was qualified to receive—the bulletin said that communion was for baptized persons. Her parents had never mentioned if she'd been baptized. But there was a greater reason. She just couldn't face Andrew up close, not yet, although she was longing to. She would stay back.

At the door of the church, Andrew had greeted Shelby and Tisha. He had begun to reach out toward Shelby for at least a hug, but then looked sheepishly at the parishioners around them. Maureen came up just then, and they all shared introductions. It had been Maureen's idea to have lunch at the local restaurant.

Shelby studied Andrew in his black clergy shirt, with the white clergy collar. He looked distinguished, like some kind of visiting church dignitary from England. She shook her head, as she tried to juxtapose that image with him, bloodied and covered with mud and pine needles.

Andrew couldn't stop looking at her from across the table, and she loved it. But the polite conversation kept her from saying what she wanted to say. As much as Shelby loved

Tisha and Andrew clearly respected Maureen, it felt like Andrew and she were bashful teenagers on a first date, with their chaperones.

Maureen looked at Andrew. "So, Father, that sabbatical was very short, but clearly you learned something. That sermon was amazing. It's what I always knew you had in you." Now, she gave Shelby a smile like they'd been friends for years. "And, Shelby, it's wonderful to meet you. I suspect you've had something do with what Andrew's learned."

Tisha also turned toward Andrew. "We drove Friday night and all day yesterday to get here. Andrew, I've gotta say, you're just about as cool as this woman said you were." She nodded her approval to Shelby. "I've got to warn you, though, and don't say I didn't tell you, this woman is wild. But from what I saw back at church, you're a little wild, too. So, maybe … just maybe." She ended her comment with a wicked smile.

Andrew nodded, mouth open, at Tisha, "It's good to meet Shelby's best friend, but I'll confess, I'm still in shock." Now, he focused his eyes on Shelby. "The last thing I expected to see today was you. I thought …" He had to stop to clear his throat that was filled with emotion. "I thought I'd never see you again."

Shelby opened her mouth to speak, but just then the waitress came to take their orders. She would never remember what any of them ordered.

Tisha said, "So, Shelby's been a busy girl. Are you gonna tell him everything that's gone on?"

"First, I want to know how that young man is doing." Shelby leaned forward with concern on her face.

"Blake is going to be fine, but it was touch-and-go for a while. He had two surgeries. Everyone is very grateful this morning."

That was good news, and it told her everything she needed to know about how the troublesome Buck had behaved.

Tisha popped in again. "Well, if you're not going to tell him …" She turned toward Andrew. "Shelby, the great detective, solved the mystery of that guy you were searching for."

"Oh my," said Andrew. "How did—"

"And she got her job back. With a pay bump. That assho—" She stopped and looked at Maureen. "That awful person, Rudy, got what was coming to him."

"Well, that's good to hear," Andrew said half-heartedly. He licked his lips, looked down for a moment, then added, "I mean, that's really good news. So, you're all set, I guess."

Shelby leaned forward and said, "Well, there's …"

As Shelby paused, Maureen spoke up. "You've got some news to share, too. Right, Father?"

Andrew finished chewing a bite of food, then said, "So, on Friday morning, a lot of things had become clear to me. I called the Bishop, and I was fortunate to get right through to him. He's a busy guy. Then I called Maureen. I haven't told anyone else yet." He gave her a warm look, almost like a son would look at the mother he adored. "I told them I had decided to resign from my position at St. Timothy's."

"You what?" gasped Shelby. "Is everything okay?"

"It couldn't be better," said Andrew.

Shelby's surprise quickly turned to doubt—*Lord, did I cause him to quit?* "Why would you do that?"

Maureen spoke up. "Andrew's been our rector for eight years. He's been a wonderful priest. I will hate to see him go. But I've been worried about him. He seemed to need a fresh start. He said once that he felt like he had become stagnant. But I don't think that was the case at all. I think his restlessness was because God has something new planned for him." Maureen dabbed her mouth with her napkin and took a sip of water. "But of course," she said with a twinkle in her eye, "there seems to be another reason it was a good time for Father to launch out." She shot Shelby a sweet look that said she didn't need to add any further elaboration.

Tisha said, "Okay, I've been trying to get Shelby to tell you her really big news. Shelby, put your fork down and tell him."

Shelby was still reeling from Andrew's shocking news. But, then, she had some shocking news of her own. She said, "So, yeah, it was great to get my job back and everything. But after I thought about it for a while, it became clear what I wanted."

She savored that memory now. After talking with Liz, she had marched back into Johns' office, didn't even knock this time. Seymour had stood, shocked.

SEYMOUR: Shelby, what are you—?

SHELBY: Just came back to tell you, Mr. Johns, that I don't want to work here anymore. So, I'm handing in my resignation, effect—

SEYMOUR: Now, Shelby, let's not—

SHELBY: —effective immediately.

Later she and Tisha had met at The Quartermaster, no more than an hour before they packed Tisha's car and headed for High Plains. Shelby had expected Tisha to tell her what an idiot she was. After all, she was almost broke, and here she was walking away from a job in which she had been vindicated and got a pay raise and benefits to boot.

But Tisha had surprised her. "So, it would seem like just when you finally had it made, you walk away from it. You were out in the storm, but now you had found your refuge." She had hoisted her Happy Heron—they would only have one, because, even though they hadn't hatched their road trip plan yet, they would be leaving soon—"Here's to my wise friend, who knows that sometimes you must leave your refuge."

Shelby couldn't take her eyes off Andrew. She was quiet for a moment before saying, "Yeah, so I quit, too. And I came. I don't know what will happen here. But I came anyway. I had to come."

Chapter 63

Finally, Maureen said, "So, Tisha, I'd love to show you some of the historic buildings around our beautiful downtown."

"I still have to finish my …" Tisha caught the twinkle in Maureen's eye. "Of course, I'd love to, Maureen." Pushing her chair back from the table, she said, "Shall we go now?"

As they headed for the door, Shelby whispered across the table, "I love Tisha, and I know how you feel about Maureen, but I thought they'd never leave." Then she stood and moved around the table.

Andrew met her halfway. They stood facing each other awkwardly. "So you really quit?" he asked.

"I was just going to ask you the same question." She inched closer to him.

"We're both unemployed." He took a half-step closer to her.

"Having second thoughts?"

"No. My only thoughts are about being here with you right now," he said.

"We're being impractical romantics you know." They were almost touching now.

"I kinda like being a romantic for once," he said.

"Me too," she whispered.

"Maybe someone needs to give us silly kids a good talking to."

"We wouldn't listen anyway, would we?"

"Probably not."

Then she was in his arms. Their kiss was long and passionate. Finally, Shelby pulled away. "Oh, my goodness," she laughed, "the priest is making out rather indiscreetly right here in front of everybody."

Andrew looked around like he was only now aware that other people were there. Quite a few of them were, in fact, gawking at them. Then, looking back at Shelby, he said, "I was away from you for three days, and it almost killed me."

"Me, too." Shelby, who was usually successful at not crying, couldn't hold back the sobs.

"Shelby, I can't wait any longer to say this. I'm totally in love with you."

Shelby thought she was going to melt. But then she stiffened. "There is one more thing, and it's better to think about that now."

"What?" There was an edge of anxiety in his voice.

She pulled back in apprehension. She knew the possibilities of what could happen next. Forcing herself to look directly into his eyes to see his reaction at the moment, she said, "There's a fair chance that I'm pregnant."

He said nothing. *Oh, God, here it comes. Dear Lord, I will be stronger this time. Please help me be stronger.*

Andrew looked down, seemed to be carefully preparing his words. When he looked up at her, he said, "Of course, I know that's possible." He placed his hands on her shoulders, held her at arm's length, and locked into her gaze. "You know, Shelby, there is nothing that would make me happier than to have a baby with you."

She tried to say, "I love you, too." But it came out all blubbery, as she pressed her face against his shoulder. They both shuddered with laughter, and it seemed like he held her forever.

Chapter 64

Four weeks later

I-76 stretched out ahead of them, and late-afternoon shafts of sunlight streaked across the golden grassland. Just appearing on the horizon to the west was a blue wrinkle of landscape, still almost unnoticeable, but growing with each mile. The Rockies. That's where they were headed.

They had left High Plains only this morning, after a wild month.

The Bishop had asked Andrew to stay on at St. Tim's for another four Sundays, giving the parish time to prepare for his departure and to begin the process of finding his successor. Shelby moved into the guest room at Maureen's, but she spent a great deal of time at the rectory.

Back home, Tisha had received quite a surprise. Turned out that Seymour Johns' poor handling of the sexual harassment cases had not gone unnoticed by the higher-ups. Abruptly, Seymour had been transferred to a nonsupervisory position in some small village way up north. Within two weeks, the new postmaster, Tisha Reynolds, was hired.

During that time Shelby and Andrew had also gone through premarital counseling with Fr. Morrison, down in North Platte. And a week before Andrew's final Sunday at St. Tim's, they were married at St. Tim's, with the Bishop presiding. The whole parish was in attendance, and both Shelby's and Andrew's parents made the trip to celebrate with them.

Before the marriage ceremony, there was another ceremony. Two weeks earlier, as Shelby and Andrew were taking an evening stroll around the historic downtown district of High Plains, right there in front of Sam's True Value, she had stopped and turned toward him. "I've been doing a lot of thinking." His eyes searched hers. "And praying, too. I want to be baptized."

Andrew had listened attentively, although she could sense a joy that he was working to conceal. He'd never said anything to her about baptism, and she valued that. He respected her too much to push her. This decision had to come from her. And it did.

Shelby's baptism took place the day before their wedding. Tisha and Maureen were her sponsors. Of course, they both would be part of the marriage ceremony the next day, Tisha serving as Maid of Honor and Maureen as Best Woman.

Shelby had stood in the center of the church, and at the appointed moment, leaned in over the baptismal font, as the Bishop poured water over her head, and said, "Shelby Sims, I baptize you in the Name of the Father, and of the Son, and of the Holy Spirit."

The congregation said an enthusiastic "Amen."

When Shelby raised her head, with water still flowing down her face, she felt a glow like she'd never experienced. She looked immediately at Andrew, who unsuccessfully fought back tears.

Now she leaned back in the hard bench seat of the Tundra, her feet up on the dash. She was pregnant—the home pregnancy test had confirmed that. She wasn't showing yet, but her body certainly was telling her. And the doctor in High Plains had confirmed it and prescribed prenatal vitamins.

"Not sure I want to drive that nine miles in the dark," Andrew said. "Why don't we find a place to camp, then head in tomorrow morning?"

"I'll text Lupe and let her know we won't make it tonight."

"Two mommies-to-be will have a lot to talk about."

"I can't wait to see her."

They hadn't taken much with them. Closing out each of their homes had been a lot of work, but neither of them had much. They gave away pieces of furniture and unneeded clothing and packed what would fit into the back of the Tundra. Shelby had her two duffel bags full of clothes, but this time she had more Levi's, a pair of tough boots, and some warm clothes for camping out. Of course, she brought the Tartan blanket, which, on the colder nights in the back of the Tundra, would go over the mustard-yellow sleeping bags. Andrew had packed clothes into his backpack (which had been found and returned to him) and loaded a separate bag with as many books as he could fit in—Shelby only needed her Kindle; she still hadn't finished *Nobody's Fool*. And, of course, he brought his guitar—he was already talking about the songs he'd sing for those kids in Refugio.

Lord, they felt like a couple of hippies hitting the road.

After Refugio, they would see Olivia in Golden, unless she had gotten a sudden call about a new emergency somewhere. In that case, maybe they would just go with her. Then, they'd finally get to see Sedona, who, Shelby had learned, was back in her condo in Loveland. Last of all, Rocky Mountain National Park. Shelby had already booked their campsites.

"So, what are we going to do with the rest of our lives, Ms. Sims?"

He was still calling her Ms. Sims, even though she was now Shelby Logan. And she never wanted him to stop.

What *were* they going to do with the rest of their lives? Sure, they'd have to find new jobs at some point. Andrew could find a new clergy position, with good recommendations from the Bishop and Maureen, although he'd been talking about hospital chaplaincy. And Shelby could count on an excellent recommendation from the new postmaster. But she had been thinking about nursing school.

She considered this man next to her. This man who had literally walked out of the forest and into her arms. He noticed her stare. "What?" he laughed.

She leaned toward the radio. "Just wanted to know if you want me to find some music."

"As long as it's country," he said.

If you enjoyed Mail Girl, please consider
posting a customer review at Amazon or Goodreads.

Acknowledgements and References

I am very grateful to my editor, Susan DeFreitas, who made major contributions to this book.

Many thanks to Sarah Hameister Schendel for teaching me about the job of a rural mail carrier.

I thank my sister, Patty, a skilled editor, for carefully reading the manuscript several times.

Lupe and Shelby's singing of "I Want Jesus to Walk With Me" (Public Domain) was inspired by Imani-Grace Cooper singing this song at the Washington National Cathedral, April, 2020.

The multi-church efforts at Refugio were inspired and informed by the author's experience during the recovery work in New Orleans, following Hurricane Katrina.

The Myers-Briggs character types mentioned in the book were identified using *Please Understand Me: Character and Temperament Types*, David Keirsey, Marilyn Bates, (Prometheus, 1984). Andrew was indeed an NF type, and Shelby is a mix of ESFJ and ESTJ.

It was risky and perhaps ill-advised for me, a white male, to portray Tisha as an African-American woman. I did so with trepidation, and to the extent I fell short of authenticity, I apologize to the reader. I did not want Tisha to be a stereotype from a shallow rom-com. But I also did not want to avoid having a Black female character just because it was difficult. I'm indebted to many sources for helping me better understand the character of Tisha, especially *Black Dignity in a World Made for Whiteness*, by Austin Channing Brown; *How to be an Antiracist*, by Ibram X. Kendi; and the *Internalized Oppression*

Retreat, sponsored by The Episcopal Church Office of Black Ministries, Christ Episcopal Church, Whitefish Bay, Wisconsin, August, 2020. I believe a part of the healing of our culture lies in trying to understand each other's stories. I still have much to learn, and I am working on it.

Quotations from *The Book of Common Prayer* are taken from the 1979 version.

Quotes from Muir and Leopold are:

Another glorious day ..., from John Muir, *My First Summer in the Sierra* (1911), p. 231.

Oh, these vast, calm ..., from John Muir, *My First Summer in the Sierra* (1911), ch.2.

Climb the Mountains and ..., from John Muir, *The Mountains of California*

Of what avail are forty freedoms ..., from Aldo Leopold, *A Sand County Almanac* (1949), "Chihuahua and Sonora: The Green Lagoons," p. 157-158.

Quotes in the beginning of each part of the book were:

Mary Oliver: from the poem "When Death Comes," from Mary Oliver, *Devotions* (New York: Penguin Press, 2017), p. 285.

Luke Bryan: from "I Believe Most People Are Good," from the album *What Makes You Country*, 2017.

Finally, I thank Mary, my wife, for reading various versions of the manuscript and offering important insights into improving the story. She is my most enthusiastic encourager.

About the Author

Jim Trainor grew up in LA and lived much of his life in the West. He now lives in the upper Midwest with his wife Mary. When he's not writing, they are travelling the country in their campervan and hiking in the wilderness. They have three grown children.

Jim is both a Ph.D. physicist and ordained pastor. He's a former deputy director of the Physics Division at Los Alamos National Laboratory and has authored over seventy articles in physics. As an Episcopal priest, he has served congregations in New Mexico, Texas and Wisconsin. He is active as a speaker on the relationship between science and spirituality.

Jim is the author of seven books.

More information on Jim and his books at
www.JimTrainorAuthor.com

Also by Jim Trainor
www.JimTrainorAuthor.com

"Compulsively readable."
The Booklife Prize

What if you went to your high school reunion and everyone there thought you had died at age 18? And then you learned that they were right. Ed Turner was an ordinary guy, not ready to swept up in a whirlwind of danger, romance and parallel universes.

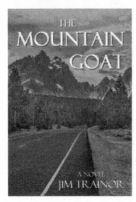

"... skillfully captures the magic of starting over in this memorable road trip novel."
Publisher's Weekly

Honorable Mention in Literary Fiction, 27th Annual Writer's Digest Self-Published Book Awards, 2020

Ryan Browning's headed out in an old campervan, on a roadtrip through the American West and through the intersections of grief and faith, art and science, love and deadly danger.

For Wil Weathers, who's lost his job and his girlfriend, a backpacking trip might just be a cure for the blues. But while waiting for a late-night bus in a small northern Wisconsin town, Wil finds a body. When he returns with help, in the form of the attractive Sally, the body has disappeared. Come up north, where Wil and Sally now find themselves the target of unknown killers and on a collision course with an eco-terrorist gang preparing to destroy the lives of millions.

Karen hopes that Maui will rekindle the fire in her marriage. But the flames that engulf her are of betrayal and murder, from which there may be no rescue.

The Sand People takes us to beautiful Maui, amidst posh beachfront resorts, then draws us deeper into the Maui most tourists never see: rural onion fields, the county jail, a funeral and a run-down bar far from the beachfront glamour. It blends laughter and tears in grappling with issues that plague our lives: broken relationships, addiction, shame and death -- and pointing toward the victory of hope over failure.

Honorable Mention
Foreward Reviews 2012 Book of the Year

Josh and Evangelina have little in common, until they are thrown together and pursued by unknown killers. In a desperate flight for survival, they take refuge in a run-down nursing home in rural northern New Mexico. In this place of helplessness, they must confront old demons, as they are catapulted toward a final deadly showdown that means reaching for strength that may be beyond their grasp.

We have big questions about the meaning of life.

Join Jim Trainor, physicist and pastor, in exploring the intersection of science and religious faith. *Grasp* leads you deep into the heart of the matter, bringing together thoughts of great scientific and religious thinkers with the real-life stories of people who have grasped for the truth.

Fred → Jim

Typos

p. 174 "overhauls"
"moving slowly"

p. 230 "convinced" NOT convicted

p. 282. "Lust see"

p. 293. "lust" has a pejorative (sinful)
religious connotation. Another
word? love? affection? or to get laid
or who he wanted sex with.
"object of" too stilted.

"? for God's sake"

298 -
306 - lust again.
330 - ? shrilly a known predator

Made in the USA
Middletown, DE
03 February 2021